THE
GLASSWRIGHTS'
APPRENTICE

VOLUME ONE IN THE
GLASSWRIGHTS SERIES

THE GLASSWRIGHTS' APPRENTICE

MINDY L. KLASKY

OPEN ROAD
INTEGRATED MEDIA
NEW YORK

ISBN 978-1-4976-4057-3

This edition published in 2014 by Open Road Integrated Media, Inc.
345 Hudson Street
New York, NY 10014
www.openroadmedia.com

To Mom and Dad,
who taught me I could go anywhere
with a book in my hands

Original Acknowledgments, 2000 Edition

This first novel would not have been possible without the support of an extraordinary number of people, especially Richard Curtis, Laura Anne Gilman, Deb Givens, Jane Johnson, Bruce Sundrud, the Washington Area Writers Group, and my family.

Additional Acknowledgments, 2010 Edition

This book would not have happened without the love and support (and never-ending techno-patience!) of my husband, Mark.

I love keeping in touch with readers! Please stop by my website, http://www.mindyklasky.com, to learn more about me, my books, upcoming appearances, etc.

CHAPTER I

Rani Trader pushed through the throngs in front of the cathedral, sparing only the Pilgrims' dusty robes from her sharp-elbowed thrusts. Fighting the crowd gave her an opportunity to spend some of the rage that pulsed in her thirteen-year-old veins, and she barely remembered to protect the precious basket that was slung over her arm.

The day had begun far too early, with Cook splashing a cup of icy water in her sleeping face, swearing at her to get her miserable bones down to the kitchen. As Rani crouched on the icy flagstones, dispensing threads of dried cotton to the faintest of smoldering embers, she shivered so hard that her teeth ached. Still, she managed to fill her lungs with breath after breath, blowing life into the fire that her fellow apprentice, Larinda, had let die during the night.

Of course, Rani could not speak out against Larinda, even when Cook kicked her for being so slow at building up the flame. Apprentices needed to stand by each other no matter what the assault from journeymen, masters, or servants.

That miserable dawn had only been a harbinger of a terrible morning. Rani had helped Cook stir the great cauldron of sticky porridge, ignoring the protest of her own belly as she ladled the noxious stuff into bowls for the masters and journeymen. Even if the food had been palatable, Cook never made enough for the apprentices to eat their fill.

When Rani's parents had bought her way into the

prestigious glasswrights' guild, it had never occurred to them to question the fare that would be served at the apprentices' table. Now, there was not a night that Rani's belly did not cry out in hunger. Even when Cook prepared enough food for all, it was difficult to swallow the rations, thinking of the mice that swarmed in the pantry.

Rani knew that she was learning humility. She knew that she was learning patience. She knew that she was learning the blind obedience that paved the way to the highest level of her chosen craft. Still, when her belly growled and the sun had only climbed halfway to noon, it seemed that she would never be an Instructor.

Now, in the cathedral square, a Pilgrim stepped backward and ground his leather-heeled boot into Rani's inadequate soft shoe, unaware of the girl behind him. She stifled a cry and caught her large basket before it toppled to the cobble stones. Nevertheless, she heard glass clink hard against metal, and she offered up a quick prayer to the Thousand Gods that the knife had not cracked the jar of lemon water.

Thinking of the tart-sweet drink, Rani swallowed hard, and for the hundredth time, cast aside the shameful thought of sneaking a hand into the basket and extracting a morsel from the treasures Cook had ordered her to bring to Instructor Morada. Rani bore fresh-baked caraway bread and a plump sausage, the latter newly carried in from the smokehouse. She had watched as Cook counted out a half-dozen tiny, tart apples, and she had almost swooned when she was required to cut a slab of rich, creamy cheese to complement the feast. Almond honey cakes anchored the basket, and Rani could smell their heady fragrance over the less enticing odors of the perfumed and over-heated crowd.

She would not dishonor the guild. She would serve Instructor Morada with humble obedience, even if she fainted from hunger.

Directing a well-aimed kick toward a Touched brat who refused to let her pass, Rani permitted herself an angelic smile, indulgently dreaming of the day she was presented with her Instructor's sash. Instructors were glasswrights who had completed both their apprenticeship and their journeys and returned to the guildhall. Treated with the greatest esteem, they were courted daily by the guild, enticed to stay and impart their knowledge to worthless wretches of apprentices, instead of setting up profitable masters' workshops.

Rani's immediate concern, though, was not instruction, but making her way through the thick crowds closest to the cathedral doors. Everyone hoped for a glimpse of Prince Tuvashanoran in his Presentation regalia. It was not every day that a living king stepped down as Defender of the Faith, in favor of his eldest son. Even though King Shanoranvilli would retain the throne and all the secular power in the kingdom, he was transferring his role as religious leader of this people. The honor bestowed on Tuvashanoran was great; in fact, the event was unusual enough that Rani's guild had been commissioned to re-glaze one of the cathedral windows in commemoration.

Even now, Instructor Morada was putting the finishing touches on the work, making certain that the glass had settled well in its armature. Ideally, the window would have been completed well before Presentation Day, but there had been countless delays. First, they had not been able to get rare cobalt glass from the eastern province of Zarithia. Then, when the glass finally did arrive, the yellow stain had refused to take to the blue, leaving muddy streaks across the surface instead of the expected grassy green. Even after new glass was found to replace the faulty stuff, work had gone slowly. Designs had been mistakenly erased from white-washed tables, and a dozen grozing irons—used to cut the planes of glass—had gone missing from the store-rooms.

As late as yesterday morning, Rani had blended pot-paints for Morada to stipple into the final design, adding the last touches to the window as it rested in its cathedral armature. Morada had climbed down the scaffolding to view her handiwork in the full light of the previous noon, only to decide that a little more stippling was needed in the Defender's face, filling out the fierce features that symbolized the heart of the Pilgrims' faith. Of course, the paint could not be added once the sun had passed to the cathedral's western side—it was impossible to see the effect on the glass. Morada contented herself with rising at dawn, forcing Rani to re-mix the pot-paints in the sleepy hours after she had served up Cook's glutinous porridge.

Now, as the sun lent autumn's warmth to the cathedral wall, Rani stood at the foot of the scaffold. Often, she thought that scaffolding was the reason she had yearned to be a glasswright in the first place. She loved climbing, loved the feeling that she was moving above the workaday world. Slinging Morada's lunch over one shoulder, Rani tossed back her short, black cloak and grasped the narrow wooden supports. Her hands were well-used to climbing, and she started up the structure with a scant breath of prayer to Roan, the god of ladders. Roan had watched over Rani since she first climbed to her bed in the loft of her father's shop.

The touch of wood sliding beneath her fingers was comforting, familiar, and Rani was almost at the top of the scaffold before she realized that the usual rope supports had been pulled up to the plank platform at the top. Before she could question that oddity, she was confronted by Morada's look of outrage. "Ranita! What are you doing here?" Sheer fury coated the Instructor's words as completely as yellow stain on glass, and Rani bowed her head in an apprentice's immediate apology. Morada towered over the girl, the grey streak in her jet hair lashing out like a cruel whip. The Instructor set her bony hands on her hips, and even as Rani averted her gaze, she could make out the spider web of white glass-scars on the woman's fingers.

"I'm sorry Instructor Morada. Guildmistress Salina sent me with your lunch. She said to bring it to you before the Presentation."

"I don't need any lunch! Can't you see I'm finishing the window? I don't have time to be interrupted by a stupid apprentice."

Rani didn't like Morada much under any circumstances, and she was particularly rebellious after her fight through the crowd. It took a full count of ten before she yielded to the guild's precepts. "I am sorry, Instructor, if this apprentice has failed to meet your expectations." Rani remembered to lower her eyes, which was just as well, given the smoldering resentment she was unable to quench completely. In fact, she imagined that her anger gave off the acrid stench of burning. "I beg your pardon, Instructor, and I beg leave to assist you in your work."

"No!" Morada's outraged cry was enough to cause Rani to meet her agate gaze, even though she knew she would pay for the insolence. The cold hatred that greeted her sent a shiver down the girl's spine. Morada was not taunting her with an Instructor's typical cool superiority; she was not channeling the tight rage that Instructors reserved for slow or recalcitrant students. Rather, the woman's lips were white with suppressed fury, and she lurched threateningly to where Rani huddled on the edge of the scaffold platform. "Didn't you see that I pulled up the rope support? Even you are old enough to know when Instructors do not wish to be disturbed."

Rani's eyes darted to the pile of rope beside the scaffold's wooden ladder, coiled high against the cathedral's stone wall. "Instructor, I merely acted on Guildmistress Salina's orders—"

"Apprentice, you 'merely' violated one of the most basic guild rules. If you want to do anything other than grind paint for the next ten years, I strongly advise you to stop talking back to your superiors and leave this scaffold. Now." Rani wanted to explain, to soothe Morada with a joke and a story, but the Instructor's fury cut her off. Under guild rules, Morada was wholly in the right, even if Rani had had no choice but to follow Guildmistress Salina's instructions.

Rani set the basket of food carefully on the scaffold platform, edging aside a coil of lead stripping.

Lead stripping.

Lead stripping had no place at the cathedral. The Defender's Window should have been fitted entirely in the workshop, colored glass laid into a sturdy lead frame on the surface of a white-washed table. Now Rani could place the acrid smell she thought she had imagined—Morada had lit a brazier to heat the lead and bend it to her needs. Such a menial task was far beneath an Instructor, especially an Instructor as famed as Morada. And Rani, having witnessed Morada humbling herself to an apprentice's job, was certain to be penalized.

"If you please, Instructor Morada," Rani could hardly speak past the constriction in her throat as she tried desperately not to see the offending metal coil. "Would you like me to tend to the brazier while you finish your work?"

Morada's hand flew faster than Rani could follow, and then the girl's cheek stung; her eyes watered involuntarily against the slap. "I would like you to remember your place, Apprentice. Get your miserable carcass down the scaffold, and return to the guildhall. You have shown nothing but insolence since you were ordered to assist on this window. You merchant-rats are all the same—too stupid to follow directions and too stubborn to learn."

Protest bubbled in Rani's chest, the words fueled by her stinging cheek. Still, Morada was the Instructor, and Rani only needed to swallow twice before managing the guild's formula. "Yes, Instructor, you speak the truth, imparting wisdom to this Apprentice."

"A mynah could say as much. Go, wretch! I'll see you in the Hall of Discipline when I return to the guild."

"Yes, Instructor." Rani turned to the rope guide, ready to toss it down to steady her descent.

"Apprentice!" The word cracked out in the autumn air, brighter than the sunlight on the cathedral's new copper roof. "You climbed up here without the rope. You can certainly make your way down without it."

This time Rani could not keep from gaping at Morada. Anger was one thing—Rani constantly set the Instructors' teeth on edge because she had not mastered the obsequious tones of her fellow apprentices. But to be forced to descend the scaffold without the rope, when one was perfectly available.... Rani might have been confident in her climbing skills, but it was a foolish risk to descend without a guide rope. "Or perhaps you'd like a faster way down?" Morada's eyes were furious, and Rani had no doubt that the woman would follow through on her threat—at the very least giving Rani a shove to help her down the wooden ladder.

"No, Instructor." Rani scurried to the platform edge, catching her lower lip in her teeth as she steadied her feet against the suddenly too-smooth wooden rungs. She silently appealed to Roan, and despite one slip in the middle of the structure, the god of ladders guided her feet safely to the ground. Only when she had made her way to the bottom of the scaffold did she indulge the hatred that simmered beneath her heart, spitting onto the ground to get a nasty taste off her tongue. Merchant-rat! Rani's parents had paid good money to get her into the guild—better money than Morada would earn for the Defender's Window, whatever the Instructor's mastery of her craft.

Even now, the guild payment forced Rani's family to live like paupers. Her older brother, Bardo, who had hoped to make his Pilgrimage this year, had had no choice but to postpone his journey. Of course, he could walk the Path of the Gods here in the City, but that was not the same. Every night, as Rani fell asleep in her closet of a room, she tormented herself with the knowledge that she—she alone—was responsible for her family's failure to complete the Pilgrimage and gain immediate passage to the Heavenly Fields upon their deaths, long may those be in the future.

Such speculation drove her to the familiar verge of tears. After all, it wasn't as if she had asked for the privilege of coming to the guild. Certainly, she had shown skills in that direction—even as a toddler, she had enjoyed laying out the trinkets at her father's stall in the marketplace. Unlike Bardo and her other brothers and sisters, she was not interested by the mere glint of sunlight on silver. Unlike her mother, she did not care whether the goods were of the highest quality, imported from mysterious Zarithia. Unlike her father, she did not give a tinker's dam if the till were full at the end of the day.

Rather, she felt the way the goods should look on their

table; she knew how the wares could best set off their own attractions. Her parents quickly learned that when she set out the boards, more trinkets were sold. After a brief training period—an apprenticeship, Rani grimaced—she had been assigned that duty on a regular basis. It was her accomplishments that let her merchant family sell more, her skill that permitted her folk to buy her way into the guild.

Now that she lived in the chapter-house, her family was reduced to setting out its own displays, to its unaided attempts to seduce passing customers. So, when Instructor Morada berated Rani for buying her way into the guild, the woman did not know the true edge of her cutting words. Rani had cost her family their spiritual blessings, their savings, and—most importantly—their future, since their stall would not generate equal profits without Rani's gift.

By the time Rani worked her way around to the front of the cathedral, she was completely convinced that her suffering at the guild's unsympathetic hands was unwarranted. She, the poor glasswright's apprentice.... She had done nothing to warrant scorn from her Instructors. She had done nothing to garner the beating that she would certainly get at the hands of the disciplinarian—a beating that would hurt all the more since it would fall on top of the bruises still painted across her back from last week's exploits.

No, there was nothing to be gained by speeding back to the guildhall. And, looking around at the crowd, Rani realized that there was everything to be gained by watching the Presentation. After all, it was not every day that religious ceremonies flooded the City's streets. If the disciplinarian were going to beat her, Rani might as well give him good cause. She might as well enjoy this Presentation Day. And if Larinda had to work harder back at the guildhall, then so much the better. After all, Larinda had let the fire burn down, and turn about was fair play.

Brushing a hand against her still-stinging cheek, Rani began the steady process of worming her way to the front of the crowd. She had a distinct advantage over the other people in the cathedral square—because she was dressed in an apprentice's somber uniform, her short tunic of black wool and her simple cape left her free to dart into places that appeared smaller than a toddler. For once, she was grateful that she was short for her age. At one point, though, she pushed too hard, and a velvet-clad woman—the wife of a Soldier by her complicated hairpiece—reached out a jeweled hand to grab at Rani's shoulders. The glasswrights' apprentice actually laughed out loud as she evaded the woman's grip, darting forward in the ranks as the woman's absurdly stiffened gown forbade her from following.

It wouldn't do to have a Soldier after her in all this chaos, Rani chastised herself. That would warrant special attention from the disciplinarian—if a Soldier broke caste to come to the guildhall and complain about her behavior. Still, he could only complain if he caught her outright, and that was not likely. As Rani ducked in front of a line of Noble children, all dressed in identical regalia, she barely resisted the urge to make a face at their wailing protests. Heraldry was one of the many studies that Rani would master as an apprentice, but for now, she contented herself with memorizing the emblem on their coat of arms. She would check later to see which family she had offended.

Rani's heart beat faster, and she realized that for the first time since she had joined the guild she was actually enjoying herself. And why not? Guildmistress Salina could not know how long it would take to deliver Instructor Morada's lunch. She could not guess how long it would take for Rani to work her way through the crowds, to return to the tedious job of scrubbing down the glaziers' white-washed tables. If Rani planned properly, she could be gone for the better part of the afternoon, and her absence never missed. Larinda might even be required to scrub clean the tables, all by herself. And the pots from the morning's porridge.

Ducking past a heavily-perfumed woman who sported several chins, Rani suddenly found herself on the lowest step of the cathedral entrance. She was surrounded by Nobility; each extravagantly-robed person around her was related in some distant way to the prince who would be Presented that morning. Conditioned since birth to yield to the strict lines of rank and privilege, Rani was assailed with doubts for the first time since leaving the scaffold. It was one thing to frolic for an afternoon, free of the guild's over-watchful guardians. It was another to flout social tradition and set foot inside the cathedral during a Noble feast day. Before she could finish measuring her desire against her wisdom, the crowd carried her forward, depositing her on the cathedral's doorstep, in front of the chief royal herald.

That man, dressed in the crimson and gold raiment of the king's household, looked down his impossibly long nose at her. Rani itched to pick up a piece of charcoal, to sketch out the scene on the cathedral steps. She would capture the pointed arch of the doorway, the carved ranks of the gods who waited to escort Pilgrims to the Heavenly Fields. Against it, she would sketch the herald's flowing cape, his austere dignity reinforced by the waves of glass. His hair, coiffed in the accepted style of a king's servant, would also be frozen in her drawing, and then she would apply all of her skill to record the man's disdainful sniff. Rani would have laughed aloud at the pompous man preserved forever in the windows of her mind, but the herald chose that moment to notice her.

"You!" he barked. "You have no purpose here for the Presentation!" His staff of office crashed down on the top step.

"Begging your pardon," Rani bobbed into the deep curtsey appropriate to offer a Noble, for the herald assumed his master's rank when he dealt with a lowly Guildsman. "I have been sent to the cathedral on guild business, good sir. My Instructor is finishing the Presentation Window even now." Well, that much was true, Rani assured herself, trying to smile against the thunderhead that clouded the herald's face.

"Go around to the transept door, then, Apprentice Glasswright. There are good people waiting to honor their lord this Presentation day." The man sniffed at her costume before turning his attention to the next Noble party that craved admission to the spectacle.

"Begging your pardon," Rani began again, scarcely bridling her impatience. "I need to get inside the cathedral."

There. She did not precisely lie. She did not say that she needed to enter the cathedral on guild business—if she had done that, the disciplinarian could not find a punishment brutal enough. No, Rani merely told the truth—she did need to see the Presentation if she was ever going to capture the momentous event in glass of her own.

She could see that the herald did not believe her. Before the man could speak, though, the crowd surged forward, grumbling its impatience with a hundred hundred voices. For one instant, the herald glared at her, furious that she dared to challenge his authority. Then, a Noble woman was shoved by the crowd and kept her balance by planting one long-nailed hand in the middle of Rani's back. Startled, Rani coughed as the breath was forced out of her, and she, too, caught herself on the nearest available object—the herald's staff of office. The herald, predictably, squawked his outrage and directed a well-aimed kick toward Rani.

The crowd's fury raised in pitch—fury that a Noble woman should be left sprawling before a herald, even if that herald sought a petty revenge. Reading the reaction with the skill of his office, the herald immediately stepped forward to assist her ladyship, steadying the woman in her voluminous skirts. His solicitousness was eloquent testimony to his fear of losing his appointment. The woman would have none of it, and she brushed away his impertinent fingers with her handkerchief, keening as if his touch burned her. The crowd's hum turned into a distinctly hostile murmur.

Rani took advantage of the confusion to duck inside the cathedral.

The massive nave was the greatest in the world, stretching seventy paces to the crossing tower. Rani had already studied the windows that lined the aisles on either side, mammoth planes of glass depicting, on the left, the story of the World's creation from the breath of First God Ait, Man's creation

from the breath of the World, Good and Evil's creation
from the breath of Man. The right aisle told the story of
Jair, of his humble birth among the casteless Touched and
his unparalleled rise into the castes, first as a Merchant of
trinkets from a blanket in the square, then as a Guildsman-
weaver, fashioning similar blankets. The windows displayed
the battles that Jair had fought as a Soldier, his miraculous
saving of the City, which was even then old beyond memory.
The last row of windows approaching the transept contained
Jair's final transformation, from Soldier to Noble-Priest.

The cathedral windows, surmounted by roundels showing
dozens of the Thousand Gods, were stunning because they
formed the Final Route for pilgrims. Five windows were
singled out to reflect the specific stations of Jair's Pilgrimage,
the four castes. Huge altars nestled beneath each of the
pilgrimage windows, and banks of candles flickered in the
shadowy cathedral. Rani was drawn to the Guildsman's
altar as surely as if a tether tugged her.

Glancing around to make sure that she did not attract
undue attention from the mostly Noble crowd, Rani dug into
the small pouch at her belt, reluctant fingers excavating a
copper that she had saved for boiled sweets. She could hardly
attend such a momentous event as Prince Tuvashanoran's
Presentation without lighting her own candle, sweets or no.
Her family would never live down the shame—as if they had
not taught their Merchant-daughter how to worship in the
cathedral. She hesitated only an instant before depositing
her coin in the convenient cask, then she selected the longest
candle in the nearby basket, to make up for her sacrifice.

Rani lit her taper and muttered the Guildsman's Prayer,
words that had already become familiar in the short months
since her apprenticeship. Every morning, under Cook's
watchful eye, she muttered the Prayer upon awakening. She
spoke it before each meal, before each artistic undertaking,
before each installation of finished glasswork, in penance
before the disciplinarian and—finally—at the end of every
day, on her knees beside her pallet. "May all the gods look
upon my craft with favor, and may they take pleasure in

the humble art created by my hands. May Jair Himself be pleased with the humble offering I make, and may the least of my works bring glory to the world. May my works guide me to the Heavenly Fields in my proper time, as the gods do favor. All glory to the Thousand Gods."

Despite her best intentions, Rani rushed through the last few words, unable to pry her attention from the crowd. Not surprisingly, with the vulture of a herald standing guard over the door, most of the folk were Noble. Of course, each of the major Guilds was in evidence—the Tilers, the Embroiderers, the Painters, the Armorers, others that Rani could not see from her current vantage point. Each guildmaster or guildmistress wore a heavy robe of office, surmounted by a cloak emblazoned with that particular guild's symbol. Rani did not immediately see the glasswrights' Guildmistress Salina, but she calculated a path that would keep her as far from the other craftsmen as possible, eager to avoid a confrontation. Nowhere in the cathedral did she espy another apprentice.

Rani's evasive course took her down the right aisle, bobbing beneath the masterful Pilgrimage windows. In fact, with a final elbow placed sharply in the side of a Noble girl (a child too young to complain to her non-observant mother), Rani made a space for herself at the edge of the south transept. Craning her neck, she could just make out the massive window where Instructor Morada toiled. From inside the cathedral, the glasswork looked complete, with all its lead stripping in place. That completeness, though, may have been a deceptive trick of the light, for the sunlight was brilliant—strong enough to hint at the scaffolding just beyond the window. Rani noted that those rays focused through the window exactly as the guild had intended.

There, at the foot of the transept altar, was a pool of brilliant blue light. Blue, because that was the color of the King's heir, the color of pure intention and noble goals, the color of the Defender of the Faith. The clear light focused through the glazed robe of the Defender in Morada's masterpiece, untempered by other hues, even by the riot of color streaming through neighboring windows. Pride filled Rani's narrow chest and straightened her spine.

She might have boasted to her neighbors, or at least flashed the guild-blazon on her cape a little more flamboyantly, if the Defender's procession had not begun at that precise moment. Trumpets rang out as if a battle loomed, and a strained hush fell over the crowd. The fanfare was repeated once, then twice, and then two times more—a total of five to match the Touched and the four castes that Jair had lived.

With each repetition, pockets of worshipers fell to their knees—first the few Touched who had been permitted to enter the cathedral as servants to Nobles. In rapid procession, the scattered Merchants knelt (Rani almost forgot and fell to her knees), followed by Guildsmen (Rani gratefully remembered her new status), Soldiers, and finally Nobles.

The trumpets gave way to a choral antiphon, sung by children who were secreted in the clerestory aisles far above the worshipers. Those clarion voices rang out like chimes on the gates to the Heavenly Fields, and Rani shivered at the unexpected beauty. As the fluted notes echoed off the cathedral's ceiling, Prince Tuvashanoran processed down the aisle.

Each royal step was marked by the crowd's gasp of awe and admiration. Trapped at the edge of the south transept, Rani was tempted to pinch her way to the nave, but she restrained her twitching fingers, knowing that she had an uninterrupted line of sight to the azure puddle of light and the Presentation itself.

And she was not disappointed.

Prince Tuvashanoran was easily the most popular Noble in the City's history. Not only was he breathtakingly handsome, but he was the very flower of knighthood. He had won the golden spurs with ease in the Spring Tourney, treating his opponents with compassion and respect. Various princesses from rich and fabled lands to the north and east were presented at court on a regular basis, and the Prince entertained them all—singing in his rich baritone, playing his lute, and showing off his horsemanship in the castle's central courtyard. But he was more than a courtier.

Last spring, when the thaw was late and wet snow was still deeper than a man's chest, wolves had coursed down the hills outside the City. On a damp, foggy night, Prince Tuvashanoran came across the Pilgrim's Bell unmanned, despite the clear danger to the travelers who made their way through the misty countryside. Rather than send for servants and waste valuable time, the prince stood by the bell himself, tolling the heavy metal through the night with such calm precision that not a single person in town realized anything was amiss. Five Pilgrims straggled in during the fog-ridden night, one with tales of narrowly escaping a giant beast, a Wolf of the Underworld.

Prince Tuvashanoran led a hunting party that very day, despite having not slept the entire previous night. He rode the beast to earth and presented the gigantic pelt to the High Priest so that the warm fur could be distributed to the needy among the Touched.

Now, the legendary Tuvashanoran strode down the nave, golden fillet catching the gleam of tinted light from the clerestory windows. Each step was a ballet of grace; each turn of his head was a symphony of responsibility.

When he reached the altar, Tuvashanoran knelt, bending his regal knee before the impossibly ancient High Priest. The old man's face was obscured beneath a high, jeweled miter, his age-wasted body enlarged by a voluminous cope. The High Priest beamed at his spiritual son, then raised shaking, liver-spotted hands to hover over Tuvashanoran's raven hair.

As the children's antiphon reached its musical climax, the prince bowed his head in complete submission to the Thousand Gods. The High Priest's lips moved in unheard prayer before the old man helped the young lord to rise, turning him back to look at the gathered masses. Tuvashanoran was visibly touched by the homage proffered by the worshipers, and he spontaneously raised his hands to echo the High Priest, gathering in his people's adoration like a lowly merchant-farmer bringing in sheaves.

The echoing antiphon faded, and an acolyte stepped forward, moving with a careful choreography that contrasted with Tuvashanoran's spontaneous gesture. The prince shrugged off his cloak, stepping away from the jewel-encrusted garment that was worth more than the glasswrights' guild could command in an entire year of commissions. The acolyte staggered under the heavy garment as one of his fellows spread a golden cloth before the altar.

Only when the fabric was an unrippled puddle of metallic silk, did Tuvashanoran return to his kneeling posture. He offered up his joined hands to the High Priest, tendering the sort of fealty usually reserved for the Crown. The High Priest, expecting the honor, took those royal hands between his own, nodding solemnly before setting palsied palms upon the Prince's bowed head. There was a long moment during which not a rustle of silk or velvet could be heard, and then the Priest's voice echoed up to the clerestory. "Who brings this man before the altar of the Thousand Gods?"

"It is I, Shanoranvilli ben-Jair, King of Morenia, Lord of the City, and Defender of the Faith, who brings my son to the altar." Rani started guiltily; she had not even seen the king process down the nave. From the crowd's indrawn gasp, Rani realized that few others had watched their liege approach, so captivating was Tuvashanoran.

Looking across the dais, Rani could see the entire royal family looking on in pride. Beside King Shanoranvilli stood his young wife, the exotically beautiful Queen Felicianda. Prince Halaravilli was there as well, scarcely two years older than Rani herself, and Prince Bashanorandi, Rani's own age. A flock of princesses rustled on the platform, craning their young necks to see what their eldest brother was doing. Or half-brother, Rani amended mentally—Prince Bashanorandi and the princesses were all Queen Felicianda's children; only Tuvashanoran and Halaravilli survived from the king's first marriage.

The High Priest did not appear to be concerned with the complicated relationships in the royal family. Turning to King Shanoranvilli, he intoned gravely, "Defender of the

Faith, you call yourself. And what proof do I have that you bear that title?"

While the king's voice might quaver, there was nothing weak or yielding in his stance on this brightest of bright days. Keeping his eyes on the High Priest, Shanoranvilli raised sere hands to the heavy chain of office encircling his neck. Even at this distance, Rani could make out the massive, interlocked J's of the chain, the letters so ornate that they were hardly recognizable. J for Jair, J for the royal house. "I wear the Defender's Chain, Father, symbol of my obligation to the Thousand Gods and reminder of the power that those gods give to me."

"And why do you come into the Gods' House today?"

"I come to transfer this Chain, to one who, in his youth, can Defend the faith better than I."

The High Priest looked down at the king, as if he were considering this offer for the first time. Rani shivered at the expression in the Holy Father's eyes, for she had seen such a look once before—the night she forsook her parents' house for the guild. There was pride there, but it was buried beneath sorrow, the emotions so keen they sliced across the cathedral's charged air.

"And do you come here of your own free will?" The priest asked at last, his bushy eyebrows arched high so that they merged into one commanding line above his far-seeing eyes.

"Aye, I come of my own free will."

"And you, Prince Tuvashanoran, do you take up this burden of your own free will?"

"Aye, I take it up of my own free will." The Prince's voice was proud and strong, hurtling up to the windows with the vigor of youth.

"Then let the Church prepare you for your duties." The High Priest raised a trembling hand, and a cloud of acolytes swarmed about the dais. Rani knew that the boys were her own age, apprenticed to the church and its priests even as she served the guild. Still, they looked like little children as they darted about the kneeling Prince, averting their eyes to the stony floor rather than gaze directly at their liege.

The whole thing was ridiculous, Rani scoffed—these same boys were Tuvashanoran's cousins, his closest family. Only royalty would be permitted to participate in a ceremony as important as Tuvashanoran's Presentation. The royal boys could not truly have been overwhelmed with awe in the space of a few hours.

The old man, for his part, merely gave a curt nod, indulging in a single wave of a liver-spotted hand to confirm that the child was acting in the justice and light of all the Thousand Gods. Only when the Prince managed a spare nod as well, did the boy actually summon the nerve to lift up the golden fillet, to hold aloft the symbol of worldly commitment. Thin lines of enamel-work caught the cobalt sunlight, flashing brilliantly to the crowd.

As the acolyte stepped away, bearing the worldly burden, Rani felt the urge to shout with pride for the glory of her Prince. The High Priest raised his arms, as if summoning the force of the heavens. "Welcome to the house of the Thousand Gods, my son. Welcome to the most holy seat of the Pilgrim. As you set your feet upon the Defender's road, you must let the gods know of your desire to serve them, of your desire to be their sword arm in the battles of the world." The High Priest gestured to a naked sword that lay upon the altar, unadorned steel glinting with a deadly power.

"Before you take up this new weapon for your battle, drink of this cup, the stirrup cup for the journey you now undertake to serve your people, the kingdom of all Morenia, the community of the faithful." The priest held out one withered hand and an acolyte stepped forward to pass the old man a gilded chalice. The goblet was heavy, requiring two trembling fists to raise it before the awed people. With a bow, the priest passed the chalice to Tuvashanoran, who paused for a moment to settle the weight of metal and jewels in his own grasp. When he raised the cup, he found the exact focus of light from the Defender's Window, making every facet of each embedded jewel wink at the congregation. Then, Tuvashanoran drank deeply, swallowing the holy wine with relish, with the fanaticism of a soldier riding off to battle. Only when the massive cup was drained did he hand the treasure back to the high priest.

The old man nodded proudly. "Now, my son, prostrate yourself in the house of the Gods, before the Pilgrim's Table, and offer up any thoughts that would make you impure to carry out your mission in the world."

Rani heard the congregants' collective sigh as Tuvashanoran followed the Priest's orders. The prince moved like a cat, fully composed, aware that every eye in the cavernous nave was tied to him. Touching his brow to the base of the altar, Tuvashanoran unconsciously flicked the edges of his undertunic, causing the snowy linen to billow into angelic wings. Then, before the image could be lost and the Prince could become just an ordinary man kneeling before an ordinary block of marble, Tuvashanoran prostrated himself before the altar of the Gods.

A lump of pride grew in Rani's throat as she watched. She might only be an apprentice. She might only be the youngest child of a merchant family, a family that had scrimped and saved to buy her way into a guild. Still, she was a part of the force that had painted the portrait before her, part of the brotherhood that crafted the regal image of a Prince shedding his temporal crown to take up his spiritual one. Rani could not keep from casting her eyes up toward her small contribution to this pageant, to the window that Instructor Morada had scarcely finished in time for the Presentation. Whatever panic had been in the guildhall, whatever rage Morada had expressed on the scaffold, it had been worthwhile, for that rush and fury had created this perfection.

As Rani glanced up at the window, something caught her eye. A year ago, she would not have seen anything out of place in the careful leaded design. A month ago, she would not have recognized the outline of a bow against the glass. A week ago, she would not have realized that the bow was not part of the intricate armature. But only yesterday, she had white-washed the table that had borne the drawings for this window. She had scrubbed for hours, wiping out Instructor

Morada's charcoal lines; she had studied the precise pattern of lead and glass that created the masterpiece. Rani knew that there was no need for lead in that precise arc.

An archer's bow leaned against the window.

Even as Rani recognized the danger, the bow was pulled away from the glass. She could imagine an assassin stepping back on the scaffold, moving the tip of a carefully fletched arrow to a single missing pane of glass. Rani thought she could hear the arrow nocked to the string; she could feel the tension of calloused fingers pulling the string to the archer's ear.

And all the while, Prince Tuvashanoran lay before the altar, unknowing. Rani struggled for breath in the suddenly close cathedral, clambering to her feet. In the silence of the praying congregation, her voice rang out, piercing and shrill. "Your Highness! To arms!"

Guards leaped forward before she had completed the four words. Tuvashanoran jumped into a fighter's crouch, all holy ritual forgotten as he grasped the ceremonial sword from the altar. The motion tore him around in a half-arc, already searching for the threat carried on a child's voice.

For one instant, there was nothing. Utter stillness gripped the congregation, the priest, the prince. Then, with the impossible momentum of a swooping hawk, a flash of light cut through the cobalt pool. The silence was cloven by a man's outraged bellow, and Prince Tuvashanoran whirled around to face his people. Even as the crowd surged toward the altar, Rani could see the black-fletched arrow blooming from the socket of the prince's right eye.

CHAPTER 2

Rani threw herself against the guildhall's majestic gates, hitting the wrought iron with enough force to make the posts screech in their stone moorings. "Brother Gatekeeper!" she panted, trying to force a scream behind her ragged breath. "Brother Gatekeeper, let me in!"

She looked behind her with a wild eye, desperately trying to fill her lungs. She had been running for nearly two hours. In the stunned silence following her shout in the cathedral, Rani had not even tried to make her way down the endless nave. Instead, she had ducked out the transept portal, using all her strength to push open the heavy oaken doors.

Even with adrenaline pumping in her veins, she had nearly been unable to get by, for the wooden mass of Morada's scaffold blocked the door's full swing. As it was, she needed to scrape sideways to edge through, and she did not spare a thought for the short black cloak that she left snagged on the doorframe.

The crowds near the cathedral had still been thick with disappointed citizens hoping for a glimpse of the Presentation, and the hordes became even more resistant to passage as rumors began to fly. When Rani finally cleared the Cathedral sector, she sprinted in panic in the opposite direction from the guild, winding through the Soldier's Quarter for a solid hour before she could untangle the streets.

By the time she worked her way to the familiar byways

of her childhood home in the Merchants' Quarter, a dust of panic had sifted over the City. Twice, she saw platoons of soldiers jogging down the narrow cobbled roads, grim rage scarcely suppressed as lieutenants called out the marching cadence. Merchants pulled in their trestles while the sun still shone, and frantic mothers summoned children into the safety of dark doorways.

Rani had been tempted to run to her own family, but she realized reluctantly that she needed to warn her guild. She was an apprentice now, not a merchant, and she needed to tell her brothers and sisters of Morada's evil, even if that meant revealing her own unplanned complicity in Prince Tuvashanoran's death. Although half the City sprawled between her and the stricken prince, Rani could still see the streaks of crimson across Tuvashanoran's pale, pale flesh. There was no chance that he still lived.

"Brother Gatekeeper!" she cried again, desperation ripping her throat as she wracked her brain to remember which of the guildsmen was assigned gate duty. Her cries remained unanswered, and she abandoned the gate to duck down the alley that lined the guild's garden, all the while imagining a ravening crowd sweeping around the bend in the street, bent on bloody vengeance against Morada Glasswright.

The deserted mews gave Rani some feeling of safety, and she dashed one hand against her cheek, leaving dirty streaks in the tracks of her tears. Stone walls towered over her as she fought back sobs, letting her fingers trail against the rough rock as she stumbled down the alley.

This was all a nightmare. Tuvashanoran was the greatest warrior who had ever lived. He could not be felled by a single arrow. He could not be murdered in the house of the Thousand Gods. And Morada could not have committed the murder. Still, Rani could see the lead stripping coiled on Morada's scaffold, and she could hear the wicked anger in the Instructor's voice. Morada had removed at least one pane of glass from the Defender's Window, and she'd been prepared to cover up her action with hastily applied lead. Morada had been furious when Rani discovered her.

If the Instructor had not murdered Tuvashanoran, she had certainly been directly involved in the attack.

Now, standing in the alley, Rani was startled by a crow's harsh cry. Reflexively, she reached for a large stone amid the broken cobbles. Years of working before a board of shining pretties had taught her excellent aim—she could frighten off the largest crows that were intent on stealing from her hard-working family.

The bird was perched on a low branch of a straggling apple tree—possibly even the tree that had borne the apples that Rani had carried to Morada that morning. Remembering the fruit made the girl's stomach clench in hunger. For a moment, she was ashamed—how could she even think of eating when the greatest hero of her people lay dead in the cathedral, cut down by an arrow because *she* had called him from his prostration before the altar? Perhaps, without Rani's unintended assistance, the archer-assassin would have missed the prince. Perhaps Tuvashanoran would have lived. Rani might not have plucked the bow, but she had surely summoned Prince Tuvashanoran to his bitter, untimely death.

Thrusting aside her guilt, Rani studied the immediate problem of gaining entry to the guildhall gardens. The apple tree was at least fifteen feet above her, the wall itself the height of two men. Casting about the alley, Rani discovered a quartet of broken barrels. Some of the staves were cast in on each of the casks; the coopers had deemed them past repair. Still, Rani made short work of rolling the barrels to the wall and balancing them to create a rickety tower.

She was still far from the top of the wall when her stomach clenched with hunger, bile painting the back of her tongue. There was no help for it. Dusting her hands against her grimy doublet, she set her jaw and pawed for a handhold amid the stones.

She may have only worked in the guildhall for a few months, but in that time, she had been forced to stir innumerable pots of paint. She had scrubbed endless acres of whitewashed tables. She had trickled cornmeal into countless cauldrons, and then stirred the resulting mush until it thickened to Cook's revolting expectations. Her arms trembled with her new strength, and she found hand-holds where none were visible, tiny gaps where she could force her fingers. Like a horsefly loose in the pantry, she made her way up the stone wall.

Only once did she get stuck, and that was when the crow realized that his territory was being invaded. The giant bird cawed harshly and swooped upon her. His beak clashed against the flashing gold thread of Rani's guild emblem; the thieving bird was after the apprentice's wealth just as its brothers had tried to steal from the merchants' boards. Rani, thrusting away the image of bloody talons and beak, fended off the crow's attack with a stiff-fingered hand. That instinctive maneuver made her slide down the face of the wall; she only caught herself by flattening her belly against the stone and skinning both knees.

The crow, not to be deterred, beat at her with its wings, and Rani cried out as she imagined the sharp beak ripping her flesh. The bird cawed again, flapping its huge wings in excitement over Rani's glittering guild-patch. Rani could picture her skin being ripped as she heard the fabric tear, but then the crow stroked away on his broad wings, trailing the golden threads that had secured Rani's multi-colored badge of office.

Anger gave way to relief, and Rani clung to the wall for a moment, panting out a prayer to Fairn, the god of birds, who had seen fit to send away that particularly nasty minion. Without the looming crow, Rani made short work of the rest of her climb. Arms quivering, she pulled herself atop the wall, and it only took a minute to summon the nerve to leap to the apple tree.

Once she was secure in the tree's gnarled branches, she began to shake uncontrollably. Suddenly, she was chilled—her arm was bare where the crow had ripped the fabric, and she missed the cloak she had been forced to leave at the cathedral. A steady breeze stiffened against the tear-tracks on her face, and Rani realized that her hands were still trembling when she reached for a rosy apple.

For just an instant, the ripe fruit melted into the blood streaking Tuvashanoran's fine face, but she shuddered past the image, squeezing her eyes shut and bringing the fragrant fruit to her lips. She chewed mechanically, then grabbed at another and another.

Only when the worst pangs in her belly were quelled did Rani descend from her perch. She paused at the base of the tree to gather several windfalls and stuff them into her doublet's hidden pockets. The orchard was eerie in the late fall afternoon; autumn-bare branches straggled across a darkening sky. A breeze skirled through the trees, rattling dry leaves like prayers for the dead.

Rani ducked into the guildhall unseen and made her way through strangely silent corridors. Usually, late afternoon was the time of greatest activity—instructors finishing their classes for the day, apprentices scurrying to complete their tasks before scrubbing up after their brothers and sisters.

Today, though, no one roamed the halls. Rani passed by the great chamber where the whitewashed tables squatted, awaiting a glasswright's hand to sketch complex charcoal designs. Not a glazier was in sight. Certainly, the ragged tail of a fire twitched on the grate, but even that was faded almost to embers. Rani almost stopped to bank the coals, in an effort to limit her work later in the day.

Afterwards, Rani could never be sure what drove her to the Hall of Discipline. Maybe, it was Instructor Morada's angry words, delivered on the scaffold, ordering Rani to report for punishment. Maybe, at the back of her mind, she heard the ghosts of voices in the guildhall's deadly still, and she decided to seek them out. Maybe her steps were guided by one of the Thousand Gods.

Whatever the reason, Rani made her way to the dimly lit Apprentice's Corridor, a narrow passage that skulked behind the Hall of Discipline. She had spent more time in this darkened space than she cared to admit. The stone walls curved above her, hulking to barrel vaulting without even the narrowest of windows. Indeed, the only light in the oppressive passage came from the candles that burned on altars spaced down the corridor. Each altar was dedicated to a different god—Lene, the god of humility, Plad, the god of patience, Dain, the god of contemplation.

Altogether, there were a half dozen altars, each littered with trinkets offered up by straying apprentices. Rani had studied her fellows' offerings on many occasions; the most censured apprentice each week was charged with replacing the massive tallow candles that smoked on each altar. The candles were as long as Rani's arm, and as thick around as her neck, and she needed to stretch on her tiptoes to light them.

Now, she fought the compulsion to lug out replacements for the low-burning candles on the cluttered altars. Such attention to detail would have been absurd—Tuvashanoran was dead. The prince had died because *she* had called him; *she* had cried out. Rani did not need to be a soldier to know that the deadly arrow would have passed harmlessly over Tuvashanoran's head, without her interference. If she had just kept silent, Tuvashanoran would have been spared. No burning wax in a darkened corridor was going to absolve Rani this time.

She might ignore the candles, but she could not dismiss the final altar, at the end of the shadowy passage. This was the single place within the guildhall where Rani had spent the most time since her tumultuous arrival. The altar itself was fashioned out of a massive block of stone, and its front was inlaid with dark tiles of smoky glass. The altar was sacred to a deity almost entirely foreign to Rani—Sorn, the god of obedience. It was customary for an apprentice who was summoned to the Hall of Discipline to kneel before Sorn, to ask forgiveness before punishment could be meted out by the guild disciplinarian.

Sorn was a harsh master, as Rani had learned too often. A kneeler was fashioned at the foot of his altar, ostensibly to provide greater comfort to petitioners who sought divine guidance. Rani knew, though, that the kneeler was just another element of the disciplinarian's craft, for its wooden surface was embossed with the tools of the glasswright's trade—grozing irons and coils of lead stripping, pincers and rectangular glass tiles. It was impossible to kneel upon that narrow bench without transferring those sharp-edged images to tender knees.

Nevertheless, Rani could not approach the Hall of Discipline without at least a token obeisance. Traditionally, the disciplinarian's first move was to check a petitioner's knees. If Rani showed up without a visible symbol of her worship, she would merely be sent back until she *was* marked. Sighing, Rani lowered herself to the familiar kneeler.

She should not have been surprised to overhear the conversation in the Hall of Discipline. After all, the altar was especially situated so that one apprentice could make out the ... instruction of another, thereby fostering greater discipline through the imagined penalty. Many a time, Rani had emerged from her own instruction at the hands of the disciplinarian, only to face the whey countenance of another apprentice, looking up anxiously from Sorn's altar.

Still, when Rani realized that the voice was Guildmistress Salina's, she caught her breath, the better to make out the hissed words.

"Of course it did not go as we wished!"

Rani could not make out the other person's response, but it rumbled around the corner, a man's timbre.

"We knew there was risk in using our scaffold," Salina insisted, "but we never intended to call attention to a glasswright in the *middle* of the plot. Since that brat cried out, there's no way the guard will see us as innocent victims. The glasswrights are certain to be the first suspects. The only reason they've delayed so far is to muster troops."

Rumble.

"No, we must accept the cards the gods have dealt us. It was ill luck and blatant disobedience that led that merchant-rat to be in the Cathedral. She's been a thorn in my side since I took her family's money—I never should have kept her around. She's too strong to bend to the good of the guild;

she's stubborn enough to break first, just to show who she thinks is mistress."

Rani's indignation was so sharp that she almost stormed into the Hall. Only the rumble of the unheard speaker stilled her, his rumble and the icy fingers that closed around her heart at Salina's dismissive tone.

"Contract be damned. She may have shown some promise with patterns, but she's more trouble than she's worth. Those merchant-brats almost always are. Now, the soldiers are certain to come looking for her—her guild insignia was perfectly clear, even if no one knows her by name. I saw it myself, on the cloak she left hanging on the cathedral's side door. I instructed Brother Gatekeeper not to let her in—at least we'll be able to claim that we don't know where she is."

Rani's skinned knees smarted, and tears stung her eyes. Guildmistress Salina was supposed to act as her mother; the woman had sworn she would love Rani as her own daughter. Even the chronic annoyance in the guildmistress' voice would hurt less than her current dismissive tone.

"I've got all the guild in the refectory for now—they know that Tuvashanoran is dead, and Instructor Parion is leading them in prayers for his soul." The old woman's grim laugh crept down Rani's spine. "We may have planned a different messenger, but our missive has been delivered, all the same. Don't worry, Nar—"

Perhaps the guildmistress would have spoken three syllables, labeling her companion as a guildsman, or four, which would mark him as a soldier. Rani would not even have been surprised to hear five syllables spilled across the Hall of Discipline, denoting the conspirator one of the princely caste.

She was not to learn the man's identity, though. Before Salina could finish her sentence, a tremendous crash echoed down the Apprentices' Corridor. The guttering candle flames all but died, and Rani tumbled back onto her heels, ignoring the stinging pain of her embossed knees.

Steel-shod feet clattered against the stone flags of the discipline chamber, and leather creaked against mail. Rani heard Salina's cry of outrage, and then a man's bellow, cut off in a sickening, wet gurgle.

Rani's heart pounded in her chest like a chick pecking through its egg, and she clambered to her feet. What was it Salina had said? The guild was assembled in the refectory. Rani ran down the Apprentices' Corridor, ignoring the fact that the breeze of her passing extinguished some of the dangerously low candles.

The refectory—there would be companionship there. There would be other apprentices who would understand this most recent injustice. There would be Instructors who could explain to the soldiers, who could make everyone understand that this was all a horrible mistake.

Rani never made it to the refectory, though. The soldiers moved faster than she had thought possible. She had scarcely reached the door to the Apprentices' Corridor when a great monster of a man came crashing through from the Hall of Discipline. He bore a sword, and even in the dying candlelight, Rani could make out the sheen of sticky crimson on his blade. Surprising even herself, she screamed, and the soldier swivelled in her direction like a blind beggar.

His sword swept across Lene's altar, and Rani cried out as the carefully balanced offerings to the god of humility crashed to the floor. Horror at the sacrilege rose in her throat like bile, and she almost turned back to defend the holy altar.

Almost, but not quite. Rani might have been raised to respect all the Thousand Gods, but she certainly was not going to die for them, not here, in a darkened hallway of the guild that despised her. Harnessing the desperate strength of the pursued, she snatched up the velvet altar-skirt dedicated to Lene, pausing only an instant to toss the cloth at the warrior before rushing headlong from the corridor. The soldier bellowed his rage as he freed his wicked sword from the dusty cloth.

The maneuver gained Rani precious seconds, and she fled into the heart of the guildhall, unfettered by sword or mail. She heard the berserker warrior behind her, leaving a trail of destruction, but she knew the corridors of the guildhall like the lines on her palm. Often enough she had been summoned to bring a pot of tea to an Instructor in the dark hours after moonset, and she had ferried laundry, glazing tools, and other endless burdens along every inch of these passages.

Instinctively, Rani dashed toward the refectory, but she traveled by way of the obscure and twisting servants' corridors rather than the main hallways. Gaining a narrow alcove near her destination, she huddled in the shadows, drawing her pale arms inside her dusty jet tunic and crouching against the dark floor. She caught her breath as her pursuer rounded a corner, his mail clashing against the stone walls.

Either Rani's prayers to all the Thousand Gods were answered or the soldier's military helm obscured his vision. Whatever the cause, the berserker stumbled down the hallway toward the refectory, snarling rage at his prey. As soon as the mad soldier had clattered out of earshot, Rani sprang toward a recessed stairway just across the corridor. She took the steps two at a time, recalling when—only a fortnight after her arrival at the guildhall—she and Larinda had first explored this passage. Then, they had thought to escape the completely unreasonable wrath of the Instructors at some misdeed.

The stairs were steep, and Rani's breath stuttered from her lips as she climbed the last dozen steps and emerged onto the narrowest of balconies, perched high above the refectory floor. Stone-carved stands indicated that the space was originally intended for musicians, but the luxury had long since been abandoned—Rani had never dined to the accompaniment of a musical serenade.

From this vantage point, she could make out a milling horde of Instructors, guildsmen, and apprentices. Clearly, the glaziers had been surprised at their afternoon work— many people clutched the tools of their trade. In happier times, Rani might have grinned as one particularly absent-minded Instructor held a piece of crimson glass to her eye to check for impurities, looking for all the world as if she were daft. Rani felt the urge to cry.

Cook was in the refectory, too, holding a wooden spoon coated with evil-looking glop. Even from this height, Rani could hear the woman complaining that her meal was being ruined, that the fire was burning too high, that an apprentice should be in the kitchen stirring the pot.

The soldiers who burst into the refectory obviously did not care if the guild went hungry for the night. Rani recognized her pursuer from the hallway below, but it took her several minutes to realize that all the guards were looking for her. In fact, it was only as one particularly burly man with a filthy, tangled beard pushed Larinda to her knees near the dais that Rani even realized what was happening.

One by one, the apprentices were cut out of the crowd. As the guildsmen and Instructors recognized the wolves in their midst, they attempted to shelter the children. Parion, the Instructor whom Salina had appointed to guide the guild in prayers for Tuvashanoran, swept off his cloak and settled it around the shoulders of one of the most senior apprentices.

The subterfuge, witnessed by a soldier, merely won Parion a backhanded gauntlet across his mouth. Rani felt ashamed when she saw the Instructor's hand come away from his split lip, a trickle of blood glinting even at this distance. As the apprentices were herded to the far end of the refectory, the leader of the guard stormed through the door, his face apoplectic beneath his ornate helm. He sent the heavy wooden door crashing back on its hinges as he pushed Guildmistress Salina into the hall.

The dramatic entrance was heightened by Salina's appearance. Her hair had come undone during her struggle in the Hall of Discipline, and cottony wisps of grey haloed her face. A gash stood out on one pasty cheek, and her quivering hand drifted to the narrow trickle of blood as if she could not believe her fate. Before any of the soldiers could stop Parion, the Instructor moved to his mistress' side, offering Salina an arm to lean on. The guildmistress accepted the assistance with a humility that was more devastating than anything Rani had yet witnessed.

The captain of the guard glowered as Salina lowered herself onto her chair on the dais. Only when the soldier towered over the seated guildmistress did he speak, immediately claiming the undivided attention of all in the room. "I am sent by Shanoranvilli, king of all Morenia, to convey this message to the Glasswrights' Guild. It is known that you have conspired against the heir of Shanoranvilli, the Prince of the People, the man who would have been Defender of the Faith. Tuvashanoran is dead, and Shanoranvilli has decreed that this shall be the penalty."

The guard's words evoked rumbles among the glaziers, protests that they were innocent. The soldier ignored the glasswrights and continued in a stony voice. "At least one of your brotherhood stood on the scaffolding outside the cathedral. We know that you delayed completing your commission until the Presentation Day. We have found the missing pane of glass that let the arrow fly. Even if, by some miracle of the Thousand Gods, a glasswright was not the person who shot the arrow, your brotherhood bears full responsibility. You gave access to the assassin. You summoned His Highness, Prince Tuvashanoran, from his holy meditation to his death."

It was a warning! Rani wanted to cry out. I was trying to *save* the Prince's life! But she held her tongue. Tuvashanoran had been beloved; all Morenia would be set on revenge. No one would ever believe in the innocence of a glasswrights' apprentice, in her very bad luck. The guard continued his pronouncement: "Before my soldiers leave this hall, they will question each of you. Guildmistress Salina has already denied any knowledge of the glasswright who stood on the scaffold, and she has paid the penalty for her ignorance."

The soldier reached behind him and dragged Salina to her feet. As the guard pulled the woman forward, he jerked her right arm up, applying enough force to dislocate her shoulder if she had hesitated in the least. Now, as Salina swayed before her guild, the source of her disorientation became readily apparent. A ragged bandage slipped loose, revealing a crimson flower that bloomed against the length of her forearm.

"Shanoranvilli claims the pledge of blood fealty from every glasswright—Instructor, guildsman, and apprentice alike." Rani's stomach turned as an aide glided forward, slyly displaying the symbols of the guild's blood oath to the king. In one hand, Rani could make out a golden cup, still tinged with crimson. In the other was a glass knife—sharper than any metal blade, Rani had heard, and able to cut as deep. The instruments of the Oath differed for each guild, but the principle remained the same. The king could demand fealty of any of his vassals upon any whim, ordering his subjects to prove their loyalty with an oath sealed in blood. And even the most bitter of protesters would say that unveiling Prince Tuvashanoran's murderer was more than mere whim.

The captain returned to his proclamation, certain now that he had the glasswrights' full attention. "Each of you will be questioned, every morning and every evening, until the identity of the glazier on the scaffold is known. Each of you will be required to swear the oath of blood fealty every time that you are questioned."

There were angry murmurs among the crowd, and Rani clutched the balustrade with rigid fingers. The room seethed against the injustice of the king's order, but Rani raged against Salina. The guildmistress could have named Morada. The guildmistress could have saved her people from the terror and the pain that the soldiers were now certain to distribute. Crouching in the gallery, Rani tried to remember if any other guildsman could name Morada, if there was a single brother or sister who could spare the others from Shanoranvilli's justifiable wrath. For that matter, Rani thought for the first time to search the refectory floor for Morada herself.

Before Rani could complete her review of the ranks, the officer continued. "We know that the glasswright on the scaffold was not the only malfeasor in the cathedral. We will find this guild's apprentice, the whelp who cried out to Tuvashanoran to bring him into range for the assassin. That name, at least, Guildmistress Salina has provided. We know we look for Ranita, and we know she is not among the apprentices gathered here."

Rani's fury was a physical thing. The guild was supposed to be her *family*. It was supposed to take the place of the flesh and blood she had turned from, the folk whom she had abandoned to the market's vagaries. Even as Rani stared at the bloody bandages about Salina's wrist, even as she imagined the sting of salt rubbed into the bloody line of the guildmistress' treacherous fealty oath, tears sparked in her eyes.

She was abandoned, and for a crime she had committed all unknowing.

Again, Rani's attention was recaptured by the captain of the guard. "Aye, we know the name Ranita, and we know the look of the traitor we seek. And we suspect that you know her as well, and at least one of you harbors her even now, in your misguided plot to bring about the fall of the house of Jair. As loyal soldiers to that house, we must do all within our power to help you recall your loyalty to your king."

The soldier made a curt hand gesture, and one of his men swooped into the herd of apprentices that milled at the foot of the dais. Rani squelched a cry as the soldier emerged from the chaos of frantic arms and legs, dragging Larinda forward by her hair. Before any of the stunned glasswrights could move, the soldier whipped a blade from his waist. Larinda did not even have a chance to pull away before she was screaming, holding up four fingers and a bloody stump where her thumb had been. The soldier kicked away the digit and, at the gestured command of his officer, gagged the shrieking girl.

Rani swallowed the sudden sickness that rose in her throat, taking a deep breath against the vertigo that threatened to pitch her onto the refectory floor. Even if she had retched, it was unlikely the sound could have been heard above the turmoil in the room. Instructors and guildsmen cried out, and the herd of terrified apprentices threatened to stampede past the soldiers' bared swords.

"You bastards!" Salina's voice rose above the chaos. "She's only a child!" Salina held out her arms, and Larinda took shuddering refuge, burying her face in the guildmistress's voluminous robes, even as Parion stepped forward to staunch the wound. The captain of the guard took a menacing step toward the trio, but drew back when the glasswrights' hum reached the frenzied pitch of a wasp's nest.

"Aye, she's a child," he settled for grumbling. "And the traitor who called Prince Tuvashanoran to his death was a child as well. We shall mark one child, each dawn, until you deliver your murderous rat to us."

Rani's first thought was to flee the gallery, to run back to the safety of her childhood and the luxury of her mother's embrace. Her second thought was more honorable, and she ordered herself to run down the narrow gallery stairs, to force her way into the refectory to save her fellow apprentices. Her third thought, though, won out. There was no way that she would survive a confrontation with the guard. They were certain she was guilty; they *knew* she had murdered Tuvashanoran.

Indeed, she could hardly argue in her own defense—she *was* guilty, because her words had summoned the prince to his execution. Her actual innocence would hardly be considered by a man who was willing to lop off the thumb—the thumb!—of an innocent child.

And so Rani stayed in the gallery, gripping the stone balustrade as the guardsmen finished their job. She was hardly surprised when a young soldier entered the refectory, bearing aloft the Orb that symbolized the power of the glasswrights' guild.

Each guild in the City had its Orb, consecrated to its particular god and blessed by the High Priest in annual ceremonies of great solemnity. Even now, Rani could envision the Holy Father standing in the guildhall's convocation chamber, invoking Clain, the glaziers' god, while Defender of the Faith Shanoranvilli presented Salina with a large purse of gold coins, rewarding her for royal commissions well completed in the prior year.

The glaziers' Orb, as appropriate to their craft, was fashioned of glass. The workmanship was ancient, the globe's lead tracery as fine as spider's silk. Each fragile metal frame held a panel of glass so thin that it shimmered in the air. Blue swirled into red and green and yellow—dramatic colors presenting a map of all Morenia, fashioned to appear like a globe of all the world.

When Rani was first presented to the guild, she had sworn her apprentice oaths upon the Orb, and she knew that each confirmed master spoke his words of commitment and brotherhood before its delicate glass planes. The Orb was the guild's heart, the core of the glaziers' power.

Even at this distance, Rani could see her fellow guildsmen's awe, inspired by the Orb. The globe's essence was tangible across the room, and a few of the glaziers relaxed visibly in the soothing familiarity of that energy. For Rani, though, the presence of the Orb was anything but soothing. Soldiers who could mutilate a child—what would they do to a bauble of glass and lead?

In an instant, Rani's worst fears were confirmed. The young soldier presented the globe to his captain, scarcely bothering to hide his gloating smile as the burly soldier hoisted the fragile thing. His voice, when it poured across the refectory, was oily and gloating, and Rani was more chilled than she had been to witness Larinda's maiming. "I speak in the name of Shanoranvilli, King of Morenia, lord of the City, and Defender of the Faith. 'My forefathers gave the glasswrights' guild its charter, and in times past the glaziers have served my family well. In remembrance of that old service, I am merciful, and I do not yet demand the life of every man and woman in the guild. I offer this mercy despite the fact that the guild has stolen the heir of my body.'"

The captain raised the globe above his head, even as some of the instructors made a furtive religious sign, muttering gratitude to their individual gods that their lives were to be spared. The soldier continued, unresponsive to the whispered prayers. "'I, Shanoranvilli, have harbored an asp at my breast, in the glasswrights' guild. Therefore, I order the guild destroyed, and all its members outlawed in the eyes of the land. I order its buildings razed, stone by stone, by the labor of the former glasswrights. I order its wells befouled so that no man, woman, or child may think to take shelter in the ruins. I order its lands sown with salt so that no loyal citizen of the realm will pollute his faithful soul by eating of the fruit of the traitors' guild.'"

"Have mercy!" Salina cried, awkwardly setting aside the maimed Larinda and falling to her knees before the captain of the guard. "We are innocent, my lord!"

The soldier ignored her. "'Henceforth, the sign of the glasswrights' guild will be a sign of treachery. Anyone seen wearing the badge of the aforementioned guild will be beaten for a first offense. A second offense will warrant branding—an image of grozing irons crossed upon the brow—to forever mark a traitor. A third offense will be paid for with the traitor's life, worthless as that coin may be.'"

The outcry was probably more than the captain had expected—his men needed to lay about with the flats of their blades before any semblance of order could be restored to the hall. "So speaks Shanoranvilli, King of Morenia, lord of the City, and Defender of the Faith. Let any who defies his will taste the justifiable force of his anger." The soldier raised the Orb above his head, turning it for a moment to catch fitful torchlight. Then, with a flick of powerful wrists, he dashed the glass and lead to the floor.

Glints of color skittered across the flagstones. A collective cry came from the guildsmen, and Rani felt the power that was released as the leaden frame crumpled against the floor. The energy of the disbanded guild was a physical thing, pressing in upon her mind, and she remembered the touch of that power when she had sworn her eager apprentice oaths only a few months before.

The captain, though, did not waste his time with somber reflection on the disbanding of a guild that had been an honorable part of the City's structure for generations. Instead, he gestured to his men to move through the room, and the soldiers ripped away every visible symbol of the glasswrights' now-outlawed brotherhood. Fine fabrics were torn, badges stripped from sleeves. Jeweled tokens were plucked from stunned breasts and pocketed by soldiers, with an eye toward selling valuable stones and melting down gold and silver. The guards were harsher, more avaricious, than the crow that had stolen Rani's own insignia.

Only when the guildsmen stood before the soldiers, silent and shivering in the aftershock of the destruction, did the full import of Shanoranvilli's edict reach Rani. The glasswrights were now deprived of caste. They were no longer the guildsmen they had been since birth, unless they could find some brother guild brave or foolish enough to take in a putative traitor. Every glasswright in Morenia had just been converted to one of the casteless, to one of the Touched.

That realization, more than any other ruthless action by the soldiers, made Rani realize that she must flee the guildhall immediately, if it was not already too late. Forcing herself to set aside the image of the shattering Orb, she scampered down the gallery stairs. She could hear the soldiers in the refectory, once again cutting out the apprentices for imprisonment and execution of Shanoranvilli's bloody orders. Before the confusion could be sorted, Rani sprinted down the stone hallway to her bedchamber.

Once there, she found surprisingly little that she needed. Her scant clothing, all proudly bearing her guild's badge, was as good as a death sentence. As an apprentice, she owned nothing; by contract, all of her possessions belonged to the brotherhood. Still, she reached beneath her mattress, extracting the few treasures she had hoarded.

There was the steel blade from Zarithia her father had given her, her first reward for laying out the merchant's stall and luring passersby. There was a four-sided coin from some distant land to the south, pierced and threaded onto a rawhide thong by her oldest brother, Bardo. There was a doll the size of her hand, made out of a knotted rag by her mother when Rani was a babe. There was a piece of cobalt glass that pooled in her palm, smooth and flawless, rescued from a trash heap the first day that Rani had swept the Instructors' workroom. And there was a mirror that had been her birth-gift from the Merchants' Council. Its perfect circle was solid silver, with a raised boss on the back, showing a lion attacking a mountain goat. Her fingers automatically caressed the sinewy cat's body. "Brave as a lion, fleet as a lion," she muttered, remembering her father's incantation as he entrusted her with the treasure when she had left for the guildhall.

Rani shoved her meager possessions into her pockets, forcing them down among the windfall apples she had recovered in the garden. A quick glance outside her door proved the hallway still deserted, but she knew her luck could not hold.

Indeed, Rani had just gained the guildhall doors, the massive stone portals that opened onto the gardens, when she heard the crowd stir in the refectory. The soldiers spoke in harsh voices, and it was apparent that they were driving the apprentices to Shanoranvilli's legendary dungeons.

Rani darted outside, but even in the twilight, she could see the guards at the gate. There was no time to climb her apple tree and scale the wall; an alarm would surely sound. Rani ducked behind the hall's west wing, dashing to the massive glass kilns that squatted on their raised stony platform.

Used to fire glazes onto panes of glass, the ovens were fed dry oak by over-heated apprentices. Rani knew that the nearest oast had last been used to fire Morada's Defender Window—it had been empty for at least three days, for Rani herself had borne the responsibility of keeping the kiln fueled. Still, the ceramic oven held heat for days after a firing, and she could feel the warmth radiating from the clay walls in the cooling autumn night. She tugged at the heavy door, leaning back with all her weight to make it swing outward.

The wave of heat was like the summer sun baking a field of obsidian. Before Rani could draw back, though, she heard the commotion outside the guildhall. Soldiers' voices were loud in the night, and there was the clang of metal on metal. Rani had no idea how long it would take for the soldiers to begin to raze the hall, but she was certain to be captured if the captain set a guard about the grounds tonight. Above the pounding of her heart, Rani could just make out a soldier's order, "I want the perimeter secured before we bring out the guildmistress. There's no telling what these treacherous dogs will do in the dark."

Rani's last hesitation was squelched as a young voice called out from the corner of the building. "Yes, sir!" The guard made no secret of his mission as he swept his sword from its scabbard. Rani could make out the weapon's moon-shadow as the soldier approached the corner of the guildhall.

Rani took one deep breath of the cool night air and ducked into the kiln. She barely managed to pull the door closed before the guard's booted feet crunched on the oven's gravel platform.

CHAPTER 3

Rani watched in horror as Tuvashanoran rose from the altar, lifting his iron-sinewed hand to pluck the arrow buried deep in his eye. As he pulled the quivering shaft from his flesh, it writhed in his fist, shriveling into a stub. Blood still dripped from the end, crimson droplets that steamed on the marble dais, and Rani realized that the Prince did not hold an arrow; rather, he grasped Larinda's severed thumb. Before Rani could scream her horror, Tuvashanoran turned to where she knelt in the suddenly empty cathedral, drilling into her with his steely eyes. "It was not enough to murder me," he intoned. "You needed to strike your sister apprentice as well."

"No!" Rani cried, and the single word dragged her up to consciousness. Her heart pounded in her chest, and her tunic was drenched in sweat. For a long minute, she was too terrified to open her eyes, too afraid that the gritty floor beneath her would be in the cathedral, with Tuvashanoran standing in judgment over her.

Her breath came in short gasps, snagging normal thought, and she struggled to untangle herself from her nightmare's clinging shroud. Opening her eyes, she did not recognize the strange closet surrounding her, or her hard bed. No wonder she had had such foul dreams—she must have offended Cook yet again, committed some arcane violation of the guild's rules that she certainly could have avoided if only she'd been born to the guildsman's class. Her penalty had clearly been sleeping in the sweltering pantry, futilely warding off mice from the Instructors' flour.

Sighing against Cook's barrage that was certain to accompany her morning appearance in the kitchen, Rani sat up, striking her head against the ceiling and discovering that she certainly was not in the pantry. Memory flooded back as she rubbed her forehead—visions of fleeing the berserker warrior, Larinda's bleeding hand, and the vengeance King Shanoranvilli had declared against the guildhall.

Now, Rani could recall her narrow escape from the king's guard, crouching in the steaming oven, certain that a soldier would throw open the door at any minute. She had regretted her impetuous hiding place almost as soon as she pulled the door closed. She could not see prospective invaders, and the stone thoroughly muffled any approaching footsteps. More than once, Rani imagined the door grating open against the brick platform, and she crouched against the kiln wall, fingering her Zarithian blade.

Ultimately, though, exhaustion eroded terror, and she slipped into an uneasy sleep peppered with horrific nightmares. Now, her stomach clenched, and she remembered that she had not eaten since devouring those few apples yesterday afternoon. Sweet as they had been, the fruit was no substitute for missed meals, and Rani rummaged in her tunic pockets, rooting out the apples she had hidden away. Her first bite was bruised, the flesh mealy and tasteless. Rani wrinkled her nose and started to toss away the fruit. Just as she began to flick her wrist, though, she realized that another meal might not come easily. The second and third apples were just as bruised, but Rani was a little less ravenous when she had finished them.

Of course, food was only part of the problem. Rani's hands were sticky with apple juice. Her clothes stuck to her body in uncomfortable patches on the outside, and her bladder pressed painfully from the inside. Grimacing in the dark, Rani crept to the kiln's door, easing open the heavy stone so she could peer outside.

Blinking in the sudden light, she dashed away involuntary tears. Only after forcing her eyes to stay open in the brilliance did she realize it wasn't actually bright at all. In fact, she was peering out at night-time, and only a single torch flickered in her line of sight. One torch, and an army of soldiers.

Rani froze like a deer startled by hunters. Straining her ears, she could make out an incessant scraping sound, a noise so persistent she wondered how she had ignored it so far. A shiver crept up her spine, changing almost to a convulsion as fresh air slapped her sodden chest. Trying to place the totally unfamiliar sound, Rani set her teeth and dared to edge her prison door open a little wider. The kiln door gritted on its stone platform, the sound echoed by the cavernous oven until it seemed that the alarm would summon every soldier in the quarter. Rani nearly compounded her error by crying aloud when she learned the source of the scraping noise. Stone by stone, the proud guildhall was being leveled. Rani stared in horror as teams of glasswrights struggled in rope harnesses, leaning forward under the steely eyes of Shanoranvilli's soldiers. Instructors stood on the crumbling walls, wedging metal bars into the ruined hall, prying out great blocks of stone. Hesitating workers were immediately confronted by uniformed soldiers, and Rani gasped indignantly at the crack of a whip—a whip!—as if the guildsmen were nothing more than dray animals!

Indignation melted to guilt in a heartbeat. How could she have brought this upon her guild, upon the folk who had adopted an unworthy merchant brat and pledged to teach her a valuable craft? For an instant, she thought to present herself to the soldiers, to creep from her hiding place and confess that she had summoned Tuvashanoran to his death. Her admission might ease the misery painted before her, and it would be better than huddling helplessly on the kiln platform.

Before she could move, though, a tiny voice murmured in the back of her skull. *She* was not responsible for the destruction of the guildhall. *She* had nothing to do with the attack on Tuvashanoran. Besides, the soldiers had spoken plainly enough in the refectory—they sought vengeance, and nothing could save the glasswrights' guild now. The hall would be razed, the fields sown with salt, the well fouled, and Rani's sacrifice would change nothing.

Thoughts of the well forced Rani's mind back to her current predicament—thirst made her tongue thick in her throat. Sighing, she looked about her cubby hole, ascertaining that she had left nothing behind. She took a deep breath and forced the kiln door open another spare inch.

The air flowing into the oven was freezing, and Rani's teeth chattered, despite her terror that the soldiers would overhear. As she crept from the oast, a breeze picked up, blowing some of the guildhall's dusty corpse into her eyes and nose. She smothered a dry cough and stifled a sneeze, clutching her arms about her to ward off the midnight air.

It did not take military prowess to realize that Rani's only means of escape was back in the apple orchard. Reversing the process of her inauspicious arrival, she could scale the wall with the help of the gnarled trees, make her way down the abandoned alley. As Rani huddled against the brick oven, the orchard looked impossibly distant—she needed to cross the entire kiln-yard and Cook's vegetable garden. Listening to the scrape of stones from the guildhall, a sound like the grating of bones, Rani was too afraid to move.

Too afraid, that was, until the captain of the guard took the decision from her. "You! Aye, you, you good for nothing sack of bones!" Rani's heart clenched in her chest. "Get your miserable arse over here and lend a hand with these prisoners! The kilns are coming down next—every last stone of them!" Only then did Rani realize the captain spoke to someone else, someone dangerously near her hiding place.

A soldier materialized out of the gloom, muttering under his breath and settling a hand on the hilt of his broadsword. Swearing an atrocious curse, the man kicked open the kiln door, muttering about the grit and the heat. The soldier had been lounging in the shadows on the far side of her kiln; Rani had escaped detection by a matter of minutes. As it was, he might peer into the gloom between the ovens at any moment, glimpsing the white gleam of her eyes in the midnight murk. If she hoped to make her escape, the time had come.

Drawing a deep breath and tugging at her tunic, Rani ducked from the deep shadow of her kiln to the next. No soldier cried out in rage; no alarm disrupted the glasswrights' steady labor. Her successful jump gave her confidence, and she ducked to the next oven, and the next, until she was at the end of the row.

From there, it was a simple dash to Cook's garden. Fortunately, Rani had been delinquent in completing her chores; she had not yet cleaned up the garden's autumn debris. Tangles of squash vines massed at the edges, and towering stalks waved where the onions had gone to seed. Rani crawled through a tangle of melon vines until she reached the corn, and then she was able to jog down the narrow rows, running nearly upright. She tried not to think about how many times Cook had ordered her into the garden, how many times she had complained about the endless platters of vegetables, without a hint of meat for a hungry young apprentice. She was grateful she had knelt in the fresh summer earth, pulling weeds and coaxing the garden to robust life.

She only wished that she had not been quite so zealous in harvesting the garden's riches for the guildhall kitchen. One melon—was that so much to ask for? So much to have overlooked?

Gaid, the god of gardens, must have heard her petulant demand, for she stumbled even as she thought her desire, and her hand came down hard on a feathery plume of greens. Tugging at the vegetables, Rani was rewarded with a cluster of thick carrots. She resisted the urge to gnaw on one of the orange roots then and there. Instead, remembering how grateful she had been for the apples she had tucked away before her night in the kiln, she shoved the roots deep into a tunic pocket. She clutched for more bounty but discovered that there were limits to Gaid's generosity.

Rani worked her way to the stone-lined edge of the garden,

ready to dart past the well and melt into the orchard like a midnight shadow. She almost cried out in frustration when she discovered that soldiers had beaten her to the spot. Yet another of Shanoranvilli's iron-clad captains strode about the edge of the plot, roaring at a crew of glasswrights as if they were his personal slaves. "You miserable beasts! You think I don't know what you're doing? You think I don't see how every last one of you is plotting and planning, waiting to murder again!"

A crack rang out closer than Rani had expected, and she crouched lower behind her screen of dried vines as the soldier curled up his long whip. "You, goat-face!" Rani followed the captain's gesture into the night, realizing with a gasp that the soldier was berating Cook—and that the old woman was a scant meter away. "You put your back into that work, or I'll lay such stripes on you, you'll wish your dam had never spread her legs."

Rani braced herself for the furious explosion that was certain to follow. Cook never permitted anyone to gainsay her, even when she was dumping an extra handful of salt into the stew. She certainly would not tolerate such foul language, even if the speaker *was* of a different caste. The soldier, oblivious to his imminent peril, continued, "Aye, you old hag! You put your back into hauling, or you'll find yourself *on* your back, if any of my men is desperate enough for a poke!"

Now, Rani understood that the workers were dragging stones to the well, razing the careful garden borders at the same time that they blocked off the guild's water supply. The rocks nearest the well were already gone, and the workers were forced to range farther afield. Cook had chosen a stone near Rani's hiding place.

The apprentice was close enough to see the hatred set in Cook's thin lips—close enough that the old woman looked up when the child gasped at the soldier's brutal words. Rani shut her eyes, scarcely bothering to offer up a fruitless prayer to Jun, the god of night, that he might take her under his wings and shield her from the soldiers' eyes, even if Cook had spotted her. "You ninny!" hissed the all-too-familiar voice. "Open your eyes so you can see where you're going!"

Rani was so startled she broke off her prayer in mid-word. Cook stood less than an arm's length away, the old woman's face contorted in fury as she went through the motions of struggling with the heavy stone. "Count to ten, then run for the wall." When Rani only shook her head, uncomprehending, Cook called on the god of kitchens: "Lan bless us, you'll only get one chance. Find Morada and *prove them wrong!*"

Before Rani could question the old woman, before she could ask where she was to go and who she was to enlist in her battle to find the missing Instructor, the soldier's whip sang through the air, whistling just above the apprentice's head. "Don't waste your breath on prayers, old hag! Not one of the Thousand Gods would spare you the time of day."

The whip licked the woman's cheek, leaving a trail of blood, black in the moonlight. Then, Cook launched herself from the ravaged garden, hurtling her rocky burden at the soldier with a lioness' single-minded courage.

The guard was surprised by the attack, and his terrible oaths rang out in the night. Other guildsmen stared stupidly, already too dulled by their labor to find liberation—or even encouragement—in Cook's brave rebellion. The captain of the guard hollered from his post by the kilns, and the ground trembled under metal-clad feet as soldiers gathered from all over the compound.

Rani sprang away from the commotion at the well, leaping for the orchard and lunging from gnarled trunk to gnarled trunk in a frantic effort to melt into shadow. She wriggled up one particularly knobby tree near the edge of the copse, ignoring the scrape of bark against her palms. Reaching the last branch broad enough to support her weight, she took a single steadying breath and launched herself at the wall.

There was one horrifying instant when she discovered she had miscalculated her leap, and the breath was crushed from her narrow chest as she came up sharp against the wall. She gasped for air and stifled a sob, certain she would feel a soldier's gauntleted hands on her legs at any instant. Driven by blind terror, she caught her bottom lip in her teeth and forced first one leg to the top of the barrier, then the other.

She lay across the top of the wall for a long second, gathering her breath and bracing herself for the hue and cry the soldiers were certain to raise. Ignoring the sting of scraped palms and knees, she clutched the stone like an orphan and offered up a prayer, calling on Lan, whose help Cook had already enlisted.

Even though she knew she was looking back at certain death, she could not refrain from one last glance at her adoptive home. Already, the guildhall's familiar outline was destroyed, the jagged teeth of its rotted towers lurid in the torchlight. A crew of soldiers swarmed in the kilnyard like maggots on a corpse, and Rani could scarcely believe that her sheltering oven was already reduced to rubble.

That destruction was nothing, though, compared to the tumult closest at hand. Cook was surrounded by half a dozen soldiers. The woman's cries floated across the orchard. "You drunken sots! The guild had nothing to do with the prince's murder! By First God Ait, I've never seen men as foolish as you!"

The woman's taunts were met by gauntleted fists, and Rani heard the crunch of breaking bones, even across the orchard. "You blooming idiots!" Cook's voice shrilled against the pain. "In the name of Lan, find the true murderer—find Instructor Morada and leave us to mourn the Prince!"

Rani knew Cook directed those last words at her, even as the soldiers surged forward, pummeling the woman into silence. Rani forced herself to look away, ordered herself to exploit the distraction as all the soldiers focused their attention on one rebellious old woman.

Dropping over the stone enclosure, Rani barely remembered to roll when she hit the ground. The breath was knocked out of her, and it took a long minute to recall how to climb to her feet, how to gather her arms and legs and run—run as fast as if wolves pursued her under the cloak of night.

Soon, though, Rani was forced to stop her headlong flight, brought up short as she gasped for exhausted breath, sobbing like a baby. Gulping from a fountain at the heart of the Guildsmen's Quarter, she remonstrated with herself. Her behavior was ridiculous. She had not cried when she *arrived* at the Guildhall, when she was all alone in the world. She certainly wasn't going to disgrace herself and her guild now, bawling like an infant in the night. Cook would expect more of her. The old woman would never forgive Rani if she dishonored the glasswrights with tears that only proved she was too weak to belong in her current caste.

In fact, Rani should be husbanding the new strength that she had found, the new power that sharpened her wits and lent strength to her body. It was as if Cook's cries to Lan had been answered, as if the kitchen god had truly adopted Rani as his own. How else could one lonely apprentice escape an entire platoon of soldiers bent on her capture?

Rani vowed to light a candle to Lan when she next had the chance. The kitchen god... he was an odd patron for a merchant girl turned glasswright. But if Lan had seen fit to respond to Cook's prayers, who was Rani to protest? Who was Rani to gainsay her elders and her betters?

Rani's silent tongue-lashing worked its magic, and she retreated to a deep doorway, gathering her thoughts close with her ragged tunic. Search out Morada, that's what Cook had said. How was she supposed to do that—one disenfranchised apprentice wandering the City's streets without even a penny to her name?

Rani's head began to ache, and she remembered the soothing herb tea her mother made whenever she was ill. The thought brought fresh tears to her eyes. She imagined her mother's cool hand laid across her brow, smoothing back her hair, forcing away fear and exhaustion and childish nightmares.

Her family may have bought her way into the guild, and they might fear the wrath of Shanoranvilli's soldiers, but they would certainly take her in. That's what family *meant*.

Rani picked her way through the streets. Except for the

Pilgrims' Bell, tolling steadily in the foggy night, the City was quiet now. The constant clang was comforting; Rani had heard it every night of her life. She carefully schooled her thoughts away from the memory of Prince Tuvashanoran and his daring feat of manning the abandoned Pilgrims' Bell. Those stories were past, as dead as the man who inspired them.

Rani picked up speed as she made her way to the Merchants Quarter. Now, she knew the streets. She had played in them as a young child, roamed them to bring customers to her family's stall. She knew the way the cobblestones buckled in this patch, and she automatically ducked through a stone gateway to cut through the potter's tiny yard on the corner near her family's home.

Despite her shivering exhaustion, Rani let a smile cross her lips. She would come home, and her mother would gather her up in fat arms, pressing Rani's head against her breasts in the way that usually drove Rani to squirm away with a wrinkled nose of disgust. Rani's father would listen to her gravely, shaking his head in disappointment that his daughter had gotten herself meshed in such misdeeds. Bardo, her brother, would be the one to help her. He would let their mother shed a tear or two, and he would let their father rant and rave, but it would be Bardo who would lead Rani through the streets in the dawn. He would walk her to the Palace, her hand neatly folded in his, and they would explain what a terrible mistake had been made.

Bardo would make everything right.

Rani rounded the last corner, reassuring herself that her brother had the power to set the world straight. She was so intent on thinking about Bardo that she forgot to look where she was going. She came up short on a sooty flagstone, her hand raised to knock on a non-existent door.

Her home was reduced to smoky rubble.

Rani stared at the charred ruins in disbelief, staggering back to the stone curb across the narrow street. She could smell the remnants of the fire, and she could see lazy smoke spiraling up from the collapsed beams of her parents' house.

She could taste the soot on the back of her tongue as clearly as if she had kissed the blackened lintel of her home.

"Get away from here!"

Rani jumped at the hissed anger, stifling a cry as she whirled to face a midnight shadow. "Varna!" Rani was so relieved to see her childhood playmate that she almost chanted the name. She took a step toward the tinker's daughter, coating her words with gratitude that she had finally found an ally in her struggle. "You won't believe—"

"I won't believe any words from your lying mouth!"

Rani stepped back as if she'd been slapped. "Varna, it's not true, whatever they've said."

Varna spat at her feet. "Aye, Rani. Just as it wasn't true when you told me we'd work the stalls together this summer. Just as it wasn't true when you told me you'd never go to some guildhall, to be a snotty apprentice."

"Varna, you *know* I didn't want to leave you. But my parents were willing, were able to pay for me to join the hall, to make the glass—"

"Glass! They say the arrow you shot had a glass tip, and that's why the prince died so quickly."

"Varna, I didn't shoot the arrow. I *couldn't* have—I was inside the cathedral. I saw the whole thing."

Varna did not let facts cut short her tirade. "Aye, you were inside the cathedral, where no merchant child had a right to be. They say you cried out and Tuvashanoran rose to his death. You killed the prince, whether you shot the arrow or merely cleared the way for one of your *sisters* to do it."

"Morada was not my sister! Morada was a nasty Instructor who could care less whether I lived or died. Varna, Morada was worse than any of the customers we ever served. She was mean, and rude—"

"I wouldn't expect you to say anything else. How foolish do you think I am, Rani? I believed you when you said you'd never leave the Merchant's Quarter. You lied then—why shouldn't you lie now, telling me how terrible the guildsmen are? What did you say to them about the people you left behind? What did you tell them about me?"

Rani gaped at Varna, amazed at the transparent jealousy in her friend's voice. "Varna, I never mentioned you to them."

"So, even your closest friend was not worthy of mention in the guildhall! Rani, you forgot everyone when you left behind your family. Merchants have no business in a guildhall."

"Varna, that's not fair! You were just as happy as I was when the guild agreed to take me in. You know how I can draw, how I can design the glass—"

"I know how you promised to be my friend."

"Varna!" Goody Tinker's voice sliced through Rani's strangled response. "I told you to wake me if those god-forsaken fools came back." Before Rani could duck away into the night, Varna's mother stepped into the doorway of her soot-stained house, cradling a sleeping infant in one brawny arm.

"Goody Tinker!" Rani exclaimed. "What happened? Where is my family?"

"Get away, witchling!" The woman's fingers flew in a sign of warding. "You've worked your evil on the prince, now don't think you can come back to destroy the homes of good people."

"Destroy the homes? Goody Tinker, I had nothing to do with this! Where are my mother and father? Where is Bardo?"

"Gone! As you should be! Whatever fate they meet, it's too good for them!"

"Goody Tinker, I don't understand! I don't know what you're saying—"

"Aye, and we didn't know what the soldiers were saying when they dragged us from our beds. They barely gave me time to waken Varna and pull my Dona from her cradle— they would have harmed my babes just like that." The woman snapped her fingers in front of Rani's nose. "If they hadn't stopped to confiscate your father's trinkets, we all might have smothered in our beds, with the smoke billowing about."

Rani stared at the scorched flagstones, at the heat that had twisted her neighbors' stalls. Certainly, the tinker's home was left standing, but the fog had lifted enough to show that the fancy-painted sign—the board Goody Tinker had taken such pride in only a few months before—was black with soot as it swung in the night breeze.

"You've brought shame on us, girl! You plucked the flower of Shanoranvilli, and the City will never be the same. Get away from here—you don't belong with civilized folk."

"Please, Goody Tinker, let me explain—"

"Guard!"

Rani scrambled into the night, frantic to leave behind her home, desperate to escape the safety she had sought only a few minutes before. As she rounded the corner, she realized that the voice that had summoned the guards was Varna's. Rani's own friend had turned against her.

This time, Rani fled without any conscious plan. She was exhausted; her sleep in the kiln had completely failed to refresh her. Nevertheless, she was able to avoid the guards easily, familiar as she was with this quarter. The fog assisted her escape, and she drifted in and out of the clammy banks, with only the tolling Pilgrims' Bell and her pounding heart to break the silence of the sleeping City.

The entire time she ran, Rani wondered about Goody Tinker's words. Her mother, her father, all her brothers and sisters... They couldn't be dead; Goody would not have spoken about them in the present tense. Rather, they must be taken into Shanoranvilli's dungeons, reluctant companions to the glasswrights' apprentices.

That conclusion was easier to dwell on than the other lesson she had learned on the tinkers' doorstep. Varna hated her. Varna, who had been her best friend, whom she had pledged to love as a sister for her entire life.... Varna had called the guards.

When a stitch daggered her side, Rani slowed her headlong pace and set aside her bitter thoughts. She staggered down deserted streets, stumbling over her own feet in utter exhaustion. Pulling her tunic closer and cinching in the waist, she wished that she had managed to keep her cloak. When her fingers snagged in the ragged hole where her guild badge used to be, she could only stare stupidly at the trailing threads.

That evil crow had done her a service. Tuvashanoran's edict against the Guild would have forced her to sacrifice the shiny emblem herself; better that some living creature profit from the loss. *That* thought was so drenched in self-pity that Rani could not keep a solitary tear from leaking onto her cheeks. The tear turned to a sob, and the sob to a torrent. Huddling in a shadowed doorway, a thirteen-year-old disgraced apprentice cried herself to sleep, accompanied only by the tolling of the Pilgrims' Bell, summoning wanderers from the fog-shrouded hillsides around the City.

CHAPTER 4

Rani woke before dawn. At first, she was not sure what had summoned her from her uneasy dreams. Then, she realized that it was her turn to light the kitchen fires, and she'd best hurry or Cook would be furious. That thought, of course, reminded her that Cook *was* furious, if she wasn't dead. And that reminded her that she had promised to light a candle to Lan. Rani rolled over and forced her eyes to open.

And closed them again when she saw the ring of eyes staring back at her.

"Cor!" came a harsh exclamation. "Ye've gone 'n' woke 'er, Rabe!"

"I dinna *touch* 'er! She woke 'erself!"

"Ye breathed so loud she could 'ardly 'elp 'erself, could she?"

The Touched! Ever since she'd been a baby, Rani had been threatened with banishment to the casteless Touched when she'd been lazy or had done wrong. "Sweep the hearth, or I'll turn you out among the Touched," Rani's mother had grumbled. "If you don't polish that silver buckle, you might as well go run with the Touched." The Touched were dirty and cruel and more than a little jealous of any proper merchant girl, or a guild-sworn apprentice. Rani watched through slitted eyes as a boy—Rabe?—reached out one grimy finger to poke her side. He managed to find the bruises she had gathered against the guild wall, and the pain throbbed beneath her skin. "Go ahead. Tell 'er I dinna wake ye, or we'll 'ear nothin' else fer a week."

Rani opened her eyes again, swallowing hard before turning to the children's apparent leader, the girl who had spoken first. Rani had to clear her throat before she could make herself understood. "I woke myself. Because I remembered I have to work in the guildhall."

"Ohhhh," the girl breathed. "The *guild* 'all. Beggin' yer pardon, milady." The Touched child faked a curtsey, a look of disgust twisting her filthy features, and the boy snorted. "And what guild would that be?"

"The gl—" Rani started to answer, then remembered the soldiers' horrible charge. Who knew what stories had already spread to the streets? What would these children do to her, if they knew the king desired her death? Shaking away the last cobwebs of sleep, Rani forced herself back against the alley wall. One hand crept inside her tunic pocket, closing comfortingly around her Zarithian knife. "What difference does it make to you?"

"What difference?" the girl crowed. "What difference! We wouldna want t' 'ave a' 'undesirable element' roamin' th' streets at night, now would we? After all, King Shanoranvilli 'as 'is reputation t' think of. Wouldna want pilgrims t' fear for their lives i' th' city streets, eh?"

The boy jabbed a sharp finger into Rani's breastbone. "'N' I don't think ye're from any guild, if ye're sleepin' 'ere i' th' street."

"I can sleep where I choose!" Rani protested, raising her chin defiantly.

"Aye, 'n' what's yer name, that we may be th' judge o' yer choices?" The boy took a step closer with his challenging words, and his breath stank as he forced Rani to lean away.

"My name is Ra—" Rani caught herself before she voiced the second syllable. What was her name? If she gave her birth name, Rani, then the Touched would know that she belonged to a merchant family. They could surmise that her presence in the streets, alone in the cold night, meant that she had been driven from her family home for some unfathomable shame. If she gave her guild name, Ranita, that would only give rise to more unwelcome questions, inquiries that could not stand against Rani's torn tunic. She swallowed hard and restated her assumed name with pretended authority. "Rai."

The girl shook her head scornfully, spitting out the single syllable. "Rai. Ye're stakin' claim to a Touched name, then, are ye?"

"Touched or a God," Rani muttered, wondering if she would actually have to use the metal knife that warmed beneath her fingers. Her blasphemy drew an unexpected laugh from the girl.

"Ach, ye're no Touched girl, but ye've figured our way o' thinkin'. Touched, Gods, we draw no lines 'ere i' th' streets. What've ye got t' share wi' us, Rai?"

"To share? I don't have—" Rani remembered the carrots she had dug reflexively from Cook's plot. "I've brought carrots from the garden."

"Garden! We Touched don't 'ave *gardens*, girl. Don't make me call ye a liar."

"Not *my* garden. The garden of the gl—" Rani's assumed scorn melted as she realized she could not even speak the name of her former home. These Touched brats might just be waiting for the opportunity to summon the guard. Everyone knew you couldn't trust the Touched, especially not the bands of ragtag children who roamed the City unsupervised while their parents worked as servants for the nobles and the priests. Rani swallowed a tight knot of fear and reformulated her retort. "The garden at the stone heap Shanoranvilli's soldiers are destroying. I ducked through the wall they're tearing down and helped myself. Those miserable guildsmen won't have any need of *carrots* when the king is through with them."

Either the swagger in Rani's voice was convincing, or the children were awed by her bravery in facing down Shanoranvilli's men. The crew stepped back, and even the leader paused before settling her possessive hand on the filthy roots. "Been chased by th' kings' men m'self, I've been. Can make a soul 'ungry." Strong teeth crunched on carrots, and Rani dutifully produced roots for each of the other children. Rabe snatched two, and Rani was left with only one gnarled carrot for herself. Her loss was swiftly forgotten as the Touched's leader extended a grimy hand. "Name's Mair."

Each of the other children took their cue from their leader, and Rani found herself shaking one dirty paw after another. She barely resisted the urge to rub her hand against her thigh after each filthy contact, especially when a challenge sparked from Rabe's eyes as he squeezed her fingers tightly.

"So, Rai," Mair continued. "Ye dinna talk like ye're from th' City, at least not fro' th' Touched. Ye might watch that, y'know. If th' guard 'eard ye, they'd ask 'ard questions. They've been a little crazed, since 'Is Lordship took that arrow in 'is eye."

"May the Prince's soul rest in peace," Rani mumbled, lapsing into the etiquette her mother had pounded into her. The piety merely garnered a newly appraising look from the Touched children.

"P'r'aps ye're a Pilgrim's child, forgotten i' th' City streets?"

"No, I—"

"A *Pilgrim's* child might not know our ways, 'n' she might say th' wrong things at th' wrong time 'n' be o'erlooked. By th' Guard. Or by others i' th' Streets."

Before Rani could respond, a clatter of boots on cobblestones echoed from the far end of the alley. "Soldiers!" hissed Mair, and the children scattered into doorways and scraps of shadow. Rani, taken by surprise, did not leap with the same agility and was left exposed in the middle of the street.

"Rai—" came Mair's strangled warning, bitten off as the guard turned down the narrow lane. It was too late— Rani would only endanger the other children by following them into a doorway now. The soldiers would not hesitate to round up the entire group, meting out whatever justice a band of Touched urchins could expect on a misty morning when a prince had just been murdered.

Muttering a prayer to her new patron, Lan, Rani drew herself up to her full height as the soldiers emerged from the mist. "On your knees before your betters, brat. We heard your whispering, and the curfew not over for another hour yet. Who were you talking to? And why shouldn't we cut you down on the spot?"

Rani froze as even more soldiers loomed out of the fog. Their voices were harsh against the mist, and she surprised herself by bursting into explosive tears.

"Aye, you stand there! Keep your hands where we can see them!" The guard's harsh orders fed Rani's sobs, and she hiccuped for breath as she dropped her gnawed carrot to the cobblestones. Even as she wept, though, a plan formed in the most devious corner of her mind. She measured out a little more despair into her tears and peeked up at the troops' leader from beneath silvered lashes.

"P-please, your honor," she stammered, then let her voice tremble away into another shuddering gasp. From the corner of her eye, she saw her words begin to have their desired effect; the soldier who had circled around to her right let his sword droop toward the cobble stones. She sniffled and tried again, "If you please, your honor, could you direct me toward the marketplace?"

"And what would a gutter rat like you want with the marketplace, an hour before dawn?"

Rani despaired at the man's harsh tone, and her voice quavered as she spun out her answer. "My da said I should meet him there if I ever got l-l-lost in the City!"

"And who's your da?"

"Thomas Pilgrim, your honor. We've walked all the way from Tyne-on-Shane."

"Tyne-on-Shane? I've never heard of it."

"There's no reason your honor should have," Rani responded quickly, neglecting to mention that the village had not existed a few heartbeats earlier. "We are a humble little village, far to the north. Your honor could not know the home of every poor Pilgrim who walks in Jair's footsteps." Rani hastily made a holy sign as she spoke the name of the

First Pilgrim, remembering to sniffle a little as the guard furrowed his brow.

"If you're a pilgrim, where's your Star?"

Rani burst into new tears; she had been so hopeful she could carry off this sham. Of course she would be discovered—all pilgrims carried the Thousand-Pointed Star as a symbol of their mission. A Star would have been her ticket to inns along the road, through the City gates, into the holiest of chapels in the cathedral. With the Star, she was a sacred wanderer who commanded the religious dedication of the guard. Without it, she was only a street urchin.

"Th-that's why I'm here," she choked on the lie. "I had my Star when I came into the City, and I lost it in the streets. The Touched attacked me in the alley there, and they ripped it from my clothes. If I don't find it, my da'll have my hide."

Her conscience twinged as she accused Mair and her cohorts of crimes against her imagined Pilgrim self, but she rapidly translated her guilt into vulnerability, adding to the image by rubbing her thin arms in the chill fog. Her pitiful sobs proved too much for the kindly soldier on her right. "Don't cry, little pilgrim." Burly arms pulled her to her feet, and Rani had to discipline herself not to shove away the raspy uniform. "We'll take you to the marketplace. Your da will come for you at dawn."

"My da'll never speak to me again!" Rani managed to exclaim as the guard extracted a grimy kerchief from a pouch at his waist.

"Nonsense. He'll be so relieved to get you back he'll forget your wandering off. Blow." Rani obediently cleared her runny nose, acting as if she were the infant this soldier apparently expected, rather than a self-possessed girl of thirteen. "You're just lucky it was the guard that found you. You can never be too wary of the Touched, and other miscreants roaming these streets."

"Miscreants?" Rani's voice trembled over the unfamiliar word.

"Aye, little pilgrim. You must be new to the city, if you have not heard our woes. An evil girl has helped to murder

Prince Tuvashanoran. Just tonight, she tried to break into a tinker's shop, stealing food and threatening to set fire to an infant's cradle."

Rani let a little of her residual anger at Varna—at her *former* best friend—spill into her words. "No one could be so evil!"

"Aye, little pilgrim, so you might think. But not all girls are as obedient as you." The soldier wiped away Rani's tears with an avuncular thumb. "Come along, little one. We'll take you to the marketplace. It's not safe to wander these streets alone. You've already found the Touched—you don't know what other evil you might encounter."

Rani could see that the captain of the guard was not as tender-hearted as this man, but she let her adoptive savior settle his military cloak about her shoulders. The garment was long on her, fluttering about her knees. Before Rani could be grateful for the warmth, the soldier exclaimed, "What ho!" He poked his fingers through the ragged hole in her tunic, through the threads that had sported her glasswright's badge. "What's this?"

"That's where my Star was! That's where my ma stitched on my Pilgrim's badge, so I could pass through the City protected by all the Thousand Gods!" Real panic tinged Rani's voice, and she tried to wriggle free from the guard's grasp. The captain harrumphed, and she tried to translate the sound to either disbelief of a murderer's tale or disgust at a pilgrim's clumsiness. Her adoptive soldier flashed a look at his superior.

"Permission to accompany this child to the marketplace, Captain?"

"Who's to say she's not the brat we're looking for, man?"

"Look at her! Does she look like she was part of a plot to kill Prince Tuvashanoran? This little one could hardly blow her own nose!"

Rani swallowed her indignation at the man's patronizing tone, hunching her shoulders to make herself appear even smaller. The captain stared at her pitiful form and snarled to his man, "Go ahead, then. Take her to the market. If her father's not in sight, hand her over to the Council, and let's be about our watch."

The soldier saluted, and Rani bobbed her head in wordless gratitude. She remained silent as they worked their way through the streets, not even crying out when shadows flickered in the fog and she just made out the shapes of the Touched children she had befriended—and betrayed. She did not know if Mair traveled to help or to seek vengeance against Rani's accusations.

Even with the threat of the Touched children, Rani looked for an opportunity to slip away from the soldier. As soon as the sun rose, he was likely to look at her tunic again, to realize that the missing Thousand-Pointed Star had not settled on her right sleeve, but rather on her left—typical location of a guild insignia. For that matter, the guard was likely to reflect on the wisdom of believing any grubby child alone in the streets—pilgrim or no.

The decision was soon taken from Rani. Arriving at the edge of the marketplace, she scanned the bustling folk who scrambled about to display their wares for the new day. Graceful stone pillars marched across the square, their intricate stonework supporting heavy tarpaulins that sagged with morning dew. The rising sun tinted the sky, rose light seeping into misty grey. Row after row of stalls stretched across the market.

The soldier led her deeper into the narrow streets, passing temptingly near the food stands. The pungent scent of cheeses wafted through the air, and a number of butchers had set up stalls beneath a fly-buzzing canopy. Pyramids of vegetables towered to her left. Already, buyers swarmed, pressed close against each other as late-arriving merchants choked the pathways with their trestle tables.

"So, child," the soldier said, resting a proprietary hand on Rani's shoulder, "where were you to meet your family?"

"My father said he would wait by the scale-masters. He said men charged with maintaining the king's measures would protect a lost child." Rani was improvising. She knew that the scale-masters were in the very heart of the marketplace, manning their brass balances so that customers could complain about merchants' short measures.

"There we go, then." The soldier began to force his way through the congealing crowd. Rani waited until the man was turned sideways, edging between a donkey-cart and a permanent stand whose owner was setting out the last of her several dozen eggs.

"Papa!" Rani exclaimed in a shrill voice. Scores of men turned toward her cry, including a knot of pilgrims several yards away. The soldier looked up, startled, then let an easy smile paint his face.

"You, there!" he called to the black-robed worshipers. "You seem to have mislaid a treasure along the Pilgrim's Road!"

Rani waited just long enough for confusion to blossom on the pilgrims' faces, and then she shrugged from under the soldier's hand, ducking beneath the table that held the towering eggs.

The result was more spectacular than she could have imagined. The soldier, kind as he was, was still a trained man-at-arms, and he was not about to be stopped by a mere table. Lunging for his escaping charge, he crashed through dozens of eggs. The liquid clatter startled the donkey that had blocked his way, and the beast began to bray and buck, toppling its flimsy cart and striking out with sharp hooves against everything around him.

Rani exploited the chaos to duck down another aisle toward the crowded heart of the marketplace. Farmers cried out at her passage, and more than one well-laid board flew into the air. Pots of golden honey fell victim to her mad rush, and a pyramid of particularly fragrant melons rolled to the ground.

Despite the chaos—or perhaps because of it—Rani found it easy to melt into the crowd. The soldier's cloak she wore *was* darkest crimson, and the sun was not yet completely over the horizon. Wiping a mixture of egg yolk, honey, and pulpy bread from her face, Rani dived beneath a curtained stand, huddling beneath a pile of carrots and potatoes until the outcry faded around her.

As she squinted through a gap in the cloth of her sheltering trestle, Rani's heart raced. Her lone guardsman was soon isolated in the middle of the market. Rani, a merchant-child at heart, was fully aware of the conflicts between her caste and the soldier's. The merchant-farmers were no different from her own family of trinket-sellers; they had certainly suffered beneath the guards' tyrannical attention in the past. There were soldiers notorious for offering "protection"; most merchants tithed to the guard, whether they cared to or not.

Now, as Rani crouched in hiding, an old woman discreetly swept up a sodden cabbage and lobbed it at the soldier. The man swore and started to round on the crone, but the hum of disapproval rose to an angry buzz.

"I warn you!" the guard growled, "That child might be a traitor! She might be the witchling who called Prince Tuvashanoran to his death! If the king finds you sheltering a conspirator, you'll all be gibbet-meat."

"Aye, you can't keep your hands on a pickpocket, and so you threaten us!" The cry rang out from the fringe of watching farmers, and agreement echoed down the ranks.

"A traitor! Ha! If you'd been doing your job, the Prince would still be here to say how foolish you sound!"

"Incompetent guard!"

The cries disintegrated into a jumble, and the guard turned in a wary circle, measuring the sweep of his sword against the citizens' mounting outrage. Rani could read the thoughts creeping across his face, as clear as painted glass windows. He did not actually *know* that Rani was a murderer. She *could* have been a panicked child, springing after her father in a crowded marketplace. Pilgrims *were* accorded virtually unlimited courtesy under the law.

The soldier counted the angry merchants and recognized futility.

Jamming his sword into his sheath, he raised angry hands to shoulder level, showing his good intentions, even as his face raged against the crowd. The assembled marketers let the lone man escape, shouting only an occasional epithet. Rani's heart went out to the soldier—he did not deserve such shame when he had merely acted to help a lonely, frightened child.

Well, for that matter, she had not deserved the full scale manhunt that still threatened her. And the Touched had not deserved her accusations. And Cook had not deserved to be assaulted on the edge of her own garden. And Tuvashanoran had not deserved to die.

The Thousand Gods built mysterious cities.

Rani crouched beneath the trestle until her pulse returned to normal. By then, the market was in full swing. Touched women who served as cooks in nobles' houses jostled merchant wives set on finding the best bargains. Rani peered out at the spectacle, measuring the pace of the morning market in the well-worn leather shoes passing before her barricade. When the square appeared to sport enough people that she could melt into the crowd unnoticed, Rani pushed aside her sheltering fabric curtain.

Ducking from beneath the trestle, she immediately realized the magnitude of her mistake. Two men stood on either side of her hideaway, hammy fists on hips, severe frowns creasing their jowls. One wore the traditional leather apron of a baker, but the other—the one nearest her—wore a bloody linen apron that had once been white. Both boasted brooches on their left breasts, carefully fretted hemp tied into the familiar knot of the Merchants' Council.

The baker and the butcher took two ominous steps forward, and Rani's stomach turned as the sweet-rotten smell of animal gore assaulted her nostrils. The butcher closed his fingers around her upper arm, pinching the meat against her bones. "What have we here?"

"Looks like a rat has gotten into the market." The baker spat through a huge gap in his front teeth.

"Let go of me! I'm the daughter of Thomas Pilgrim. I've come to the City on the holy pilgrimage of Jair!"

"Aye, and I am Quan, the harlots' god." The butcher jerked her arm sharply, dragging her down a small byway toward the market's heart. "Come along, my little magpie. To the Council with you."

The Council. The word quivered through Rani. Her father had longed to serve on the Merchants' Council his entire life. He sold outside the marketplace, though; he'd never been powerful enough or wealthy enough or popular enough to wear a Councilman's hempen knot.

Rani thought she might prefer another confrontation with Shanoranvilli's guard to a meeting with the Council. From everything her father had ever said about them, they were a mighty force, striking terror in the heart of any trader who dared disobey the caste's rules. Her father's words had been laced with jealousy and suspicion—there was a never-dying tension between the merchants who sold their goods in the marketplace and those who—like Rani's family—sold their wares in the streets of the Merchants' Quarter.

Since the merchant class had no desire to submit to constant visits from the king's soldiers, it had evolved the Council to serve as its own police force. The Council was not empowered to take military action, and it could not mete out any formal punishment for violations of the King's Peace. Theft, assault, and other crimes against the King's Peace were still handled by the guard. But marketplace disputes were reviewed by the Council; the merchants kept their own strictly in line.

Rani certainly was not put at ease by the brawny baker and butcher who forced their way through the crowd. The men bellowed when customers or merchants got in their way, and neither hesitated to apply a hammy fist to ease their passage. Rani, glancing over her shoulder in half-hearted contemplation of escape, saw the old egg-woman parading behind their little procession, holding her head high, even as gummy yolk solidified on her apron.

Sooner than Rani cared for, she was pushed toward a dark little hallway that led to the covered portico at the core of the marketplace. Ironically, the Council sat near the scale-masters where she had fantasized meeting Thomas

Pilgrim. The intricate stone ceiling writhed with beasts and flowers, filtering out most of the morning's rosy light.

"Morning, Your Grace," the butcher said, and Rani peered into the shadows, trying to discern a body in the gloom. As her eyes adjusted, she could make out a tall man sitting in a folding wooden chair, his bony hands relaxed on carved arm-rests. Shrewd eyes glinted beneath his bald pate, and shadows made a skull out of his sunken cheeks. The dim light picked out a fist-sized hempen knot secured to his left breast.

"It's too early for disturbances in the marketplace." The man's voice was old, and Rani wondered who held the post of Chief Councilor this season. The job rotated among the most respected merchants; so far, it had remained far beyond her father's grasp.

"Not too early for the likes of this gutter rat." The baker spoke this time, pushing Rani forward, so that she fell to her knees. "Broke all of Narda's eggs, she did."

"Narda, do you seek the judgment of the Council?"

"Aye, Borin." The woman managed to make her two words a pitiable plea for assistance, even as she gloated over being the center of attention.

"And you," Borin directed his words to Rani. "What are you called?"

Rani ran through the possibilities. "Ranita" would likely do her more harm than good; she could scarcely demand to be handed over to guildsman justice when she could not name her guild. "Rai" would earn her a severe beating, if not worse—merchants considered the lawless Touched children an unfortunate blight, like flooding, drought, and insect infestation. There was little point in appending "Pilgrim" to her name—she certainly had no Star to mark her pilgrimage, and a quick inquiry at the cathedral would clarify that no panicked Pilgrim Thomas sought his daughter. Shrugging in resignation, she managed to voice the two syllables, "Rani."

"Rani." The old man's voice was as stony as the canopy above his head. "Do you have family to stand beside you as the Council decides its verdict?"

"No, Your Grace." Rani longed to name her father, longed to throw herself on the mercy of the Council for help in finding her missing family. Such a request, though, would only raise nasty questions, impossible questions. Better to stand alone than to stand surrounded by the King's Guard.

As if acknowledging her decision, Borin nodded before turning to the butcher. "What happened to Rani in the marketplace?"

Rani listened as her exploits were recounted. Even though her knees itched where they were caught between two bricks, she did not shift position. She did not like the tone of the butcher's voice, but he was fair enough in his words, describing how she had fled Shanoranvilli's guards and upset various tables, including the one bearing all of Narda's eggs.

"And what other damage did she do?"

"Tarin lost two dozen melons—they were bruised enough that he'll likely not sell them. Rordi claims she trampled his squash, but two other merchants say he damaged his own goods, hoping for a Council verdict and a free afternoon. Others lost their displays, but their wares were not destroyed."

Borin nodded slowly, weighing the personalities involved, measuring out his own knowledge of the merchants under his supervision. Rani remained enough of a merchant's daughter to take pride in the Council's smooth governance, even as she feared the penalty Borin would extract.

"Rani, do you have anything to say for yourself before the Council speaks?"

"No, Your Grace."

"Do you have any money to pay for disturbing the Market's peace?"

"No, Your Grace."

"Do you have any reason that the Council should not announce its verdict, binding you and the merchants you have wronged today?"

"No, Your Grace."

"Very well. The Council gives this verdict. Rordi suffers punishment enough, in not having his own wares to sell.

Rani will scrub down Tarin's stall every night for two weeks, and she will mind the stall for him during the noon hour for those same two weeks. A Councilor will watch from nearby and make sure that all the coins owed to Tarin get to him each day. As for Narda, Rani will be her servant for a fortnight, doing her command in all things at all times, except for those hours when the child meets her obligations to the other merchants. The Council will pay Narda from the Common Fund for today's loss of eggs."

Narda crowed her delight, but both the butcher and the baker satisfied themselves with tight nods. Borin's sentence was a fair one. The old man looked Rani directly in the eye. "You hear the Council's verdict. By your name, you are already sworn to abide by the Council. Will you stand by that oath, or do you demand the King's Justice?"

Rani hung her head and forced a whisper. "I will abide by the Council."

"Then rise up, Rani, and go to your appointed duties. In a fortnight, the Council will review your actions and determine if further sanctions are necessary. I release you into Narda's care. The egg-woman is responsible for feeding you during your service. Beware the Council and the King's Justice if you fail to do as you have sworn."

Rani bowed her head in the gesture of submission she had used before her father for years. Authority was authority, whether in the guise of a parent or a judge in a crowded marketplace. Borin nodded, and the baker dug into a coffer, counting out coins to remunerate Narda for her losses.

As the woman hid away the coppers, she turned to her charge. "Come, girl. What do they call you? Rani? Well, Rani, we've a long day ahead of us, don't we?"

Rani followed the diminutive merchant back through the stalls. No one took notice of them now; the marketplace was flooded with townsfolk filling their larders with fine goods. Rani quickly ceased to have time to watch the shoppers. Narda handed her a rag and a small wire brush and ordered her to get to work, cleaning the toppled egg-stand. Narda, unexpectedly freed from a day's labor in the marketplace, took her settlement funds and made her way to a distant stall already setting out tankards of ale.

Rani quickly discovered that the eggs she had broken were not the first to paint the table. Glue-like yolk crusted the cracks between planks, and the trestle legs gleamed with an albumen glaze. The rag helped to wipe up the worst of the morning's misadventures, but Rani settled down to a long day's work with the wire brush.

The labor proved no more difficult, though, than many of the tasks she had mastered at the guildhall. The scrubbing created its own rhythm, and Rani hummed to herself as she wielded her tools. She vaguely remembered despising such jobs when she worked for her parents, but she had learned the true value of labor during her life as an apprentice. At least the sun was warm in the sky above her, and here in the marketplace, there were no embers to burn her, no lead fumes to inhale. She would not be cut by daggers of near-invisible glass. All things considered, her binding to Narda was no more difficult than her obligation to the glasswrights had been.

Most importantly, she had time to think as she sat cross-legged in the marketplace. She needed to formulate a plan. The guild was likely in ruins by now, all the glasswrights chained in Shanoranvilli's prison. Another apprentice was probably thumbless, maimed in the service of Rani's escape. Cook was almost definitely dead, Lan keep her. Rani's family was certainly arrested, if not worse, and her home was burned.

Tears stung at the corners of Rani's eyes, but she swallowed hard, berating herself that she was merely reacting to the pungent smell of egg yolk, freed from the wood trestle. If only she had not been ordered to bring Morada's lunch to the cathedral....

Morada. There was the key.

Rani did not believe that Instructor Morada had murdered Tuvashanoran. In the first place, Rani could not imagine actually *knowing* a cold-blooded murderer. In the second place, although Morada had been angry on the scaffold,

Rani had tormented her siblings enough to know that the Instructor's anger was rooted in fear, not in murderous rage. In the third place—and most importantly—Morada had a glasswright's body. Her fingers were nimble and deft; she could cut a plate of glass into the most intricate of designs. The woman's arms, though, were a craftsman's; she could not pull a bowstring taut; she did not have the skill to hit a target hundreds of ells away.

Fine. Morada was not the murderer. Nevertheless, she had welcomed the murderer to her scaffold. Certainly, that was the meaning of the Instructor's nervousness when Rani arrived with lunch; that was the reason for the cold hatred that Rani had read in Morada's grey eyes.

Rani wiped a trickle of sweat from her own eyes. The sun was warm in the marketplace, and the soldier's deep crimson cloak soaked up the heat. Sitting back on her haunches, Rani removed the garment and folded it carefully on the ground, setting it in the shadows of the stone-walled stall. Here, in the crowded marketplace, no one would notice a soiled cloak. Even with the gaping hole where her guild badge had been, Rani would be practically invisible.

The apprentice almost laughed out loud as she realized the import of her thought. The market was the perfect place to disappear.

And disappearance would be even more important to Morada than to Rani. Morada had a reputation in the City; she was known to various nobles who had paid dearly for her glasswright services. Besides, Salina was certain to talk at some point, or the soldiers would ultimately take a census of the imprisoned glasswrights. They would learn that Morada was missing, and a search would begin.

Morada would not be safe anywhere in the City. No friends would take her under their roof, for fear of Shanoranvilli's retribution. Even public taverns would be closed to her. The establishments that served nobles would never let her in the door. The soldiers' drinking houses were too fraught with risk. The merchants, counting out the day's till, would not welcome a stranger. The guildsmen would embrace one of their own—even a stranger—but only if that stranger could show a token of mastery. No glasswright's token would provide passage today. Morada would be alone.

So, Rani congratulated herself on her deductions, Morada would have to make her way to the marketplace if she intended to eat or drink. Rani merely needed to study the crowds, the good folk come to spend their coins on fare for their kitchens. Rani breathed yet another prayer to Lan, grateful that Cook had shown her the path to the kitchen god.

Given Lan's help and enough time, Rani was certain to find her prey. And Rani *would* find her. Instructor Morada, by assisting Tuvashanoran's killer, was as guilty of murder as if she had pulled the bowstring herself. Murder, the guildhall's destruction, Larinda's maiming, Rani's own parents disappearing into the night as their home burned to its foundations.... Morada's list of misdeeds was long.

Even as Rani wallowed in vengeful thoughts, Narda returned. "So, my little eggcup, how is your work progressing?"

Rani had smelled alcohol on adults' breath before, but never in such quantity, and never so early in the day. She executed a judicious bow as she made way for Narda's inspection. "Just fine, mistress. I've almost finished this leg of the table."

The old woman stared at the stand, examining it with a care usually reserved for fine jewelwork. One gnarled hand rubbed against the wood, and Rani saw that callouses marked the horny flesh. Narda cocked her head to one side, looking for all the world like a tipsy crow. "Aye, you've done a fine job with your work so far." The words were pulled grudgingly from the woman's throat. "Don't let me keep you from the rest."

Rani felt uncomfortable working beneath the woman's watchful eye. It wasn't that she planned to shirk her punishment—far from it, Rani knew justice when it slapped her wrist. Rather, when Narda watched, Rani felt a peculiar itch against her shin, and then a niggling tickle on her scalp.

She squirmed like an infant trying to break free of swaddling clothes.

The old woman cackled, and the alcoholic fumes were nearly enough to knock Rani back on her heels. For just an instant, she thought of asking the woman to breathe on the table; surely the spirits on her breath would loosen that particularly stubborn patch of egg yolk. The image of Narda, exhaling like a dragon, made Rani smile. The smile turned to an open grin when the old woman chose that moment to yawn, marking her action with a distinct roar from somewhere deep in her gut.

"Well!" the egg-woman exclaimed, "You take to your labors like kidneys to pie! Mind you, finish that table by tonight, or you'll be explaining your laziness to Borin. For now, though, I'd best take you over to Tarin. You're to mind his stall while he takes his lunch." Narda took Rani by the hand and led her through the marketplace.

Stepping up to the melon-merchant's stall, Rani felt the market's power in her bones. She knew that Council watchers were eyeing her, but she could not keep a smile from her lips as she sold Tarin's wares, counting out coppers with flashing precision. Rani was born a merchant; she thrived in the marketplace. Try as Guildmistress Salina might, with words and prayers before altars to the Thousand Gods, with frequent petitions to Clain, the glaziers' god, the guild had been unable to dig out Rani's roots.

Once, looking up from the stand, Rani glimpsed a figure on the edge of the market, a shrouded woman who kept her face well-hidden within her cloak. Rani caught a glimpse of a white streak in dark hair, and she almost cried out Morada's name. Before she could make a move, though, one of the Council's women stepped into view, her fretted badge clear on the shoulder of her tunic. Reluctantly, Rani dropped her hand, settling to the business of making change for a peck of fruit.

When Tarin returned, he was surprised and pleased with her handiwork, and he presented her with a melon—a little dented on one side to be sure, but fragrant in the midday sunlight. Narda, too, held true to Borin's edict, handing over a large loaf of bread when she fetched Rani from the fruit-stand and led her back to her scrubbing. Further pleased with the progress on the table, the old woman splurged on a meat pie for supper, drawing on the coppers that Borin had awarded her for the loss of her eggs. Even as Rani ran a surreptitious finger down the front of her tunic to scrape up a stray daub of gravy, her eyes darted around the market, hoping against hope to catch another glimpse of the figure she was increasingly certain had been Morada.

Few shoppers remained in the district; even the tardiest of cooks had gathered up remnant herbs and produce to prepare their evening meals. Narda, finishing her own pie, eyed the detritus of the day's market shrewdly, then walked around her trestle table with an inebriate's false balance. She barely managed to strangle a cry as the last rays of sun glinted off the stand. "Cor! You've done a fine job, girl."

Rani's narrow chest swelled with pride at the compliment. She *had* done well—the table was stripped of its egg glaze to reveal sturdy oak trestles and planks. Rani had polished the wood until it gleamed, using all her skill as both merchant and guildsman to bring out the whorls in the oak. Rani imagined smooth white eggs arranged on the surface, inviting tomorrow's shoppers with their perfect shape.

"Aye," Narda completed her circuit around the table, "you've done well by your family. Almost makes me hate to do this."

Before Rani could startle away, the old woman withdrew a heavy chain and a manacle. She clapped the iron around Rani's wrist, anchoring the chain on the leg of the trestle.

"Mistress!" Rani gasped out her surprise.

"What else would you have me do, little merchant? You've paid your way today, but Borin allotted me another thirteen days of your labor. I'd not have you count out the coin in your own fashion and conclude your debt paid. You can keep watch here in the marketplace for the night. Don't worry. It'll be dry enough."

"Mistress Narda, you can't leave me alone!"

"Nonsense. Stop that blubbering! You're a big girl, and you must learn to accept responsibility."

"But the Touched—" Rani gave voice to her long-standing merchant-child's nightmare, ignoring the pangs of conscience that reminded her she now had *names* for the Touched. Old habits died hard, and the limits of caste were the oldest habits of all.

"If you need assistance, you can always call for the guard. Here. This will sweeten your night." The egg-woman produced a sweet cake from her satchel, only a little the worse for its leathern stay. "Sleep well, little merchant."

Rani stared as the woman staggered away to complete her studies in tavern alchemy, transforming the last of her copper to ale.

Rani had not realized how fatiguing her day had been; she found herself drifting off to uneasy sleep before the sun had set. She curled protectively around Tarin's half-eaten melon, her gnawed loaf of bread, and the untouched sweet cake.

She was swirling into dreams when a hiss hurtled her back to wakefulness. "Shhhhh. We'll see if she's got any eggs on 'er!"

The words shocked Rani into a sitting position, and she immediately reached for her Zarithian dagger. Rabe materialized out of the twilight, his earnest face twisted into a sneer as he saw her blade.

"Not much good that'll do ye now. I'd kick yer wrist, an' th' knife'd go flyin'. Why don't ye drop it, and spare yerself th' pain."

"Rabe." Rani twisted around and saw Mair watching her lieutenant from the shadows. She nodded a cautious greeting, and the girl stepped up to Rani's side.

"Ye were expectin' First God Ait, p'r'aps?" Mair settled onto the trestle table, swinging her legs as Rani clambered to her feet. "Afraid of us Touched, are ye?"

"And why wouldn't I be? I've heard tales." Rani raised her chin defiantly.

"Tales!" Mair chortled. "If ye 'eard 'alf th' stories we

could tell ye! About thieves 'n' murderers 'n' ghosts seekin' bloody revenge i' th' night!"

Rani blanched, certain Mair was referring to Tuvashanoran, wondering whether the Touched leader would give her up to the Guard. "You're just trying to frighten me."

"Ye've done a fine job o' that yerself. What sort o' rot 'ave they been feedin' ye about my sort?"

"I don't know what you mean."

"Did they tell ye we skin cats in the night alleys? Did they tell ye we kidnap babes 'n' drink their blood?" Mair's laugh was deep in her throat, and her fingers closed tight on Rani's wrists as she pried loose the glinting Zarithian blade. "Those're pretty bangles ye're wearin', Rai."

"Please...." Rani swallowed her fear—these were the same children she had faced down last night, the rag-tag band who had gladly eaten her carrots. They could not mean her harm. Rani repeated that irrational mantra as she held up her manacled wrists. "Can you help me out of them?"

Mair set the knife on the table with a curious glance at Rani. "*That* we canna do. We 'ave our own peace with th' Council. We don't brook their justice, 'n' they let us creep th' market."

Rani thought of the shadowy figure she'd seen at noon, and she pounced on the opportunity. "You can really go through the marketplace as you will?" Mair nodded. "Then we can work a bargain." Rubbing her arms against the gathering night-chill, Rani described the Instructor she sought, stressing Morada's ragged cloak, and the distinctive white stripe in her jet hair.

"'N' if we find 'er for ye, what'll ye give us?"

"If you *look* for her, I'll share my food. Today Narda brought me a full loaf of good bread, and Tarin gave me a melon for my labor. If you find her, all you need to do is follow her, tell me where she's hiding." Rani proffered the half-melon that she had been saving to break her fast in the morning. She hesitated only an instant before adding Narda's cake to the bait. Mair snatched at the food like a starved animal, sniffing at the cake before handing it to her lieutenant.

The Touched leader kept her eyes on Rani as she spat into her palm, and then offered her hand to her new partner. "Deal."

Rani spat onto her own hand, clattering her chains as she clasped Mair's palm. "Deal."

Mair did not ask why Rani sought Morada, and Rani volunteered no information. The Touched leader forced Rabe to hand back Rani's dagger before the children melted into the market shadows.

After that, Rani's days settled into a pattern. Narda appeared each dawn, trundling her barrow through the waking streets, eggs teetering dangerously. Rani rose from her chilly bed, helping to steady the load and lay out the wares, alternating smooth white eggs with brown ones. Narda shared a breakfast of fried dough, or boiled eggs, or fat bacon, and then the woman disappeared into the growing crowds. Rani sold eggs all morning, adjusting prices to match the buyers, scrupulously collecting pennies into the leather pouch Narda had provided. The egg-woman returned whenever she needed more coins to finance her tavern visits, bringing food and praising Rani for her labor. Tarin came at noon and at dusk to claim her services—she minded his stand for an hour when the sun was directly overhead, and she scrubbed down the vegetable debris at the end of the day. She offered up at least half her food to the horde of Touched children every night, and Mair reported on the ever-disappointing status of the hunt.

Rani never faltered in her submission to the Council's verdict. She never failed in her responsibility to Narda, never shirked her work for Tarin. She never received shelter at night, even when a steady drizzle dampened the entire marketplace. She never saw Morada.

Until the last day of Rani's two-week sentence.

That morning began like all the others, with Rani groggily waking in her rough bed beneath the trestle table. She stretched in the early morning dawn, rubbing her arms against the chill that shivered through the autumn sunrise. Soon, merchants trundled in their wares, narrow handcarts jostling in the tight marketplace aisles.

Narda was late, and Rani was getting impatient as she peered down the ranks. She had followed Borin's edict to the letter, and her chains chafed more this morning than they had at any time since she left the guildhall. The destruction of her guild still haunted her nightmares, and Cook's order echoed louder in Rani's skull. Cook had charged her in the name of Lan, in the name of the god who had watched out for Rani so far. Rani could no longer duck her responsibilities. But the apprentice knew that she needed her freedom if she were ever to find Morada.

Offering up an exasperated prayer to the kitchen god, Rani pivoted about, staring toward the heart of the market in case she had somehow missed Narda's initial approach. During the preceding fortnight, Rani had learned the secrets of the marketplace; she knew its shadows and nooks as well as she knew her former guildhall, as well as she knew the streets of the Merchant Quarter where her own family had sold their wares. Glancing toward Tarin's stall, Rani saw immediately that *that* particular patch of black did not belong.

She started to cry out, to warn Tarin of a thief, but the lurker chose that moment to move into a patch of foggy sunlight. Rani's shout died in her throat as she recognized Morada's profile.

The Instructor's hair straggled about her pinched face like drowned snakes, and the glasswright's skin was a pasty grey. If Rani had come across her under other circumstances, she would have worried for the woman's health; she might even have summoned one of the priest-leeches who served as chirurgeon for the lower castes.

At that moment, though, Rani's heart secretly soared at Morada's haggard appearance. She recognized the tang at the back of her throat, the sharp craving for revenge. Rani wanted vengeance for Tuvashanoran's death, for the havoc at the guildhall, for the ashes of her family's home and the personal indignity of chains in the marketplace.

As Rani strained at her metal bonds, Morada flicked a nervous glance about the market. The apprentice watched as wiry glasswright fingers danced over new-dug potatoes, and suddenly the woman's ragged pockets bulged with pilfered riches. Rani swore softly under her breath, breathing the most hideous words she'd ever heard her brothers use. She yanked on her fast-held chain. Where was Mair? Where were the Touched who could go about the marketplace with ease? How could Lan's gift of Morada go unused?

Rani was almost whimpering with frustration when a heavy, dirt-encrusted hand fell on her shoulder.

"There you are, my pretty!" Rani started like a rabbit caught outside its burrow. Narda cackled, rummaging in her pocket for the key to Rani's chains. "A cart was upset at the Merchants Gate—fresh melons all over the road. Sorry to delay you, and this your last day in my service." Rani rubbed at her wrists, trying to smooth away the angry red welt where she had strained against her bonds, the better to keep Morada in sight. "I wouldn't have it said I starved you, girl. Here's a penny—find yourself breakfast and come back within the hour."

Rani was so astonished she scarcely felt the coin fall into her outstretched palm. She almost missed Narda's remonstration: "And there's another penny for you, if you come back with a flask of ale! Might as well have a drink before we receive Borin's final judgment!"

Rani scarcely thought of the Chief Councillor as she darted through the crowd, intent on keeping Morada's black cloak in sight.

CHAPTER 5

For one desperate minute, Rani thought that she had delayed too long, and the Instructor would be lost in the crowds. Then she took a deep breath and plunged into the heart of the marketplace. In the past fortnight, she'd polished her merchant skills, learned to measure the crowds of meandering buyers. Rani knew there was enough room to glide between the stands *there*; she knew she could duck beneath *that* trestle and emerge in the proper aisle to keep the Instructor in sight.

By now, the merchants were familiar with the sight of this serious child on her errands, and more than one seller raised a hand in greeting. Rani nodded to acknowledge the attention, but she did not stop to gather up the proffered treats—an apple here, a wedge of cheese there.

When Morada reached the market's edge, Rani hovered on the fringe of tables, hesitant to move beyond the clear boundary. Narda had given her coins to buy breakfast and ale; the egg woman had assigned her a very specific mission. If Rani stepped beyond the merchants' range, she was likely to negate the fortnight of service she had almost completed. Nevertheless, if Rani lost Morada now, there would be no redeeming her family, no explaining Tuvashanoran's death.

Glancing about frantically, wondering if she were being observed by Borin's Council Watchers, Rani found herself face to face with the statue of the Defender of the Faith that guarded the market's northern edge. Although the marble face was well-worn with age, Rani could easily imagine Tuvashanoran's features graven in the stone. This was the role the Prince would have assumed in the Cathedral; this was the title he would have claimed if he had been spared the assassin's arrow.

With the mechanical obedience of a well-trained child, Rani bobbed a curtsey before the commanding statue, inclining her head beneath the outstretched arm. Mourning citizens had left offerings to the murdered prince at the marble feet. When Rani glanced at the sad carved eyes, she could see Tuvashanoran as he had last stood during life— tall and rigid with pain, an arrow blooming out of his eye, out of the stone socket. Rani's mind supplied the cobalt light of the cathedral windows, and she almost cried out at the vision, cried out as she had during Tuvashanoran's ceremony.

Almost, but not quite. Rani had a mission, and she would not let guilt sway her from pursuing the Instructor who bore the truth. Consciously choosing to read the Defender's marble arm as a benediction rather than a curse, Rani realized what she must do, regardless of the Councilors who patrolled the market with their knotted hemp badges.

She stepped outside the market.

Morada's filthy cloak was just flitting around a distant corner. At first, Rani followed the Instructor through well-known streets. Although Morada slunk in the shadows, Rani had no problem keeping the older woman in sight. Even as Rani racked her brain to figure out where the Instructor was heading, Morada took a series of obscure turns, leaving the Merchants' Quarter altogether. Rani had a vague notion they were worming toward the cathedral close. The buildings were close together on the narrow streets, and in many places, the upper stories had toppled toward each other. Evil smells seeped from the gutter, and Rani tried to breathe through her mouth.

Morada seemed oblivious to the raucous laughter tumbling from behind warped doors, and she did not even start when a piteous wail drifted through a decrepit shutter.

Rani had begun to doubt she would ever find her way out of these dark streets when Morada ducked into a hovel on the corner of two refuse-ridden alleys. Stepping over a slimy pile best left unexamined, Rani huddled against the daub and wattle, taking only an instant to pull her clothes closer, to protect her skin from the filthy building.

The wall was as unwholesome as the rest of these streets but, for once, the decay worked to Rani's advantage. She could put her ear to a crack beneath the cracked window frame and listen to the movement inside the hut. Even as Rani crouched by the foul building, a man's voice hissed, slurred with drink and perpetual ill-will. "What have you got under that cloak, woman? You were gone long enough."

If Rani had not been listening for Morada's reply, she never would have recognized the Instructor's voice, miserable and whining. "You know bloody well I couldn't get back any sooner. That damned Council runs the market like a military camp. I almost wasn't able to get these." Rani imagined Morada presenting her meager hoard of potatoes.

The man snorted. "It's the height of harvest, and this is all you manage?"

"By all the Thousand Gods, Larindolian, you try my patience." Rani was so startled to hear Morada pronounce a noble name, she almost gasped aloud. "You know as well as I that it would mean instant death if my face were recognized. You could have sent any servant to the market with money to buy the finest sweetmeats, or you could have gone back to the Palace to eat. I brought you food. I stole when you told me to. I've proven my loyalty to you and your cause—let's get on with our plans."

The silence that greeted Morada's irritated outburst was long and when Larindolian spoke, his voice was a dangerous cross between a purr and a growl. "*My* cause, eh? I thought you had sworn loyalty to our common leader, Instructor. I thought you had embraced our mission. I would have expected your guild to teach you the meaning of dedication."

"My guild taught me all the lessons I need. I understood

dedication long before you came along, Larindolian—you and your keeper."

"Watch your tongue, Instructor! When you joined our cause, you swore loyalty to one far stronger than I."

"When I joined your cause, I believed we would bring justice to the City! Tuvashanoran was a better instrument for that justice than any I've seen among your colleagues."

Rani recognized the sound of an open hand on flesh, and the scrape of furniture testified to the force behind the blow. "Tuvashanoran was a rutting dog, and don't you forget it, you lily-livered cow. Defender of the Faith! That man was not fit to lick the shoes of the one we serve!"

Rani could not help but thrill to hear Morada chastised, even if the mysterious Larindolian insulted the sacred memory of the Prince, even if he hit a woman. Certainly, the Instructor deserved her comeuppance, given her complicity in Tuvashanoran's death and her long history of lording over the guildhall apprentices. Gambling that Larindolian's anger would make the nobleman incautious, Rani rose beside the rotting window sill, peering inside the dilapidated house. To Rani's right, Morada sat in a chair, shaking her head as if trying to clear out cobwebs of confusion. A handprint whitened her cheek, rapidly flushing to angry red. When the Instructor spoke, her words fell into the still room like pellets of ice.

"So much for the Brotherhood of Justice, eh, Larindolian? So much for equality before the Thousand Gods."

"Justice and equality," the man sneered, and his handsome features contorted into a mask of contempt. Even in the gloom of the dilapidated shack, Rani could see that the nobleman's eyes were eerily light, a frightening blue so pale it was like ice. "Justice and equality are merely words that the weak use to keep us strong folk enchained. Things are changing in the City and I, for one, will not be tied to weaklings who snivel about 'justice.'"

Morada snorted. "Those 'weaklings' are your sworn brethren. Are you fool enough to challenge the Brotherhood here and now, with Tuvashanoran's body not yet set on its pyre?"

"You should not try to guess what I intend to do with the Brotherhood, little sister."

The Instructor stared at the man in shock, a look of horrified realization flushing her features. "You *are* going to challenge them, aren't you? Even with the oaths you've sworn, you believe you're better than the rest of us!"

"You cannot know what I believe, woman!"

Morada jutted her chin defiantly. "Is this the drink speaking, or have you decided that Shanoranvilli is the next to die? Have you selected your coronation robe yet?"

The man's fury seemed all the greater because no emotion flicked across his face. He gathered his tremendous strength in his forearms, lashing out at the Instructor with fists like flour-sacks. Rani cringed at the window, and Morada twisted to keep the raging nobleman from breaking her jaw. The woman's escape was hindered by her chair, and wood splintered beneath her as Larindolian landed a glancing blow on her collar bone. Morada yelped—in fear or pain— and the sound enraged the nobleman further. The sound of ripping fabric was loud in the squalid chamber as another glancing blow caught the Instructor's gown.

Before Larindolian could move to complete his discipline, Rani glimpsed bare flesh. Drawn around the Instructor's bicep, in blue tracery more delicate than any leaded window, was a tattoo. Four strands were woven into one, a quartet of ravenous snakes feeding on each other.

The tattoo would have been surprising under any circumstances—proper women simply did not have drawings drilled into their flesh. The image on Morada's arm was even more striking to Rani, though, because she *knew* the design. She had seen those four snakes twined about another arm.

Suddenly, Rani was no longer a thirteen-year-old apprentice huddling in a sordid alley, spying for her life. Instead, she was five years old and playing on her parents' doorstep, lunging after a leather ball Bardo had brought from the marketplace. The toy had been all the more magical because there was no reason for her brother's generosity. Bardo was laughing his hearty laugh, playing with her, keeping the ball from her grasp.

Rani, never one to yield to supposed authority, leveled a hard kick against her brother's shins. When he stooped down to gather up her flashing legs, to still his annoying gnat of a sister, Rani grabbed onto his arm, pulling his sleeve with all her might. Even now, crouching in the filthy streets of a strange quarter of the city, Rani could remember the shadow that had passed across her parents' doorstep.

Bardo's fury was immediate as she bared his arm. She glimpsed the bulge of muscle beneath his tattoo—four angry snakes turning red pin-prick eyes on the suddenly cowering girl.

Bardo had bellowed his rage and shaken her off his arm to crash on the stone doorstep. He backhanded her before she even realized she'd been knocked breathless. His fingers closed around her own arms, and he shook her with such violence that her teeth rattled inside her skull. She heard her eyes slosh in their jelly, and she could not blink away the sapphire, ruby, and citron lights that flooded her vision.

"You cursed fool!" Even now, Bardo's words seared Rani, and she swallowed remembered tears. "Don't you *ever* tell anyone what you've seen! Do you understand me? Don't you mention one *word* of this to anyone!"

As if for good measure, Bardo had settled his thick fingers against her throat, and the ominous pressure had made her gag. She had managed to choke out an apology, a promise that she would never mention the curious design.

And that had been all.

Bardo had covered his arm, and then he had offered her a dirty kerchief to wipe her tear-streaked face. He had instructed her to blow her nose before leading her to the baker's, and he let her choose the largest pastry she could find. The leather ball was gone when they returned home.

Rani marveled that she could have forgotten the incident. Her beloved Bardo had slapped her like … like a child. *Bardo had beaten her....* And all because she had discovered a tattoo that matched the design Morada sported on her arm.

Now, the Instructor panted at Larindolian, capturing the raw fury Rani remembered in her brother's voice. "You blasted idiot! I don't have anything else to wear, and even *you* can't want me to answer questions about what this means."

Larindolian's fingers strayed to his chest, as if he felt crawling snakes across his own flesh. Before he could react further, a tumult thundered from the far end of the narrowed street. The cadence of marching boots echoed off building walls. "Soldiers!" Morada exclaimed, interpreting the sound faster than Rani did. The apprentice ducked into the shadows of a neighboring hovel as a troop of Shanoranvilli's armed guards swung into view.

The helmed captain stopped on the doorstep of Morada's ruined hut and announced his royal warrant with a snarl: "Open in the name of King Shanoranvilli, that justice be done in the name of all the Thousand Gods." Before any human could have responded, soldierly boots crashed against the door, and the splinter of wood was lost in the clatter of armed men passing through too small a space.

"Here's the murderess you're searching for!" Larindolian's voice rose above the tumult.

"Traitor!" Morada cried. "You summoned the king's men!" Then, even before the soldiers could react, dark velvet flashed by Rani, and the apprentice just made out the shape of a man in the alley's gloom. Head bent low and face obscured against his shoulder, Larindolian was escaping.

"Hold, witch!" cried one of the men inside the hut, and Morada howled her rage, shrieking epithets that brought grim responses from the assembled soldiers. Even without seeing the confrontation in the filthy room, Rani recognized the sound of fists on flesh, and the duller impact of boots. Morada's flaring anger turned to raw-voiced pain as she pleaded with her attackers to look to Larindolian.

The desperate words merely heated the soldiers' blood, and the men sprinkled imprecations amid their brutal punishment. "Murdering witch!" Rani heard, and "Blasted whore!"

Suddenly aware of her own danger if the guards' rage were not sated by attacking the Instructor, Rani glanced up and down the vile street. She did not know her way in this quarter; she could not hope to escape trained military men who were well-heated by vengeance. Before she could choose to brave the streets or wait out the horror inside the little house behind her, however, the decision was taken from her.

The soldiers emerged from the hut, man-handling their sobbing, twisting prey from the ramshackle room. One of the guards chanced to look over his shoulder as Rani gaped from the shadows. "Aye, brat," he spat toward her feet, "let this be a lesson to you. Mind your caste, and you won't have to worry about a visit from the King's Guard." The man hitched at his belt and hustled to catch up with his fellows, taking the opportunity to land a solid punch in the small of Morada's back. In seconds, bitter silence filtered over the street.

Mind your caste.

As if Rani belonged in these abandoned city streets. This was a zone fit for no decent person—only the Touched would live in these filthy shadows.

Rani glanced around, half expecting to see Mair and her spirited troops lurking in the ruined doorway across the street. Instead, a toothless bundle of rags stirred on the rotting threshold, turning a bandaged head to look at her from a single crazed eye. Rani jumped, astonished that she had not noticed the creature before. "Aye, little one!" cackled the ancient Touched. "Mind yer caste!" The voice was high and reedy and Rani could not tell if the speaker was male or female. "Oh, yes. If ye want t' be safe, little one, mind yer caste!"

The bundle of rags dissolved into an ancient creatures' diseased limbs, a skull bobbing on the end of a spine grown twisted and deformed with age, rickety legs shambling toward the terrified girl. Before Rani could shrink away, a bony finger poked at her throat, burrowing into the V of flesh and cutting off her breath. Rani tried to back away, but she was trapped by the rough daub and wattle behind her, rooted to the spot and transfixed by the horrific smile that stretched the skeleton's thin lips.

"Ye're wastin' time, little one. Yer Instruct'r won't last th' night i' th' king's Black 'Ole."

"I—" Rani cleared her throat to force words past her revulsion. "I don't know what you're talking about."

"Step smart, little one. Th' Instruct'r'll 'ave more 'n th' king's good 'ealth on 'er mind, after that last fight with th' noble 'un. Ye talk to th' Instruct'r 'n' ye'll learn th' answer to all yer questions."

"How do *you* know?" Rani struggled to keep her voice respectful, fighting fear and revulsion.

"I mind me caste, little one!" The ancient Touched cackled, chanting a holy mantra. "Mind yer caste. Mind yer caste."

"I don't understand!"

"Mind yer caste...." The skeleton tumbled the words over its sere lips, jostling them about like knuckle bones in a cup.

Rani recoiled and started to turn away from the mad speaker. Old habits died hard, though—she could hardly leave her elder, and a victim of madness besides, without some token of respect. Rani fished deep in her pocket for Narda's coppers. She was already in for an ell with the egg-woman; she might as well plunge for a mile.

"Here you go," Rani proffered the coins from a safe distance. "Buy yourself some food."

Before the apprentice could spring back, steel fingers closed about her wrist, a tighter grip than Rani could have imagined. Now, face to face with the Touched creature, the apprentice could see the fire burning deep within those ancient eyes. "Don' ferget yer lesson 'ere today. Ye can learn things when ye least expect t' learn."

The skeleton leaned closer, and Rani's stomach turned at the stench of rotten food and decaying teeth. For one terrifying instant, she thought the Touched was going to kiss her, and she lunged backwards, bruising her shoulder blades against the house. "Aye, Rai, Rani, Ranita. Don't ferget t' seek out all yer Teachers."

The creature's tongue moved in its mouth like a slug on bruised apples, and Rani twisted away in horror. As the Touched's laughter echoed off the decaying buildings, Rani fled the deserted quarter.

She got lost following the street that she thought Larindolian had taken. She wandered through more twining lanes, past more shadowed doorways, and finally she squeezed past a pile of rubble where some ancient ruin had collapsed, emerging in the cathedral close. The holy building loomed over her, and she could not help but glance at the glasswrights' scaffold, still standing beneath the Defender's Window. Morada's rope continued to hang from the smooth wooden uprights, and Rani imagined an assassin scaling the rickety structure, bow in hand.

An assassin who was an archer.... Of course, soldiers learned to handle a bow, but so did others. Every noble learned archery in childhood—it was one of the skills befitting the Court, showing the culture and grace of the noble caste.

Tuvashanoran himself had been a fine archer. Rani dashed away unbidden tears, recalling how the noble prince had hunted for venison when he was little more than a child himself. A famine had plagued Morenia as drought seared crops for the third consecutive year. Tuvashanoran had led a hunting expedition with his noble brethren. Two days from the City, the Prince had found and shot a magnificent buck, slaying the beast with a single glass-tipped arrow. Tuvashanoran, ever-mindful of his obligation to his people, had shared out the venison on his way back to the City. Wherever a family ate of the rich flesh, rain fell. The Thousand Gods smiled on the Prince.

Making a holy sign, Rani muttered a prayer for Tuvashanoran's soul, directing her holy words to Bern, the god of rain. Halfway through the invocation, though, she changed her appeal, speaking instead to Doan, the god of hunters. Doan seemed more appropriate, after all, since Rani had become a hunter herself. Or the hunted.

Either way, she was likely to become a shackled prisoner if she did not return to the marketplace and excuse her absence in some satisfactory manner. Even now, her heart pounded at the thought of Narda's wrath and the Council's judgment. As Rani wound her way back to the marketplace, she practiced her excuses.

She had found a small child, separated from its mother in the terrifying market. She had discovered another merchant, selling eggs that looked at first to be of a higher quality than Narda's. She had heard rumors of a merchant selling ale at half the normal price, in dire need of unloading his wares that morning.

Each of the stories rang false in her own skull, and she came to the edge of the marketplace without a plan for deliverance.

Rani had scarcely passed beneath Tuvashanoran's outstretched marble arm when she was shadowed by two of the Council's Watchers. If she recalled correctly, the pair of cheese-merchants were husband and wife, although they looked enough alike to be brother and sister. Each wore the symbol of Council rank fastened to a pungent tunic, the hempen knots bobbing like wise men's heads. Rani held her chin high and walked through the market as if she were wholly in the right. She forced herself to think of the cheese-sellers as a royal escort.

As Rani stepped up to Narda's trestle, a customer bustled off into the crowd, nestling her new-bought eggs in a carefully woven basket. Narda blinked foggy eyes at her erstwhile assistant, and Rani heard disappointment in the old woman's words. "I had hoped not to resort to the Council."

"You don't need to, Mistress!" Rani responded automatically.

"I don't see my ale. I suppose you've managed to lose my coins, somewhere in the marketplace?"

"You need not add 'thief' to my name, Mistress," Rani

cast a nervous glance at the Council Watchers, afraid that they would cut short her response.

"'Thief.' 'Vandal.' I name the names that fit. I gave you coins and you return without ale—what else am I to say?" At Narda's angry gesture, the Council guard dogs stepped closer.

Rani had not spent her life as a merchant's daughter without learning one basic principle: all people could be bought. Plunging her hand into the sack at her waist, she finally hatched a plan. Even as her fingers fumbled past the Zarithian knife—a tool she dared not use now—she felt the cool kiss of an incised metal coin. Her hand emerged from the sack, and she stared down at the square metal in her hand.

Rani could still remember her excitement at finding the foreign coin, caught upright between two cobblestones outside her family's house. She could hear Bardo's voice— *Bardo had beaten her* as he drilled a hole in the foreign coin, carefully hoarding the spirals of sheared silver. "Here you go, little one. A rare find this is—someone'll be sorry to have lost it in the City."

Rani had worn the coin on a leather thong around her neck, treasuring it not only as money from a foreign land, but as a thing of beauty her brother had crafted for her. Even now, she remembered Bardo's easy grin as he slipped the coin over her head. "Fine jewels for the Lady Ranikaleka," he had joked, turning her name into a noble one, and she had laughed at the silly sounds, even as she thrust out a proud chest to better display her wealth. Because Bardo had drilled it for her, because Bardo had made it for her, Rani valued the silver coin far more than she would have valued the handful of boiled sweets it might have bought.

In fact, she had worn the coin until she began her life in the guild hall, often dreaming of the wealth and good luck the exotic token would bring her.

Now, she could scarcely bring herself to touch the metal square, remembering that Bardo had worked it. What had her brother done? How had he charmed her? How had she forgotten his raw fury when she discovered the tattoo inscribed on his arm?

Thinking back on the punishment she had received so long ago, Rani felt rebellion sprout in her belly. Even if she had forgotten Bardo's rough treatment, she now knew he was not merely the loving brother he had seemed. The tattoo was a secret sign, and Rani knew its entwined circles lay at the heart of Tuvashanoran's murder. There was more to her brother than met the eye.

"What have you got there? More goods that you've stolen from some unsuspecting merchant?" Narda's harsh words jarred Rani back to her present dilemma.

In one tragic morning, the coin that Bardo had strung for her had lost its power as an amulet against all things that frighten young girls. Now, it could serve one final purpose— freeing her from the Council's punishment—if only she could spin out a game of marketplace bidding. To that end, she thrust out her lower lip into a credible, childish pout. "Your words hurt me, Mistress Narda. I had thought to surprise you with all the ale this coin can buy." She paused for effect before twisting the four-sided treasure in front of Narda's calculating eyes.

Whatever excuses the egg-woman had expected, she was clearly startled by the sight of foreign silver. She dropped the egg she was holding, ignoring the resulting saffron splash down the front of her stand. Rani stifled a sigh at the egg-stain—she remembered too well the pain of scrubbing the old table clean. Mentally, she nudged her price upwards.

"Pish," Narda sniffed. "The money changers would have no idea how much to give you for this."

"They may not know the coin, but they can weigh silver."

Narda shrugged elaborately. "*If* it isn't alloyed. Something like that ... you couldn't buy more than ... a gill of ale."

Rani swallowed her smile—Narda may have begun the bidding low, but the merchant had been intrigued enough to make the first offer. "A gill, mistress! You must have misspoken! This coin will certainly buy you a gill of ale— every day for the rest of your life."

"How dare you curse me! Limiting my life to a few weeks—that is all your little coin will ever add up to."

"Alas, fair mistress, you misunderstand. I did not mean that your days are numbered. Perhaps I should have said this coin would buy a gill for each of the Thousand Gods to drink every day for a week. I would gladly hand those riches to you, my mistress, my mentor, my guide in the City's marketplace."

Narda was not invulnerable to the merchant ploys she used every day, and Rani watched the woman preen with pleasure at the thought of her power in the market hierarchy—power nourished by gallons of ale. Rani rushed in to close the deal. "Come now, Mistress—you must already be warm this morning, and heat breeds thirst. Let me give you my coin, and I'll stay here to mind the stall. I'll clean up that spill there," Rani nodded to the runny egg, "and I'll sell the last of your wares. We can go to the Council this evening, and you can tell them I've served my time." Rani set the coin on the edge of the stall, purposely turning it so that the sun glinted off the metal.

"You drive a hard bargain, my little eggcup!"

"Only because you've taught me so well, Mistress."

"Very well, then." Narda snatched the coin, hiding it from prying eyes. "Done."

Rani should have felt joy at bargaining for her release. She should have felt a flush of victory at beating Narda at her own game. She should have felt giddy at her success. Instead, she watched her treasure disappear into the old egg-woman's fist, and she resisted the urge to cry out, to beg for the return of Bardo's gift.

Before Rani could forfeit her advantage, one of the forgotten Council watchers stepped forward, a bemused smile on her face. "I take it, Narda, you no longer wish to invoke the Council's power against this one?"

For just an instant, Rani read the threat of betrayal in the egg-woman's eyes, but then the danger evaporated like a mist. "Nay, Marni. Thank the Council for keeping watch.

I guess my little helper was looking out for me after all. I should not have gone to Borin so soon."

Marni looked steadily at the old egg woman. "Come to the Council at the end of the day, as you were instructed in the first place. Borin will pass his final judgment then."

"Aye, we'll be there," Narda nodded.

Marni scrutinized Rani for a long moment, and the erstwhile apprentice squirmed under the gaze. She wondered just how much the Councillor knew, just how long Rani had been tracked by the watchers. Had one of Borin's people followed her to Morada's secret meeting?

Rani quickly cast aside the thought. Certainly, if the Council knew that they had Tuvashanoran's murderer, or an accomplice to that evil-doer, anywhere near their grasp, they would have summoned Shanoranvilli's guards already.

Rani realized Narda was delivering her last words of chiding instruction, and the apprentice nodded meekly before the egg-woman disappeared into the crowds, leaving Rani to make the rest of the day's sales. Clicking her tongue in disgust, the girl saw that Narda had not even bothered to lay out the eggs in an attractive pattern. How could she expect to sell her goods if she did not take the most basic steps to attract customers? The stand truly would go downhill after today's obligations. Narda had good reason to fear Rani's release.

Moving the smooth eggs into position to please her customers, Rani ruminated on the lessons she had learned outside the market. Morada certainly was involved in a larger plot—a plot that was intertwined with at least one nobleman. Rani squelched a shudder in the bright noon-day glare as she recalled Lardindolian's blue eyes, the dagger behind the noble's gaze that Morada had apparently never seen, or seeing, had not heeded.

Frightened even in the Market's bright safety, Rani pushed her thoughts away from the icy nobleman. Instead, she thought of the mark she had seen on Morada's arm, the strange tattoo the Instructor had tried to keep covered. Four writhing snakes, twined into one. How could Rani have forgotten Bardo's arm? More importantly, why had Morada worn the same tattoo as Bardo?

Rani sighed, paradoxically wishing that Bardo was near, purposely setting aside her fear and anger. She loved Bardo. He had always protected her. She wanted him beside her.

"Such a sigh, 'n' from one so small! I dinna think ye were gonna get out o' that un, mate."

"Mair."

"Aye, Rai. Quick thinkin' that, givin' her yer only coin i' th' world."

"How do you know what coins I've got?"

"Oh, I know, Rai, I know." For all the snaggled smile Mair spared, Rani's heart pounded at the thought of Touched hands—Rabe's jealous, creeping hands—prowling through her belongings while she slept, all unawares.

"What else was I going to do?" Rani demanded. "I couldn't go back to the Council to ask *their* mercy."

"Nay," Mair answered seriously, "Ye took th' only course ye could. We won't 'old that against ye."

"'Hold it against'—Who says you get to judge me at all?" Rani's misgivings heated her words.

"The Thousand Gods say, merchant girl, 'n' dinna fergit it. Each o' us 'as our place i' th' City, 'n' we Touched aren't about t' fergit ours. It's like th' Old One said, 'Mind yer caste.'"

"How could you know that?" Rani squeaked, recoiling as Mair's fingers echoed the skeletal Touched fingers on her cheek. "If you were close enough to hear that, why didn't you help me?"

"Who says I 'eard anything? I know what I know, Rai, but I'll ne'er tell one o' yer sort where I learned it."

Mair's smirk made Rani's blood boil, and the apprentice stepped up to the trestle, longing to take out her frustration on the Touched girl. Rani glanced around for the loyal troop of children certainly secreted among the nearby stands, but she saw none of Mair's allies. "You followed me!"

Mair caught Rani's fists before she could do something she'd regret. "I promise ye this, Rai. I dinna follow ye."

"Rabe, then. You sent him to do your evil work."

"Rabe was nowhere near ye; I've better things fer my lieutenant t' trouble 'imself about. Believe me, Rai, I've got no cause t' lie t' ye. I've got no cause t' fight ye, either, but if ye force me, I'll beat ye black 'n' blue."

Before Rani could respond, she was distracted by a commotion at the end of the market aisle. Shoppers exploded in a bevy of shrieks, and more than one market basket was dropped in the confusion. Even as Touched children swarmed from the stands to snatch up the spilled goods, Rani made out the trumpets that cleared the way for King Shanoranvilli's officials to move through the marketplace. She scarcely hesitated before clambering up on Narda's trestle table for a better view, balancing amid the few remaining eggs.

Her stomach turned at the sight that met her eyes, and she almost tumbled from her perch. Six men-at-arms forced their way through the crowd, bearing a wooden platform smeared with offal. As the soldiers pushed through the market, a cry went up among the merchants. Over-ripe melons smashed against the men's burden, but the soldiers bore the abuse stoically. A hastily crafted banner was slung across the litter, but Rani could not make out the crude letters.

"Cor!" Mair exclaimed, and the Touched leader startled beneath Rani's frozen hand. "Well, Rai, ye'll not be searchin' fer yer Instructor friend again!"

Rani forced her eyes to the litter, even as a wilted lettuce smashed into the guards' burden. Instructor Morada gazed out at the marketplace, agate rage already grown cloudy beneath a bloodied stripe of stark white hair. A brutal pike secured the disembodied head to the foul litter as Shanoranvilli's guard exhibited their evidence of the King's Justice. The soldiers passed in front of the egg-stand, and Rani could at last make out the words on the befouled banner: DEATH TO ALL TRAITORS.

CHAPTER 6

"And do you have any further words to speak in your defense before we pass our judgment?"

Rani forced herself to take a calming breath, to remember all the phrases she had rehearsed so carefully during her fortnight in the marketplace. "I've tried my best, Your Grace, even when things were not easy or fair." Unbidden, Morada's bloody face floated before her eyes, and she had to blink hard to drive away the vision of crimson-stained pepper-and-salt hair. Perhaps Rani had *not* actually tried her best; perhaps if she had put more effort into her work, she could have questioned Morada before the Instructor's death. Possibly, she could have learned more of the strange Brotherhood that the glasswright and the nobleman had discussed just before Morada was captured.

"And do you submit to our judgment, without reservation or contradiction?"

"I do, Your Grace." Belatedly, Rani thought to kneel, easing herself onto the ragged brick floor, ignoring the pinching pain against her knees.

"Then by the power granted me by King Shanoranvilli, I pronounce your sentence served. You are free to walk among the people, with no stain of your former wrongdoing upon your brow." Borin leaned back in his throne-like chair, and Rani struggled not to sigh with relief.

Borin's acceptance of her service was a mixed blessing.

Of course, she was free again, to come and go as she desired. Nevertheless, she had nowhere in particular to go, nowhere that was certain to be safe, sheltered from prying eyes. With an uneasy sense of foreboding, Rani wondered if she might not have spent her four-sided coin more profitably than in securing Narda's acquiescence.

"Stand, Rani." The Chief Councilor probably meant the command to be an honor, but Rani's unsettled mood made the order seem more like a threat. "It is rare that the Council finds a merchant with the care and respect you show for its rules. Your family should be proud of you." Rani swallowed uneasily. It would not do for Borin to ask questions about her family. She realized that the Chief Councilor was waiting for some response, though, and she managed a brief curtsey. "I hope they are, Your Grace. I certainly hope they are."

Before Borin could reply, there was a commotion at the edge of the room. Rani turned to find Borin's Council colleagues stepping aside, shuffling in vaguely-disguised dissatisfaction to allow a newcomer to enter the room. Only when the person stepped into the dim light did Rani realize that it was Mair.

Rani almost cried out her Touched friend's name, but she had no chance before Borin registered his visitor. The Chief Councilor crossed the small room with the speed of a striking snake. Rani could see his fingers dig into the meat of Mair's arm, and he hissed "What are you doing here?"

Mair stood her ground. "My troops've learned a few tidbits, Yer Grace. Ye'll want t' know my secrets, I can assure ye. Ye'll want t' know them *now*." Her tone was urgent, and Borin glanced back at Rani, the dim light reflecting off his bald pate.

"Very well," the merchant scowled, and dragged the Touched girl outside the room.

Rani caught her breath, hoping to overhear some whisper of their conversation, but she could make out nothing. She sighed, thinking of Mair's bravery. Rani would never have dared to make demands of Borin in his own chamber, especially when the Chief Councilor was so clearly busy.

These Touched folk.... They refused to live by the rules of the other castes.

Rani's speculation was cut off as Borin returned to the chamber. The man ran a hand over his skull and shot a glance at his fellow councilors who were waiting placidly.

"Rani, there *is* one more service you can provide, and it would further your reputation among all the merchants of this City." Borin cleared his throat and took a deep breath, as if steeling himself for a difficult task. "This is an honor we would normally assign to one of our own, but we cannot overlook your loyal actions and your faithful words since joining our ranks." Borin signaled to one of his minions. "Katrin, your roll of record."

The summoned councilor looked up in surprise. "Borin," she protested, "we do not owe our tithes until tomorrow, until Hern's feast day."

"Do you think I've forgotten the calendar?"

"Of course not, but—" The woman shifted uneasily beneath Borin's incisive gaze. Other councilors fidgeted, and Rani caught a muttered oath directed at Hern, god of merchants.

"But?" Borin pushed, and there was a sharpness to his voice that Rani had not heard before. "Are you challenging my leadership?"

"Of course not, Borin," Katrin protested. "But what am I to think? A Touched brat comes in, interrupting the Council's business, and the next thing I know, you're ready to confer our highest honor on this little criminal!"

Before Rani could bristle, Borin exclaimed, "No! That's where you're wrong, Katrin. Rani Trader is no longer a criminal. She has served her sentence well and honorably. All taint of her past is removed by that service."

"Still, Borin—"

"Any further challenge, Katrin, you must take before the full Council. Are you willing to do that?"

For a long minute, Katrin stared at her leader. It occurred to Rani that perhaps Katrin had thought to claim the mysterious honor for herself. Before the first blossom of pity could open in Rani's chest, Katrin collapsed in a stiff, angry bow. "No, Borin. I'll follow your will."

"Very good." The bald man held out his palm, ignoring the sting as Katrin slapped a roll of parchment across his fingers. "Rani Trader. It is this Council's custom to offer tithes to the priesthood on our feast day—a sampling of all our wares to see our brother priests through the coming year. Tonight our offerings must be conveyed to the cathedral close, to the end of the Pilgrim trail. Will you serve as our ambassador to the priests, bearing all the merchants' gifts, good wishes, and prayers for the coming year?"

Rani stared at the man, slack-jawed. The honor he mentioned was legendary—one that she and Varna had play-acted as children. Bardo had served as the Council's messenger one year, carrying the market's riches through the streets, amid much pomp and circumstance. Rani still remembered his boastful pride, especially that he had been chosen over merchants who sold their goods in the marketplace. That the Council would proffer this office to a child—to a rebel who had merited punishment for violating all her caste's rules.... Had *Mair* said something to Borin to bring about this honor? Rani sank back to her knees in honest humility, forgetting to put on the airs of her assumed identity and her false story. "Your Grace, you honor me too greatly."

"Nonsense, Rani. I honor you with your due. You have borne your punishment—even your chaining at the stall— with a grace clear to everyone. When you have your own stall in the marketplace, it will be a model for your fellow merchants. The tithing embassy is yours, if you wish it."

"I am honored, Your Grace. I will gladly go to the priesthood."

Borin might have breathed a sigh of relief. He certainly spoke faster: "Mind your caste, then, Rani, and go forth as our ambassador, bringing honor upon all our people." Rani's eyes shot up as she heard the words that had been muttered by the huddled Touched creature in the alleyway, but Borin seemed unaware that he had said anything unusual. Instead, he gestured imperiously, and Katrin rustled forward, bearing a small wooden cask.

Rani had imagined a cart piled high with goods, a dray swaying beneath the combined weight of all the offerings. She almost yelped as she recognized her mistake, giving up the enticing image of riding into the cathedral close, balanced atop a mound of cloth-of-gold. Her disappointment must have shown in her earnest features.

"Not what you anticipated?" Borin's smile was tight.

"Oh no, Your Grace," she began, shaking her head. "It's just that...."

"We've reached an agreement with the priesthood. They have no storehouses for our wealth, and they don't want aged goods. Beginning this year, we send them promises— inscribed on golden paper and settled in this box." Borin opened the wooden casket, and Rani caught a whiff of cedar as a delicate slip of gilded paper curled over the side. "Throughout the coming twelve-month, they need only present these receipts to the Council, and we will provide them with the finest goods at our command."

Rani nodded, measuring the advantage to the Council: the merchants could continue to claim ownership over their goods if any delicate negotiations arose with moneylenders. A flush of interest spread across her cheeks. She had never dreamed that life as a merchant could be so full of intrigue and dealing. There was no need to escape to a *guild* to arrange things and craft structures of beauty. She could do that right here in the Merchants' Council.

Borin, though, misread the flush on her face. "You are shamed by your mission, now that you know you will not bear your caste's visible wealth?"

"No, Your Grace!" Rani stumbled over her words in her effort to gainsay the Chief Councilor. "I was merely struck by the beauty of your system."

Borin swallowed a sour smile, as if he did not believe a word she spoke. "A beautiful system, well, yes. Enough of these flattering words. If you leave now, you'll still reach the Pilgrims' Compound before dusk."

Rani accepted the wooden box with a stiff bow. Borin made as if to follow Rani to the market's edge, but when they reached the eaves of the covered portico, a phalanx of armed soldiers appeared. Rani darted a quick glance toward Borin, but he seemed unsurprised by the soldiers' presence, as if he'd had advance notice of their invasion.

"Borin, Chief Councilor of the merchants?"

"Aye." Rani could barely make out the single syllable above her pounding heart. She considered dropping the box of receipts and fleeing the market in a whirlwind, as she had arrived.

"We have reason to believe that the merchants in this marketplace are harboring a vicious criminal, the murderer of Prince Tuvashanoran."

Borin looked concerned, and he settled a protective hand on Rani's shoulder. "Surely that was the traitor whose head you carted about the market this very day?"

"That was only one of the criminals. She spoke before she died, and now we search for the executed woman's apprentice."

Borin grimaced, apparently unaware that Rani had begun to shudder beneath his hand. "In the marketplace? I can't say I follow your logic. But these words are certainly not necessary for a child to hear. Go along, Rani Trader. Go about your business."

The councilor stressed her last name, as if he were telling the soldiers that she could not possibly be the murdering guildsman that they sought. The captain of the guard merely scowled in annoyance, letting Rani pass. "I warn you, Councilor, this is a serious matter."

"Yes," Borin agreed. "Of course. Come into my chamber and tell me all that you suspect."

Rani did not wait to hear the guard's response. It was all she could do to make her legs move forward, to keep her fingers clasped around the sharp corners of the casket that held the tithing slips. She had enough presence of mind to raise the wooden cask to her chest, using the smooth wood to cover any rip in her garments that might be noticed by enemy eyes. She had not needed to worry about her missing guild-badge for all the nights that she slept alone, chained in the marketplace, but now that she was returning to the streets....

The box was not heavy, but it was awkward in her arms. As soon as she was out of the soldiers' sight, Rani shifted the casket to her shoulder. Keeping her eyes on the cobbled streets, she tried not to think about the soldiers in the marketplace behind her, about where she would rest her head that night. As she walked, the casket grew heavier, and she sighed deeply as she shifted the wooden box to her other shoulder.

"Gettin' tired, are ye, Rai?"

"Mair." Rani jerked back to the present, startled to see the Touched girl in the street, as if she had just come from the cathedral close. Rani kept walking, and Mair obligingly turned about to keep her company.

"Ye might turn a smile toward th' one friend ye got i' all th' world."

"Friend!" Rani scoffed.

"Aye. Who else would come t' Borin 'n' warn 'im that th' soldiers were comin' fer ye?"

"Warn him?"

"Aye. I woulna want t' see ye missin' yer 'ead, like that Instructor o' yers. I was watchin' out for ye, see? No need t' fear me."

"I'm not afraid of you." Rani shifted the casket on her shoulder and jumped when Mair reached out a hand to steady it. Rani reached for her Zarithian blade, all too aware that she carried the wealth of dozens of merchants.

"Easy there!" Mair exclaimed. "Afraid we'll be stealin' her goods? That rat-pricker wouldna stop us if we 'ad a mind t' steal yer scrip."

"I'm not afraid of anything," Rani's chin jutted defiantly.

"Make sure ye can talk without yer voice quakin' when ye try that line on a stranger!" Mair's grin was easy, but her teeth glinted in the fading sunlight.

"Borin would not have entrusted me with this mission if he didn't think I could handle the likes of you."

"The likes o' me! Cor, ye *do* believe anything ye're told, don't ye? I'm sorry t' bear th' bad news, girl, but Borin chose ye t' avoid choosin' among th' real merchants vyin' fer th' 'onor!"

"I am a real merchant!" Rani retorted hotly, and a full minute passed before her curiosity got the better of her. "Why would he have to choose?"

"Ye claim t' be th' daughter o' merchants—ye should know well enough yerself. There're two groups o' merchants i' th' City—those sellin' i' th' market like yer precious Narda, and those sellin' other places i' th' Quarter. Borin dinna want t' favor one over th' other; he dinna want t' choose a messenger as 'is favorite."

"But he did! I'm from..." Rani trailed off as she tried to complete the sentence. Was she her father's daughter, representing the Quarter Merchants? Or was she Narda's aide, representing the marketplace?

"Aye, Rai, ye're from where'er ye claim t' be."

Despite the mocking tone, Mair's words rang true. The only real explanation for Borin choosing Rani was to ease other Council burdens. The crafty old councilor was outwitting his fellow merchants, beating them to the punch before they realized that the annual fight had even begun. Rani struggled to reweave her proud dignity. "And if I'm so unimportant, then why are *you* here?"

"Maybe my friends 'n' me, we wanted t' steal yer scrip so we c'n chew on a few extra apples winter nights." Mair laughed as Rani backed away, casting about a furtive eye for Rabe's shadowy presence. "'N' maybe we wanted t' warn ye o' other dangers. Keep yer eyes peeled in th' close. It'll likely be yer only chance t' learn what 'appened t' yer Instruct'r friend."

"She wasn't my—" Rani began to argue by habit, but modified her response. "What do you mean, 'what happened' to Morada? I thought that was clear enough." Shifting the casket once again, Rani set aside the memory of Morada's gelling head.

"Then think on *why* it 'appened. Cor! If *I'd* caught a traitor, ye can be sure I'd torture 'er a good long time before I let 'er die. Someone killed 'er outright, before she could say too much. I'd want t' know 'oo that person was."

"Maybe someone took pity on Morada, and executed her to spare her pain."

Mair chortled, a heartless sound that scraped Rani's nerves. "Aye, that mun be it! A woman kills th' Defender o' th' Faith, a city searches fer a fortnight, 'n' when she's found, the king takes pity on 'er and 'as 'er executed like a noble gone astray."

"You don't have to make me sound stupid!"

"*Sound* stupid! That wasna my intention, Rai."

Before Rani could grouse about Mair's choice of words, the girls emerged into the cathedral courtyard. The sun was setting behind bloody bandages of cloud, its last rays reflecting off the near-opaque windows. As Rani looked pridefully at the work of her former guild, the entire side of the building was coated with a viscous crimson light. Unbidden, Morada's specter gazed down at Rani from the splay-legged scaffolding. The apprentice froze, grasping Mair's arm as her vision flooded with the memory of Tuvashanoran's bloody death.

Mair continued on a few steps before realizing that she had lost Rani, and urgency spiced her words as she turned back to the apprentice. "Ye'd best get back t' work, Rai. Ye wouldna want Borin's councilors t' come lookin' fer ye 'n' callin' ye thief."

"Aye," Rani agreed, nodding and shifting the Council's casket closer to her narrow chest. With a nervous glance to the shadows, she followed the path past the scaffold, making her way to the pilgrims' compound at the back of the close. Only when a priest stepped forward to challenge her did she realize that Mair had melted into the shadows, disappearing like the Touched wraith that she was.

"Well at last!" huffed the overweight religious who stood

at the gate. "Father Aldaniosin's been expecting you for over an hour—it doesn't do to keep him waiting." The man hustled Rani through the gates, wheezing as he locked the stronghold behind her. The Pilgrims' Bell tolled ahead of them, sending out its first steady summons against the rising fog.

"I'm sorry," Rani managed. "Borin only gave me—"

"Save your excuses, child. I'm merely the gatekeeper. I'm just the brother assigned to stand in the rising mist, with all manner of mischief lurking around me, threatening in the dark..." The man's grievances were deep-carved with a familiar blade, and Rani stifled a sigh of impatience. It was hardly *her* fault she had been late—the Council should have summoned her earlier.

Before she could complete her justification in her own mind, the gatekeeper ushered her toward a low building, well set off from the other structures in the quiet compound. "Here you are," he huffed. "Don't waste any more of Father Aldaniosin's time, child." Just before Rani ducked through the doorway, she heard a swell of prayer rise from a building across the green. The pilgrims must be sitting down to their dinner, breaking the long day's fast with simple fare.

The comforting chant spread like warm balm, all the more soothing for the sad memories stirred by the words. Somewhere in the dining hall were men like the mythical father she had created to fool the soldier, the loving, caring Thomas Pilgrim who had searched frantically for his daughter. Not for the first time, Rani wondered what she would do if she never saw her father again, if she never felt her mother's strong arms about her, if she never teased with her brothers and sisters, about silly things like who got the last sweet cake during a hurried breakfast. Her family had not managed to get word to her when she was easy to find in the marketplace. How could they find her if she retreated to the life of a skulking spy, trying to find Tuvashanoran's real murderer? Could they find her at all, imprisoned as they were in King Shanoranvilli's dungeons?

All these thoughts—and more self-pitying words—rolled

over Rani as the distant pilgrims ended their chant and, presumably, settled down to their meal of hearty bread and thick soup. A breeze skirled across the courtyard, reminding Rani she was not only orphaned, but hungry as well. Her life as Narda's well-fed servant glimmered more appealing every moment. The thought forced a heavy sigh from her lungs.

"At last!" boomed a voice from the shadows of the nearest building, thunderous in the darkness, and Rani was so startled, she almost dropped her carved box.

"F-father Aldaniosin?"

"Of course." The man's voice was sharp with annoyance. "Who else would be fool enough to stand here in the dark, waiting for a tardy child? Come in, girl. If the incense seeps out, we'll just be here further into the night."

As Rani stepped over the threshold into the small outbuilding, she was buffeted by the sound and the smell and the sight of death.

The sound came from a black-robed trio kneeling at the far end of the room. Their voices rose and fell over familiar syllables, chanting the Summoning of the Gods over and over, including in each repetition the name of another one of the Thousand Gods. The words jumbled together in Rani's ears, the hasty formula marked off only by the click of beads as each decade of prayers was completed, each round of appeals measured and clipped in a neat skein of ten.

The smell reminded Rani of her last visit to her father's ancient mother, before the old merchant-woman found her own way to the Summoning of the Gods. A heavy perfume of rose oil and smoky incense failed to mask an underlying sickly sweetness, and after an explosive sneeze, Rani sneaked shallow breaths through her mouth.

Even as she huddled on the doorstep, reluctant to step into the smoky chamber, she translated the scene before her. Three stone tables rose out of the earthen floor, solid and steady, like misshapen tree trunks. The right-most table was mercifully empty, its smooth surface reflecting the flicker of torchlight and the steady notes of the three chanting worshipers. The other two, however, bore grisly burdens.

On the middle platform, atop the highest surface, lay Tuvashanoran's body. Even with a bandage wrapped about his brow, even with his right eye obscured by herb-steeped linen, Rani recognized the royal figure. Unconsciously, she sank to her knees, bowing her head and sketching a holy sign before the man who would have been Defender of the Faith.

And in that motion, Rani caught a glimpse of the third table, to her left. For just an instant, her mind refused to register the horrific sight. If she had stood at the foot of the platform, she might not even have recognized what confronted her, but there was no mistaking the rotting robe, the filthy hands with their broken nails and criss-crossed scars, the bruised arms. The third table held the mortal, headless remains of Instructor Morada.

"Enough of that!" snapped Father Aldaniosin, drawing her attention back to Tuvashanoran. "There will be ample time to honor the Prince at his pyre. We've still got to bury *this* one tonight." The priest spat on Morada's ragged cloak, and Rani's head jerked upright.

"B-buried, Father?" Certainly, she had expected retribution against a woman accused as traitor, but condemning her flesh to worms! "There's been a mistake—" Rani started to choke out.

Father Aldaniosin hardly heard her; he was already moving to the prince's alabaster body. "A mistake? Certainly there was a mistake. I don't know what Brother Hospitaller was thinking, binding His Highness' mouth with comfrey. Still, there should be no harm done if we place your ladanum on his tongue now. After all, it's the voice he speaks through the fire that matters, the words that reach the Thousand Gods when he's released from this earthly shell." The priest signed himself piously.

"Ladanum?" Rani repeated.

"Certainly. That's the formal name for the herb in your casket. I suppose Brother Herbalist called it by its common name when he sent you—myrrh. It would poison a living man, but to the dead...."

At that moment, the trio of worshipers completed a century of their chant, concluding the sequence of the Gods of Nature. Rani almost recoiled as they began to chant to the guilds' gods, and she caught herself listening for mention of the glaziers' special protector, Clain. Perhaps King Shanoranvilli's eradication of the glasswrights had not yet penetrated to the Cathedral's lists. Perhaps the glasswrights' guild lived on in some form. Before Rani gave over all of her attention to the chanters, Aldaniosin smoothed down the snowy linen covering the Prince.

"Come along now. We haven't got all night. Bring the herbs closer."

"But Father,—"

"No more excuses!" The priest towered over her quaking form. Rani had planned on being a good child; she had planned on confessing that she had only come to deliver the merchants' tithes. Nevertheless, she was drawn by Father Aldaniosin's firm command, by the imposition of solid, adult direction on her life of disarray.

Her fate was sealed when the priest softened his tone to paternal guidance. "Come along, child. The first body you care for is always the hardest. This is a crucial part of your training, if you wish to be a priest. You should be honored to serve the Prince in this last glory."

Serve the Prince. So far, Rani had failed miserably in that regard, despite her best attempts to heed the order of the City's castes. Far from serving the nobility, as a good merchant should, she had *caused* Tuvashanoran's death. Still, Father Aldaniosin proffered some meager way to atone for her sin; he offered deliverance from the guilt that stalked her conscience. If she could ease Tuvashanoran into the world of the Thousand Gods.... If she could guide his footsteps to the path carved by Pilgrim Jair, then she might begin to atone for her own role in the Prince's demise—however unwitting her cathedral outcry had been.

At least she had handled the dead before—the little babe

her mother had borne when Rani herself was six years old—the nameless little brother who did not live out his first night breathing the City's cold air. But the office the Priest demanded was one reserved to those under holy vows, at least the preliminary ties of acolyte. Rani hesitated beyond the circle of Father Aldaniosin's lantern, afraid to commit the sin of handling the dead, afraid to confess that she was not a member of the priestly caste.

Father Aldaniosin, misreading her hesitation, clicked his tongue in exasperation. "I don't know where we get our postulants these days." Without warning, he grasped her arm with claw-like fingers, pulling her toward the altar. Plucking the wooden casket from her hands and setting it on the edge of Prince Tuvashanoran's bier, Father Aldaniosin seized her wrists and planted her stiffened fingers on the prince's dead flesh.

"There!" he exclaimed. "Was that so terrible?"

After the initial shock, the form on the table was not as frightening as Rani had imagined. The Prince's skin was so cold, he might have been made of wax. Nothing of the man remained. Surely, the Thousand Gods would not punish her for attempting atonement, when that action merely required her to handle this shell of a former man. After a surprised pause, even the chorus of worshipers resumed their chanting. Rani resisted the urge to make a holy sign as Clain's name tumbled from their lips. So, the glasswrights were not completely eradicated from the City.

Rani realized Father Aldaniosin was waiting for an answer. "No, Father," she managed. "Forgive my foolishness."

"Forgive, forgive, forgive—that's all you postulants say. Now, let's get to work—we'll finish using the myrrh in that box there, before we shift to the herbs you were sent for. We certainly won't be wasting any on *that*." Father Aldaniosin glanced daggers at Morada's body, and Rani's confidence in her new-found vocation wavered. "Here. I'll hold him while you wind the sheet. Sprinkle the ladanum evenly—you'll need more there."

Rani swallowed a burning taste in the back of her mouth

and began to unroll the fine-woven linen, taking care to avoid touching the Prince directly. Father Aldaniosin waited until she had made her first few passes around the royal feet, and then he observed, "It would not be amiss for you to recite with the worshipers."

Rani nodded and waited for the trio to complete their antiphon. She joined them with her treble voice on the next pass, only hesitating for a moment as she realized they had completed reciting the guilds and were moving on to the merchant gods. "Hail Hern, god of merchants, guide of Jair the Pilgrim. Look upon this pilgrim with mercy in your heart and justice in your soul. Guide the feet of this pilgrim on righteous paths of glory that all may be done to honor you and yours among the Thousand Gods. This pilgrim asks for the grace of your blessing, Hern, god of merchants."

The formula was an ancient one, repeated for centuries in and around the cathedral. They were the first words Rani remembered hearing, for her mother prayed to Nome, the god of children, every morning and every evening, paradoxically invoking prayers for the passing of a life in her quest to preserve the little ones she loved.

So, the words were familiar on Rani's lips, but the sequence of the gods was not. Certainly, Rani knew a few of the links, stringing together each of the City's recognized merchant callings. The goldsmiths came first, then the tinkers, the leatherworkers, the tailors.... There was no reason for the order—no logic other than Jair's own word, for he was the one who had first recognized the Thousand Gods and recorded their presence in the life of a common man.

Rani let the worshiping trio carry her along, occasionally lapsing into silence on the second word of the prayer, allowing the professionals to determine who would be the next focus of adoration. All the while, she wrapped the prince's limbs in the flawless pyre-linen. Father Aldaniosin continued to shift the body, rolling the dead weight from side to side as Rani added purifying herbs to the snowy cloth. She skimped on the ladanum when she could, desperate to avoid opening the casket she'd carried to the cathedral.

The recitation of merchants lasted for the time it took Rani to work her way up the noble legs. She was relieved to find that Aldaniosin had already covered the Prince in a modest loin cloth, and she scarcely hesitated as she worked the winding cloth over Tuvashanoran's smooth belly, across the expected scars of a warrior leader. She kept her eyes focused on the narrow field of the marble flesh just beneath her fingers. She did not want to think of that cold body as an entire man; she did not want to be reminded of the living, breathing prince who she had summoned to death. Her conscience panged her as she pretended to add ladanum to the binding, sprinkling the scantest layer of herbs on the snowy cloth. She wiped her green-stained fingers frequently against the linen, adding to the appearance of coverage.

The worshipers had just shifted to the Dark Gods—the terrible, necessary lords of pestilence and illness and evil—when Father Aldaniosin shifted Tuvashanoran onto his back, reaching beneath the heavy torso to remove the last sheltering drapery so that Rani could perform her function. She had filled her left hand with the fragrant myrrh, and her right was tangled in the winding cloth. The worshipers took a deep breath before they began the next decade of their prayer, and Rani started with them, "Hail Tarn, god of death—" when she looked at the undraped torso before her, letting her eyes take in the next field of her labor.

Father Aldaniosin had crossed Tuvashanoran's arms on his marble chest, splaying the fingers in a clammy attitude of prayer. Rani scarcely bothered to register the telltale discoloration around the nail-beds, clear sign that her labors were necessary and almost overdue.

Rather, Rani looked at the Prince's muscular arms, at the once-proud flesh now collapsed in a heap of limp meat. Father Aldaniosin adjusted his grip on the body, and Rani saw that she had not imagined what she first suspected.

Bound about Tuvashanoran's right bicep, indigo tattoo gaudy against the pallor of lifeless skin, was a band of four snakes, twined about themselves and glaring at Rani through pin-prick crimson eyes.

CHAPTER 7

Rani completed her tasks mechanically, doling out the precious ladanum as if it were her own lifeblood. She blinked hard to drive away the images that roiled her thoughts. First Bardo, then Morada, now Tuvashanoran ... all bearing the twisted snakes. What did the strange tattoo mean? What cause could join together Bardo Trader, Instructor Morada, the wily nobleman Larindolian and, now, the noblest of all men? What had Larindolian called his circle? The Brotherhood of Justice.

Father Aldaniosin misunderstood Rani's blinking; he thought his acolyte was exhausted by her trip to the City for myrrh. He clicked his tongue over a child so weak, so unable to uphold the glorious standards of the Thousand Gods. His condemnation distracted him enough that Rani managed to palm the last fistful of myrrh from the priest's casket, making it appear that she withdrew the precious herb from her own carved wooden box. Rani prayed furiously to all the Thousand Gods that Father Aldaniosin would not hear the rustle of gilded papers as she snapped shut the merchants' casket.

The Gods, at least, stood by Rani, and she was able to avoid detection, able to stretch the ladanum to finish wrapping Prince Tuvashanoran's body. At last, afraid to speak and reluctant to remain silent, Rani gathered up her cedar chest. Finished with her grisly assignment, she was determined to find the Brother Provisioner and be done with the priests.

Father Aldaniosin, still unaware of the mistaken identity, pointed Rani toward the kitchens and Brother Hospitaller, and she dragged her feet across the courtyard. In moments, Rani found herself inside the low refectory building, drawn forward by rush-light, the aroma of plentiful food, and the harmonious good cheer of the penitent.

As Rani hovered just over the threshold, one of the faithful looked up from a bowl of fragrant soup. "There now, young pilgrim! Come to join us for supper, are you?"

Rani recognized the accent from King Shanoranvilli's easternmost territories; she had heard a few such travelers while she tended her father's shop. Lured forward by the promise of good food and comforting companionship, she started to accept the seat, but drew back when she realized she would be doomed without a pilgrim's Thousand-Pointed Star. Instead she managed a curtsey, still holding her cedar box awkwardly. "Thank you, goodwife, but I'm only a merchant from the City, sent to deliver a message from the Merchant Council."

"A merchant's daughter!" the old woman exclaimed. "Then you must sit with us—my husband and I are tinsmiths from Zarithia, and we have missed the comfort of our people on the long Pilgrim road."

The woman's husband overheard their conversation and turned to Rani with a scrutinizing eye. "A merchant in the City, are you? You look a mite scrawny to be a *true* merchant's daughter."

"Hardu, mind your manners," the woman shushed before turning to mother her new charge. "You do look like you could use some meat on your bones. Come, sit beside me, and tell me what it's like to live in the City."

"Begging your pardon, ma'am, but I must deliver this box to the priests."

"Nonsense. No priest is going to transact business during a meal. Even the religious caste knows we must feed our bodies before we can feed our spirits. There, Hardu, move down so this little one can join us."

The man shifted his weight on the bench, and Rani resignedly took the proffered place, declining to point out that far too many priests *were* conducting business during the meal—at least the businesses of corpse-wrapping and prayer-offering. The woman—Farna, she introduced herself—was solicitous of her new charge, offering the choicest tidbits from her own trencher. Even as Rani's stomach clenched at the rich aroma, Farna settled her warm woolen cloak about the girl's shoulders, clucking her tongue at children's insistence on running about the streets half-clothed, with no regard for a winter wind, or the threat of grippe, or any number of other looming disasters that only a mother could discern.

Resignation melted into relief as Rani tucked into the fine pilgrim food. Only occasionally did she have to swallow hard, catching a breath of myrrh on her hands.

"We've left our own daughter back in Zarithia," Farna babbled on. "She's older than you, dear, old enough to run our market stall without us keeping an eye on things. We've given her her head before, to make sure she can manage for the six-month we'll be on the Pilgrim Road. Isn't that right, Hardu?"

Hardu grunted his assent, and Farna sailed on to her next conversational gambit. "We could hardly believe the misfortune of our timing, taking to the Pilgrim Road as bad luck falls on the City! Prince Tuvashanoran—did you ever see him?"

Rani swallowed an unfortunate piece of gristle and managed to choke out, "Aye, he was a great man. He came through the Merchants' Quarter frequently. He held all the City's castes near his heart, as Defender of the Faith."

"Defender," grunted Hardu. "He never quite became that, did he?" The man punctuated his question by reaching for a hefty length of bread, worrying at the crusty loaf with one of the cathedral's use-dulled knives.

"This City needs more Zarithian wares." Rani managed

to deflect the question, wincing as Hardu levered the dull blade through the bread and released a shower of crusty flakes. "I've got one myself," she couldn't resist adding the boast, patting the satchel that now rested beside the merchants' carved box.

"A dagger, then? Do you hear that, Hardu? The child can recognize the value of our goods, even here in King Shanoranvilli's City." Hardu snorted, as if certain his wares would be valued anywhere, and reached for a bowl of the thick stew that was the base of the Pilgrims' meal. He ladled the stuff onto his plate, carefully selecting slivers of meat and barely restraining a grimace as Farna plucked out the richest morsels to give to Rani. Rani, not wanting to disappoint the kind woman, swallowed the fine fare almost without chewing.

"So," Farna babbled on, "what do you bear in that chest? Something as precious as Zarithian metal?"

Before Rani could answer, she noticed a priest hovering behind her, cocking his head with a suspicious glimmer in his eye. While Farna was oblivious to Rani's sudden discomfort, the woman could not fail to sense the religious' gaze, and she turned with a hearty laugh. "Father! This little one seems hungrier than we thought. Could we have more stew?"

The priest's hawk-visage registered annoyance for just an instant. While the pilgrims might follow in Jair's footsteps, he seemed to think, their demands could be annoying at times. As he came forward, he gave Rani an eagle glance. "Little pilgrim, you are not wearing your Star. Jair would frown on such a breach of pilgrim custom."

"Oh no," Farna interjected, before Rani could craft an excuse. "This little one isn't a pilgrim. She belongs to your City. She was just telling us she's a merchant's daughter. She has some sort of message for you." Farna patted Rani on the head, soothing her as if she were a restless pup. "There, dear, *that's* how you get the priests' attention. Now you can deliver your box." The motherly woman sat back, immensely pleased with herself.

Rani managed not to frown her displeasure. Instead, she invested all her thoughts into devising an escape from the suddenly too-solicitous priest. All her calculations came to naught as the religious reached forward, mistrust wrinkling his brow. "What have you got in that box?" Rani had no choice but to offer up the casket, hoping the brother would value the gift and forgive the bearer.

She never learned if absolution was to be hers.

As the priest set his hands on the box, a tremendous force pounded open the refectory doors. Cold night air burst into the hall, blowing reeds and clothing with reckless abandon. Startled pilgrims cried out, and more than one journeying soldier reached for a sword that was absent in this holy place.

Rani, already jumpy for fear of being unveiled as an imposter, scrambled underneath the long refectory table. She pushed her way between Hardu's feet, clutching at Farna's cloak and covering her terrified shoulders with the woman's dark wool. Quivering, she could make out the scene in the refectory from her sheltered vantage point.

Fearsome warriors swept the hall like a tempest, overturning benches and tables as if the furniture belonged to dolls. The marauders grabbed at jabbering pilgrims with vicious hands, and many voices wailed for Jair's intervention. Rani heard her erstwhile questioner's priestly voice, shrill with reciting the Mercy Prayer.

In the tumult, the merchants' casket tumbled from the bench, carved top shattering on the stone floor. The wooden remnants rolled about, spewing forth their curling papers. The receipts swirled like golden snow, and Rani fought the urge to sweep up the offerings, to preserve them from trampling, heretical feet. Even knowing the danger she faced, Rani might have darted out to gather up her caste's offerings, but she was frozen by a sudden realization. The tissue of the merchants' receipts was the *only* metallic glimmer in the chaotic hall.

There was not a bared weapon among the marauders.

If the invaders had been a band of soldiers, each would have been armed. Instead, the only sign uniting the invaders was the scrap of black mask bound across each brow, hiding eyes and nose from pilgrims and priests too terrified to examine their harriers.

Certainly, the refectory was filled with a fearsome amount of noise. The invaders hollered as if they would awaken Prince Tuvashanoran from his untimely sleep, and several women's voices shrilled in the bone-shivering ululation of graveside mourning. Pilgrims cried out to be delivered from the ravagers, some screaming in terror, others fervently commending their souls to the Thousand Gods for safe-keeping.

Nevertheless, despite all the tumult, the sharpest knife Rani could spy was the dull blade for the bread, and that was brandished by a pale-faced Hardu.

Unbidden, Rani's memory flitted to her games in the City streets—joyful rounds of Free the Princess, played with her then-friend Varna. In their carefree games, Rani had often crafted a show of noise and strength, just like the marauders'. She had always had one specific purpose—to distract the Princess' appointed guard.

But where—and what—was the article that represented the Princess in *this* tumult?

Rani spared a passing thought that her cedar box of merchants' receipts was the figurative Princess. Certainly, *she* had never seen such riches assembled in one place—all the merchants' tithes for an entire year. Rani had never been charged with as much responsibility as now swirled about on the refectory floor in the form of flimsy golden papers. One slip chose that moment to flit across the flagstones, and Rani reflexively grabbed it, making out the torn and soiled letters—"one dozen cloaks of fine grade wool, with emblems to be determined by the bearer."

Before Rani could complete her thought, a half-dozen of the marauders discovered her hiding place, heaving back the massive wooden table with a roar of rage. Even as Rani's shelter crashed against the flagstones, she scampered across the floor, sending up a flurry of gilded treasure as she huddled beneath the illusory shelter of Farna's borrowed cloak. Who knew that Rani had borne such riches to the cathedral? Borin, of course, and some of his fellow merchant councilors. And Mair. Could the Touched girl have acted so rapidly, pulling together members of her casteless hordes to raid the pilgrims' compound? Rani shivered, remembering Mair's apparently coincidental appearances, first in Borin's shadowy market stronghold and then, again, as Rani had approached the cathedral close.

Even as Rani scrambled for some new lee, she came face to face with one of the plunderers. For just an instant, she was startled into immobility, frozen by the banshee screams that echoed in the dining hall. Then, rough hands reached toward her, fingers curved with a murderous tension, palms latticed with scores of tiny scars. Rani knew hands like that; she had hoped and prayed to be admitted to a brotherhood that would grant her the same cicatrices.

The marauder was a glasswright.

Rani was so startled, she almost missed the invader's strangled intake of breath, the gasped, "You!"

Even as Rani's gaze was drawn to the pursed mouth, she caught the flaring eyes behind the black mask—eyes that had glared at her every day that she worked in the guild. "Guildmistress Salina!"

Rani bobbed into her accustomed curtsey without thinking, forcing down the swirling questions of how the guildmistress had escaped the king's dungeons, how she had come to stand in the cathedral close like a free woman.

Amazed and tangled in Farna's too-long cloak, Rani almost missed the most important aspect of the woman before her. Stitched into Salina's mask was a delicate tracery of black on black with eight scarlet pin-pricks—four intertwined serpents, with evil teeth glinting across the bridge of the guildmistress' nose.

As Rani made out the now-familiar sigil, the meaning of this strange attack suddenly became clear. One glance toward the still-open refectory door confirmed the apprentice's suspicions—shapes moved across the courtyard, midnight shadows against darkest night on the far end of the cathedral

close. If the invaders had been more familiar with their
territory, they would not have needed their faint glimmer of
lantern-light; they might have escaped all unnoted.

But the marauders had never expected to need to invade
the cathedral close. The invaders were stealing back the
evidence that linked them to Tuvashanoran's murder. They
might be taking Morada's brutalized body, doing away
with the snake tattoo that would connect the Instructor to
the dead Tuvashanoran in any way more obvious than her
treacherous act. Or—and Rani trembled at the thought—
they might be stealing Tuvashanoran himself. What lengths
would the mysterious Brotherhood go to to keep the City
from learning that both Morada and the prince bore the
sign of intertwined snakes?

Rani knew she should summon help. She should identify
Salina as one of the vicious glasswrights sought by the king's
men. She should let people in power know the true danger
behind this attack.

But there was nothing she could do.

No one was prepared to help a terrified child in the
midst of the cathedral chaos. If she unmasked Salina—
literally or figuratively—she would need to answer sticky
questions about how she knew the Guildmistress. Even
if the old woman were revealed, there was no guarantee
that the shocked and weaponless pilgrims would rally to
attack; Rani realized how preposterous it sounded to blame
a shriveled old woman for Tuvashanoran's death. Almost
as preposterous, she sighed, as to claim that she herself was
innocent as an accomplice. There was no way to implicate
Guildmistress Salina without throwing herself beneath
justice's rough-shod feet.

Trapped like a baited lion in King Shanoranvilli's
Amphitheater, Rani did the only thing she could think of.
Muttering to her newfound patron, Lan, she lowered her
head and ran directly at Guildmistress Salina. Her tough
skull took the old woman just below the breastbone.
The apprentice scarcely had time to gloat over Salina's
tremendous *ooommmph* of expelled air before the masked

woman fell back, crashing onto the flags and sending up a new flurry of gilded paper and bruised rushes.

Rani took advantage of the chaos to scurry for the refectory door.

The cold night air slapped her as she gulped great breaths, trying to slow her pounding heart. As much as she longed to hide in the cathedral outbuildings, to seek refuge in one of the prayer chapels scattered about the courtyard, she only permitted herself to disappear inside Farna's midnight cloak, to clothe herself in the deepest courtyard shadows as she crept to the hut where Father Aldaniosin had prepared Morada and the prince for their final rest.

One quick glance confirmed the marauders' success. Rani began to tremble as she recognized the priest's formal robes, as she made out the distortion of blackest iron protruding from his dark-stained belly. The invaders had not withheld their steel here, at the site of their true mission. The rampage in the refectory had been staged to cover the sound of murder.

Rani stepped over the steaming pool of Father Aldaniosin's blood. She was obscenely drawn to the bleeding and tangled ruins that had been the three worshipers. "Hail Tarn, God of Death..." Rani heard in her memory, and she tried to rub out the prickle of terror against the nape of her neck.

Turning to the three altars, Rani confirmed her suspicions.

Tuvashanoran continued to lie in state, his myrrh-scented bandages untouched by marauding hands. Now, though, the prince was flanked by two empty platforms; Morada's mutilated corpse was nowhere in sight.

Rani became aware of a sound louder than her rasping breath, angrier than her pounding heart. Someone had gained the Pilgrims' Bell and was ringing the heavy metal furiously, sending up a klaxon into the heavy autumn night. Shanoranvilli's soldiers were being summoned to the rescue.

Once again, Rani acted on impulse, abandoning rational thought. Gathering her midnight cloak tight and lifting a fold over her pale, pale face, she slipped toward the gates of the cathedral compound. She paused only a moment, to look back at the riotous mess in the courtyard, to try to thrust away the image of Father Aldaniosin, bleeding his last drop in service to his Prince.

As Rani drew a regretful breath, a dark shadow emerged from the refectory door. She was not even surprised to hear her Guildmistress' voice raised high on the freezing night breeze. "Halt! Stop! The glasswrights' apprentice!"

Rani melted into midnight as the pounding of soldiers' feet echoed after her.

"So, you can see, I had nowhere else to go."

"Aye, Rai, we c'n see that." Mair paced in front of Rani, shaking her head, even as she fingered Rani's new cloak, obviously assessing the value of the stolen goods. "At least ye 'ad th' presence o' mind t' steal th' cloak." Rani started to protest that theft had never been her intention; she had merely grabbed the garment in terror. She thought better of the confession, though, and settled for an eloquently mysterious nod. "Pity ye dinna think t' grab some o' that scrip from th' dinin' 'all floor—we could've used new goods fer barter 'n' whatnot."

Rani resisted the urge to make a fist around the one slip she *had* managed to save the receipt for woolen cloaks. "The merchants would hardly have redeemed their stolen scrip. You'd only be fingered for what happened in the cathedral close."

Mair laughed throatily and shrugged. "It'd be worth a try. Th' City's not ready t'admit we Touched 'ave th' strength t' pull off *that* sort o' campaign."

Rani pulled her cloak close. She had wandered the streets in the Merchants' Quarter for a frightened night, snatching only a few minutes of sleep huddled in an alleyway. When she was awakened by Mair and her troop, Rani was genuinely pleased, and she had willingly followed the Touched children into the no-mans-land between the City's Quarters.

Now, thrusting away yet another unwelcome image of Instructor Morada's stolen, headless torso, Rani asked, "Do you? Do you have strength enough to raid the cathedral?"

"An' wouldna ye like t' know? No, Rai, we'll not be tellin' ye all our secrets til ye join our ranks fer good."

"Join you?" Unexpected tears of relief prickled Rani's eyes at the thought of joining anyone.

"Aye. We've traded wi' ye an' learned from ye, but we'll not tell ye more about th' Touched til ye swear ye'll stand wi' us 'n' not agin us."

"Stand with you against whom?" Rani's voice sounded impossibly formal against the Touched girl's rough brogue, and she started when another one of the ragtag band answered.

"Aw, Mair, let 'er go. She 'asn't a clue what it means t' be Touched."

Mair glowered at the filthy Rabe. "Aye, Rabe, 'n' I mean t' teach 'er. Ye got a problem wi' that?"

The boy scuffed dirt in the general direction of Rani's feet, close enough for the apprentice to ball up her fists in angry response, but far enough away that she need not fight to retain her honor. "No un 'ad t' teach me. 'R ye, fer that matter."

Mair's voice was tinted with a deadly warning. "An' 'oo's t' say we canna do more fer our newest recruits?"

"And who's to say I'll do whatever you're asking me to do?" Rani interjected. "Why do *you* want *me*?"

Mair turned to stare at her, dark eyes glinting in the wan light of a new day. "Don't ye worry about that, Rai. We want ye." The leader of the troop snapped her fingers and held out one commanding hand. A young child slid forward, lugging a half-filled wine skin. Mair took the leather and turned to face the children under her command. "I propose that Rai join us, as a full member o' th' troop. Any o' ye want t' challenge me?"

Rabe squirmed and tried to dig his toe into the cobblestones, but he did not speak out against Mair's impetuous act. The leader waited a full minute for rebellion to bloom before she turned to Rani. "'N' ye Rai, do ye want t' stand by us, instead o' agin us? Do ye want t' be recognized as one o' th' Touched in Shanoranvilli's City?"

For just an instant, Rani hesitated. She was proud of her merchant's breeding, mindful of the glory of her caste in a City where all was measured by birthright.

Nevertheless, she had sold that birthright once, electing to become a glasswright, for something as intangible as an artist's blossoming sensibilities. Now, she was offered far greater riches—companionship, food, allies against enemies still unknown. "Aye," she managed the one syllable. Rabe snorted his disgust, but Mair stared him down.

"Fine then, Rai. Take this," the leader hefted the wineskin toward Rani, who flinched under the unexpected weight, "'n' answer this. Do ye, Rai, swear t' join yer brothers 'n' sisters among th' Touched, t' stand wi' them agin all injustice, 'n' right all wrongs i' th' City?"

Rani's eyes had grown huge and solemn, but she nodded her agreement. At a twisted smile from Mair, she managed to choke out the words, "I do."

"Then drink wi' yer brothers 'n' sisters, 'n' be one o' us." Rani hefted the awkward leather sack to her lips and sipped at a liquid she quickly realized was more powerful than wine.

Even as the heady whiskey startled Rani's tongue, Mair leaned forward, pumping the supple leather with a vicious squeeze. Rani spluttered as the alcohol burned down to her lungs, and her choking brought tears to her eyes. When she could breathe again, she turned an accusing gaze on her mentor. "Why did you do that?"

"If ye plan t' live as one o' th' Touched, ye'll do nothin' by 'alf measures. Ye wouldna want t' starve 'cause ye dinna eat all yer cakes, would ye?" Rani shook her head, still dazed by the fiery beast that clawed its way to her belly. "Good. Now, there's only one other thing, if ye're goin' t' be one o' us." Mair cast a meaningful eye toward the pouch at Rani's waist.

Suspicion creased Rani's brow. Had that been Mair's plan all along—to get Rani drunk and then steal her meager possessions? Rani covered her pitiful sack of treasures with a mistrusting hand.

"Exactly!" Mair chortled. "Ye know what we're goin' t' ask before we do it! Ye're meant t' be one o' us, 'n' that's fer sure!"

"What do you want from me?" Rani's panicked question was slurred from fear and the tightening clutch of whiskey, and her careful words sounded more like Mair's patois than the fine speech of a merchant child in the King's City.

"A pledge o' faith t' yer new people."

"What?"

"Nothin' ye couldna been forced t' give us weeks ago." Mair stared at her steadily, waiting for Rani to measure out the demand. The apprentice felt the other children's eyes crawl like worms across her skin, and she reached into her sack, her fingers moving over her treasures as if taking inventory, verifying that the Touched had not somehow pilfered her meager riches while she was unaware.

The Zarithian knife, gift from her father.

The rag doll, gift from her mother.

The smooth circle of cobalt glass, found at the guild.

And the silver mirror, birth-gift from the merchants' Council, embossed with its fierce lion pulling down a goat.

As Rani touched the last of her possessions, she knew that the precious silver was already lost to her. Even beneath her fingers, the metal shrank away, predator and prey cringing from her attention. "Brave as a lion; fleet as a lion," she muttered as she pulled out the delicately wrought treasure. The mirror was her sole remaining link to a merchant's life; it was the first item she would have sold had she lived out a normal life in her caste, had she stepped up to finance her very own merchant stall.

The polished metal glinted wanly in the daylight, and Rani felt the hunting lion and its hapless prey brand her palm. Even as Rabe darted out a grubby hand for the prize, Rani pulled it back from the greedy boy, unable to part with her final link to the world she had once known, the easy past she had been born into.

Rabe scoffed as Mair prodded, "What's yer problem, Rai? Is th' price too 'igh? Do we ask too much t' bring ye into our family? T' 'old you as one o' ours no matter 'oo is askin' after ye, or fer what?"

Rani's head whirled, and she wished she had taken no part of the whiskey. Certainly Mair's words made sense. Rani's entry into the calamitous glasswrights' guild had cost her parents far more than a silver mirror. Nevertheless, Rani's bonds to her family, to her heritage, were tied to the silver disk like silken cords. She managed to mutter, "I can't give it to you. It was a gift to me, from the Merchants' Council."

"Fro' th' Council!" Mair crowed. "Th' Council, great Rai! Why ye're the girl 'oo came from nowhere! Now ye claim t' 'ave a gift from Borin 'imself!"

"I was a merchant the day I was born! The Council gave me this mirror so I could start my own stall!" Rani answered hotly, the words bubbling past the knot of reason and restraint that had come all undone in its whiskey bath.

"'N' now we're afraid!" Mair exclaimed. "We're all tremblin' i' our boots." As if to underscore the scorn in their leader's voice, the Touched children huddled closer to Rani, craning their necks for a glimpse of the silver caste birthright. An excited hum infected even the littlest ones. "'N' don't go thinkin' ye can grab fer yer knife," Mair warned. "We'd stop ye before it cleared th' bag."

As much as Rani longed for the simple life she'd left behind forever, she had not gone entirely soft in the head. Even as her breath came fast, she knew she would not fight this Touched band. She had no desire to bleed out the last of her life in a dilapidated alleyway in some unknown quarter of the City. Instead, she swallowed the bitter mixture of pride dissolved in hatred. Mair and the Touched had stood with her throughout the past weeks of tumult.

Without realizing she'd made a decision, Rani held out the mirror, turning it about so that the children could see the raised lion. "I'll not lift my knife against you. I meant my oath when I swore my faith to the Touched."

Mair waited for a long minute, spinning the tension into palpable yarn. When the older girl took the mirror, Rani felt a cord sever in her chest, a bond to the family and caste and life she had always thought of as her own, even when she had been in exile at the guild. Mair hid away the treasure, apparently unaware of the mirror's true value.

Fighting back a prickle of tears, Rani took the only action she could think of.

Raising her right hand to her lips, she spat into her palm. When she extended the whisky-scented mess toward Mair, the leader of the Touched looked surprised, as if she could not remember thus binding Rani to silence in the marketplace, not so many nights ago. Then, with the other Touched children looking on, Mair spat into her own palm and clasped Rani's tightly. The two girls eyed each other steadily, holding their pose until many of the other children shifted restlessly.

"Fine, Rai. Welcome t' yer life among th' Touched."

Rani ignored the swoop of relief at Mair's words. Perhaps her trade had been well-made. Hitching at her belt, she managed to add a swagger to her step as she turned around to survey the ramshackle quarters. "I don't expect we're going to find any breakfast *here*, are we?" Mair laughed, and the horde soon made its way back to the safer sections of Shanoranvilli's City.

In fact, the troop of children made its way to the Nobles' Quarter. Rani had never explored those streets; she had only traveled there once, with her father, when he was delivering a well-worked set of bowls to some high-caste family. Now, she saw how the nobles' houses were better faced than any she had seen before. Music drifted from many balconies, a delicate strum of lutes, and tremulous female voices twined through the air like fragile roses on a trellis.

Soldiers stood in front of many houses, their broad chests covered with their employers' livery. Rani could breathe in the scent of autumn flowers—rich blossoms that were carefully tended in lush gardens, sheltered by stone walls. The nobles' lives were so different that Rani might have been in another land, on a world as distant as the moon.

The Touched children ignored the wonders of this new setting, spending their considerable energy on darting unseen from doorway to doorway. Rani was quickly led off the main streets into the quiet alleys that spread like blood vessels behind the nobles' villas. Each estate had a passage behind it, and Rani marveled at the extravagance of a life well-lived. In one alley, they found a keg of ale, half stove in, but with several inches of good beer left in the bottom. In another, a flock of starlings chittered over the heels of a dozen loaves of bread. The birds proved no match for the children; they were driven off by Rabe's energetic suggestion that the Touched feast on starling pie.

All the time, Mair led the troop, looking around blind corners to make sure a soldierly protector was not unfortunately stationed. She issued final decisions on all items that bore a noble coat-of-arms. Always, she balanced safety against treasure, protection against wealth. More than once, Mair informed her company that they had to leave behind a cloak or a tunic or—in one surprising instance—a sluggish hound puppy, for each was clearly branded by its noble owner, and each might be begrudged in the long run, might be missed if found on a Touched child, even if those treasures had been discarded like so much trash.

Rani was exhilarated by the search. She imagined herself on one of her father's buying missions, finding treasures to enrich the merchant stall.

Once she nearly came to fisticuffs with Rabe over a pair of leather gloves. They must have been cut for a lady—the leather fingers were narrow, and short enough that they fit the children. Rabe found the left glove on top of a rubbish heap at the same time that Rani found the right, blown against a stone wall in the alley. Turning back the soiled cuff to hide a worn seam, Rabe demanded that Rani hand over her treasure.

Rani did not care for the gloves until she saw how much Rabe wanted them. Then, the blue-dyed leather took on a special allure, becoming the perfect complement to Farna's cloak. Rani thrust out her chin as she anchored her feet in the alley's debris. Ultimately, Mair refereed the dispute.

Rani wore the gloves for the rest of the day, even though they hindered her efforts at some of the dirtier scavenging.

That night, the troop settled into makeshift quarters, back in the thready streets that unraveled between the City's established quarters. Mair had seen that each of her charges had enough to eat, stopping to chat with every child and exclaim about some treasure or other. As the ragged band settled down to sleep, Mair appointed the first guard, then came to sit beside Rani.

"Ye did just fine, fer a girl 'oo never combed th' Nobles' locks before." Rani stretched out her fingers, taking advantage of the moon's glimmer to study her treasured gloves. Mair shifted to a more comfortable position, producing a ragged blanket from her well-packed satchel. "Rabe'll not be comin' 'round t' friendship if ye keep lordin' yer roots over 'is."

"Lording!" Rani exclaimed, but lowered her voice as sleepy eyes focused on the pair. "*He's* the one who's been lording it over me. Ever since you asked me to join your group."

"'E's afraid, Rai. 'E fears losin' th' only family 'e 'as in all th' world."

Rani snorted. "I'm not likely to cut him out of his place with you."

"Ye've got *my* blanket over yer knees, don't ye?" Rani almost squirmed from beneath the wool throw as Mair sighed. "Ach, 'e's not long fer takin' comfort wi' us, i' any case. It's almost time 'e found 'is own way. 'E could lead a 'andful o' Touched as well as I. Or 'e could find 'imself a solid job, a man's job i' almost any noble 'ouse."

"I didn't mean to—"

"Aye, Rai, you dinna mean t' do anything t' upset th' lives o' yer Touched kin." Mair's words were so matter-of-fact— and so disbelieving—that Rani could think of no response. Leaning against the crumbling wall, she heard the muffled breath of sleeping children around her. Mair's body was close to hers, and the blanket settled over them like a warm pudding. Rani let herself drift, thinking how far she had roamed that day, and how much she had learned about life in the City that she thought she'd known her entire life. Her legs were heavy with fatigue, and her eyelids drooped.

"Rai?" Mair's voice was leaden with her own drowsiness, and Rani almost failed to produce an answering grunt. "What's it like t' live in one o' them houses, wi' a mother 'n' a father, 'n' brothers 'n' sisters around all th' time?"

Tears of self-pity soaked the back of Rani's throat. "It's like... It's like all the sunlight in the world, streaming through the Cathedral windows."

"Why don't ye go back then? Ye couldna 'ave done somethin' so bad yer own ma wouldna take ye back."

"They're gone." Rani's voice cracked. "I did something— or the King's Men *think* I did something—so terrible they've taken all my family away. I think they want me to come to the prison, to ask for my folk to be released."

"We'll go tomorrow," Mair promised, as easily as if she were agreeing to steal a pie from a window sill. "What're their names?"

"Jotham and Deela Trader."

Mair's breath whistled between her teeth and her body stiffened beneath the blanket. "Ye're th' one they're seekin' then. Th' one 'oo killed th' Prince."

Rani froze, conscious that her next words could save or destroy her. "I'm the one the soldiers *say* killed the Prince. I didn't, though."

"Ye're Ranita Glasswright. Rani Trader."

"I'm Rai."

There was a long moment of silence, and Rani watched Mair decide whether to summon the night-watch, to hand over a murderous fugitive. The apprentice forced herself to calculate the angle she would leap to be free of the blanket, to flee down the alley when Mair set off an alarm.

"I've got bad new fer ye."

"What?" Rani barely managed to force the syllable past her pounding heart.

"Yer parents weren't just taken t' Shanoranvilli's dungeons. Th' soldiers 'ad their sport. It was all th' capt'n could do t' rein in 'is angry men after th' Prince was killed. Jotham and Deela Trader'll be feelin' no pain now."

Rani felt the air pressed out of her lungs, but she forced stunned questions past her lips. "And my brothers? My sisters?"

"Th' same, they say. They're all at peace now, Rai."

"Even Bardo?" Rani could scarcely manage the two words in her disbelief. Even when she was abandoned in the marketplace, she had not imagined her entire family *dead*. Imprisoned unjustly on her behalf, yes, tortured and starved—but executed!

"Bardo? Yer brother is Bardo?" For the first time, Rani heard fear in Mair's voice—fear, and the sharp note of discovery as the Touched girl fit together her bits of knowledge. "If ye're Bardo Trader's sister, Rai, that's another story. Another tale entirely." Mair pulled the blanket from Rani's legs, huddling deep within the wool as if hiding from a nightmare. Rani shivered in the sudden midnight chill, but managed to force words past her swelling throat.

"Then Bardo still lives?"

"Mair's answer was pulled from reluctant lips, and the Touched girl's fingers flickered in a protective sign. "Aye. Or so the rumors say."

Rani heard more, though, volumes left unspoken. "Tell me, Mair. Tell me about my brother."

CHAPTER 8

Uncharacteristically, Mair looked away from Rani, gathering up the blanket and feeding it through nervous fingers, as if she were shelling peas. Rani waited impatiently for several minutes, blinking in the moonlight, but finally curiosity roughened her voice. "What? What could be so terrible that you can't even tell me?"

"We're caught in th' dark o' night, Rai, 'n' there're things better said i' th' day, if they 'ave t' be said at all."

"Oh no you don't! I'm not going to sit here all night, imagining all sorts of terrible things!"

"Whatever ye're imaginin' it's no worse'n th' truth."

The grim words clutched Rani's heart, and she swallowed hard but she forced her voice into a coaxing wheedle. "Come, Mair. It can't be as bad as all that. It can't be worse than what you've already told me—that my family is all ... gone." The words did not sound real as she pleaded. "Tell me what you know, and we'll figure out the truth of things."

Mair sighed deeply. Rani felt the leader's body relax against her own, and she managed to release her own pent breath, aware that Mair had come to a decision—a decision that Rani might regret. "All right, Rai. But you willna like what ye're goin' t' 'ear."

"There's a lot about this whole thing I don't like. At least I know you're going to tell me the truth."

"Aye, Rai, at least ye know that." Mair jutted her chin

toward a sleeping shape, some distance down the alley. "Ye've surely noticed that Rabe isn't th' easiest among th' Touched."

"I've noticed," Rani said wryly, unable to resist flexing her fingers inside her hard-won gloves.

Mair noticed the movement and restrained a grim smile. "'E 'asn't always been wi' us. Not all th' Touched children roam in troops like us, ye know."

"Of course," Rani snorted reflexively. Until she managed the two words, it had not occurred to her that she knew next to nothing about how the Touched lived—other than Mair's little group of followers and the adults who were fortunate enough to find work as servants. For Rani's entire life, the Touched had been merely the most lively of countless wonders scattered about the City quarters. They were the lowest of the castes; technically, they *had* no caste. In Rani's closed mind, the ragged folk were no more citizens of King Shanoranvilli's realm than the carving on Noble houses and the fine signs outside merchant shops. The Touched simply were, and for all Rani knew, always had been.

Mair was no fool, and she apparently read Rani's two words as a confession of ignorance. "There're 'ole Touched families, just like ye 'ave among th' merchants 'n' whatnot. A mother 'n' father 'n' a passel o' kids." The leader waved a hand to take in all her charges. "We're t'gether because we chose t' leave our families, or because they left us. One way 'r another."

Rani could hear a surprising ripple of sorrow beneath Mair's words, but she did not want to interrupt the lesson to pry into Mair's own story. "Well, Rabe," Mair continued, apparently unaware of Rani's curiosity, "'e came from one o' those families. 'Is mother was always plottin', always schemin'. She was good enough t' mint coins in th' alley, she was." Mair's voice was quiet, respectful, and Rani realized that Mair had dreams of being the best Touched thief and beggar in all the City—just as Rani had once been certain she would be the best merchant and, later, the best glasswright. "One day, Rabe's ma came up wi' her riskiest plan."

Mair's whisper fogged the night air, and Rani had to lean close to catch the scarce-breathed words. The leader might have chosen Rani over Rabe where the gloves were concerned, but she clearly had no intention of hurting her lieutenant with overheard tales of his family's past. Rani's breath froze in her throat as she tried to capture the whispered story. "Rabe's mother was goin' t' steal from a merchant—rare goods that weren't likely t' be found elsewhere i' th' City—'n' then she was goin' t' sell back th' treasures, later, when th' merchant realized how much 'e needed th' goods. She'd worked out th' 'ole thing, stealin' while an apprentice was i' th' shop, sellin' back to th' merchant 'imself. She figured she'd make a finer penny if she worked over a merchant in th' Quarter instead o' th' Market—th' Council's too strong there, keeps too sharp an eye on th' likes o' us. No, she worked out 'er plan well. I'll not bore ye wi' th' details; suffice t' say she stood t' make a tidy profit."

Rani nodded; she had firsthand knowledge of such a scam. "Someone did that to my father." She shuddered, remembering her family's rage, remembering her own horrified guilt. "A ragged old woman came in at the end of the day and managed to steal a set of pewter spoons. Spoons and a pair of shoe buckles."

What Rani neglected to tell Mair was that *she* was the one responsible for the theft. It had been the first day her father had ever left her alone in the stall. He had been gone for scarcely half an hour. For some long-forgotten reason, Rani's mother and siblings had been occupied elsewhere. Even now, Rani could remember watching the grubby Touched woman enter the shop. Rani knew that no Touched woman had any legitimate reason to be in her father's stall. Nevertheless, Rani was a young child at the time, and a respectful one, and she could hardly order an elder out into the street.

Of course, that was precisely what she should have done, as her father had told her in no uncertain terms. He'd realized the spoons and buckles were missing immediately, and he had berated Rani for not keeping a closer eye on his goods. Late that night, she had finally fallen asleep, exhausted after sobbing through supper and evening prayers and all her household chores. Her father had not even permitted her the dignity of paying back the stall from her small store of hoarded coins; even though the lost goods were only made out of pewter, they were worth more than all of Rani's meager accumulation. Rani could still remember the confused hope that had tightened her chest when the Touched woman re-entered the shop a fortnight later. The crafty old witch had taken care to scrub the pewter wares, doing her best to mar their smooth surfaces, and Rani's unschooled eye actually did not recognize the treasures. Even as Rani's pulse quickened, Bardo had stood beside her, and he lost no time establishing that the goods were those that had been stolen. There was something about the buckles—they came from a distant corner of the realm, and they had a special clasp on the back, a unique twist that no other merchant could boast.

Looking back, Rani could still remember the angry fire that had burned in Bardo's eyes. He had hidden his knowledge, though, that he was buying back his own wares. Bardo had bargained with the Touched woman, striking the deal as if his heart was not truly in the negotiations. He paid out precious silver, counting it into the thief's filthy palm without seeming to realize that he was paying at least three more coins than Rani knew the goods were worth.

That night, Rani wrestled with terrifying dreams as she slept beneath the rafters, tossing and turning on the sea of her sisters' snores. She imagined that she heard the shop door open and close at least twice, and many times she woke from a fitful doze, expecting to find a lawless band of Touched plundering the store.

Bardo was late coming to breakfast the next morning. Rani's mother clucked her tongue over her hard-working son, shaking her head when Rani's father suggested that Bardo had gone down to the docks to review the most recent shipments of goods. Only when the porridge was reduced to sodden lumps and the tea was cool enough for Rani's childish lips did Bardo return to the house.

Even as he swung open the door, she could see the savage glint of victory in his eyes. He smiled broadly as he set a sack on the kitchen table, reaching in like Wair, the god of gifts, distributing treasures to all the family. For his mother, he had the sweetest honey, and for his father, the flower-scented balm that eased the shopkeeper's persistent lumbago. Each of the girls received a delicate flower crafted of metal, intended to clasp her cloak, and each of the boys crowed over a sharp-bladed knife.

And Bardo brought Rani a special gift, in addition to her flower clasp. As she turned her grateful face toward him, he tousled her hair. It seemed an afterthought that brought him down to kneel beside her, digging deep in his pouch for the last of his treasures.

At first, Rani did not recognize the gift. Then, as Bardo settled it into her lap, she realized she held a drawing slate and a chalk stylus. "For you," Bardo had said simply. "So you can practice those drawings that take all your time."

Rani had flung her arms around Bardo's barrel chest. He understood! He knew the trembling excitement that beat in her fingertips, the compulsion that forced her to arrange and rearrange the goods in her father's stall.

"Bardo," her mother scolded, even as Rani grasped the generosity of the gift, "You shouldn't tempt the child! How is she to learn that her place is with the merchants? Such a toy is better suited to a guild-child!"

Rani felt tears prickle at the corners of her eyes. "Now, Mother," Bardo chided, settling a protective arm around Rani's shoulders, "I find my way into a little profit, and you do everything in your power to take away the fun of my gifts. You're working against the Thousand Gods, you are." He drove away his mother's scowl with a wicked grin. "In any case, who's to say a merchant child doesn't need to learn her figures? This slate is perfect for that. Come now,

Mother. You wouldn't want me to think my night's labors were for no good cause, would you?"

As he asked his question, Rani felt the tension in his muscles, communicated through the wiry fingers that still rested on her shoulder. Wondering what labors Bardo could have undertaken in the dark of night, Rani waited through a painfully long pause, watching as her mother and father stared at their son. Either might question his comings and goings, might demand to know the source of the wealth he spread throughout the warm little room. The answers might not be pretty, and all the little treasures might be rejected. After a century of panicked heartbeats, Jotham Trader extended his hand to his eldest son. The dangerous moment was past, and Rani had nothing to mark it but the confusing memory of the tempered steel she had glimpsed in her brother.

No one else questioned their good fortune, and Rani was soon excused to store away her most valuable possession. In the following days, she had made a great show of working out sums on the slate, using at least half of her precious chalk for calculations befitting a merchant. Only in the quiet corner of the room that she shared with her sisters did Rani exploit the slate for her own desires, sketching out the delicate tracery of stained glass windows, working out her own elaborate shorthand to indicate the stunning colors for her guildish drawings. Ultimately, her work with the slate had proven instrumental in convincing her mother to let Rani go to the glasswrights' guild.

Now, huddled in a dilapidated doorway in an abandoned City street, Rani forbade herself to dwell on the family she had lost, on the parents who would never scold her again. Instead, she forced herself to think about Bardo's gift, about her slate and chalk. She had put them in her satchel to take to the glasswrights' guild, but then she had removed them, worried that the nub of chalk would not be fine enough for her newfound companions, ashamed that she would question Bardo's gift. She had slipped the slate between the cornshuck-filled mattresses in her attic room. Now, its sooty remains must lie in the unraked ashes that drifted over the ruins of her home. She would never see Bardo's gift again.

"'N' 'ee never saw 'er again," Mair concluded, her voice grave with her ominous news. "One day, she was th' center o' 'is world, 'n' th' next she was gone, not even 'er bones lyin' i' an alley. All because th' goods she chose t' work 'er grift were rare i' th' eyes o' a merchant-man."

Rani shuddered, coming back to her grim present with the sheepish realization that she had heard nothing about Rabe's mother. Already knowing the unwelcome news she would confirm, Rani fished for more information, trying to hide the fact that her attention had wandered. "And did he ever find out what happened to her?"

"That's just it!" Mair hissed, and Rani was grateful the Touched leader felt constrained by her sleeping companions. "Th' last person t' see 'er alive said she was goin' t' meet wi' th' merchant she 'ad stolen from, goin' t' set things right. A bloody meetin' it was, i' th' eyes o' all th' Thousand Gods."

Rani's stomach turned a queasy flip as she realized that Mair's story and her own recollections might tell one tale. Excuses began to tumble from her lips. "But you can't be certain that he killed her! Anything could have happened—the merchant might have had her tossed out of the City, for theft. That might have been kinder than branding her a thief. You've said yourself these streets aren't safe."

"But there's one more thing t' th' story, Rai. Rabe's mother's belongings were returned t' 'er family, left outside their doss. 'Er shift 'n' 'er cloak, both stained wi' more blood than any child should see. 'N' th' 'ole was wrapped 'round wi' a belt, a belt wi' a pewter buckle, a buckle wi' an odd little twist, like th' ones that were taken. But th' belt, it 'ad been changed. Some one took a knife and cut into th' leather. They made th' design deep. Four snakes, all twisted 'round themselves. 'N' their eyes were painted i' blood."

Perversely, Rani could not picture the bloody snakes. Rather, she could only see Bardo, standing tall and straight in her memory, proud and protective of her family. She shuddered as she thought of the gifts that her brother had borne that morning long ago, the slate that she had boastfully enjoyed.

She felt sick, aching in the pit of her stomach.

There was a long silence before Rani could speak. "So what are you saying, Mair? Are you saying I should tell Rabe that Bardo is my brother?"

"Oh no, Rai, I'm not sayin' that at all!" For the first time, Rani heard a note of alarm in the Touched leader's voice. "I'm not certain I could control Rabe, if 'e thought 'e 'ad to fight ye t' preserve 'is mother's memory, 'n' 'is father's."

"His father, too?" Rani swallowed the question that leaped to her lips: "What did Bardo do to his father?" Just in time, she rephrased her question. "What happened to his father?"

"Th' man ne'er recovered from findin' 'is wife's belongings. From findin' 'er things, 'n' ne'er findin' 'er, that is. 'E still wanders around th' streets, sleepin' in whate'er doorway'll give 'im shelter. Rabe goes t' find 'im whene'er 'e can, t' bring 'im food 'n' put a blanket around 'is shoulders."

Rani thought she might be sick, right there in front of Mair. Certainly she knew that children grew up to care for their aged parents; she had fully expected to bear responsibility for her kerchiefed mother and father when they were too old to run their store. She had even envisioned little plays of revenge, determining when her parents could spend a copper on sweets, or when they could shirk their work as she ran *her* merchant stall with their assistance.

It had never occurred to her, though, that she would need to nurture her father gone soft in his brain. She had never imagined either of her parents alone and adrift in a city that offered little solace to the poor and broken members of each caste. Again, the nagging guilt that Bardo could have caused such injury made Rani shift beneath Mair's thin blanket.

"There must be all sorts of folk bearing any number of tattoos," she managed at last. An image of Prince Tuvashanoran's strong arm leaped to mind, the snakes twined across his frozen, death-hard muscles. She thought of Instructor Morada as well, and when she spoke, she was unconscious of the admission she was making, the confession that Bardo was branded. "Almost anyone could bear the sign of the Snake, not just my brother."

Mair stared at her, eyes penetrating even in the midnight gloom. "Th' only ones that bear *that* sign keep it t' themselves, Rai. We don't know much about 'em. We know they don't show their symbol in th' City streets. We Touched never find 'em in our passageways, 'n' th' other castes would never let 'em settle i' th' finer quarters of th' City, at least not openly. We Touched don't want t' start somethin' th' other castes are smart enough t' steer clear of, not when we already 'ave t' worry about th' soldiers runnin' us out o' th' City. That's part of what makes us so leery of th' Brotherhood."

"The Brotherhood," Rani repeated, and she remembered Larindolian sneering at Morada in the dilapidated shack, tangled in the City streets. The Brotherhood... The Brotherhood of Justice.

"Aye, they call themselves th' Brotherhood of Justice, but we know 'em by another name. We call 'em th' Brotherhood o' th' Snake."

Rani heard the title, and a gulf of despair opened beneath her heart. She might deny that Bardo had beaten her. She might deny that Bardo had anything to do with Rabe's tragic tale. There was no way, though, for Rani to ignore the tattoo she had seen on her brother's muscled arm. Bardo had proven "brother" to more than Rani.

"But who are they?" Rani pushed for more information. "What does the Brotherhood do?"

"We canna be certain, but we 'ear rumors. They say they want t' do away wi' th' castes; they say they want a life i' th' City where all men stand b'fore th' Thousand Gods like equal brothers."

"And you don't believe them?" Rani asked before she could even process the notion, before she could imagine what it would be like to live in the City without the comfort, the stability of knowing her station in life. Before Mair answered, Rani recalled Instructor Morada taunting Larindolian in the hut, asking the nobleman if he'd abandoned his belief in equality.

"We Touched dinna believe anyone wi' a caste sayin' he'd gi' it up. Ye dinna exactly see folks flocking' t' join us, now, do ye?"

Rani heard the question like an accusation. But who would want to be *Touched*, to be without a caste? Of course, Mair had been born Touched; she'd had no choice. And Rabe, too—Rabe, who had lost so much to the Brotherhood, to Bardo.

Rani realized she had no right to huddle with Mair beneath the Touched girl's blankets. Rani's family had stolen from Rabe all of his world; she could hardly complete the theft by taking the boy's place with the only family left him. Sighing, she began to push back the blanket.

"Where're ye goin'?" Mair asked sleepily, clenching her teeth against the sudden draft.

"I'm leaving, Mair. I didn't come to steal Rabe's place with you."

"Ye think ye could steal *anything* from me?" Mair managed a prideful chortle, even as she settled her head more firmly against her satchel pillow. "Ye're not that good, Rai. Not yet, anyway. Lay yer 'ead down, 'n' get some sleep. Rabe'll be after ye in the mornin', pokin' t' see if ye're ready t' part wi' those gloves. Ye'd best outfox 'im on a full night's sleep."

Rani shook her head, determined not to shame her family any farther than Bardo had already managed. "I can't—"

"Ye can't make me freeze t' death, Cabbage Brain. Lay down, or leave my blanket, but dinna be invitin' th' night air in!"

"Fine, Mair. But I promise you this. I'm going to find the Brotherhood, and when I do, I'll learn the truth of what happened to Rabe's mother. I'll get the Brotherhood's wergild for her, the price that Rabe deserves for his loss."

"Right, Rai. Ye'll get th' wergild, an' we'll all eat cake. Go t' sleep now, though, in case ye 'ave t' steal tomorrow's breakfast."

Rani sighed and settled the blanket about her shoulders, reluctant to admit how comforting she found the warmth and trust radiating from the Touched leader.

As it turned out, Rani did not have an opportunity to atone with Rabe, even by making the hollow gesture of handing over the indigo gloves.

She was sleeping soundly the following morning, having threaded her way through a grim and confusing forest of nightmares. She had finally thrust away the images of Morada's headless body, Bardo's raging fury when she discovered his tattoo, and her mother's misplaced pride when Rani had joined the glaziers' guild. All that remained, in the grey cocoon of the last hour before dawn, was a warm place beneath Mair's blanket and the slow, steady breathing of Rani's newfound friend.

Thus, she could hardly be blamed when she could not struggle up to wakefulness. The stomp of soldiers' boots was familiar by now, a recurring background to her waking thoughts. This time, she was scarcely aware of the military beat until her entire body throbbed with the message. Full realization only came when Mair whipped off the blanket, exposing Rani to the bitter morning cold.

"Wh-what?" the startled apprentice gasped, but Mair was already heading away, marching down the alley and poking a leather-bound toe into the exposed sides of a few still-sleeping children. Rani followed, jealously noting that Rabe was on his feet, moving parallel to Mair, shaking awake the troop with rough attention. One youngster rubbed a filthy hand across her eyes and looked as if she were about to cry, but a stern bark from Rabe knocked her into silence.

"Come along," Mair cajoled, holding out a crust of bread to the last awakening child, a ragamuffin who looked to be little more than four years old. "Today isna th' day t' tarry, little one."

"What's today?" Rani asked as she slunk up to the little domestic scene. Pride forbade her to admit that the crust of bread in the child's grimy hand looked appetizing. One thing about all this roaming the City streets—she felt as if she'd never eat her fill again.

"Turnin' Out Day." Rabe answered, his features pulled into a grimace at her ignorance.

Rani felt a sick turn of horror in her belly. She had seen Turning Out from the safety of her parents' shop. Soldiers drove the Touched hordes from their parasitic sites, making the four quarters of the City clean and safe again for Jair's favored castes. Even as Rani tried to swallow her panic, Mair turned her attention to the anxious faces that looked up at her. "All right, troops. 'R' ye ready? Pell, where'll we meet on th' outside?"

A young boy, peering through matted hair that hung to his shoulders, flashed his gap-toothed grin at the leader. "We'll meet at th' stagin' area fer th' merchants, outside o' th' Merchants' Gate."

"Aye," Mair nodded, reaching out an authoritative hand to tousle the child's filthy hair. "'N' when'll we gather there? Trace?"

A coltish girl flashed a nervous smile about the group, ducking her head shyly. "We'll gather at th' third hour after noon, Mair."

"Brice, Felt, where 're ye goin', as fast as ye can make yer way?" Mair picked out two of the smaller children, grimy twins who had made a formidable team during yesterday's scouring of the Noble's Quarter.

"We'll run t' th' Touched Core, 'n' let everyone know we're rousted but well." Brice answered immediately, his freckled face serious as if he contemplated a mental map of the City's tangled streets.

Mair nodded. "'N' tonight? When we're back inside th' walls?"

Felt answered, his filthy brow puckered in deep thought. "We'll be findin' ye 'n' reportin' back any word fro' th' Core. We'll look fer ye i' th' marketplace one hour after th' Pilgrims' Bell starts ringin', and then ever' hour after that."

"Right, then! Good luck, all. Keep yer eyes peeled 'n' yer ears clear." Mair held out her filthy hand, setting it in the middle of the half-circle of children. Within seconds, each member of the troop had added a fist to the collection. Rani hesitated only a second before she, too, floated her hand among her fellows. Excitement trembled through their fingers, arcing across her taut skin like the crackle of static electricity. "T' th' Touched!" Mair cried.

"T' th' Touched!" the children echoed, and one or two added, in piping voices, "T' Mair!"

Before the leader could acknowledge the salute, the pound of soldiers' feet became a thunderstorm, and a phalanx of armed guards rounded the corner. The men walked four deep, the soldiers in the first row sporting heavy, boiled-leather shields. All the men wore fearsome masks, gruesome features carved out of hardened leather and wood. Rani recognized Sorn, the god of obedience, and Tarn, the god of death. There was Cot, the god of the soldiers themselves, and a warlike depiction of Pelt, the god of Order.

As the soldiers pounded forward, panic pulsed through Rani's body. As soon as the armed company saw the Touched, they broke ranks, each man working with two or three of his fellows to encircle a terrified child. The Touched were driven like a herd of disorganized sheep through the streets. Any attempts to break away were brutally suppressed.

As Rani watched her colleagues scramble, the full weight of Mair's warning swooped down on her. The soldiers were actually driving the Touched children from the City, punishing them for daring to beg, daring to live outside the caste system. It hardly mattered if the children did not survive their sojourn beyond the City walls. There were always more Touched brats.

Every day of Rani's civilized life, she had heard of the horrors beyond the City walls. Life outside was hard in countless ways. King Shanoranvilli's protection was less certain in the countryside. The Pilgrims' Bell, summoning travelers into the safety of the City, away from ravening wolves, was only one symbol of the safety that Shanoranvilli offered his people. Rani knew that highwaymen traveled the roads, and there were tales of strange illnesses that descended on unprotected villages and destroyed every man, woman, and child in a single night. She had heard of one group that branded children for entertainment, carving off their ears and noses and etching evil runes on innocents' foreheads.

As a merchant, as an apprentice, if Rani had ever bothered to think about Turning Out, she would have concluded that it was the only way to deal with casteless hordes. After all, it wasn't permanent banishment, merely a warning, a show of the power that the king *could* exercise, if he so chose.

Now, her blood pounding like the warning klaxon of the Pilgrims' Bell, Rani convulsed at the thought of being cast outside the City walls. How could these soldiers throw her to the wolves outside the City—the beasts both animal and human that would certainly plot her death? How could grown men condemn children to torture and maiming?

Rani stumbled and came down hard on her knee, crying out as tears sprang to her eyes. For just an instant, Mair turned around, snarling at the guards in an attempt to break through to her fallen companion. A flame-edged spear convinced the leader of her foolishness, though, and Mair threw up her arms in fury. "Remember, Rai! On th' outside!"

Before Mair could offer further encouragement, her shepherding soldier landed a heavy blow across her face. Rani's cheeks flushed hot with shame. Here she was, afraid of pain on the outside of the City, and her only friend in all the world was being beaten *inside* the supposed safety of the City walls. Beaten, the apprentice realized, because of Rani's own fear and weakness.

"Lan," Rani prayed, "look upon me with your blessing. Keep me safe from harm outside the City walls." Rani continued to extemporize her prayer as she swallowed hard, bracing herself to make a break for the City gates. She hesitated too long, though, and found herself hopelessly outdistanced by her companions. She glanced about, frantic to find a means of escape, but before she could make her desperate dash, she was cut off by a well-armed soldier.

The man was a full head taller than Rani's own father, and his arms bulged from his leather jerkin like joints of meat hanging in a butcher shop. He wore his hair in a warrior's clout, but his beard was not so tamed; ancient grease competed with that morning's bread crumbs to tangle the russet strands. As the man opened his mouth to bellow at the cowering child, Rani reeled beneath a wave of foul-smelling breath, and she saw that the soldier lacked more teeth than he boasted. Rani, stomach churning, planted her heels and faced down the man.

"Ach," the guard bellowed, "What have we here?"

"Rai!" Mair called over the tumult, tossing out a lifeline into the maelstrom of Rani's panic. "Don't fight th' soldiers! We'll meet ye on th' outside! *Outside!*"

"Aye, gutter rat, go meet your pack on the outside." The soldier leered as he spat the last word, and Rani felt slippery cobblestones beneath her leather soles. Contradicting his own speech, the man cut her off from escape.

"What are you going to do with me?" Rani's voice quavered as she tried to remember how to breathe.

"Do with you?" The man threw back his head and laughed humorlessly, chilling Rani to the bone. "Quite the fierce tiger cub, aren't you?" The man reached out a broken-nailed hand, clearly intending to grasp the meat of Rani's arm. Catching her breath at the indignity, Rani gave up a sound like an animal caught in a trap. Too late, she realized that the only person in the alley who heard her cry was the soldier; the rest of the king's men had completed their sweep of the streets, driving the herd of surprisingly calm children to the City gates. Rani was alone with an opponent who bettered her in weight, experience, and sheer gall. "Let's see if this little cub remembers how to suck milk."

Closing his massive hand around Rani's throat, the man forced her against the wall. Even as he cut off her breath with cruel fingers, his free hand fumbled with the lacing of his trews. Rani's struggles only excited the man more, and his breath came in short, evil-smelling gasps. He leaned close to cover her mouth with his own, and she tossed her head with the desperation of a horse trying to throw off a bit. She was rewarded by a knee driven, sharp and hard, between her legs, and the soldier's heavy body pinned her firmly.

Rani began to cry, forgetting that she was no longer a merchant's daughter, that she was not even the lowest of apprentices in the glasswrights' guild. She was only a Touched child, separated from her troop in the City streets.

The soldier recognized helplessness when he saw it, and laughter rose from deep in his belly. "Aye, little tiger. Mewl for your mother to come and free you! I've news for you, tiger cub. Your mother is dead and skinned."

The soldier had finally succeeded in loosening the tie on his breeches, and he leered at Rani as his beefy fingers closed around her neck, forcing her to kneel on the cobblestones. "No, little tiger, there's no one to help you now." His breath panted between clenched teeth as he drove Rani's head back against the wall.

She twisted away, stiffening her fingers as if they truly were tiger claws. When she struck out at the man's gut, though, she was rewarded only with a surprised laugh. As the soldier towered over her, Rani raised her hands for one last defense.

The soldier's uniform was so filthy, Rani would not have known he wore Shanoranvilli's gold and crimson if she had not first seen him with his fellow guards. The fabric was stiff with dirt, and Rani's fingers scrabbled for a purchase as she tried to push away her leering attacker. His breath came hot and foul above her, and her desperate fingers tangled in the rigid laces on his breeches. To her horror, the rotten uniform fabric split open at the seams, and a torrent of curses rained down upon her.

"My uniform! There'll be no saving you now, girl!" The soldier's rage turned his face as crimson as his breeches should have been. "Your own mother couldn't help you now, tiger cub. Nor your father, nor all your sisters and brothers!"

Rani, though, knew better. She found herself staring at a nightmare pattern, an outline so familiar that she knew she had dreamed it all her life, and all the lifetimes she had lived before. Four snakes, eight eyes—she hardly had to count any longer. The tattoo writhed on the soldier's thigh, snaring the girl's attention more thoroughly than the man's now-meaningless nakedness.

Staring at the pattern, she raised suddenly fearless eyes to the fighting man. "And if my brother is Bardo Trader? What then, soldier? Who will save you then?"

CHAPTER 9

"I'm telling you, if I could take you to the Brotherhood tonight, I would! By Cot, you're a nuisance!" The soldier kept his voice low, but he pounded his fist on the mess hall table, nearly upsetting his tankard in his frustrated rage. Rani glanced about the room nervously, but none of the other soldiers even acknowledged Garadolo's outburst.

She suspected that they would pay the same attention if he suddenly pulled a knife and slit her throat, and that suspicion reined her voice to a hoarse whisper. "And I'm telling you, you'd best find a way to take me to Bardo. Don't you understand? There's a reward in it for you—more beer than even you could drink in a year." Gluttony gleamed in Garadolo's eyes, and Rani pressed her advantage. "Besides, if you don't take me to him, I'll find someone who will. And when Bardo hears some of the stories I can tell him about the dangers of living in the City streets...." Rani let her voice trail off, and Garadolo shifted uncomfortably on his wooden bench.

"No need to spread tales, girl. No need at all." He waved over a serving lad, indicating that Rani's bowl should be filled again. Garadolo might be a drunkard and a lout, but he was generous with his soldier's rations.

Rani tucked into the fare greedily, enjoying watching the man squirm. When she had revealed her family ties, he had lost all semblance of lust. It had taken only a minute for him to rewrite his actions, to whine that he had only been jesting. He was a compassionate man, he vowed. He was not about to leave Rani on her own, with only the lice-ridden Touched for companions. He swore he would not let Rani out of his sight until he had restored her to her brother.

Rani was no fool. She heard the thoughts beneath his solemn words: there was no telling what trouble a Touched brat might bring on a soldier who had forsworn his loyalty oaths to his king and his birth-vow of conduct as a member of the soldiers' caste. There was no end to the danger of a snake tattoo.

Rani had been forced to twist her own tale around the truth. She could describe her brother readily enough, leaving no doubt in Garadolo's mind that she did, in fact, know Bardo. She clearly recognized the intertwined snakes, and she took every discreet opportunity to remind him of the tattoo's ominous connection with the Brotherhood. Nevertheless, she had been forced to admit that she did not presently know where Bardo was hiding. While she hinted at some secret family mode of communication to track him down, Garadolo had seen that she had no way to access her notorious brother directly. At least not promptly.

Rani was repulsed that she needed Garadolo's assistance. Independent by nature, she was loathe to trust a man who pawed young girls. Still, there was no one else that she could turn to. While it seemed that half the City bore the cryptic sign of the snakes, she knew the whereabouts of no other *living* person with the Brotherhood's tattoo. As disgusted as she was by the soldier, and as frightened as she would never admit to being, she knew that he was her most likely tool for finding Bardo. She forbade herself to imagine what she would do if he proved as prone to accident and death as all the others she had found who bore the Brotherhood's insignia.

Now, using a crusty heel of bread to mop up the last of her stew, Rani watched Garadolo drain his hefty tankard. The froth still infected his moustache as he pushed back from the table. "I'm heading back to the barracks. I don't know where you're going, but you'd best not let the guard catch you in the streets after curfew. Today was Turning Out day, you know."

The man thought he was so clever, chortling at his own sarcastic advice. Rani bristled, and resisted the urge to rub at her left bicep, where Garadolo's fingers had left ugly, purpling bruises. If only she had listened to Mair, had run for the City Gates with the other Touched children.... If only she hadn't been afraid. "So I heard," she muttered. "We'd best be on our way."

As Rani intended, Garadolo was completely flustered by her matter-of-fact pronouncement. She swung down from her bench as he spluttered, fixing him with a steady eye. "I should be near you when you contact the Brotherhood. If I'm forced to find Bardo myself, things will not go well for you. If he hears I was delayed returning to him, he will not be pleased."

Garadolo started to swear, dragging the words through the snarls in his filthy beard. His breath came in rapid, fetid puffs. "No need for you to say that, girl. No need at all."

"Then you *do* know how to get to Bardo."

"I know how to start the process. And believe me, there's nothing I can do tonight. Come along now, back to the barracks for a rest. You must be tired running with those Touched brats."

Rani longed to tell this boorish oaf that she would not have been tired if she had not needed to fight *him* that day. In fact, she longed to be quit of him altogether, but her choices were severely limited. On the one hand, she could wander the streets alone and afraid, trying to track down Mair's troop, or at least the "Core" that the children had spoken about. On the other hand, she could stay with Garadolo, searching out Bardo.

The only problem with choosing Bardo was that she had to face Garadolo. Well, she sighed, there were nasty things she'd managed to accomplish every day of her life—the soldier could hardly be any worse than emptying chamber pots or fishing out pickles from foam-scummed brine.

Rani almost took back that resolution, when she caught another whiff of the fighting man's stale breath. Forcing herself to breathe through her mouth, she responded to the hope behind his words. "I'm not tired, and the Touched are not filthy. I'll come with you, though, so that I can reach Bardo more quickly."

"Aye, you can speak with Bardo Trader in the morning."

Garadolo led the way through the streets. A few shops huddled in this warriors' quarter, but they were closed up for the night. Signs swung in the night air, and Rani could just pick out their blazons in the moonlight—one merchant sold armor, another appeared to sharpen swords and other deadly blades.

This was a strange quarter of the City, a tangle of streets that Rani had never fully explored. Her family had made a living selling finer stuff to more thoughtful patrons. She tried to recapture her caste-bound sense of superiority as Garadolo led her deeper into the maze, past various check points where the foul man saluted the guards, surrendering the night's password like the most valuable of coins.

Each time Garadolo drew himself to attention, he set a disgusting claw on Rani's shoulder, pulling her closer to his stinking leather jerkin. She tried to squirm from his touch, from the uncomfortable nearness of his ripped trews, but she quickly yielded before the guards' suspicion.

At the next check point, Garadolo muttered the password, but the guard peered down at them, swinging his lantern closer to Rani's face. "Now who've you got there?" queried the soldier, casting a knowing look at the sorry military specimen before him.

"Ranimara." Garadolo improvised a soldier's name. "A recruit for the elite corps of His Majesty's Guard." The man at the gate laughed knowingly and waved them through.

The charade was repeated twice more before they arrived at the barracks, and Rani had no illusion that the sentries served to protect her. They were certain they had seen a young soldier girl, intent on rising through the ranks by any means necessary. The events were common enough that they saw no need to question a child's pinched face in the torchlight, or a soldier, groping at his swelling trews.

By the time Rani and Garadolo arrived at his quarters, she was nearly asleep on her feet, trembling from cold and exhaustion, and other, more frightening emotions. When the soldier pushed her through the doorway, she stumbled into the center of a tiny room. The remnants of a cold fire reeked in one corner, clearly extinguished by the contents of an upturned chamberpot. A mattress sagged against the far wall, stained and lumpy, and Rani did not look too closely for the vermin she was certain to find. A few other accoutrements of military life were scattered about the room—a well-worn scabbard in one corner, a dull iron knife by the threshold.

Garadolo closed the door behind them, turning a massive key in a lock that looked so shaky Rani had no fear that she could break free if need be. The soldier ambled to a shuttered lamp, fiddling with a wick until a sickly light flickered through soot-stained glass. When the mottled flame leaked into the room, Garadolo turned to his captive, stopping to scratch himself thoroughly, as if his bedbugs had already begun their nightly feast.

Rani made her way to the far corner of the room, the corner without the sodden ashes. She thought about taking out her Zarithian knife, letting it flash an eloquent warning in the lamplight, but she knew she would not be a match for the man's strength if he became truly intent on stealing her prize possession.

Instead, she settled for bowing her head in prayer, speaking her words aloud. "May Jair and all the Thousand Gods keep us safe in the darkness of night. May Set, the god of Travelers, guide our feet upon the proper path tomorrow. May Fell, the god of Families, watch over me, and see me reunited with Bardo in the morning." And may Lan protect me, she added silently.

Garadolo looked as if he had not said his own night-time prayers since a nurse stood over him, ready to beat the words from his reluctant soul. Nevertheless, he refrained from any untoward discussion of their bedding arrangement, and Rani's final reminder of her brother-protector wiped the leer from his face.

"We'll get a message to your brother in the morning, then, Ranimara." Calling her by her newest name without apparent irony, Garadolo gave a final hitch at his torn breeches before strolling over to his bedroll. "It's warmer here, by the lamp," he gestured. When Rani fixed him with a glare more icy than the night-time air, he shrugged. "Can't say I didn't try. Let yourself be cold, Ranimara." He chortled at her snort of disgust.

Any delusion that Garadolo might have worried about her physical comfort was dispensed within three short minutes, as the soldier fell into snoring, alcoholic sleep. Rani covered her ears with the indigo gloves she had secured from Rabe. When that proved fruitless, she tried to force her breathing to match the man's, but she soon grew dizzy with the depth of his snores. Finally, she resigned herself to a sleepless night, leaning against the plastered wall and pulling her knees close to her chest. She passed the time by offering up prayers to Lan. Clearly, the kitchen god had smiled upon her—he had heard her pleas to stay within the City walls. Against all odds, he had guided her to Garadolo, to the Brotherhood, and to Bardo.

Rani must have slept at last, because she was alone in the sordid room when she awoke. A finger of greyish light pointed across the floor, prying apart the wall through a jagged crack beside the shuttered window. Outside, she could hear the troops stirring, accompanied by a great deal of clanking metal and creaking leather. The symphony was accented by frequent curses, and Rani could picture the army of men, jostling each other in the chilly dawn with the camaraderie she had often observed among her brothers.

Her brothers! Where was Garadolo? Was he bringing Bardo to her even now?

Rani stood up and stretched a crick from her neck. Her clothes were grimy, telling a tale of too many nights spent in the streets. She ran filthy fingers through her hair, reminding herself that she would soon have a comb and a mirror; she would soon be returned to the comfort of family.

The thought brought momentary tears to her eyes—she had strictly forbidden herself to think about the bitter news Mair had brought about her family's death. The Touched leader might have incorrect information, after all. She might have been spreading vicious rumors, created by Bardo's enemies, or by marketplace merchants who were jealous of her family's success in the Merchants' Quarter. Rani would know the whole truth shortly. However reluctant Garadolo might have been, he would bring Bardo to her. He would reunite her with her favorite brother, and then this nightmare would end.

As the daylight seeped into the room, blushing with a semblance of rosy life, Rani looked about, realizing she would be deeply embarrassed if Bardo saw her in such squalor. After all, the last time she had seen her brother, they had stood inside the glasswrights' prestigious Guildhall. Now, she was reduced to utter poverty, to the depravity of a filthy soldier's kept girl. Her surroundings were foul; her clothing was ragged. She was a sorry excuse for a well-raised merchant child.

Rani berated herself for accomplishing so little since Tuvashanoran's murder. She had run from situation to situation, letting the guild be destroyed about her very shoulders, letting one lead after another disappear in the City's brutal, bloody streets.

Remembering how Bardo always preferred the counters of the family shop to be orderly and neat, Rani looked about Garadolo's quarters. She might be the disgraced daughter of merchants, she might be the castout apprentice of glasswrights, but she was still Rani Trader. She knew how to put a home in order.

On the floor beside the door, a wooden bucket leaned on its side, mute witness to Garadolo's disgusting hygiene. Rani fetched the pail, surprised but pleased to discover that its bottom was solid. There had to be water somewhere here in the Soldiers' Quarter; it was just a matter of finding one of the City's many wells.

Rani made her way through the narrow streets, walking a spiral path from Garadolo's door. She was careful to count the turnings so that she did not become lost. As it turned out, she did not have far to go—her sensitive ears soon picked up the music of water falling from a fountain. Sure enough, Rani rounded a building and found herself in the middle of a cobbled square.

Water flowed freely from a tall font, a robust statue fashioned like a soldier. The fighting man wore the king's uniform, and he leaned his sword against his shield. That shield bore the head of a lion, and the lion's mouth opened to send an arc of water into a spreading pool. Rani grinned at her success, surprisingly pleased to discover she was not alone at the fountain.

A line of women—no more than girls, really—stretched around the jet of water, each bearing a bucket or a water flask. The girls chattered among themselves, taking their time as the line moved forward slowly. Rani took her place at the end of the queue, raising the empty bucket to her shoulder in imitation of the two girls in front of her.

One of those girls turned to face her, brushing stray brown locks out of her eyes as she inspected Rani from head to foot. "What's yer name?"

Rani almost choked on her answer. It was a simple question, really, and one that she should have been prepared to give. Nevertheless, she did not know if she should say her birth name—betraying her caste as merchant—or if she should call herself Ranimara, a soldier girl. From the accent behind the girl's question, Rani's companion was one of the Touched—a single syllable might suffice.

Rani covered her confusion by coughing, dragging out the subterfuge until the other girl pounded her between the shoulder blades, almost making Rani drop her wooden bucket. "Easy there," the girl crooned. "Take it easy." When Rani finally let herself take a deep breath, she thought the other girl might have forgotten her question. That wish proved too optimistic. "All I asked was yer name. Ye needn't get so frightened." The girl leaned closer, casting a shrugging glace toward their companions. "Ye're new 'ere is all. We all know what it's like. We know 'ow cold th' streets can be at night. There's no shame i' it, keepin' 'ouse fer a soldier."

Rani started to protest—she was not so naive that she mistook the meaning behind the girl's words. She started a rambling argument to redeem her honor, but then remembered that she was playing a role. If this girl was going to believe her, she could hardly protest in her merchant's well-bred accent. Rani let herself slip into Mair's patois. "I ne'er been 'ere before."

"Ye'll find it's not so bad. The soldiers always 'ave bread 'n' wine, 'n' they're more 'n 'appy t' share, if they think it'll keep ye i' their bed."

A hot blush painted Rani's cheeks, even as her belly twisted at the thought of yielding to Garadolo's attentions. She was more glad than ever that she was Bardo's sister. By now, the girls were up to the fountain, and Rani filled her bucket behind her companion. As they stepped away from the water, the other girl flashed a smile. She was missing a tooth on the side of her mouth. "Welcome t' th' Soldiers' Quarter. I'm Shar."

"Rai," Rani responded.

Before she could scrape up more conversation, Shar let out a surprised yelp. "Dalarati!"

Rani looked up to see a young soldier standing on the edge of the square. His hair was jet black, swept back from his forehead, with lines of a comb still furrowing the strands. His eyes were laughing, and Rani's breath caught in her throat. He was one of the most handsome men she had ever seen, almost as handsome as Bardo.

"Dalarati, what are you doing here?" Shar grinned, and she dug her toe between two cobbles, affecting a delicate shyness. Rani noticed that she turned her face to the side, hiding the gap of her missing tooth.

The soldier smoothed his tunic's pleats, and his strong fingers did curious things to Rani's pulse. "We're moving to the night shift, starting with sunset. We've been given the day to prepare."

"Th' 'ole day?" Shar crowed, shifting her pail to one hand and reaching up to play with the careful lacings at Dalarati's throat. Rani thought that she should look away.

"The whole day," the soldier confirmed, "after you've broken your fast." He produced two sweet rolls from the sack at his waist, proffering both to Shar.

"Oh, Dalarati! You remembered me!" Shar pulled him close, coming dangerously close to sloshing water on his leggings.

"How could I forget," he answered wryly, when he had finished kissing her thoroughly. He traced a finger along her throat. "Now, are we going to stand in the square all morning, or are we going back to my quarters? I've got a lot to do before duty tonight."

"A lot to do?" Shar pouted, starting to turn away from her handsome benefactor.

"Aye," he laughed at her posturing and reached out a loose fist to chuck her lightly on the chin. "I've exercises to complete." His supple fingers closed around Shar's waist. "And weapons to polish." Shar giggled, and let the man lead her toward the edge of the square.

Rani was still staring in a bemused combination of shock and jealousy when the Touched girl wriggled out of the soldier's embrace. She darted across the square, coming to a breathless stop in front of Rani. Before the apprentice could speak, the Touched girl thrust one of the sweet buns into Rani's hand. "But—" Rani began to protest.

"Take it! I'll not 'ave time t' eat both." Shar giggled and glanced at Dalarati, who was feigning impatience. "Welcome t' th' Soldiers' Quarter, Rai."

Rani barely managed to wait until the pair was out of sight before she tore into the roll. She was hungrier than she had imagined, and the sweet almond filling left her licking her fingers unabashedly. On her way back to Garadolo's lair, she imagined the meals she could feast on in the Soldiers' Quarter. Feast, that was, if she were willing to pay the price.

Of course, such thoughts were sheer foolishness. She would be leaving the Quarter before supper time. Bardo would be there by noon, taking her away from the dingy room and the frightening filth, carrying her off to whatever life he had built for himself.

Rani occupied herself with such thoughts as she set about straightening the small room. As the morning ripened, she found herself singing "The Merchant's Blue-Eyed Daughter." The song had always been Bardo's favorite, and before the sun set that night, Rani would make him sing it aloud, rolling his rich bass voice over the notes.

As she sang, she set about loosing the locks on the shutters, but when the morning light streamed into the room, she almost wished that she had not bothered. A layer of grime covered wood, plaster, everything in the chamber, as if Garadolo and an army of predecessors had never washed their greasy hands, but had fondled every surface. Repeatedly.

Sighing, Rani set her pail of water by the door. The shreds of some garment were tangled on the floorboards—it appeared that Rani was not the first person to rip Garadolo's rotten clothes. She set her lips in a grim smile as she salvaged the filthy cloth, so full of holes that it could serve no legitimate purpose.

No legitimate purpose, that was, except as a rag. Rani shivered when she plunged her bare hands into the bucket of cold water, and she needed to wring out the cloth three times before the water ran clear. Still, she started in the corner, cleaning out a circle of human living space.

It took her the rest of the morning and a good part of the afternoon, but the room was reformed when she was finished. She had listened to the cathedral bells toll noon, unable to resist waiting on the doorstep for Garadolo to show up with Bardo, but she had been sorely disappointed. Now, as she added a sheen to the rippled glass reflecting sunset in the window frame, she fought a wave of despair.

Despite the chill in the air, she left the door open and sat on the front porch. She had made several more trips to the well for fresh water, and her arms ached. Her belly roared with hunger as well, and she fought back the suspiciously salty taste of tears as she leaned against the doorframe.

The sun had set before Garadolo returned to his room. He strode jauntily down the street, beefy legs rolling in new trews that he had apparently cajoled from the quartermaster. The spring in his step faded visibly when he saw Rani sitting on the doorstep. "Still here, are you?" he grunted.

"Of course. Where's Bardo?"

"Where's Bardo?" he mimicked, pushing her into the room. "Don't be saying his name aloud in the streets! What do you want, for the entire quarter to know the mark I bear?" There was honest fear behind his words, a cowardice that fed Rani's disappointment. "What in the name of Cot! What have you done with my room?"

"I cleaned it." Rani resisted the urge to add an epithet to her simple declaration. "You told me you'd bring Bardo to me. You lied!"

"I didn't lie, little tiger." Garadolo looked around as if in shock, seeming scarcely to recognize the neat bed roll against one wall, the shimmer of glass behind dust-free shutters. Stroking his greasy beard, he turned to her with a leer he doubtless intended to be soothing. "I tried to find him, honest I did. It's not easy for one as low in the Brotherhood ranks as I. I tried to see my commander, to send a message up the ladder. Your Bardo has himself better protected than a spider in his web."

"Fine," Rani seethed, nearly yelping as Garadolo left streaky fingermarks on the clean window. "I'll find him myself, then. I thought one of Shanoranvilli's own soldiers could get things done, but I clearly was mistaken."

"Those words are creeping close to treason, little one. Don't be dragging the king's name through your own muck."

"My—" Rani started, anger crystallizing to push her fingers toward her Zarithian knife.

"And don't think you can pull a knife on one of the King's Guard." As if to underscore his meaning, Garadolo set one hammy fist on his own much longer dagger.

"If you won't—"

"There's no 'won't' about it. I *could* not, not today. The whole City was crazed, with heralds standing on every street corner, crying out the search for that cursed Ranita Gl— that cursed guild-girl. Tuvashanoran's pyre was lit at noon, you know." Rani had not known, although she should have remembered. Her thoughts flashed to the ladanum she had worked among the winding sheets, to the shroud she had prepared. Garadolo harrumphed as Rani slunk away from him; she could not tell if he knew her true role in the prince's death. When she merely stared at him sullenly for a long minute, he swore and repeated, "I tell you, I *could* not! I've sent a message, and tomorrow I should receive a response. Of course, I'll need to pay the messenger...." He trailed off meaningfully, twisting his fingers in the air.

Rani clutched at her pouch, her meager hoard of treasures. "What do you want from me?"

"I'm just a poor soldier, girl. I can't be paying bribes for you. What have you got in the sack?"

Reluctantly, Rani had to admit his claim was reasonable— he *was* only a soldier. Sighing, she dug into the pouch, pulling out first one indigo glove, then the other.

"These'll fetch a fair price. They were worked for a noble family."

Garadolo inspected the gloves in the glimmer of the lamp Rani had trimmed so carefully, and he seemed pleased with what he saw. "They should do the trick. What do you say we eat now?"

"How can you eat, when you need to steal from me for a messenger?"

"Your messenger is out of the ordinary, girl. Eating is what soldiers do, every day and every night. Come along."

Rani was hungry enough that she dropped the fight. Reflexively, she set herself to remembering the twists and turns as he dragged her along, and she managed to snare at least one of the passwords as they passed a bristling checkpoint. Soon, she found herself in the soldiers' mess hall, eating stew out of a hollowed loaf of bread. She washed down the chunks of meat with ale, doing her best to ignore the fact that she had to share her tankard with her keeper.

Garadolo was intent on letting everyone know that Rani was his companion for the evening. He settled a heavy paw on her shoulder as often as he thought he could get away with it, and more than once, he decried the appetite of his little tiger. The grizzled men leered at their companion, and Rani wished that she could sit on the far side of the room, where the men were quieter, more sedate, even though many of them also sported female companions.

When one of Garadolo's peers indulged in a particularly graphic speculation, Rani was spared the need to respond by the wholly unexpected arrival of Dalarati and Shar. The handsome young soldier looked about the room and seemed about to join his quiet, orderly brethren at the far side of the chamber. His eyes caught on Rani, though, and he darted a quick look of ill-disguised disgust toward Garadolo.

Dalarati grimaced and leaned down to whisper something in Shar's ear. The Touched girl started to protest, but Dalarati set the palm of one hand against her cheek in a soothing, fleeting caress. Nevertheless, Shar dragged her feet as Dalarati crossed the room to Rani's side. Obviously, Dalarati and Shar were accustomed to sitting on the far side of the room.

"Evening, Rai," was all the soldier said as he straddled a bench. Shar took her place beside him, apparently forgetting her momentary displeasure as her young man fed her snippets of meat from his trencher. Dalarati held his tankard to her lips for her to sip delicately at his ale. Rani felt a rat of jealousy burrow into the hollow space behind her heart, even as she was grateful for their companionship.

The meal began to break up as the soldiers with consorts headed toward the door. Rani delayed as long as she could, engaging a thoroughly uninterested Shar in a discussion of raids in the Nobles' Quarter. Shar humored her new friend, even pretending not to notice the occasional lapses in Rani's adopted accent. Nevertheless, the other girl leaned against

Dalarati, steadying herself by looping suggestive fingers through his belt.

Dalarati could not ignore such attention for long, and he turned an open grin on Shar. "Ready to return home, are we? Fine enough—we've an hour before the night watch calls." Amid the chorus of good-natured suggestions of pastimes, Dalarati managed to gain his feet, conducting his clinging companion to the door. The sharp night air, though, apparently reminded him that Shar's shawl remained at the soldiers' table.

Rani handed the garment to the handsome guard, contriving to let her fingers brush against his. "Thank you for joining us," she managed, swallowing hard against the pounding of her heart.

"The pleasure was mine, my lady." He delivered a mock bow, using the motion to dig into the small pouch at his waist. "Buy an almond bun in the morning and think of Shar and me." Rani caught the coin and stifled a gasp, and then the dashing soldier was gone.

Garadolo decided to leave shortly thereafter, and when they entered his quarters, Rani immediately took her belongings to her corner. Garadolo began to laugh harshly, and Rani had to raise her voice to be heard. "You'll be seeing Bardo tomorrow, won't you?"

The soldier swallowed a curse, but his ardor was clearly quenched. "Aye, little tiger. I'll see you delivered tomorrow. You have my word on that."

Garadolo's word was worth as little as his soldierly oath to defend the poor and the weak.

Rani waited eagerly through the next day, too excited to think about eating, about cleaning, about any details of daily life. She reminded herself that her indigo gloves had been well-spent if they brought her brother to her. She tried to order her thoughts, to think of the questions she would ask Bardo. She wanted to know why she had seen the snakes in so many places, how the mark was connected to Tuvashanoran's murder. She wanted to ask Bardo why he had not sought her out, how he could have let their merchant shop be burned to the ground, let their family meet with unspeakable horrors in the king's dungeons. She wanted to know how he could be mixed up with the Brotherhood when she heard such terrible tales about them, when she had witnessed the destruction that they had created in the cathedral yard.

Bardo had always had answers before, and Rani longed to hear his deep voice, serious and slow as he explained it all to her. She longed for the comfort of his wisdom, even as she consciously set aside memories of his rage. After all, it was her *brother* she sought, not some crazed, tattooed rebel, not some murderous vigilante who had enforced justice among Touched thieves. There must have been some mistake. Bardo would set all right. He would explain away the horror. He had to.

Despite Rani's hopes and prayers, Garadolo showed up alone at the end of the next day. He told Rani that he had sold her gloves and used the money to bribe the first of the Brotherhood's petty officials. That bribe had secured him an interview with another protector tomorrow, but he must be prepared with another bribe. The soldier paused eloquently, clearly waiting for Rani to pay her way.

She hesitated for a long minute before extracting Dalarati's coin from her pouch. The silver meant more than breakfast—it had been a gift from the handsome soldier. Garadolo tested the metal between his rotten teeth and nodded his approval before squirreling it away in the filthy folds of his clothing.

And so each day took on a pattern. Every morning, Rani waited restlessly, straightening the tiny room, cleaning surfaces that were long-since shining. Every afternoon, she sat on the doorstep, certain that Bardo was going to round the corner at any instant. Every evening, Garadolo returned home with a new excuse, a new explanation of how he had progressed in his attempts to reach the Brotherhood. Every night, they returned to the mess hall, and Rani ate her fill of the soldiers' food, despairing that she would ever see her brother.

She became creative in finding bribe money for Garadolo. Often, she cleaned other soldiers' quarters, earning a few coppers from the fighting men's kept women. Once, she slipped past the checkpoints, back into the City streets. Too proud to consider begging, she managed to pick a stranger's pockets, earning a handful of silver for her trouble. A handful of silver, balanced by the weight of her soul—she considered the trade a fair one when she thought of Bardo. Another day, she ducked into a soldier's unattended doss, digging in his possessions for anything of value. Garadolo did not ask her where the silver belt buckle came from when she handed it over, and she dared not volunteer the information.

As the days dragged on and Rani became more skilled at theft, the thought crossed her mind that Garadolo might be lying. She went so far as to threaten to leave one night, gathering up her meager belongings and opening the door to their tiny room. The soldier bellowed in rage and dragged her back inside, and when he forced her down beside the lantern, she could see his skin was pasty, and sweat poured off him in the cool night. "You can't leave! Not after you've had me approach the Brotherhood."

"You're not holding up your end of the bargain," Rani shot back at him. "I've given you more trinkets in a week than I've traded in the rest of my life, and you've returned the favor with nothing!"

"I'm working up the ladder," he muttered for the thousandth time. "I don't know how to prove to you...."

"What sort of Brotherhood closes its doors against one of its own?"

"You don't know this Brotherhood, girl. You only think you know your Bardo. He's high and mighty in his tower, protected by the longest field, lying behind the deepest moat, surrounded by the highest wall, with more arrow loops than stars in the sky."

"Have you told them who I am? Does he know his sister is the one who seeks him?"

"I've told everyone who'll listen to me. Don't you think I want you gone?"

While Rani did not trust Garadolo as far as she could kick him, she did believe he would rather have a cooperative bed-warmer than her own constant argument. Nevertheless, as she fell asleep that night, listening to the Pilgrims' Bell measuring its doleful welcome across the City, she vowed she would follow the soldier in the morning. She would trail him to his contact with the Brotherhood, and she would see Bardo before the bell tolled the next night.

CHAPTER 10

"Halt and speak the password!"

The voice hissed from the shadows, and Rani jumped, barely remembering to pull Farna's cloak close about her. She almost missed Garadolo's response as she craned her neck, tilting her head to catch the soldier's words above her pounding heart.

"Tarn keep me from the Heavenly Gates," muttered the soldier, and his invocation of the god of death sent shivers down Rani's spine. The words proved acceptable to the watchman, and Rani squinted as Garadolo slip past the checkpoint.

The night was cold here near the City walls, and Rani needed to snatch breaths through her cloak, trying not to betray her presence with a fog on the midnight air. She had spent an uneventful day tracking Garadolo, but he had cut short their dinner with the announcement that he was going to meet with Bardo that night, come Cot or the midnight watch. Rani had promised to wait in the soldiers' quarters as she handed over part of her most recently stolen bribe—a hoard of silver coins that she had ... borrowed ... only the day before. Hopefully, she would be long gone before the captain of the guard realized that someone had found his treasure trove.

The theft made Rani nervous—she had been hired to clean the captain's quarters, and she would be the most

likely suspect when the soldier discovered his loss. She had
become enough of a fixture in the Soldiers Quarter that any
of the girls who consorted with the guards would know
to find her in Garadolo's lair. Her sense of exposure was
only heightened by her knowledge that she had not given
Garadolo all of the coins; she had kept the lion's share of
the incriminating evidence herself, the better to plead her
case with Bardo's protectors when she succeeded in meeting
them.

Whatever the cost, she reminded herself, she must see
Bardo. She must learn the truth behind the snake tattoo.
She must solve the mystery of Tuvashanoran's murderer,
who still stalked the City by day and by night. She'd been
running long enough, cold and scared and hungry and
homeless. Rani longed to be through with her charade, to
return to the simple days before she had ever heard of the
Brotherhood.

Even now, she looked back to her life as an apprentice with
blinding fondness. She'd been so lucky then, so privileged
that her most difficult task had been scrubbing a white-
washed table. Her life had been good before Tuvashanoran's
murder, and her heart pounded at the thought that she might
now find her way back to that simpler time.

And so, Rani found herself crouching in a doorway in
the City's darkest sector. Garadolo had unwittingly led
her through the City's meanest streets, tracing a path
through slumbering quarters that scarcely cared whether
a soldier passed, or an apprentice, or a Touched child. By
contrast, there had been murderous caution in the voice that
demanded a password, and Rani trembled as she debated
how she could best maneuver her way past the sentry, to the
Brotherhood and Bardo.

"Step smart, little rat, or I'll carve you to the bone here
and now." The voice hissed out of the darkness, and Rani
could not entirely smother her yelp of surprise. Focusing
on the sentry ahead in the mist, she had not heard anyone
glide up behind her. A sharp blade pricked the nape of her

neck, and she dared not move as she struggled to formulate a response.

"Tarn keep me from the Heavenly Gates," she squeaked, even as she thought a more comforting prayer in her own mind.

"So, the rat has sharp ears. The better for paring, eh?" The knife-point edged her forward, and she took three reluctant steps, trying to ignore the scarcely-mastered trembling that made her knees ache. Before she could reach the checkpoint where Garadolo had passed the guard, a heavy black cloth fell over her eyes, and a blindfold was pulled tight none too gently. One stray fold cut across the bridge of her nose, and the dusty bond urged her to sneeze. The cold metal kissing her neck convinced her to stifle the impulse. "Go ahead, you spying rat. Walk forward."

The hissed command left her no choice, and Rani moved as steadily as she could. The darkness was disorienting, and she tried to test each step before planting her foot. Her captor did not give her time for exploration, though, and Rani feared that she would find her way into a deep earthen grave at any second. The knife brooked no dissent, and she commanded herself to focus on her surroundings, to learn what she could above her lungs' panting and the itch about her eyes.

The cobblestones under her boots gave way to smooth flagstones, lessening the likelihood that she would turn an ankle in her blind exploration. Even as she sighed with relief, she realized that she had passed through an entryway. The door was low and narrow, and the lintel brushed against her hood, so close that Rani wondered if her captor would have warned her before she dashed her brains out. She scarcely had time for further indignant speculation as rough hands forced her to turn sideways, to inch forward one half-step at a time as she tried to preserve her balance in the narrowest of corridors. Stone walls snagged at her cloak, and the loose ends of her blindfold caught once, leaving her a tiny slit to view her surroundings.

She could make out the torchlit walls to either side—

crumbling brick that leaned close above her. The passage
wound about itself, writhing like a serpent. The soft bricks
were broken by many jagged cracks, and crusty stains
remained where water had seeped into the structure. No
building could contain a passage so long—Rani realized
she must be moving *inside* the City walls. Unbidden, Rani
remembered Mair talking about the Brotherhood, recalled
the Touched girl's statement that the Brotherhood kept out
of the City streets, clear of the City's four quarters.

Rani continued through a passage impossibly narrower
than the tight corridors she had worked through so far,
emerging at last into a broad chamber. Without warning,
her captor hit the back of her legs with some stout object,
and she plummeted to her knees. The brick floor was hard,
and her teeth rattled in her skull, but she scarcely had time
to protest as the man ripped away her blindfold.

Torches flickered in the low room, and Rani could just
make out the warren of hallways that scurried away to
her right and left. Mosaics tiled the walls, eerie patterns
that made her cringe. Only after she saw the same shapes
reproduced on the floor did she realize what the lines
represented: four serpents twined about themselves. Eight
eyes glared at her from the cardinal points of the room,
bloody patches on the writhing wall mirrored by crimson
pools on the floor.

Rani squirmed beneath the malevolent gaze, jumping as
Garadolo spluttered from across the room, "I didn't know
that she followed me here! How could I know she would
track me? I told her to stay in the barracks—I ordered her
to stay away!"

"You fool!"

Rani squinted, trying to make out the owner of the
slurred voice that hissed from the shadows on the opposite
side of the snake chamber. Garadolo appeared to know the
speaker; the soldier fell to his knees, bobbing his head in
submission. "Begging your pardon, lord. I didn't mean to
expose the Brotherhood to harm. I didn't mean to endanger
you, lord."

"Idiot!" There was something familiar about the hissed rage, and a fading memory leaped in Rani's mind. She craned her neck to get a better look at the speaker, but was curbed by the prick of metal at the base of her skull. She settled for listening to the nightmare anger. "You cursed soldier—you don't even know what the Brotherhood stands for! I'm not your lord, you miserable excuse for a doorstop. I'm your brother."

"Aye," Garadolo bobbed, even as he visibly fought the urge to tug at a forelock. "I know that, I—, brother. You're my brother, but wiser and shrewder than I—"

"Quit your babbling!" The interrogator moved into the light, and Rani saw why his voice was familiar. Larindolian, the nobleman who had met Instructor Morada in the decaying hut, nudged her with his toe. "And you! How did you find your way here?"

"Begging your pardon," Rani bobbed her head, but purposely neglected to add a title to her salute. If the man did not want to be called a lord, who was she to gainsay him? Rani gestured toward Garadolo, who cast daggers with his eyes. "I understood that this soldier was coming to meet with you this evening, and I worried that he might forget the gift I gave him to carry on my behalf. I thought it best to bring my full offering directly."

Rani produced a knotted rag from the pouch at her waist, trying to ignore the pressure of the suspicious captor's knife at her neck, trying to forget that the man before her had betrayed Instructor Morada to her death. Rani focused instead on moving her hands smoothly, steadily, doing nothing to threaten the knife-wielding sentry. She had tied the rag tightly about her treasure, and she could not pluck loose the knots; she was forced to raise the cloth to her teeth. She tasted salt on her tongue, and tried to forget that her own blood would flow with a similar tang if Larindolian chose not to accept her offering.

"For the Brotherhood," she managed, when she at last untied the cloth. The hoard of silver glinted red in the torchlight. She managed a bow and set the coins on the floor before the nobleman.

"What ho, Garadolo! This urchin brings us more in one visit than you manage in a fortnight of escapades!" The soldier glared his fury across the small room, and Rani found herself almost grateful for the nobleman's presence. "Perhaps we're lucky this prowling child managed to trace your steps!"

"I wasn't concerned with a child, I—, with a mere child." Garadolo scarcely remembered to swallow Larindolian's title. "I had other matters on my mind."

Larindolian poked a toe at the hoard of silver, only pulling back his fine leather boot when he appeared to consider kicking the soldier. "Matters more pressing than a spy who tracked you to the Brotherhood's heart?"

"I didn't worry about that mewling tiger cub." Garadolo glanced over his shoulder and lowered his voice to a whisper. "It was all I could do to shake Dalarati when I left the mess hall."

Larindolian swore a vicious oath, whirling to slap a well-gloved hand across Garadolo's cheek. "You still have not disposed of that threat? You were ordered to act more than a month ago!"

"I've been trying to see the Brotherhood for the better part of that month," whined the soldier, terror glinting in the bloodshot eyes above his greasy beard. "It's not as easy as you make out. The man is popular with the soldiers. He's always surrounded by his fellows—on the target field, drinking draughts. I think it's not necessary to do away with him. Not yet."

"*You* think? Since when have you dared to think, Garadolo?" Larindolian pursed his lips with disapproval. "We can see the product of your *thinking* right here—with this street urchin you've permitted in our midst."

Rani had listened to all she could; she nearly interrupted the nobleman in her eagerness to focus his attention on her. "Begging your pardon, but Garadolo is not wholly to blame.

I followed him, even though he ordered me to stay in the barracks, because I wanted to see my brother."

"Your *brother*?" Larindolian was incredulous, but Rani could not tell if his surprise was from being interrupted, or if he simply could not imagine all the trouble spawned by a girl's simple desire to see her sibling. "And who in the name of all the Thousand Gods might that be?"

"Bardo Trader,.."

"What, ho!" Garadolo exclaimed. "Don't waste time with your story, little tiger!"

"Shut your trap, you stupid ox! One more word from you, and I'll feed your privates to the queen's goldfish." At Larindolian's rebuke, Garadolo gaped comically, opening and closing his mouth like a trout plucked from a stream. The nobleman turned his attention to Rani, waving back her guard with an impatient hand. "Rani Trader.... Then you are the one who was at the cathedral with Morada."

Rani sighed as the knife point was removed from the base of her skull. "Yes."

"And you are the one who summoned Tuvashanoran to his death?"

That wasn't fair! she wanted to cry out. She had not known that he would die. She had hoped to *save* the prince, not kill him! Why didn't anyone understand? Rani ignored the nobleman's question, even though she was painfully aware of the furious power scarcely contained in the nobleman, the raw anger that had attacked Morada and threatened Garadolo. "If you please, I've been looking for my brother for weeks."

"Why haven't you gone to the king, girl? Why haven't you reported all you know about the traitors who killed Prince Tuvashanoran?"

Rani forced herself to meet the man's icy blue eyes. "The king would have my life before I could speak," she shrugged. "I was in the guild, you see, and then I ran away before the king's men could destroy it. When I was with the Touched, I lied to the soldiers and told them I was a Pilgrim, and then I was in the marketplace, working for the Council and escaping their punishment. Now, I'm living with the soldiers, and I've needed to find ... goods ... to trade for the honor of an audience with you...." She trailed off, as the story of her wrongdoings seemed to magnify beneath the serpents' gaze.

"A veritable Jair, you are, changing your caste as the whim suits you." Larindolian's voice was dry, but Rani was not certain that the nobleman's quiet observation was a safe substitute for the flashing anger she had already witnessed.

"Honored be the Pilgrim's name," came Rani's belated rejoinder, and her hand fluttered in a holy sign as she sought protection against her mercurial opponent. Silently, she added an appeal to Lan, and she was rewarded when the nobleman fought a losing battle against a calculating smile.

"And what proof do we have that you are here honestly? What proof do we have that you do not come to assassinate Bardo Trader, as you have already worked to murder the Prince?"

"Kill Bardo!"

"Yes indeed, little one." Rani did not like the cold eye the nobleman cast upon her. She remembered too well his restraint as he had disciplined Instructor Morada, just before turning her over to the king's deadly guard.

"But he's my *brother*," she explained. "I love him and respect him. I'd never harm him."

"But he is 'brother' to more than you, little one." Larindolian's eyes bore into her soul. So, Rani Trader, are you prepared to join your Bardo's new family? Are you prepared to join our Brotherhood?"

The question took Rani by surprise. Certainly, she wanted to end her wandering, to be back in the safety of her family's home. She wanted to know her name and her caste, and her place in King Shanoranvilli's City. She wanted to forget about the disastrous glasswrights' guild and go back to being just plain Rani Trader, a girl who was good at the tasks she was born to. If the Brotherhood meant family, then she would throw in her lot with them.

Before she could nod her agreement, though, she was reminded of all the members of the Brotherhood she had seen thus far—Morada's fury on the scaffold, and the woman's bleeding, battered body. Guildmistress Salina, so harsh in the Hall of Discipline, shrieking for revenge against an apprentice who had acted all unknowingly. Garadolo, who clearly had his own reasons for taking in a young girl and was even now cringing at the far end of the chamber, like a craven dog. Tuvashanoran, whose body she had wrapped in linen and myrrh.

Even more, she thought of Mair, of the Touched girl who had fought the soldiers to return to Rani's side. *Mair* was afraid of the Brotherhood—Mair, who had openly confronted Borin, who had ventured alone to the cathedral close. Did Rani want to join the Brotherhood? Did she even know what the Brotherhood was?

"Please, it was never my intention to trouble you. I have lost my mother and my father, and all my brothers and sisters but Bardo. I only want to see my brother."

"Ah!" exclaimed Larindolian, as if she had spoken the true name of First God Ait. "But you can see the problem. As you know, there are people eager to murder Bardo Trader, people who have seen to the execution of all his family—"

"Not *all* his family," Rani countered hotly.

Larindolian ignored her clarification. "We'd be fools to endanger Bardo by permitting him to speak with a known criminal, particularly a criminal who has already proven her skill at assassination. May Prince Tuvashanoran rest in peace in the Heavenly Fields." The nobleman moved one gloved hand in a holy sign.

Rani reflexively repeated the gesture, even as she protested, "You *know* I did not murder the prince! There was someone else on that scaffold with Instructor Morada." Her frustration boiled over into her words. "I think Morada was right. I think you *are* deciding the cut of your coronation robe, and I think your Brotherhood would not take kindly to your actions."

Larindolian's hissed intake of breath was as sharp as the serpents' teeth gleaming on the floor and walls of the chamber. "You know too much, girl. It would be safer for the Brotherhood to slay you here and now, safer for all of us, including Bardo."

"Not safer for Bardo! I'm his sister!" Take me to my brother, and you'll be rewarded beyond your hopes."

Larindolian laughed at her brave words, brushing them off like chaff. "Prove it, girl. Make it worth my while to admit you to Bardo's presence."

Rani hesitated only a moment before pushing every one of her coins across the tiled floor to Larindolian. When her magnanimity earned no reaction from the nobleman, she muttered under her breath and reached into her pouch, extracting a man's ring, heavy with gold and set with a square-cut onyx. She had not wanted Garadolo to see the captain's signet, but there was nothing else to be done. The stone glinted in the torchlight like a baleful eye.

Larindolian's laugh stung so sharply that Rani almost dropped the ring. "What do I want with your measly coins and another man's ring?" Larindolian dug into the pouch at his own waist, scooping out a handful of gold to match Rani's hard-won silver. "You underestimate the Brotherhood, child. We have the wealth of kingdoms at our command."

The apprentice gulped, even as Garadolo whooped with laughter. "He's got you there, little tiger! Not much the likes of you can offer a lord, now is there?"

Rani flashed the soldier a dirty look before turning her attention back to Larindolian. "What do you want, then?" She was enough of a merchant to know that the nobleman would not have opened the bidding if he did not have a price in mind.

"I want you to rid us of that annoying soldier." For just an instant, Rani thought he spoke of Garadolo. She flashed a glance at her erstwhile keeper, surprising his own horrified realization that he was in danger. Larindolian barked a short laugh. "No, not that miserable excuse for the king's guard. I wouldn't bother you with garbage like that." Garadolo's quick prayer to Cot was almost lost in his spluttering indignation. "No, I speak of the one that *this* one can't manage to take care of.... Dalarati—get rid of that man."

"Dalarati!" Rani exclaimed, and the image of the handsome soldier flashed before her eyes, laughing and kind. "But he's no threat to the Brotherhood! He gave me an almond bun."

"Oh *well*, then! An almond bun," Larindolian sneered. "If you'd prefer sweetmeats to seeing your brother...."

"Tell Bardo that I'm here!" Rani demanded hotly.

"Or you'll do what? Don't press your luck, girl. I've called the king's guard on your betters, I won't hesitate to turn you in, if it'll protect the Brotherhood."

"You know I'm no threat! And neither is Dalarati!"

"You're speaking to a grown man, Rani Trader. You hardly know the lay of this land." The nobleman leaned closer; she could smell sweet lotion on his flesh. "Dalarati has already threatened your brother's life; he has publicly vowed to execute any of the Brotherhood he finds, and *he knew Bardo's name.*" Larindolian waited for his words to register. "It's a simple matter, Rani. Either you kill Dalarati, or he kills your brother."

Fear closed around Rani's chest—terror for Bardo, for the last remaining member of her family. "Dalarati could never get past your defenses!" Rani pleaded. "You have sentries and passwords...."

"But you, a slip of a girl, managed to get past them. What greater deviltry could we expect from a trained fighting man? I wouldn't trouble you, Rani, if Dalarati had not already voiced his intentions. We need you, Rani. *Bardo* needs you. Are you willing to trust your brother's safety to Garadolo, to this ... buffoon for one more night?"

Rani could only shake her head, struggling to master her disbelief. "But Dalarati is a good soldier, and true."

"True to whom?" countered Larindolian, and he sighed like a weary man. "I wasn't going to tell you this, Rani Trader, but you've forced my hand. Dalarati was once one of us. He's betrayed us before—*he* fired the arrow that slew Prince Tuvashanoran, and that was never our goal."

"Dalarati? *He* slew the Prince? And he bears the mark of the snake?"

Larindolian's gaze was rock-steady. "As surely as did Prince Tuvashanoran himself. Dalarati is a rebel. He thinks he can run the Brotherhood on his own. He decided that justice would only be done if the Defender were slain. We'd never have permitted him on the scaffold if we'd known his intention."

"But—" Rani began to protest, but the nobleman cut her off.

"Think about it. Why would we murder our highest-ranking member? With Tuvashanoran's guidance, we could have brought the Brotherhood into the open. We could have delivered our message directly to the people, to all of Morenia. All our hopes were pinned on Tuvashanoran; the Brotherhood was *grateful* that the prince was going to don the Defender's robes."

"But why would Dalarati—"

"Who can say why a madman does anything? Dalarati thought he was acting to spread justice. Somewhere along the way, the man was warped. Who knows? Maybe the Thousand Gods lured him into madness."

"But Instructor Morada had to agree with him. She had to let him on the scaffold."

"Aye, Instructor Morada." Larindolian's thin lips twisted into a grimace. "Dalarati seduced the poor woman. He convinced her of his mad plan. There's more power in a stolen kiss than in all the Thousand Gods' logic. Those two rebelled and tore apart the Brotherhood's strongest plan."

"Morada? And Dalarati?" Rani looked at Larindolian miserably, easily imagining the athletic Dalarati scaling the platform beside the cathedral. She pictured his hands on Morada's arms, his lips pressed close to the Instructor's. Larindolian nodded slowly, and when he spoke, his words were bitter ice. "You've chosen to come here, Rani Trader. You've chosen to get involved with events that are larger than a glasswright's apprentice."

When Rani merely stared in disbelief at the nobleman's words, and his offhand use of the forbidden guild's name, Larindolian cocked his head to one side, looking like a cunning fox. His tone snapped tight around his words as he tried another tack. "But perhaps Dalarati has already gotten to you, already seduced you to join his side. Let me make this easier for you, Ranita Glasswright. You've come to the Brotherhood's Inner Chamber. You know our symbol, and you've heard our passwords. You know the names of at least two of our number. We can't risk having someone run about the City, spreading lies about our deeds."

Rani reeled under the sudden onslaught, and she responded hotly, "You call yourself a Brotherhood, but you forget that I have come to find *my* brother! I'd give my life for Bardo!"

"Your life?" Larindolian did not respond with the anger she expected; rather, his smile froze his lips. "Are you prepared to make that oath official?"

"What do you mean?" A chill draft swirled about Rani's legs, and a prickle of fear snaked along her neck. Her mind was reeling from all the changes in this cold, cold man.

"If you had stayed in your guild, you would have sworn your faithfulness for life by giving a blood oath upon the Orb of power. Are you prepared to make the same commitment to the man you call your brother?"

"I do more than *call* him brother! He *is* my kin!"

Larindolian shrugged away her protest. "Will you swear the oath?"

Rani stared at the nobleman for a long moment, wondering if she trusted her life to this cruel man. Everyone knew that a blood oath was a serious thing—it attracted the attention of all the Thousand Gods. More to the point, though, Rani would be at Larindolian's mercy as he determined how much of her blood would be required to bind her to the Brotherhood. Before she could summon the courage to answer, Garadolo chuckled across the room.

"Aye, you've got her there! She says she's committed to her brother, but when push comes to shove—"

"Shut your mouth!" Larindolian snapped, but his eyes remained bound to Rani's. She felt the power of his will as if she were hypnotized. The nobleman declared, "The decision is hers. If she does not want to see her brother, who are we to force her?"

Rani raised her chin defiantly, yanking at her tunic's sleeve. "I'll see him. I'm not afraid of you."

Larindolian accepted the challenge in her words with a solemn nod, and then he flashed a dagger from his waist. In the torchlight, its blade seemed very long. "Do you know what we mean when we call ourselves the Brotherhood? Do you know what we work toward?"

Rani's memories flashed back to a dark alley, to the bitter night when Mair had shared her Touched knowledge. "I know that the Brotherhood works to end the castes. You work to make all men equal before the Thousand Gods."

Larindolian nodded shrewdly. "And do you understand what that will mean to the City? Do you understand how all Morenia will be changed?"

Rani recalled Mair's scornful declaration that people were not fighting to become part of the casteless Touched. Nevertheless, she thought of her time with Mair's troop, time when she had been treated honestly and judged fairly. She had not been held accountable for the vagaries of a marketplace beyond her control; she had not been punished for any master guildsman's mistake. She was not sworn to defend a Crown she knew nothing about, and she did not need to flatter the greater nobility above and beyond her. Rani began to glimpse that the Brotherhood might be right—the City *could* be a better place without castes. Clearly, Bardo had reached the same conclusion.

Rani met Larindolian's eyes. "I understand."

"Very well then. Speak after me. I, Rani Trader, offer up my body and heart and soul in service to the Brotherhood of Justice, and in emblem of that offering, I give the Brotherhood the blood of my body."

Rani repeated each phrase of the oath, her voice amazingly steady in the flickering torchlight. When she had finished her recitation, Larindolian grasped her wrist, slashing his blade against the vein that beat in the smooth flesh at the crook of her arm. The initial cut scarcely registered, but then the cold air stung the wound. Rani sucked in breath through her teeth, but she did not pull her hand away.

He held her bleeding arm between them, moving it and measuring the drops of blood that fell. Mesmerized by the crimson paint, she watched as eight little pools formed, one on each of the serpent eyes embedded in the floor. As she stared at the drops of her own blood, she realized that her oath was not the first to be witnessed in this chamber. The tiles were stained a rusty brown, and the grout between them drank her offering thirstily.

Horrified at the risk that she was taking, Rani managed to look into Larindolian's cold blue gaze. The nobleman nodded as he read her comprehension, her understanding that she was now part of a greater body. The malevolent twist of his lips reminded her of Morada's bloody head, but before she could cry out, walls of velvet black closed around her, cutting off her vision and seizing her breath.

When Rani regained consciousness, she suspected only a few moments had passed; her blood still glistened moistly on the floor before her. Larindolian had produced a strip of black cloth from somewhere, and he was knotting it around her arm, smothering the open cut with steady fingers. He completed his handiwork with a tight knot, and then he tugged Rani to her feet.

"The Thousand Gods have witnessed your oath, Rani Trader. You have until tomorrow night to prove your loyalty to the Brotherhood, and to Bardo." Rani flexed her fingers gingerly, taking a deep breath to beat back the midnight wings of oblivion. "I can assure you, we don't deal gently with traitors. You may long for Morada's easy death, if we are forced to hunt you down. By midnight tomorrow."

Larindolian turned on his heel, sweeping from the chamber with a flicker of torchlight, leaving Rani to be escorted to the street with Garadolo.

* * *

"Shar, don't ask any questions!" Rani fed desperation into her tone. "I don't have anyone else I can trust! I need you to go to the Core."

"'N' why don't ye go yerself?" Shar stretched on her pallet, still half-asleep in the grey light just before dawn.

"I've already told you—I don't know where the Core is. I don't know how to find it."

"Ye certainly don't!" Shar snorted. "Th' Core ain't an 'it'. Th' Core's a *she*. Well, a she now, it was a 'ee last year."

Rani made interested noises as she gathered up her friend's belongings. "See, I *do* need you. Please, take my message—I don't have anyone else I can trust."

"Who are ye really, Rai? Ye're clearly not one o' us Touched."

"I was an apprentice in the glasswrights' guild." Rani thrust Shar's satchel into her arms and knelt by the pallet to dig out the girl's sandals. A wave of dizziness rushed over her, and she took some panting breaths to clear her vision.

The Touched girl whistled softly through the gap in her teeth. "Fine, then, don't tell me. Why should ye tell me anything?" Despite her grumbling, Shar stepped into her shoes, sulking as Rani did up the buckles. "That's a foolish joke t' tell, though, Rai. *I* know ye're jestin', but th' soldiers, they wouldna be as sure. Ye wouldna want one o' them decidin' t' take revenge fer th' Prince's death, just 'cause ye dinna want t' tell me why ye're packin' me off. Ye watch yer step, girl."

"You watch your own," Rani countered as she hustled Shar to the doorway. "Go to the Core, and find Mair. Tell her I'll be with Bardo by tomorrow, and I haven't forgotten my promise. I'll bring what I owe her tomorrow morning, in the marketplace." That was the clearest message Rani felt able to deliver. She would complete Larindolian's bidding, find Bardo, and gather the wergild that she had promised Mair, the payment for Rabe's poor mother.

"And what's in it fer me?" Shar asked, finally awake enough to understand the words Rani was hurling at her. "It's goin' t' take me th' better part o' th' day t' find th' Core."

"You'll be amazed, Shar. I can only promise you'll be amazed." Rani did not listen to the girl's other questions; she locked Dalarati's door without further hesitation. Offering up a prayer to Sart, the god of time, that Shar's mission truly did take all day, Rani set about laying her trap.

"Come out, little bird! Come see what treats I've brought for you." Dalarati's voice was coaxing as Rani huddled beneath Shar's blanket. Her arm had begun to ache beneath Larindolian's bandage, but she was afraid to loosen the knot, afraid that the cut would start to bleed again. A steady hammer beat inside her skull. "How now, little bird? You said you'd be waiting for me when I finished the night watch."

Rani identified the sound of the door catching in its frame, and then the snick of the lock as Dalarati closed them in. She managed a little moan, as she thought Shar might respond to her lover in the chill light of the new dawn. She twisted about in the shadowed bed so that she could make out Dalarati's form as he strode about his room.

"It was a busy night on the walls," the soldier reported as he built up the fire. "The City's restless, as if people suspect evil in the night. It's been like this ever since the Prince was murdered. If we could just find that cursed gl—" he caught himself just in time, before he could name the forbidden guild, "that cursed apprentice, then we'd all sleep easier." Rani swallowed hard. Dalarati's words confirmed that he was a danger to her—a danger to Bardo, and to the only life that remained to her here in the City.

The soldier slapped his palms against each other, brushing off dust from the logs. "Ach! Curse them all, keeping soldiers from warm beds. Tarn take their souls and bar the gates to the Heavenly Fields!" The words prickled across Rani's skull, so like the Brotherhood's password. If any doubt had remained in Rani's heart, she now knew that Dalarati must be one of them. He must have betrayed his brothers for wealth and power in the King's Men.

Before she could bluff a response, Dalarati unbuckled his sword belt, letting the heavy weapon fall beside the hearth.

He unlaced his tunic and crossed to the pallet. "Ah, little bird," he sighed, kneeling beside Rani. "The entire watch, men were talking of ghosts and murder, but all I could think of was you. These night shifts are hard."

He paused for a moment, as if he were waiting for some ribald response, and Rani was startled by the warm flash that flickered inside her. She forced herself to remember that this was the man who had fired the arrow, this was the man who had murdered Prince Tuvashanoran. How could he sit there and woo his mistress, as if he were the soul of innocence?

"Cat got your tongue, little bird? Let's see if we can find it!" With a hearty laugh, Dalarati tugged on the mattress. Before Rani knew what was happening, she was tight in the soldier's embrace. His mouth closed over hers, and his lips teased at her own, even as his hands did distracting things beneath her tunic. His knee slid between her legs, and for just an instant, she forgot the knife that lay beside her head, the Zarithian blade she had carefully hidden beneath Shar's pillow.

"In the name of Blait!" Dalarati swore, invoking the god of lovers as he thrust Rani from him. "Rai, you crazy wench! Where's Shar?"

Before Dalarati could recover from his surprise, Rani darted across the room and picked up his sword. She dared not raise the heavy weapon against one trained to use it— she might be desperate, but she wasn't a fool. Still, she had to keep *him* from using it against her, and she could hardly open the door and toss it into the streets of the Soldiers' Quarter. Even as Dalarati untangled himself from the bedding, Rani tossed the bare blade onto the flames. Sparks flew, and the effort of heaving the weapon set her arm to a steady throbbing.

"In the name of all the Thousand Gods!" Dalarati grabbed the poker and pulled his weapon from the flames, muttering about the blade losing its fine temper. As the sword cooled on the hearthstone, he whirled on Rani, anger fighting with innate compassion. "Has Garadolo put you up to this? I know the man despises me, but—"

"This has nothing to do with Garadolo."

"I can see that you're upset, Rai. That man has used you ill, making demands no honest soldier should ask of any lass. You don't have to do this, though, whatever he's required. I'll walk you past the checkpoints myself, Rai."

"My name isn't Rai."

"What is it, then?" The man's tone was reasonable, gentle, as if he were soothing an unruly child. "Ranimara? I've heard Garadolo call you that, and if that's the name you prefer...." He was good at this dissembling, better even than Larindolian had hinted.

"Rani. My name is Rani Trader."

If she had intended her announcement to shock him into an admission, she was sorely disappointed. "Very well, Rani. Sit down here, and let's discuss your stay in the soldiers' quarters."

"We don't have anything to discuss." Nevertheless, Rani let herself be led across the small chamber, let him seat her on the edge of the pallet. She knew that she should whisk the knife from beneath the bolster immediately, that she should catch him all unawares. Still, her hand was frozen. She could not force herself to move nearer to the handsome soldier, nearer to her job as assassin. She shook her head, trying to clear away the cobwebs that obscured her thoughts.

"Ah, but there you're wrong, Rani Trader." Dalarati grinned, clearly unaware of the danger he was in. "Look, I don't know why you're here in the Quarter, why you've thrown in your lot with the Touched girls. You should know, though, that your behavior has been noted."

"My behavior?" Dalarati's admonition was as stunning as if he had slapped her across the face.

"Don't act so innocent. I've watched you some, and Shar's told me more. We know you've been stealing the soldiers blind."

"You know...." Rani thought she had been so careful. She had planned everything so well. Now, her vices were discovered by the one soldier she had thought to please, the one man she had hoped would help her in this warren of barracks.... She felt the surprising urge to sob.

"I'm trained to know," Dalarati reminded her gently. "Shar suspected something was up that first morning, by the fountain. She told me that your accent was never true to the Touched."

"Then why didn't she challenge me?"

"Who is Shar to question the Thousand Gods? Surely, they had a hand in bringing you to the Quarter, as they control all things. Though why they should choose to work through Garadolo is a question that could challenge priests for decades." Dalarati shrugged, and forced a smile to his handsome lips. Tears of frustration rose in Rani's eyes—she could not harm this man, this soldier who had seen through her lies but still protected her, still tried to keep her safe from the worst of Garadolo's depravity.

Dalarati brought up a tanned hand to brush away an errant wisp of hair from her brow. "There now, Rai. Enough of these games. I'll give you some coins and send you on your way. You should stay out of the Soldiers' Quarter for a while, give the men a chance to forget the things that have gone missing from their quarters."

"Why are you doing this?" Rani's voice quavered, and she stared in disbelief as Dalarati walked across the room, crouching to pry up a section of the floorboards. She could make out the hard outline of a strongbox, and the soldier grunted as he hefted its weight into the center of the room. "Why are you helping me when you know that I've stolen from the others?"

"Ah, Rai." Dalarati's grin was easy as he moved his body between her and the box, camouflaging his motions to open the container. "We all betray our brothers some of the time."

Betray our brothers.

Those three words brought back the full force of Rani's vow to the Brotherhood, the oath that she had sworn on her own blood. Dalarati had endangered Bardo. He had murdered his brother, Tuvashanoran, without a thought to the cost of that betrayal, without a care for all that she had suffered. He had cost Rani her family, her caste, and her safety.

In a flash, she swept her Zarithian blade from beneath Shar's pillow. Fairn, the god of birds, must have carried her across the small room, and Zake, the god of chirurgeons, guided her hand as she planted the knife in the small of Dalarati's back. It was all so easy, so simple, as if she were not merely a thirteen-year-old girl, and he were not the pride of Shanoranvilli's Men.

The soldier let out a muffled cry of surprise, and he slumped against the floor, scrambling desperately for the blade that Rani twisted once before she leaped across the room. "Ach! Rai!" The color drained from his face, and he clenched his teeth against a brutal spasm. "What have you done?"

"You murdered Tuvashanoran!" Rani's voice shook as she saw the results of her handiwork. "You stood on the scaffold and fired the arrow that killed the Prince and destroyed the guild and burned my parents' house." Tears streamed down her face, and she gasped for breath like a foaling mare.

"You're mad, Rai." Dalarati finally succeeded in pulling out the blade, but he was only rewarded by a flood of crimson blood onto the floorboards. He gasped, "By First God Ait, you're mad."

"I'm not mad! Larindolian told me! You just said that you would betray the Brotherhood!"

"The Brotherhood," he panted. "What do you know of them?"

"I know that you followed Garadolo. I know that you were trying to expose the Brotherhood. I know you want to bring down Bardo, and all he stands for. That's why you murdered the Prince."

"You little fool." Dalarati had stopped trying to move his legs, to get to his feet. His breath came in short, sharp gasps. "They've sold you a bushel of lies."

"I'm not listening to you!" Rani squeezed her eyes closed, as if that would shut out the terrible thing she had done, as if that would take back the oath she had sworn on her own blood in the Brotherhood's chamber. "You're the one who makes up stories! By First God Ait, and by Jair the Pilgrim, I won't listen to your lies."

Silence. Dalarati did not try to move, did not try to speak, but she knew that he still lived. His labored breathing shredded the small room. She fought back her tears as she whispered the Litany of Death in her own mind. The deaths of her parents, she reminded herself, the death of Tuvashanoran. Dalarati was a traitor. She had had no choice. She could not have acted in any other way.

"Rai," he whispered at last, and she jumped as if his voice were a thunderclap. "I don't know what they mean for you. I only know that they have used you—used you to wipe out the threat I represented. Bardo is working great harm—"

"Don't you speak about Bardo!" she sobbed. "His name is too good for you!"

"Fine, Rai," he gasped. "Not Bardo, then. The rest of the Brotherhood. I was close to learning their game. I told my Prince all I knew. I told him that the threat lies closest to the crown, closer than we ever feared. Don't trust them, Rai. They've murdered before, and they'll kill again." The long speech exhausted him, and he fell back to the floor, panting.

Rani could see the beads of sweat standing out on his forehead, smell the exertion on him. She wanted to run into the City streets, but she was glued to the havoc she had created. The pool of crimson crept across the floorboards, gelling in the cold morning air.

"Hal..." Dalarati murmured, but then his eyes flew open, as if he had been shoved awake. "Shar! " Rani glanced over her shoulder, expecting the Touched girl to appear in the doorway. "Shar! Don't leave me! I'm so cold...." His trembling grew more violent, his hand spasming as he reached toward Rani. "My love," he whispered.

Rani captured his right hand and clasped it to her chest, adding her tears to the gory mix of sweat and blood streaking the warrior's skin. Dalarati died in her arms as she struggled not to look at his fingers, not to see the complete lack of an archers' callouses on his well-muscled hands. Sick at heart, afraid even to think beyond her pounding chest and her gasping lungs, Rani dared not check for the tattoo of intertwined snakes that Larindolian had promised.

CHAPTER 11

"Brave as a lion, swift as a lion," Rani muttered to herself as she knelt before the statue of the Defender of the Faith at the edge of the City's market. Larindolian had outfitted her as a pilgrim before he ordered her sternly to the marketplace, and the mid-day sun beat down against her black cape. The dark costume was a near-perfect disguise. The streets teemed with pilgrims, with the thousands of worshipers who had converged on the City for this holiest of holy days, for Jair's feast day.

The heat of Rani's Thousand-Pointed Star burned through the heavy fabric of her cloak. In the shadows by the hidden passage in the City walls the air had been heavy with dankest autumn, but here in the open market, Rani felt as if she were back in the glasswrights' kiln.

She longed for the feel of her silver mirror beneath her hand, the familiar shape of the lion pulling down the goat. For all the years that she had held the treasure, she'd imagined herself to be the lion, strong and sinewy and brave. Now, she feared she might actually be the goat.

Forcing herself to wait patiently for the messenger that Larindolian had promised, Rani bowed her head over her tightly clasped hands and began to recite the holy litany for Dalarati, as if the soldier's cooling body still lay at her feet: "Hail Cot, god of soldiers, guide of Jair the Pilgrim. Look upon this pilgrim with mercy in your heart and justice in your soul. Guide the feet of this pilgrim on righteous paths of glory that all may be done to honor you and yours among the Thousand Gods. This pilgrim asks for the grace of your blessing, Cot, god of soldiers."

She repeated the incantation, calling on her private patron, Lan. It seemed like years since she had adopted the kitchen god, years since Cook had helped her escape from the garden. What would Cook think of her now? Would the old woman have deemed her sacrifice worthwhile? Shying away from her own questions, Rani began to invoke the gods of the Virtues. When another pilgrim knelt beside her, Rani knew that she should concentrate on her prayers for the peace of Dalarati's soul, but she could not restrain her wandering eyes. "Mair!"

"Aye. Ye sent fer me, didn't ye?"

"Yes, but I didn't think you'd come—not after...." Rani trailed off, her words drowned in a pool of soldier's blood. Blinking, she could still see her crimson-washed dagger in the dim light of Dalarati's quarters. She'd left the Zarithian blade behind, forgotten it in her panic to be free of the soldier's corpse.

"I shouldna be seen 'ere with ye, that's fer sure."

"But where did you get a pilgrim's robe?"

"That's 'ardly important now, is it? The better question is why *ye* are wearin' one, and what ye plan t' do now that ye've killed th' soldier."

Rani could not keep from darting her eyes at the crowd, fearful that someone would overhear Mair's harsh whisper, that Larindolian's messenger would choose that terrible moment to arrive. Fortunately, the marketplace was crowded, and no one spared attention for two small pilgrims who offered their obeisance at the feet of a stern statue. "If you know what happened, then you know I had no choice."

"I know ye sent Shar t' get a message t' me, 'n' I know she discovered th' soldier's body when she made 'er way back t' 'er only 'ome i' th' world."

"How is she?" Rani reminded herself not to cry. She must not give in to pity. Shar was better off with the Touched, better off with her own caste. Surely, Larindolian had only thought to use Shar in his battle against the Brotherhood. Against Bardo.

"That's none o' yer concern, Rai. The better question is what'll 'appen to ye. Those soldiers'd be glad to learn 'oo ye are, beneath yer Pilgrim's cloak."

Rani looked up in panic. There were more soldiers in the marketplace than usual; the entire City was set on edge as suspicion surged from quarter to quarter. Even those castes that had not deigned to note a soldier murdered in his barracks could sense the added uneasiness in a City already strained to its limits of patience. The hundreds of visiting pilgrims only heightened her feeling of anxiety. "You wouldn't dare! The soldiers are no friends of the Touched."

"Dalarati was a friend t' one o' th' Touched. A friend 'n' more." Mair moved her fingers in a holy sign. "Poor Shar. She should've minded 'er caste."

Mind yer caste. That was what the Touched creature had said outside the hut, where Larindolian had met Morada. If only Rani had listened to the warning then.... If only she knew which caste she was to mind.... Such speculation was nonsense, though. Larindolian's messenger was certain to arrive momentarily, and Rani did not want to justify her actions any further. "Mair, I can't explain; there isn't time."

"Ach, no time t' talk t' th' family ye chose fer yer own." Mair spat toward Rani's feet.

"I have other family, Mair!"

"So ye say, Rai, so ye say. Ye've an odd way o' showin' yer family loyalties, though. T' think I believed Shar when she said ye'd be payin' yer debts t' me i' th' marketplace."

Rani remembered the lie she had fashioned to send Shar on her way; she had promised to pay Mair the tribute owed to Rabe.... That, at least, Rani could make right. Afraid to look the Touched leader in the face, Rani ducked a hand beneath her black Pilgrim's robe, grabbing for her pouch. Her fingers closed immediately on the strip of golden paper, the receipt that she had stolen from the tribute offered by the merchants in the cathedral compound.

"I didn't lie, Mair. Here's what I promised, why I sent Shar to find you."

The golden paper glittered in the sunlight, and Mair glanced at it curiously before thrusting it deep inside the folds of her own robe. "A dozen robes," the Touched girl recited. "A dozen robes fer a soldier's life. Do ye think ye've traded well, Rai?"

"It's not what *I* think," she began to protest, but Mair waved her to silence.

"I'll give ye more t' th' bargain. Shar did find me wi' th' Core, though 'ow ye knew I'd be there, I can only begin t' guess. Th' Core 'eard yer message, and told me t' bring 'er own message to ye when we met. Th' Core says this: "Th' doe runs fleeter than th' buck, and she dinna get tangled by 'er antlers in th' brush.""

"What does that mean?" Rani stared at Mair as if the other girl had taken leave of her senses.

"'Ow do I know? I merely follow orders when I'm given 'em."

"The doe..." Before Rani could repeat the cryptic message, a commotion began on the far side of the marketplace. Craning her neck, she could make out the Pilgrims' progression that Larindolian had told her to expect. She was nearly out of time. "Mair, thank you for coming here. You have to believe me—I never wanted to kill Dalarati. I never wanted to hurt Shar."

Before the Touched leader could respond, a child-figure darted from the shadows at the edge of the marketplace. "Mair!"

"Rabe, I told ye t' wait fer me wi' th' others!"

"Mair, Jair's Watchers 'r' 'ere! Th' Progress is comin' t' th' market! They're choosin' th' First Pilgrim. Th' group is afraid we'll miss—"

All of a sudden Rabe looked at the small pilgrim Mair was talking to, and recognition spread across his face like a rash. "You!" he breathed, even as Mair exclaimed, "Rabe, I bind ye by yer oaths t' th' Touched!"

"But Mair, she—"

"I'll not 'ear it from ye, Rabe."

"You *'eard* Shar. You *'eard* th' Core."

"Aye, and as long as I'm th' Leader o' our troop, Rabe, I'll 'ear more than that, 'n' about more things."

The youth stared at Mair, clearly disbelieving that his leader would cast her lot with a wandering, caste-jumping murderer. "I'll not let ye do this, Mair. We'll not let ye lead us down this path."

Mair put ice into her voice as she faced down her lieutenant. "Ye'll do as ye see fit, Rabe. Just remember that ye dinna know all th' tale. None o' us knows th' full story bein' writ 'ere."

"None but that one." Rabe did not restrain himself where Mair had, and Rani felt the warm gobbet of his spit like a slap against her face. She hissed and sprang from her knees, fingers crooked as she launched at his sneering face.

"Stop, Rai!" Mair's command bit through Rani's anger like the sharpest Zarithian dagger. "Leave 'im be. 'E dinna know yer story, and ye canna take th' time t' tell 'im now."

"But—"

"I said t' stop." Mair's command brooked no argument, and Rani clenched her hands into fists as Rabe crowed his delight.

Meanwhile, the commotion on the far side of the marketplace had worked its way near. Even Rabe was silenced by the spectacle that wound through the plaza. A dozen figures, Jair's Watchers, stood at key points in the marketplace. Each was robed in solid black, with a pointed hood that obscured any human features. The Watchers were the holiest of Jair's representatives in the City, purified by days of fasting and prayer. Their presence denoted the power of this holy day, the force of Jair in all men's lives.

Hundreds of pilgrims, also gowned in black, wove through the stalls beneath the Watchers' hidden eyes. Each bore a golden Thousand-Pointed Star. Merchants cried out in religious fervor at the procession, and more than one pilgrim helped himself to the fresh fruits and ripe cheeses offered up in homage. The vendors who were favored loudly praised the Thousand Gods, grateful at being singled out in this most honored of spectacles. More than one merchant spoke Jair's name, calling on the founder of King Shanoranvilli's house, on the man honored on this holiest of feast days.

The cacophony deepened as the pilgrims chanted the Processional, calling in turn upon each of the Thousand Gods to bless their pilgrimage, to bring peace and prosperity to the City and the Kingdom and the lives of the pilgrims themselves. As the first of the black-robed holy wanderers reached the Defender's statue, Rani's stomach tightened in expectation. This was the moment Larindolian had told her to wait for; this was the reason she had been praying in the morning light.

"Mair—" She turned to the Leader of the Touched troop, ignoring the stupefied Rabe.

"Watch yer step, Rai. Ye canna see where th' serpent suns 'imself on th' rocks. 'N' dinna ferget th' Core's words. She said they would mean life 'r death fer ye."

Before Rani could respond, the pilgrim crowd surged around her, and firm hands grasped her shoulders, submerging her in the black-robed throng. Rani tossed her head in protest, but when she managed to twist around to find Mair, the girl had melted away into the crowd. Rabe was nowhere to be seen.

"Stop your fighting, you little fool!" The voice hissed into Rani's ear, and she whirled to face cruel eyes that glittered in an aging face.

"Guild—" she started to exclaim.

"Shut your mouth!" Guildmistress Salina seized her arm with iron talons, and Rani swallowed her outraged cry of pain. The old woman's claw dragged Rani into the group of pilgrims, but the apprentice did not begin to recite the Pilgrims' Processional until she felt the master glazier's fingers pinch her arm to the bone.

"Hail, Defender of the Faith. Guide this Pilgrim in the steps of Jair, first Pilgrim and greatest. Guide this Pilgrim's feet and heart in the ways of the great God ..." Rani trailed off, not certain which of the gods was being prayed to at this point in the spectacle. Ile, the god of the moon. At Salina's silent urging, Rani continued to recite, mechanically inserting the god of the sun, the god of the stars, the god of the clouds. She trembled as she passed beneath the hooded gaze of one of Jair's Watchers.

When the apprentice could restrain her curiosity no longer, she whispered, "Did Larindolian send you? How did you escape the King's dungeons?"

Salina merely tightened her grip on Rani's arm, raising her voice to chant the Processional a little louder. Rani decided not to press the matter; she knew the answer to her first question, at least. Guildmistress Salina was there in costume; she must be the messenger that Larindolian had promised. Guildmistress Salina was doing the Brotherhood's bidding, and Rani had better follow suit if she wished to see Bardo.

Suddenly, Rani thought of the words Mair had just brought her from the Core. The doe ran faster than the buck, but did not get tangled by antlers. Salina had risen high in the Brotherhood's hierarchy—higher than how many men?— but she was still free to move about in the outside world, to drag Rani through the marketplace. The guildmistress might have lost her guildhall and all her apprentices and journeymen, but she had escaped Shanoranvilli's bloody vengeance. She had managed to free herself from the deadly thicket of Prince Tuvashanoran's untimely assassination.

The thought sent a chill through Rani, centering in the ache of her bandaged arm beneath her black robes. Mair's warning had to be about Salina. The guildmistress had been instrumental in all that had gone wrong—she had snared Rani in the Prince's murder, in the burning of her parents' home, even in the power struggle between Mair and Rabe. Salina might as well have held Rani's hand as the apprentice executed Dalarati. Remembering her flight from the cathedral compound the night she had embalmed Tuvashanoran, Rani recalled the rage in Salina's agate eyes, the blunt fury behind her snake-chased mask. Salina had been there for everything that had happened; she had caused it all to fall apart. And through it all, Salina remained free to roam the City.

Rani did not have a chance to act on her new certainty, for the pilgrims were finally finishing their listing of the thousand gods. Salina drew Rani through the streets with the other worshipers, dragging her from the marketplace and the sheltering arm of the martyred Tuvashanoran's statue. What should Rani do? She was bonded to Mair like a sister; the Touched girl had brought her a warning, taking a stand against Rabe, against one of her own, to deliver it. And yet, Larindolian had promised to send a messenger, to send Salina. Larindolian had promised to reunite Rani with her true sibling, with Bardo. Whom should Rani believe? Whom should she trust?

The streets cleared for the pilgrims as they made their way from the merchant's quarter toward the cathedral. Citizens lined the narrow way, tossing tokens toward the pilgrims. Rani caught a few of the tin coins, medallions stamped with the insignia of various gods, and her fingers scrabbled over boiled sweets that were molded in the shape of religious trinkets—birds for Fairn, little ladders for Roan. In past years, Rani had been the one who had thrown the riches; she had been the one who had looked on in envy at the pilgrims who made their way to the cathedral.

Now, Rani's enjoyment of the spectacle was diluted as she tried to decipher what the Brotherhood planned for her. Salina maintained a vise-like grasp on her shoulder, making her arm throb under its tight bandage. She longed to duck out of the parade, to return to the dark quiet of her room beneath the eaves in her parents' house, to wait for Bardo to climb upstairs after a long day working in the shop.

Bardo. That was why she was here. That was why she permitted Salina's bony hand to guide her into place among the pilgrims. At one point, Rani would have darted forward, exploiting an opening in the throng, jockeying for position toward the front of the crowd of pilgrims as she had on the day of Tuvashanoran's Presentation. Now, though, Salina restrained her, reining in her enthusiasm with the pursed lips of a child's dried-up old nurse. What good was a festival, if one did not show full passion for the Thousand Gods?

Rani did not have the opportunity to argue her theological point. Instead, she found herself at the front of the cathedral, looking up at the stone steps, at a corridor formed by the hooded Jair's Watchers. At the end of the slightly ominous path, a priest held a flaming torch in one hand and a ewer of water in the other.

Each pilgrim who climbed the gauntlet of Watchers bowed his head to receive a blessing at the portal. The priest, in turn, lowered his flaming brand toward every worshiper, moving the crackling fire in the intricate pattern of a five-pointed star. The religious symbol was reminiscent of Jair's journey from the casteless Touched, through the four castes. The priest then sprinkled a few drops of water from his ewer in the hands of each pilgrim, washing away their worldly cares that each might enter the cathedral receptive to the demands of First God Ait and all the Thousand Gods.

The priest did something else, though, something far more important. As each pilgrim stepped over the cathedral threshold, the priest greeted him formally: "Welcome to the house of the Thousand Gods. Welcome in the name of Gaid." "Welcome in the name of Set." "Welcome in the name of Lart."

One by one, each of the pilgrims was greeted on behalf of a particular god. Rani felt the excitement mounting as she climbed the steps. The Watchers channeled the pilgrims, keeping them orderly despite the rising thrill.

Salina had pulled Rani back into the crowd, bridling her enthusiasm, even when one kindly pilgrim recognized the eagerness in the apprentice's soul and held back a few other travelers so that she could spring up a step or two. Rani wanted to make sure that she would be permitted in the cathedral; she wanted to observe the ritual of Jair's feast day, as if it were a cleansing rite.

After all, the cathedral was where this entire adventure had begun. Perhaps if she could worm her way back inside the stone walls, she might light a candle to the benevolent gods, find a way back to the quiet life she had known. She would gladly forfeit her status as an apprentice, if she could return to the peaceful calm of a merchant's life, settle into her easy role as her parents' daughter, as Bardo's sister. In the fervor of her sudden religious passion, Rani managed to ignore the fact that she would never again act as her parents' daughter; she would never again see her mother or father in all her living days.

The priest continued to greet pilgrims. In the name of Lene, god of humility. In the name of Sorn. In the name of Dain.

Rani wriggled, knowing that the priest was reaching the final decade of the gods. She twisted beneath Salina's grip, launching angry daggers from her eyes. The guildmistress' face was set in concentration as if she listened to some distant counting. "Please!" Rani exclaimed, barely remembering not to name the guildmistress, and Salina finally released her shoulder, just as the priest intoned, "Welcome to the House of the Thousand Gods. Welcome in the name of Tarn."

Tarn. The god of death. Rani was too late—the thousandth god was named, and she was not among the counting. Rani turned to snarl at the guildmistress. "There! I hope you're happy! You kept me from the cathedral! You kept me from the windows! You—" Rani choked on all the accusations she wanted to hurl at the guildmistress, all the bitter complaints about her lost family and friends, the life she would have enjoyed as an apprentice and a journeyman and a master.

Salina ignored the outburst, thrusting a tight roll of parchment into Rani's hands before fading back beyond Jair's Watchers, into the crowd of other black-robed pilgrims. "There now!" exclaimed the priest, and Rani turned on him with a gasp of fury, unable to channel her rage solely at the disappearing woman who had kept her from her prize. "Calm down, little pilgrim. You must straighten your robes, now, and quiet your heart. You are the First Pilgrim of the new year."

The First Pilgrim. Of course Rani knew of the honor; she

certainly would have remembered it, if she had not been so busy trying to beat Salina's game. The First Pilgrim was honored among all Pilgrims, chosen to act out the greatest of Jair's accomplishments in the coming year. Whereas all other pilgrims came from their own caste and made their journey according to their station in life, only the First Pilgrim completed Jair's story. Only the First Pilgrim was brought into the castle, to sit beside the king as a beloved member of his family. For an entire year, the First Pilgrim became one of the royal household.

Rani suddenly understood the calculation behind Salina's cruel hands. The old woman had set a high goal for her, the most noble of goals in a City attuned to the worship of the Thousand Gods. Rani turned back to the guildmistress to offer up her thanks. Too late, though—Salina was nowhere to be seen; she had melted into the crowd of black-robed worshipers as neatly as if she had never existed. Like the doe in the Core's warning, the guildmistress had avoided entanglement in the current thicket of events.

Rani swallowed hard and turned back to the priest, affecting the humility she thought a pilgrim should express. "Please, sir. I fear that I am not the proper person for this great honor."

"You are the first of the new counting of the Thousand Gods. Step forward and claim your rights—and obligations—as First Pilgrim."

As a young girl, Rani had played with Varna in the street outside their families' shops, donning black rags and processing down the "nave" of the paved road. Once, Rani had even convinced Bardo to play the role of the High Priest, standing on the threshold of the Trader shop, greeting the First Pilgrim with all the gravity of the holiest day of the year.

Nevertheless, games were one thing, and reality a completely different beast. Rani balked at stepping over the threshold, hesitated at entering the cathedral and approaching the altar where Tuvashanoran had met his death. The priest at the door seemed pleased with her humility. "Very good,

First Pilgrim. You recognize the seriousness of the course you take. Where are your parents? They shall look on as you assume the honor of First Pilgrim."

Rani's voice trembled. "My parents have crossed the Heavenly Gates."

"What! How did you make the pilgrims' journey, alone and unattended?"

Rani thought quickly. "My father died when I was merely a babe, I never knew him. My mother started out on our pilgrimage at my side, but she fell ill far from the City. We were taken in by a hospice honoring the great god Zake and tended by the chirurgeons dedicated to his holy name. My mother was several weeks dying."

"And how did you come to the City?"

"My mother would not deny my father's dying wish. He wanted to see me on the cathedral steps. She entrusted me to the care of other pilgrims who passed the hospice."

"And their names?"

"Farna, sir. Farna and her husband Hardu."

"And where are they?"

"We were separated during the Procession, back in the marketplace. I think they are already in the cathedral— Farna is uncommonly short and wanted to be certain she could see the ceremony. I had to come this last way alone, but I had the Thousand Gods as my companions."

Rani's brave resignation affected the priest deeply. He made a holy sign, in gratitude to the pilgrims who had helped Rani along her troubled way. "You are a noble pilgrim, and an honor to all the worshipers gathered here today. Come now, let us not keep the Defender of the Faith waiting."

Defender of the Faith! For just an instant, Rani raised her head, hope written clearly on her face. Defender of the Faith—maybe there had been some terrible mistake! Maybe Tuvashanoran still lived, and all of the running about, all of the hiding and scraping and horrible deeds had been a frightening error.

As Rani stepped into the incense-shrouded cathedral, though, she immediately recognized her mistake. Of course

Tuvashanoran was dead. Shanoranvilli, King of Morenia, was still the Defender of the Faith, still bowed beneath the weight of the title he had hoped to pass on, before his young, brave son was cut down on the cathedral altar. King Shanoranvilli, who had ordered all of Rani's family murdered in his dungeons....

And now that old king stood on the dais, a look of annoyance beginning to creep across his craggy features as he fingered the J's of the chain of office looped around his neck. In fact, most of the people in the cathedral looked at Rani with open hostility. They had all hoped for the honor of being the First Pilgrim; they had all completed months of pilgrimage to be in this place at this time. Rani decided not to dwell on what they would say if they knew that she had not taken one step on the long Pilgrims' Road, had not even completed the Path of the Gods here in the City, the humblest journey a Pilgrim could take and still rightfully bear the title.

Rani felt dizzy as she approached King Shanoranvilli, anchored only by the pressure of the priest's hand on her shoulder, commanding her to kneel, ordering her to incline her head. A trumpet fanfare rang out through the stone building, echoing off the marble columns and ceilings with brassy pride. Rani gulped a deep breath, swallowing the scent of rose petals scattered upon the altar behind the king. Jair's Watchers ranged themselves behind her, down the cathedral aisle.

"And who approaches the altar of all the Thousand Gods on this morning of the Pilgrim Jair's feast day?" Shanoranvilli's voice rang out to the cathedral's high vaulting, bouncing back from each pane of glass in the shimmering windows. This was King Shanoranvilli who spoke, the self-same king who had ordered Rani hunted down like a deer, who had ordered her family tortured and killed. Standing before the monarch, Rani swayed, blinking away a crimson curtain, a film as bloody as the drops she had shed for the Brotherhood. Apparently unaware of her inner turmoil, the priest nudged Rani, and she forced herself to look into the king's face.

"It is I,—" she swallowed hard, remembering just in time that heralds had been crying the name of Ranita Glasswright in the streets for weeks. She could not divulge her guild name, dared not even trust her birthname, Rani. Desperate, she thought of the Touched leader she had just abandoned in the marketplace. "Marita," she improvised, still staking claim to a guild name. "Marita Pilgrim, most honored Defender of the Faith."

She barely made herself choke out his title, barely managed to squeeze the words past her tight throat. She was unprepared for the smile he gave her, for the royal blessing that had charmed all of Morenia—soldiers and nobles, guildsmen and merchants—for decades.

"Do you have your Cavalcade, Marita Pilgrim, showing that you have completed your pilgrimage of Jair?"

Rani clutched the parchment scroll that Salina had thrust into her hands. "I do, most honored Defender of the Faith."

"Then present that Cavalcade, that I may verify your willingness to be the First Pilgrim and your suitability for that most honored office."

The scroll trembled as she proffered it to King Shanoranvilli, trembled with fear and twisted anger. He raised the document in both hands, displaying it to the crowd, which rippled with appropriate respect.

"And so, Marita of ... Zarithia," Shanoranvilli read from the Cavalcade, and Rani forced herself to pay attention. She might never see the written words that marked her supposed passage, and they would likely prove important before this charade was done. "You began your pilgrimage in the town of Zarithia?"

"Yes, Defender." Rani's response satisfied the king.

"And you sanctified your journey to which god?"

"To Charn, the god of knives," Rani improvised. Coming from a land of armorers, such a response was likely to meet with approval. In fact, Shanoranvilli nodded, as if he had expected her words. He could not know that she thought of a knife as an instrument of revenge, a tool to extract the honor owed her family.

"And you traveled by way of Borania?"

"Yes, Defender."

"And there you dedicated your stay to which god?" Once again, the King looked at her directly, and she presumed that the record of her individual dedications was not inscribed on her Cavalcade.

Her suspicion was confirmed when he nodded approval at her hastily improvised "To Nome, the god of children."

Again, a logical choice, for one as young as she. The King read through her entire Cavalcade, quizzing her on each stop of her pilgrimage. She gained confidence as she answered, naming her patron, Lan, which invoked a laugh from the assembled worshipers, who must have imagined the little pilgrim stuffing her belly before her journey. She also named the god of animals (she had always wanted to spirit a pet into her parents' home), the god of music (the trumpet fanfare still resounded in her ears), the god of flowers (the blossoms strewn upon the altar filled her nose with a wonderful, heavy scent), and the god of ladders (Roan, her old favorite, who certainly had something to do with her presence here, in light of her ill-timed ascent of the scaffold outside the cathedral.)

Shanoranvilli accepted each offering, nodding and making a holy sign as she responded to his questions. However false her words rang in her own head, the Defender was prepared to hear them. The congregation was prepared as well, and individual pilgrims cried out at her offerings, embracing her dedications as their own. Jair's Watchers looked on with apparent approval as passion built in the congregation.

"And so, Marita," Shanoranvilli concluded, rolling up Rani's scroll with obvious satisfaction, "you stand before this congregation and dedicate your Pilgrimage and the coming year to which god?"

The question took Rani by surprise, but she scarcely hesitated before her soprano voice piped to the far reaches of the cathedral. She remembered the black ashes of her home and the lost chaos of dinner at the Trader table, before she had been spirited off to the glasswrights, before her life had collapsed. "To Fell, the god of families."

If she had expected King Shanoranvilli to show remorse at her choice, she was disappointed. She named Fell as a challenge, as a gauntlet thrown at the royal feet, but the Defender of the Faith did not appear to recognize the meaning behind her words. Even as Rani dredged up memories of her own happy, murdered family, though, she saw King Shanoranvilli wrestle with his own recollections.

The steel in the old man's spine sagged, and the gulleys around his mouth deepened. Rani read his sorrow as clearly as she knew her own. King Shanoranvilli had lost family as well; he had lost his treasured son. Rani's mind spun with her own memories of the noble Tuvashanoran, and she blinked hard.

When she opened her eyes, she saw the king as more than a willful sovereign, as more than a cruel beast who had ordered her family destroyed. Now, she could view him as a desperate father, a despairing member of a family who longed for something that could never, ever be. Shanoranvilli longed for his beloved son to return from a funeral pyre.

In that instant, Rani's heart went out to King Shanoranvilli. For the first time since she had knelt in Dalarati's blood, Rani felt a modicum of peace. She had been right to execute the soldier. Dalarati had grieved the king; *Dalarati* had driven King Shanoranvilli to exact revenge against Rani's own family. By killing Dalarati, Rani had redeemed her own family's execution.

Rani felt as if a veil had been lifted from her eyes. Swallowing hard, she realized that she had more in common with the king than she had ever dreamed. She felt that bond almost as a physical thing when the Defender began to turn her toward the altar, to continue with her investiture as First Pilgrim. Something made Shanoranvilli hold back, though, and when he looked down on her, a sad smile lit the depths of his eyes. "And, young pilgrim Marita, what guild do you represent here today?"

The king clearly intended the question to be an honor, a

break from the traditional service as he recognized Rani's unique status as an apprentice and a faithful penitent. Nevertheless, she was wholly unprepared for the query, and she could not think of a response.

"Your Majesty?" she whispered, stirring a flurry of amusement among the other pilgrims.

"What guild do you represent? Your name proclaims you a guildsman, and you are surely old enough to apprentice. What guild saw the desire of the Thousand Gods and freed you to walk the path from Zarithia to the City?"

Rani's throat closed over her response. The sunlight streaming through the stained glass windows was brilliant, distracting, and she could think only of the guild she had been sworn to. If she spoke that word, though, she would sign her death warrant—all present knew that glasswrights were forbidden throughout the kingdom, and their name was anathema in this most holy of places.

"Come, child," Shanoranvilli whispered to her, a gentle smile cracking his ancient lips. "You can't become shy now. Speak to the people and tell them your guild."

Rani hated naming the lie, hated spinning out a tale for this old man who had suffered so much, like her. Still, she could not make him look a fool in front of his people. She swallowed hard, and then proclaimed her supposed guild, throwing her words past Jair's Watchers to the farthest reaches of the cathedral: "I am a bard, Your Majesty. Or rather, a bard's apprentice."

"Then you will be able to spin out the tale of your journey properly, First Pilgrim! You'll be able to entertain generations with your stories of living in the palace for a year. But before you can join the House of Jair, you must offer up the last of your worldly concerns, Marita. What burdens do you carry into this house of the Thousand Gods?"

Rani's hand automatically scrambled in the pouch at her waist. Her fingers skipped over the circlet of cobalt glass that she had hoarded from her true guild. Given enough time, she might fashion a story of why a bard's apprentice carried a fragment of pure, color-fast glass. Now, however, she was not prepared to stand by such a lie. Her soul already burdened the scales of justice; the additional weight of keeping silent about the cobalt glass was negligible.

Digging deeper, she found an offering she thought would satisfy the Defender. When she extracted her doll from the pouch at her waist, she tried to move her body, to hide it from the crowd. The poppet was a child's toy, a silly plaything that had no place in the life of a girl who had survived alone in the streets for weeks. It was a laughable prop for the glasswright's apprentice who had slain one of the King's own guard in the service of the Brotherhood. A flush of embarrassment crept over her cheeks.

"What have you there?" exclaimed Shanoranvilli, and he appeared surprised for the first time in this panoply of religious devotion.

"A doll, Your Majesty." Rani's whisper was lost in the cavern of the cathedral.

"A what?" exclaimed the king, and she might have offered him moonlight and fairy dust for all the incredulity in his voice.

"A doll, Your Majesty." Rani improvised, "My mother gave it to me, before we began our journey."

The king nodded gravely as he took the offering and set it atop the altar, but a smile twitched at the corners of his mouth. The assembled pilgrims murmured in amusement at this turn of events. While they might resent such a young First Pilgrim, they could scarcely fail to recognize the sheer entertainment of this spectacle. "You must value it greatly, to have kept it throughout your pilgrimage."

"Yes, Your Majesty. I loved my mother."

"Well spoken, Marita. We should all love our mothers." And our sons, the king might have said, for the sorrowful lines grew even deeper in the gulleys of his face. "And have you any other offerings to set aside before you ascend the altar and take on the responsibilities of First Pilgrim in the Kingdom of Morenia?"

The disk of cobalt glass weighed down Rani's sack like

an entire coil of lead stripping, but she shook her head and answered loudly, "No, Your Majesty."

"Very well, First Pilgrim. Shed the cloak of your office and the burden of your Thousand Pointed Star and prostrate yourself before this altar and the eyes of the Thousand Gods." The king reached royal hands toward Rani's black cloak, and her fingers mechanically worked the intricately woven brooch. She could scarcely believe that she—*she*, a merchant's daughter—was letting the king wait on her as if he were her own valet. Ah, the tales she longed to tell Varna. Or Mair. Or Shar.

Rani complied with the king's command to kneel before him, and then to stretch out before the altar. She reclined on her back, all the while fixing the old man with steady, trusting eyes. The sun chose that moment to move from behind a bank of clouds, and a beam of brilliant blue light streamed through the highest window in the cathedral— blue light for the Defender. Rani's gaze was transfixed by the glasswrights' final handiwork, and she was frozen by the realization that she was lying in the very pool of light that had brought death to Prince Tuvashanoran.

For one instant, Rani thought she would cry out. Her face swivelled involuntarily to the window. She could picture Tuvashanoran's handsome face, infinitely warmer and kinder than when she had embalmed his lifeless limbs. She remembered the hushed expectation that had gripped the cathedral on that other day. There *should* be an arrow waiting for *her*. She had lied to get to the cathedral. She had cheated. She had stolen. She had murdered.

The harder Rani worked to forget the events that had brought her to the cathedral, the more she longed for her adventures to end. Her breath came in sharp gasps, and her hands clenched and unclenched, as if she suffered a seizure. She wanted nothing more than to wake in her attic cot, feel the sheets tucked tight around her chest as her mother sponged away a fever from her brow. She only wanted to hear Bardo's steady voice, instructing her on how to bargain for a load of knives or a brace of buckles.

"There, there, Marita." The voice was not the one she had prayed for, but it was filled with painstaking kindness. "Be easy, First Pilgrim." Shanoranvilli offered her his dry, withered hand. "The speech of the Thousand Gods is loud, and it moves the hearts of men. How much stronger are those words in a child's ears? Rise, First Pilgrim, and take your place in the House of Jair."

Rani clung to the king like a lifeline, clambering to her feet without releasing his papery flesh. King Shanoranvilli rested his withered hands on the crown of her head, and then he bent to kiss her once on each cheek. She was still breathing the royal fragrance of musk and bergamot when the Defender of the Faith settled her pilgrim's cloak once more upon her shoulders. "Be brave, little one," the king whispered, and then he turned her about to face the crowd.

The assembled pilgrims had fallen silent at Rani's fit, struck by a child's simple faith. Jair's Watchers looked on stolidly. Such devotion was certain to bring new worshipers streaming through the cathedral doors when gossip spread through the City. Shanoranvilli settled his sere hands on Rani's shoulders as she stepped out of the flowing cobalt light, and he proclaimed, "Behold the First Pilgrim!"

Well-trained acolytes flung open the cathedral doors, preparing the way for the royal recessional. Rani shook her head, trying to clear away the fog raised by her trembling limbs. Only when she had blinked owlishly in the white light pouring down the nave did she make out the shape of one pilgrim who had already moved to the doors, who already stood beyond Jair's Watchers, on the threshold between the cathedral and the City.

Rani's cry of greeting was swallowed by the assembled pilgrims' response to Shanoranvilli's proclamation. A thousand voices cried out, "Hail, First Pilgrim!"

No one heard Rani answer with two simple syllables. "Bardo!"

Silhouetted against the noon-time sun, broad-shouldered and still, her brother had appeared at last.

CHAPTER 12

As Rani moved down the cathedral aisle, pilgrims reached past Jair's Watchers to touch her black cape. She cringed from the first grasping hands, but she sensed Shanoranvilli's strong presence behind her, and the king settled his withered fingers on her shoulders. Rani raised her chin and continued through the crowd.

"Pray for me, in the name of Mune!" croaked one man, and then the cry was taken up by others, variations rippling through as people substituted their own special gods.

"Pray for me, in the name of Zake!"

"Pray for me, in the name of Doan!"

Rani nodded at each request, uncertain of the proper response. She touched all of the hands that scrambled toward her, watching as pilgrim after pilgrim fell to his knees, muttering prayers of thanksgiving that the First Pilgrim had taken notice of a mere sojourner on the road of the Thousand Gods.

All the time, Rani craned her neck, trying to make out Bardo in the brilliant frame of the doorway. His presence drew her like an eagle to a snake.

She almost screeched in disappointment when the procession reached the carved cathedral doors and he was not there. Anger rose from her belly like a scream, and she planted her feet on the portal, determined not to give up the chance to locate her brother. As she took her stand, there was a flash of movement outside the cathedral, and a dark, tanned hand reached forward, offering her assistance over the raised wooden doorframe.

"Most honored First Pilgrim, pray for me."

Rani knew the voice from her dreams. She remembered the tone from her games as a carefree child, from the time when she was merely a merchant's daughter, doing her part to bring in custom to her parents' shop. Unexpected tears flooded her eyes as she looked up into her brother's face.

"Bardo—" she whispered, and swallowed her remaining words in surprise. Her brother looked far older than he had the last time she had seen him, when he guided her through the streets to the ill-fated glasswrights' guild. Wrinkles fanned out from his eyes, as if he had spent long nights squinting into a candle flame. Deep gulleys carved the flesh around his lips. As sunlight streamed down on him, Rani glimpsed silver threads in his hair—glints that surely had not been there a few months before.

Bardo fell to his knees like any supplicant pilgrim. "Pray for me, First Pilgrim. In the name of the great god Roat, pray for me."

The request unsettled Rani. Her own brother should not kneel before her—he was *Bardo*! He was the one sibling she had left. How could she let him kneel like one of the common Touched? She reached out a childish hand, thinking to help him to his feet.

Before she could act, Shanoranvilli interposed himself between Rani and Bardo. The king moved as if he thought that Bardo was a threat, as if he were protecting Rani from the unwelcome attentions of this persistent Pilgrim. Under any other circumstance, Rani would have been awed that the king acted to preserve her well-being, but now, she almost howled in rage.

Almost, but not quite. Before Rani could slip around the king, she heard Bardo's voice, muffled by Shanoranvilli's rich robes. "Pray for me tonight, First Pilgrim. Remember, in the name of Roat, god of justice, pray for me!"

"I will!" Rani squeaked, but before she could imagine

their reunion before Roat's altar, she was swirled down the cathedral steps, rushed along into the crowd and surrounded by the royal household guard.

The rest of the day blurred by. Rani was ushered into the royal family's private apartments. She was given a glass of watered wine, and a silver platter of buttered bread, sweet with glistening honey. She was told that she would meet the royal princes shortly. She was taken to the royal nursery.

The nursery would be Rani's home for the coming year. The First Pilgrim was welcomed into the royal family as if she had been born to it, and King Shanoranvilli seemed only mildly bemused by the tender age of his newest family member. Of course, Rani now knew that she would not be staying out her term in the Palace. Bardo was going to take her away. He would come to her as she prayed to Roat, spirit her away to wherever he now lived in the City.

That night, she would be back with her brother, back in the comfort of family. For just an instant, she remembered the anger that had blazed in Bardo's face when she had discovered his snake tattoo, the pure rage that she had awakened all unknowing. She consciously set aside that dark recollection, though. Bardo was her brother. Whatever secrets he had protected in the past no longer mattered. Rani had sworn her faith to the Brotherhood; she had bled before the snakes so that Bardo would come to her. He could no longer be angry that she had learned of his secret life.

Repeating her reassurances over and over, Rani squelched the tremor of sorrow as she realized just how limited Bardo's comfort had become, how brutally their family had been culled. She took another moment to thrust away her lingering anger at the king who had ordered their family killed. Their deaths were not Shanoranvilli's fault, she remonstrated with herself. That burden fell on Dalarati. That burden fell on the man who had slain Tuvashanoran, the man she had killed.

Tonight she would see Bardo and they would mourn their lost siblings, their lost parents. For now, Rani explored the royal nursery as soon as the king left her to her own devices. Only as she completed her review of the room did she realize that she was not alone. One of the princes was in the nursery. Halaravilli, Crown Prince of all Morenia, last surviving heir of King Shanoranvilli's first marriage, was playing with tin soldiers in the corner of the vast chamber.

Rani recognized him immediately. She had seen royal processions all her life, and she had recently watched horror spread across his face when his brother was cut down before his eyes on the cathedral dais. Halaravilli was two years older than Rani—old enough that his nurses had been replaced by private tutors. Still, the prince was expected to take his meals with his younger half-brother and his litter of half-sisters. And, apparently, he was permitted to play with his childhood playthings in a quiet window embrasure.

Tin soldiers, Rani thought. The Crown Prince of Morenia, now that Tuvashanoran was slain, and the boy was marching knights and footmen across a wooden board like a little child. She almost sniffed, remembering the stories about Halaravilli's simple mind. In fact, most people ignored Halaravilli's noble name entirely, referring to him only as "that poor motherless child."

Rani knew, as all the people of the City did, that Halaravilli had been the death of his mother. She had succumbed to childbed fever before the prince was one week old. The birth had been difficult for both mother and son. Halaravilli was widely rumored to be slow, and more than a little odd. According to loudly whispered tales, he had not spoken until his fifth birthday. Everyone in the City knew that the prince had never crawled—he went directly from sitting to staggering about the nursery on toddling legs, despite his nurses' best efforts to force him to his knees, to make him progress like a normal child.

The poor boy had never been meant for the throne—there had always been Tuvashanoran for that honor. Tuvashanoran, and a trio of other brothers who had all met with disaster. One prince had suffered a tragic riding accident, falling beneath his horse's hooves on his first ride beyond the City walls. One prince had fallen prey to the venom of a ruby mamba, a rare snake that had somehow slithered its way onto the training ground, dying in the dust of the Palace courtyard after delivering one fateful bite. One prince had taken ill of a fever on a bitter winter night, raving for a fortnight before surrendering to the sickness.

So, Halaravilli had never been meant for the crown. The prince was a slender reed to serve as a last defense for the family line, no matter how admirable his eldest brother, Prince Tuvashanoran, had been. King Shanoranvilli had recognized his dynastic obligations; after Halaravilli killed his mother with childbed fever, the king had wasted no time taking a second wife.

Queen Felicianda had come from lands far to the north, forging a powerful bond between her father's distant kingdom and the well-governed Morenia. She had served well as queen, breeding a passel of children who were nearly twenty years younger than their oldest sibling, than Tuvashanoran who had borne all the hopes of the kingdom. Queen Felicianda had dutifully presented the king with five surviving children—a son and four healthy daughters.

Now, as Rani looked at Prince Halaravilli in the nursery, the herd of the king's younger children came trampling into the room. Prince Bashanorandi—the only son of the king's second union—immediately planted himself in front of Rani. He was thirteen years old—the same age as Rani herself—and he wasted no time with polite greetings. "You don't belong here!"

"Your Highness!" exclaimed a young nurse, scarcely old enough to have a babe of her own, much less to tend this willful youth.

"I'm only speaking the truth," Bashanorandi sneered. "She's not royal, and she doesn't know how we live."

"I know how to treat a guest in my house!" Rani answered hotly, and then added a reluctant, "Your Highness."

The princesses tittered behind their hands, obviously delighted to see how their hot-tempered brother would react to this newest challenge. Bashanorandi lost no time in sighing exasperatedly, then he turned to his half-brother. "Hal, what are you doing? How could you let her come into our nursery?" Halaravilli ignored his brother, reaching instead for one of his toy soldiers and moving it into a precise position. "Hal!" exclaimed Bashanorandi. When the younger boy got no response, he swiped at the game board, scattering pieces across the room. "Don't ignore me when I'm speaking to you!"

Halaravilli looked up quizzically. "Speaking to me? Speaking to me?" The prince descanted his words in a chant. "Only a Touched would be named Hal. Only a Touched or a god. Speaking to me, speaking to me, a Touched or a god."

Bashanorandi flushed crimson and spluttered, grabbing at the inlaid game board his brother had used. His fingers slipped about for a grip, and he clearly intended to shatter the thing over his knee. "Splinters for the prince, splinters for the prince," the older boy remonstrated. "Play with the board, and you'll get splinters, o prince."

Rani could not restrain a laugh at Bashanorandi's frustrated grimace, and the youth turned his wrath on her. "You! What's your name?"

"Marita Pilgrim," she answered promptly, dropping into a pretty curtsey.

Bashanorandi started to sneer a response, but Halaravilli pinned her with a suddenly sharp look. "Welcome, Marita. You're an apprentice, then?"

"Yes," Rani nodded, sailing into her new identity. "With the bards."

"Ah, then," Halaravilli looked pleased. "A bard to tell us stories, a bard to tell us tales. You'll tell us stories of the kings, stories of the princes. A bard to tell us truths."

Rani squirmed uncomfortably. "I'm only a very new apprentice, Your Highness."

"Call me Hal, call me Hal." Rani glanced up in surprise, unable to keep her gaze from wandering to the younger prince Bashanorandi, who looked as if he would gladly strangle his brother. "I name myself, I don't let others name me. Others name me, others name me. He thinks that I am Touched, I am Touched, I am Touched. I name myself Hal."

The prince smiled conspiratorially, and Rani caught the ghost of Tuvashanoran along his jaw.

"Very well ... Hal. In any case, I am only a new apprentice, but I'll do my best to please you." Bashanorandi snorted his disgust and stalked off to the far side of the nursery, dragging the young princesses in his wake.

Hal shook his head as his half-brother settled by the hearth and began to tell his sisters a loud story about his exploits in the royal stables that morning. "I'm sorry for Bashi, sorry for Bashi. He wants to be king, wants to be king. Don't think less of him."

"Bashi?" Rani almost guffawed at the merchant's name for the spoiled prince.

"Don't let him hear you use that name. He'll knock you down, knock you down. He's knocked me down."

"But that's—"

"That's normal, normal, normal. We're brothers." Hal shrugged easily, although a shadow flirted with his brow. "Tell me about brothers, brothers and sisters, sisters and brothers. Do you have any, Marita Pilgrim? Brothers and sisters in...." He trailed off, as if unable to remember the next line of the song he was composing.

"Zarithia," Rani supplied helpfully.

"Ah, my soldiers come from Zarithia, my men are from your city!"

"I thought as much." Rani racked her brains, desperate to steer the conversation away from her supposed home. Despite Prince Hal's disconcerting speech, he might well have some concrete knowledge of Zarithia—knowledge more extensive than her own cobbled-together tales. "Um... please don't think me forward, Your Highness, but should you be playing with tin soldiers at your age?"

"I told you, call me Hal, call me Hal. And I'm not 'playing with tin soldiers', not playing at all, at all. I am winning the Battle of Morenia, winning the Battle, and using half the men my great-grandfather used. Half the men, half the men."

"Half the men!" Rani exclaimed, unaware that she was parroting the prince.

"Yes. Last week, I worked it out with three-quarters of the knights, but I still needed all of the footmen, all the footmen, all the poor footmen."

"What did you do?"

Hal looked at her appraisingly for a moment, as if she might be teasing him, or as if she might steal his secrets. "Aye," he said after a long glance. "I suppose you might be interested. It makes a good tale, doesn't it—and any bard should add to her store of tales, right?"

"Of course," Rani agreed, so pleased that he seemed inclined to forget about Zarithia that she did not notice the end of his sing-song speech.

Her conversation with Hal lasted for the better part of the afternoon. The prince told her about the original plan for the ancient battle, moving his tin soldiers into place. Then he showed her the innovations he had introduced. Twice, Bashi tried to interrupt, but both times he was driven away by Hal's chanted comments, by dancing words that concealed angry barbs. The princesses floated in and out of the discussion, and Hal took time to answer their flowery questions, but his attention remained fixed on Rani.

"And so," Rani said at last, as he showed her his final configuration for the battle, "your goal is to get your horsemen on that ridge before the foot soldiers can be cut off."

"Precisely! The bard reads the signs, reads the signs." Hal grinned, clearly excited that someone shared his interests.

"Well, what if you tried...." Rani chewed her lip, trying to envision the necessary pattern. This game of the battlefield was really nothing more than the work she had done back in her father's stall a lifetime ago, when she had set forth trinkets of tin and pewter and silver, arranging them to best suit the needs of potential buyers.

Before she could suit action to thought, though, the door to the nursery flew back on its hinges. All of the children and their attendant nurses sprang to attention. For just an instant, Rani had a flash of premonition, a hint of cold danger flowing into the room.

A man swept over the threshold, surrounded by an icy azure robe, paradoxically sharpened by its glistening ermine lining. The rich garment set off the man's fox-red hair and his long, twisted mustache. Rani wasted little time studying his raiment; her glance was immediately drawn to his frozen gaze. Larindolian stared down at her, his face as impassive as if he had never seen her before.

"Your Highness," the courtier made a stiff little bow toward Hal, then turned to the opposite side of the room, where Bashi had regrouped with the princesses. The nobleman spared a tight smile for the younger prince, and Rani thought it was the sort of look a fox might give a chicken. "My lord Bashanorandi. My ladies."

The princesses squealed their greeting, but Hal's voice was deadly serious as he inclined his head. "My lord chamberlain, lord of the chamber, chamberlain."

Larindolian permitted himself another dangerous smile. "So serious, Your Highness?"

Hal did not bend. "What duty brings you to the royal nursery, the nursery, Lord Larindolian, what duty to us?"

A flicker of annoyance pulsed along the noble's jaw, but his voice remained smooth as silk. "May I not check on my wards' safety? For you children are, of course, part of my responsibility here in the Palace." Afterward, Rani could not have explained how that simple declarative sentence sounded like a threat. Her arm set to throbbing beneath her tunic, and she imagined that her bandage was soaked through with blood from her wound. "But we should not forget our manners, Your Highness. I have not made the acquaintance of your guest."

Hal flushed at being caught in his rudeness, and he turned to Rani with a furious expression on his face, as if she were responsible for Larindolian's chiding tone. Rani curtseyed before the lord, ignoring her throbbing arm, telling herself to act as if she had never seen the man's narrow face, never seen the feral glint in his eyes. Larindolian performed his own role, nodding shrewdly as Rani regained her feet. "Welcome to the Palace, First Pilgrim. Please let us know if there is anything we can do to make your stay more ... rewarding. You will, of course, need frequent access to the cathedral, beginning tonight, I suspect. Such is the lot of the First Pilgrim."

Ah! So that was the plan! That was how Rani was supposed to reach Roat, the god of justice. "Thank you, Your Grace." Rani wished that she could leave now, run to Roat's altar, and Bardo.

"My pleasure, Marita Pilgrim." Larindolian smiled once more, a tight exposure of his eye-teeth, and then he left the nursery.

Hal stared after him with open hatred, and Rani caught the prince muttering, "Damned nobleman," and something that sounded like "a curse on his house."

Before she could comment, the nurses sprang into action, ushering the children to their suppers, and then their evening prayers. Rani took her cues from Hal and Bashi, hanging back as the princesses were readied for bed. Each of the boys had a private sleeping chamber, little more than a closet off of the main nursery. The nurses fluttered about their charges like a flock of fat pigeons, but Rani decided the women were a mean substitute for parents.

That verdict was only qualified slightly when the queen made a quick visit to the nursery at the end of the day: the nurses were a mean substitute for *Rani's* parents.

Queen Felicianda sailed into the nursery like a high-prowed ship, her exotic looks heightened by the chamber's dim candlelight. She settled a cool hand on the brow of each princess before floating to the two princes, where they huddled in the doorways to their separate chambers.

"Halaravilli," she intoned to her husband's son, to the Crown Prince with whom she shared no blood.

"My lady." The prince looked solemn in the shadows, strained and stiff.

"And Bashanorandi." A warm smile flooded the queen's

features, and her voice melted at last as she settled her fingers on her son's shoulder. "You've had a good day, my boy?"

"Fine," Bashi agreed, flashing a victorious smile toward his half brother. "Once things settled down with the First Pilgrim."

"The—" A small frown puckered the queen's brow, and then she seemed to notice Rani for the first time. "Ah, Marita Pilgrim. I bid you welcome." Rani sank into the expected deep curtsey and tried to remind herself not to think ill of the queen, of the cold mother who could spare a smile for only one of her children.

Rani even found the courage to exchange a few pleasantries with her liege lady before Queen Felicianda withdrew, rationing out one last lilting smile for Prince Bashanorandi. By the time Rani contrived to slip out of the nursery, she was exhausted by the hustle and bustle, grateful to escape the press of attention and observation. Perhaps she had been as smothered in her own family, in the narrow streets and rough surroundings of the Merchants Quarter, but she knew she had never felt so alone, surrounded by brothers and sisters who loved her.

Brothers and sisters... Like Bardo, who even now waited for her in the Cathedral. Trying to fight down her excitement, Rani gathered her cloak and her Thousand-Pointed Star close about her narrow shoulders, making sure that the holy symbol flashed importantly when the nurses attempted to guide her to her bed. When she got to the Palace's massive iron gate, she was challenged by the guard, but she gave her assumed name and the soldier stepped aside, making a holy sign and offering an avuncular warning to be cautious in the City streets. "In fact, young pilgrim, would you like an escort to the cathedral? I can call one of the household guard to join you."

"Thank you, kind sir." Rani chafed at the intrusion. "It's early enough, and I'll be on the major streets.

"But, little one, this is not a village, or even the small town of Zarithia. You are in the City now—it can be dangerous, even on a major street."

"I know how—" Rani started to leak some of her exasperation into her words, but then a shadow glided forward from the darkness in the Palace courtyard.

"Is there a problem here?" Rani's skin crawled as she recognized Larindolian's voice.

"No, Lord Chamberlain." The guard's response was tinged with a fearful respect. "I merely suggested that the lass might want an escort to the cathedral. I never intended to interfere with her worship."

"And a fine suggestion it was, man." Larindolian raised a gauntleted hand, and another dark shape emerged from the clinging night. "You must indulge us old men, Marita Pilgrim. We do not have your youthful confidence in the protection of the Thousand Gods. Marcanado here will see you to the cathedral and back. He's a fine man, in the brotherhood of soldiers."

Rani heard the hint behind the words, and she accepted the soldier's company without further protest. After all, it was not as if she would need to see Marcanado after this night; she was never coming back to the Palace. As the kindly gatekeeper watched them go, though, she could not resist hissing to her escort, "I *could* have gone alone."

The soldier blinked impassively. "My lord Larindolian thought you deserved the honor of an escort. Who am I to argue?"

Those were the last words from the stolid guard. Rani was not a fool, she knew he must be a member of the Brotherhood, or he would not have been trusted with accompanying her to her secret meeting. Nevertheless, she felt no kinship toward the silent man, and she resented his presence, resented his intrusion upon her reunion with Bardo.

She did not have long to sulk, however. Within a few short minutes, they were on the porch of the massive cathedral. Marcanado pushed open the door, impervious to the eerie creak of metal hinges, and then he took up a guardsman's position on the threshold. Rani waited for just a minute, willing her eyes to adjust to the shadowy darkness inside the building, and then she stepped over the portal.

At first, she was relieved to see that the cathedral was not in total darkness; a few of the largest tapers still burned at the altars set against the stone walls. As Rani progressed down the nave, though, she wondered if it would not be better to move through the cathedral in absolute darkness—the flickering shadows spawned ghosts in her mind.

She needed to walk the entire perimeter of the cathedral, seeking out the altar dedicated to Roat. She knew it would not be one of the large, exposed platforms beneath the glasswrights' handiwork; Bardo would choose a more secluded corner. Nevertheless, it took her a second trip around the cathedral before she spotted the god of justice's altar, really little more than a carved prie-dieu. She might have missed it the second time, if there were not a newly lighted candle burning in the center of the rough-carved platform.

Adding her own votive to the freshly burning one, Rani knelt and folded her hands on the low railing. Her heart pounded as she tried to form words in her mind, tried to structure a prayer to the god who was going to reunite her with her brother, with the last remaining member of her family. The words were hard in coming, though; her devotion was diluted by her memories of Bardo. For weeks now, Rani had sought him, desperate to be reunited with her own flesh and blood, with the older brother who had always smoothed over the rough patches of her childhood.

Bardo, though, was more than her brother. As much as Rani hoped and prayed that he would make everything right, she could not forget that Bardo belonged to the Brotherhood. Even as Rani framed her prayers to Roat, her fingers crept to the black bandage that bound together Larindolian's wound. Years ago, Bardo had slapped her for looking at his tattoo. What would he do now, now that she had sworn fealty to the Brotherhood itself? What would Bardo do, now that she had killed Dalarati? Forcing back her fears, Rani retreated to the familiar prayers of childhood, the memorized recitations that had brought peace in the past.

"Great god Roat, look upon me with favor. Bless me,

great god Roat." The words rang hollow, but she repeated them again and again, finding solace in the blunt familiarity of the simple sequence.

"Ah, Rani, ever my most devout sister." She started, and whirled around to face the cathedral's yawning darkness. The candles at her back lent a flickering eeriness to the vast room, and she imagined swooping night-demons waiting just beyond her vision. Before she could dwell on such horrors, though, there was a shift of cloth, and her brother stepped into the wavering pool of light.

"Bardo!" Rani exclaimed, launching herself across the short distance. His arms were strong and solid. "Bardo! I've been trying to find you for so long!"

"Ah, Rani," he ruffled her hair and led her to one of the low benches that crouched near the altar. "We don't have much time. People will become suspicious if you're away from the Palace for too long."

"What!" His words amazed her. If he had spoken in anger, she would have understood. She was braced for the explosive rage he had harnessed in the past, for matters concerning the Brotherhood. This was different, though. Bardo sounded solicitous, but firm. She protested: "Why am I going back to the Palace? Why can't I come with you?"

"With me!" The surprise in his voice was real, outweighing any anger that Rani feared to hear. "You can't come with me!"

"Why not? You're my brother, the only family I have left." She tried to make her words sound reasonable, even as a sob threatened to close her throat.

"But that's precisely the reason that you can't come with me now." Bardo spoke in the treasured tones she remembered. "You are too valuable to me, to risk in the places I must go. You must stay in the Palace, in the cathedral, in places where you'll be safe."

"But I don't want to be safe! I want to be with you!" She buried her face in his tunic, clasping her fingers about his arm.

He let her sob for a few minutes, and then she became

aware of his fingers smoothing her hair, of his voice crooning her name, over and over. "Rani... Rani...." The two syllables strung together like poetry, and she realized how long it had been since anyone had called her by her true name—not her assumed identity as a Touched girl, not her laughable guise as an apprentice.... She heard her name, spoken by one who loved her, and she knew that she would do as her brother bid. She snuffled loudly and dragged a hand across her nose before she pulled away from Bardo's embrace.

"Where are you going that's so dangerous?"

"I'll be here in the City the entire time. I have enemies, though—people who have more power than they should, who resent the things I must do, the things that will save the City and the kingdom."

"Things for the Brotherhood." It wasn't a question.

"Things for the Brotherhood." Bardo nodded. He did not flinch when Rani reached for the laces on his tunic, untying them so that she could pull the garment to one side, so that she could see the snakes chasing each other across his well-muscled bicep. As she raised a finger to a pair of tattooed crimson eyes, she inhaled the memory of Bardo beating her for being far less familiar. Now, he merely repeated, "The Brotherhood."

"I want to help you."

Bardo laughed and pushed away her fingers, lacing up his tunic with an easy grace. "You're too young to help."

"I'm not too young! I've already done things! Was I too young when I called Tuvashanoran? Was I too young when you made me kill Dalarati?"

Bardo's face tightened, as if he heard someone calling his name from a distance. "We never planned for you to do those things, Rani. We never wanted you involved."

"But that's the thing. Bardo, I *am* involved! K-killing Dalarati was the hardest thing I've ever done. But when I found out that he was trying to murder you, when Larindolian said that he would harm the Brotherhood, I knew I had no choice!"

"Shhhh!" Rani's voice had climbed to a shrill plea, and

Bardo's gaze darted down the dark cathedral aisle. "Rani, there are some things you must never speak aloud."

"I can keep secrets, Bardo."

He shook his head and reached out a loose fist to chuck her chin. "This isn't just some game you play with Varna."

She jerked away, muttering to the shadows, "I don't play with Varna anymore—she called the guard on me. Bardo, I can keep a secret. I haven't told anyone that you killed Rabe's mother."

Bardo's fingers tightened on her shoulder, forcing her around to face him. Rani caught a pained yelp against the back of her teeth. "What did you say?" She tried to pull free from his vise-like fingers, but he did not let her move. "What did you accuse me of?"

"I said, I've never told anyone that you killed Rabe's mother." She lifted her chin defiantly.

"Who is Rabe?"

"He's a Touched boy; I've run with his troop. I know all about it, Bardo—I know that his mother stole from me when I was minding the store, and I know that you tracked her down to get back the pewter buckles. I remember the slate you bought for me."

"The slate—"

"And the flowers and gifts for the others. I didn't think to ask about them then, because I was only a child, but now.... I don't know why you couldn't go to the Council and seek justice there, but I haven't told anyone what I know.... Bardo, please, you're hurting me!"

His fingers had shifted to the bandage at the top of her arm, closing about her healing wound with a ferocity that brought fresh tears to her eyes. Now, he smoothed the cloth over her arm, turning her about to face him. When he looked at her, his eyes burned into her own, and she felt dizzy at the vehement force he poured into his words.

"Listen to me, Rani. This is very important." She managed a trembling nod. "What I've done, what you've heard about me.... All of this is for a reason. All of this was predestined by Jair and the Thousand Gods."

"But why—"

"Why would the Gods force us to live in castes? Why would the Gods give all their riches to a few, and leave most of their children to scrimp and save, hoping forever to earn enough silver to sleep by a peat fire, for enough copper to buy a pot of porridge? Why should we be the ones to slave away when others have it so easy?"

Rani had never seen the fanatical light that flared behind Bardo's eyes. Maybe it was only a trick of the candles, but her brother's gaze flickered green. She shrunk away from his touch, pressing her spine against the back of the pew.

"Rani, our father worked his entire life to scrape together a few pennies. He hoarded his wealth with a vengeance, parceling out coins and responsibility like a miser. You're too young to understand this, but his life was miserable; he struggled along from day to day." Bardo gripped her hands and his fingers shook with the force of his belief. "The castes force each of us into submission, force each of us to give away all our possible fates at birth. Who knows what our father could have become if he had not been bound by his caste, by the Council?"

"But *I* changed castes! I became an apprentice!"

"Aye, but at what cost? Our father, our mother, all our brothers and sisters.... We poured all our riches into one pot to get you the faintest toehold on the guildsman's ladder." Bardo spoke like a priest, like a man consumed by his own fiery words. "Rani, don't you understand? The Brotherhood will change the rules. The Brotherhood will bring Justice to all the City, to all of Morenia, to all the world of the Thousand Gods."

"What are you going to do?" Rani's voice sounded fragile as a moth's wing against her brother's flaming passion.

"Ah, Rani. I would tell you if I could." Bardo sighed, and a little of the magic drained from him. "I would share my knowledge with you. But that would only place you in danger, set your life in the balance. I cannot risk the only family that remains to me, the only family to escape the tyranny of our caste. Do you trust me, Ranikaleka?"

Rani's throat closed at the tender nickname, at the playful name he had given her ages ago when her life was simple, in their father's home. She nodded, not able to speak.

"Very good. You must return to the Palace. Go back and live in the nursery. I *can* tell you this. The Brotherhood's enemies are stirring. They call themselves the Fellowship of Jair, but there's nothing about them that Jair would approve. They've been awakened by the unrest in our own ranks. The Fellowship fears us; they fear the changes we will bring. And they realize they can harm us by upsetting the balance, by swaying the power."

"But who are they, Bardo?"

"You have met one of them, and I'm amazed you've lasted so long without her betraying you."

Rani felt his words shift into place inside her skull. Who had been manipulating her life? Who had controlled her when she served her time in the marketplace, when Borin would have freed her without requiring further obligation, when she approached the sanctuary of the cathedral close? Indeed, who had manipulated her that very day, toying with her on the edge of the marketplace for so long that she nearly missed the honor of becoming First Pilgrim. "Mair." She spat the single syllable as if it burned her tongue.

"Aye. I'm sorry, Rani. I know that you believed her, believed the Fellowship's lies. But she is one of their leaders, one of their lieutenants. And this is nothing less than war."

Rani wanted to protest, wanted to explain that Bardo was mistaken, that Mair was her friend. Even as she thought the words, though, she knew she would not say them. Mair may have seemed her friend, but Bardo was her *brother*.

Besides, how could Mair be trusted? The girl was Touched, born to a life of crafty manipulation. Sure, she might have seemed like Rani's friend at times, but to what end? Mair's "friendship" always had a cost—a sweet cake, a copper, Rani's precious silver mirror.

Rani's arm throbbed beneath her bandage. Mair was part of the Fellowship, one of the enemy. It was all so confusing; nothing was ever what it seemed. The Brotherhood, the

Fellowship.... Who was Rani to understand such complicated things? She only knew one truth. Her entire family was gone, all but Bardo, who had always been her favorite, most-trusted brother. Even when Bardo had been his most threatening, even that terrible day when she had seen his snake tattoo, he had stayed his wrath. He had mastered his rage because he loved her. Bardo was her *brother*.

Now, Bardo sighed, and the sorrow of a lifetime settled over him like a mantle. "We hear rumors that someone in the Palace is planning a coup. Do you understand me, Rani? Someone is going to kill King Shanoranvilli."

"No!" She whispered involuntarily, thinking of the frail old man, of the papery hands that had settled on her shoulders—was it only that morning? It seemed so long ago.

Bardo's pained voice echoed her own thoughts. "Yes, I'm afraid. Our sources have tracked the threat to within the Palace walls, and we strongly believe it is one of the princes. The Fellowship has staked a claim to one of Shanoranvilli's living sons. One of the royal princes plots to kill his father."

"Bardo, you can't let the king come to harm!"

"We are doing all we can. We are searching for facts, for hard, cold knowledge. And that is where you can help us. Rani, we need eyes and ears, we need someone who can tell us what happens inside the nursery. Can you do that for us?"

"That and more, Bardo," Rani vowed. "The old king, it would break him to know that one of his sons conspires against him. He is not well, Bardo—he took Prince Tuvashanoran's death very hard."

"Aye, even Dalarati could not have known the force of that blow. We can only guess at the greater evil that soldier spawned before he was stopped, the secrets that he leaked to the Fellowship." Even as Rani remembered kneeling in Dalarati's blood, she felt proud of the action she had taken. Certainly the Brotherhood had called on her to do terrible things, but these were terrible times. Death lurked in every shadow. People needed to find courage in the bottoms of their hearts, and if that courage was born of fear, of respect for the Brotherhood....

"That's right," Bardo nodded, as if he had followed her thoughts. "You must be brave now. You must stay near the king. You are the First Pilgrim, Rani. You can ease an old man's sorrow and work to save him from greater harm. Will you do that, Rani Trader?"

"I will." She spoke the two words like the most solemn vow she had taken in her life.

"The Brotherhood wants you, Rani, we need you. Keep your eyes and ears open, and work your way into the royal family. There will come a time when we call on you to act, and I won't lie and tell you the action will be easy. Everything that has gone before, Rani, everything that you have done for us, is training for what we might ask of you."

Rani flashed again on a vision of Dalarati dying, but this time she was not dazed by any hint of self-hatred or doubt. Before she could speak, her brother was digging in a pouch at his waist, extracting something that he enclosed in his palm.

"You cannot come with me, Rani dearest, and I dare not give you the tattoo that would make you a full member of the Brotherhood. Accept this symbol, though, and know that we are working for you to join us, for all the City to join us in freedom and justice." His hand opened, and she saw a twist of metal, a twining of copper with eight flat glints of glass, sparking to each other across a gap of air. Bardo pushed up the sleeve of her tunic, as high above her elbow as he could reach, and then he pressed the circlet about her upper arm. For just an instant, the metal pulled at her flesh, hinting at the bruise she would have in the morning. Then, it came to rest, deadly cold against her bicep.

"This is a sign that you are bound to us," Bardo intoned. "You must not let the others see it. If you were truly a pilgrim, you would have renounced it at the altar. Now, let's get you back to the Palace."

The metal was already warming to her heartbeat, and she flicked her arm as if it were an injured wing, watching the candlelight play off the glinting snakes' eyes. "Bardo—don't leave me!"

"I'm not leaving you, Rani. By this token, I am joining you. Come to pray at night, as often as you can. I'll be here when I'm able."

She threw her arms about his waist, burying her face in the folds of his cloak. "Please! I'll do anything you ask!"

"This is all I ask, Rani Trader. Be brave, little sister. I'll see you again, and soon."

He gently pried her fingers from his cloak, and then he flowed down the aisle, disappearing into the midnight darkness as if he had never been in the cathedral. Rani, rising to run after him, stumbled against the corner of Roat's altar. The sweep of her arm as she flailed for balance was enough to make the two votive candles flicker. Before she could move away from the god of justice's altar, the flames drowned in their own wax, leaving Rani stranded and alone in the dark cathedral of the Thousand Gods.

CHAPTER 13

"Leave me alone, Marcanado! I can walk down the hallway by myself!" Rani sighed in disgust as the placid soldier followed her down the palace corridors that led to the royal apartments. She was irritated that he was shadowing her, irritated that he would not respond to her blatant rudeness, irritated that Bardo had failed to show up at the cathedral. Again.

It had been nearly a week since she had last seen her brother. In the first month that she spent in the palace, Bardo had met her at Roat's altar regularly, but now it seemed as if Rani had once again been abandoned. She edged her frustration into a high, piping voice. "I *said*, leave me alone!"

The soldier froze as she rounded on him, staring through unblinking eyes, as if she were a strange specimen of moss from the palace garden. His impassivity enraged her further, and she reached out with stiff arms, pushing against his breast-plate. "If you don't stop following me, I'll scream!"

Marcanado clenched his fists at his side, but he showed no other sign of hearing Rani's threat. Enraged, lonely, frightened, Rani threw back her head and howled, a furious keening that begged for release from the role she was playing.

While Marcanado did not give her the satisfaction of a response, there was an immediate flurry of activity up and down the hallway. Iron-clad boots clattered against flagstones as guards rushed to defend the royal family from an unknown threat. A captain shouted orders around the bend of the hallway, and then Rani was surrounded by a bristling thicket of swords, all pointing toward her black Pilgrim robes, all edging downward uneasily as the soldiers recognized the royal family's holy guest.

"What in the name of First God Ait!" The bellow came from behind a heavy oaken door, and then the soldiers were bowing, shifting uncomfortably in their armor as Larindolian crashed the door back on its hinges. "What in the name of all the Thousand Gods is happening out here?" The nobleman tugged at his flashing tunic of silver cloth, turning icy eyes on the captain of the guard. "You, man. What are you doing? Don't you realize the royal family needs its rest?"

"Your Grace," the captain of the guard nodded stiffly, issuing a tight hand signal to his men. A dozen swords slid back into sheaths, and the fighting men shifted uneasily in the narrow hallway. "We beg your pardon."

"*My* pardon," Larindolian mimicked sarcastically. "What about the pardon of the princes and princesses in their nursery? What about Her Majesty, the Queen?" The chamberlain stepped fully into the hall, closing the oaken door fast behind him. "Are you going to beg the king's pardon?"

Rani saw angry fear flash in the captain's eyes, and she knew that she could not let the tirade continue. "Please, Your Grace," she began. "The guards were only doing their job—"

"According to whom, First Pilgrim?" Larindolian turned cunning eyes on her. "Are you telling me how to run this household? Are you taking responsibility for the safety of the royal family? The only family that you have in all the world?"

The last question was a clear warning, and Rani swallowed her angry retort, remembering that she was supposed to be a pilgrim on the road to enlightenment, an orphan who had recently arrived in the City to honor the Thousand Gods. As if to drive home the reminder, Larindolian closed his hand about her arm, pressing the unseen snake-chased bracelet deeper into her flesh. His message was so clear that he might have spoken aloud—Rani must not forget that she was supposed to be alone in the royal court; she had no brother, no Brotherhood. She swallowed a defiant retort.

"I'm sorry, Your Grace." She worked to add honest remorse to her tone, but she did not quite manage the effect. "I did not mean to cause worry to you or to the guard. Please forgive this humble pilgrim, who has so much to learn about the customs of her new family."

Larindolian pinched his fingers tighter, bruising her arm beneath its metal band, but his voice was forgiving. "Certainly, First Pilgrim. We in the royal household understand the burden that you bear, the struggle to find a clear path on the road of the Thousand Gods. Go to your rest now."

Rani muttered the appropriate thanks, but she resented the need to walk down the corridor, alone but for Marcanado. She felt all eyes on her narrow back, and by the time she reached the nursery door, she was grateful for the children's guard who opened the door, even if he did look at her with weary exasperation. As if to emphasize the guard's fatigue, the four princesses chose that moment to squeal in excitement. Rani heard the flurry of the nurses trying to calm their charges, and her irritation at being penned in the palace was renewed.

When Marcanado made as if to follow her into the children's quarters, Rani rounded on him, unable to still her dagger tongue. "Enough! You can leave me now!"

Of course, the stolid soldier did not react; he merely stared at her as if she were speaking some foreign language from a distant land. "I said—" Rani started to rage.

"Marcanado, that will be enough. You are dismissed."

Rani turned to gape at Prince Bashanorandi as the soldier bowed and took his leave of the nursery. Bashi returned her gaze with an impish grin, running a hand through his red-brown hair and winking one blue eye. Ignoring two of the princesses who dove about Rani's legs in some impromptu game, Rani stammered, "How did you do that?"

"The power of command," Bashi pretended to stroke his pointed chin, as if he could grow a true beard. Rani smiled, but a chill prowled up her spine as she realized the power this younger prince bore over the household guard. If Bashi had the soldiers eating out of the palm of his hand, could it be such a great step to lust for more power, to demand more recognition as the royal heir?

Bashanorandi had done more than dismiss the meddlesome guard. Rani thought back over the past few weeks, to the other times when Bashi had shown his hand. He had made the guards play chess with him only the morning before, despite their protests that they had other duties. He often conspired with the soldiers to gain more practice time in the riding ring or before the archery targets. Bashi manipulated the soldiers shamelessly, like one born to the role. Like one ready to don a robe of power, he had revealed his true colors. How could Rani not have recognized the threat before?

Now, she longed to escape to the cathedral, to track down Bardo and tell him that she had finally unmasked the conspirator among the princes. She had solved the Brotherhood's riddle. Bashi was the son who presented a threat to his father, to the king of all Morenia.

And was it really any surprise? Bashi's mother was the proud Queen Felicianda, exotic daughter of foreign lands. Rumor said the queen's people were fierce warriors, skilled at arms and shrewd at games. How else had Queen Felicianda negotiated her marriage to the king of all Morenia? What lessons had Prince Bashanorandi learned at his doting mother's knee?

Of course, Rani could not slip out of the palace again, and she had no reason to believe that Bardo would be in the cathedral now when he had not shown up all evening, all week. Besides, the tumult in the nursery continued, with the young princesses flitting from bed to bed, upsetting their low chairs and tables, and spilling toys and playthings across the flagstones. The royal nurses were trying to reassure their

charges, bullying them back to bed with a combination
of stern orders and motherly smiles. The youngest of the
attendants had turned to the hearth at the far end of the
room, swinging a small cauldron over the open flame to
warm a soothing posset of milk and spices.

Rani took in the disarray with wide eyes, a little
frightened by the havoc she had wrought. Before she could
cross the room to her own sleeping pallet, Halaravilli spoke
from the doorway to his private sleeping chamber. "The
pilgrim returns, the pilgrim returns. Like a snake to a nest,
the pilgrim returns."

The analogy crashed against Rani's senses, and she
wheeled on the prince. "What did you say? What did you
call me?"

Before Hal could respond, Bashi spoke up, eyeing his
brother with amused tolerance. "You must ignore him,
Marita Pilgrim. He does not understand that his words
may offend those of us with normal sensitivities." Bashi
offered her a slight bow as he flashed a winning smile, and
Rani marveled at the conspiratorial jocularity in his voice.
"Besides," Bashi whispered in a tone he clearly intended his
brother to hear, "Doesn't the fool know that *birds* build
nests, not snakes?"

"Suck eggs," Hal retorted. "Suck eggs." Bashi yelped his
protest, and launched himself at his brother, adding to the
general tumult as the youths collapsed in a wrestling match
on the hard stone floor.

When the nurses succeeded in pulling the boys apart,
Bashi was nursing a ragged scratch on the meaty heel of
his thumb. Hal, for all the fact that he was smaller than his
younger brother, had emerged the better in the impromptu
battle. Bashi's blue eyes burned as he sneered his hatred for
the crown prince, his gaze made angrier by a welt that was
rising on his cheekbone. As the nurses started to chide the
boys, Hal shook his head vigorously. "Snakes suck eggs," he
insisted. "Birds build nests, snakes find nests, snakes suck
eggs."

"Yes, yes," bustled the oldest nurse. "Now sit over there

and sip your milk like a good boy." Hal caught Rani's eye as he let himself be led away like a child, sighing in exasperation and offering up an uncommon roguish grin. Rani could not help but respond in kind as she accepted her own mug.

Later that night, as the nursery finally settled to quiet, Rani thought back to the altercation in the hallway, to Larindolian's sudden appearance. The chamberlain's own apartments were not even located in the royal wing of the Palace. Where had the nobleman come from in the dark of night? Certainly not the nursery—that was at the end of the corridor. The king's doorway had been heavily guarded, even as the soldiers had challenged Rani. That left one set of rooms in the wing, one most interesting place for the nobleman to be passing a late evening with the royal family. Larindolian had emerged from Queen Felicianda's rooms.

As the crowds clamored in the marketplace, Rani hunched her shoulders forward, grateful that the day was clammy and cool. She was not immediately out of place for swaddling herself in her heavy pilgrim's cloak even though she made a marked contrast to both Halaravilli and Bashanorandi. The two princes appeared enchanted by their people, craving the attention bestowed by old and young alike.

Rani had argued against this expedition, but the tutors had thought it an excellent opportunity for the princes to see their people, to learn a little of the real life in their City. Rani could only imagine the disaster if she ran into Narda, the egg-seller who had been her mistress. For that matter, there were a half-dozen other merchants who knew her by name, and who could make life terribly uncomfortable if she were discovered in her new guise.

When she had first learned of the outing, Rani had planned to make her way to the statue of the Defender of the Faith at the market's edge, passing the mandatory lesson time on her knees beneath the statue's imperious marble arm. The tutors would hear nothing of that decision, however. Whatever rank Rani might have held in the worship of the Thousand Gods, she was still beholden to the king. Her role for the entire year was to live precisely as one of the royal family. She must be obedient to the tutors, to the taskmasters who were even now showing the boys how the scales worked at the center of the marketplace, how the Merchants' Council sat to dispense quick, rough justice.

Even as Rani worried about discovery, she realized that this excursion was a perfect opportunity to observe Bashi, to add further evidence to the docket she was filling against him. She hoped to prove that he was calculating against his father, that he schemed to take an early crown. Rani's pulse began to race as Bashi responded to a tutor's prompting, quizzing the scales-master.

"So, good man, how do you verify that the scales are in balance?"

"Your Highness," the merchant bowed and tugged at his forelock, practically scraping the ground in his eagerness to please. "If you look at this mechanism here...." the man trailed off as he indicated a complicated system of gears, "I can test the scales using these and a box of brass weights, stamped with the royal signet, of course, showing they are true and fair." He illustrated his metier with a loaf of bread.

Even as the younger of the princes nodded and prepared to look elsewhere in the marketplace, Prince Hal stepped closer to the table. "Stamped with the royal sign? Signed by the royal stamp?" Hal gestured toward the king's colors flying above the table, a symbol to all the market that the fairness and order of King Shanoranvilli held sway.

"Er... yes, Your Highness." The merchant was clearly uncomfortable with Hal's sing-song speech, and he darted a nervous glance between the box of weights, the scale, and the loaf of bread.

Bashi sighed as his brother stepped closer to the weighing mechanism. "Come on, Hal. Let's get back to the stalls. I'm thirsty, and those seed cakes look good."

"The sign shrinks." Hal ignored his brother, reaching for one of the bronze weights. The merchant swept it away from the prince's narrow fingers, scarcely swallowing a curse, and a sudden stillness settled over the crowd. "The sign shrinks,"

Hal repeated, and the merchant dug up a nervous laugh from deep in his belly.

"Your Highness, these weights are delicate things. You can't be touching them with your fingers. Your fingers will leave marks, and dust will settle—you'd change the weight."

"Change the weight, weight for change, wait for change, weighting change." Hal chanted under his breath, ignoring the growing crowd's attention. Rani was the only person who managed to tear herself away from staring at the prince with an awed fascination. She ignored his continued patter, watching the merchant instead. There was something about his nervous gaze, something beyond the tightening of his jaw as Hal continued to mutter his nonsense words. The master of the weights did, in fact, have something to hide.

"Come on, Hal," Bashi sighed. "Can't you smell the sausages? Let's go over there."

As Bashi tried to drag them across the marketplace, Hal's hand shot out, grasping the metal weights before the merchant could keep them safe. As the crowd surged closer, Hal turned the weights upside down.

At first glance, there was nothing wrong with the metal measures. Bashi stared at the smooth bronze weights and then rolled his eyes, sighing his disgust. "There! Are you satisfied, Hal?"

The older prince, though, ignored his restless brother. Producing a short dagger from the top of his supple boots, Hal gouged at the bottom of the metal marker. It took a moment of levering, but a plug of wax fell onto the weighing table, glistening in the afternoon light. Glints of metal paint flecked the table.

Prince Hal looked up to eye his brother steadily. "My name is Halaravilli," he enunciated. "I am a prince of the House of Jair, and you'll give me the respect I deserve." Bashi flushed crimson, barely managing to swallow his rage and embarrassment. Hal did not wait for his brother's response, though, before turning steely eyes on the merchant. "And *you* are a thief."

"Your Highness—" The man fell to his knees, his face

paling to the color of thin whey. He worked his hands in supplication, glancing frantically about as the pitch of the crowd rose to a frenzied hum. "I beg of you, Your Highness...."

"What? You beg mercy? Did you have mercy for the poor folk who came to you to check their purchases for fair measure?"

The merchants pressed closer, and Rani felt their outrage like a palpable flame. They had placed this man in a position of power; they had given him the ability to define right and wrong, to measure good and evil in the marketplace. Rani's own blood pounded at the thought that her birth-caste would be so betrayed, and she literally swallowed the urge to spit on the criminal. The guilty man reached for the hem of Hal's cloak. "Mercy, Your Highness...."

Hal's gaze snapped back to the royal party, clumped in the marketplace in velvets and silk. "Prince Bashanorandi!" His use of his brother's full name spoke volumes about proper respect and titles. Bashi stepped forward, pulling himself to his full height. "What is the penalty for a merchant caught short-weighting goods?"

Bashi swallowed hard and looked back at his tutors; he clearly had not memorized the Table of Penalties. Before the prince could admit his ignorance, Rani caught herself mouthing the response. "A thumb for the first offense."

Bashi must have been standing close enough to catch her murmur, or else he heard it from the crowd. "A thumb for the first offense," he parroted. "A thumb for the false weight he placed upon the scales."

"Very good," Hal nodded, although he turned his grey eyes on Rani as he issued the tight praise. The crown prince nodded to his guard. "Carry out the sentence."

"Now?" yelped Bashi, as the weights-master cried out and the crowd surged closer.

"Now." Hal's eyes narrowed as the soldiers manhandled the merchant, forcing him over to the weighing table, grappling with him to lay out his pale, pale hand against the weathered wood.

"Please, Your Highness!" The man babbled, striking out with his arms, almost succeeding in breaking free. "I beg you to take me before the Merchants' Council." At a dangerous roar from the assembled tradesmen, the man changed his pleading. "Take me to the Court, then, let me hear the King's Justice."

Hal leveled shrewd eyes on the marketplace, raising one hand in majestic reflection of the statue that stood on the far side of the marketplace, the Defender of the Faith. The gesture was regal, and even the most agitated folk in the marketplace fell silent. "I *am* the King's Justice, man. There is no appeal from my decision." Hal waited one long minute, while the crowd absorbed the power emanating from him, and then he nodded curtly at the captain of the guard. "Go ahead."

Rani could not keep her eyes from the shining steel blade, could not help but watch the sun reflect from that liquid tongue. For just an instant, she was catapulted back to the glasswrights' hall that no longer stood in the Guildsmen's Quarter; she remembered a similar knife falling on Larinda. She thought of the blood that had flowed from her fellow apprentice, and she almost cried out, almost begged Hal for mercy on behalf of a merchant, on behalf of a man who was born into her caste.

Almost, but not quite. The scales-master had known the rules of the marketplace. He had defiled his entire caste when he broke the law. Hal's sentence was fair, and mercifully swift.

A cheer went up in the crowd as the guard raised up the merchant's maimed and bleeding hand.

Hal nodded at the approval, and gestured curtly to the guard to let the merchant go free. The man stumbled through the market, ducking his head against a sudden torrent of rotting vegetables and foul debris. Only when the criminal had disappeared beneath a filthy storm did Hal turn back to his small party. "Enough." His voice was hoarse, and he panted as if he had run a mile through the City streets. The skin about his eyes was tight, strained, and Rani was surprised that his voice did not quaver. "Jair has spoken to me, spoken through me. I must pray to Jair, pray to the gods, pray to all the Thousand Gods. Let's leave the market. Leave, leave, leave."

Rani followed the princes as the guards cleared a path. She was concerned about Hal, worried about the exhaustion she read in his features. His actions had drained him, as if he had only so much power to spend in a day, and all of it had been wagered in one show of strength.

One show of strength, but what a show it was.... Rani had seen the flash in the prince's eyes as he ordered the merchant punished. She had seen the thrill of power. Hal had thrived on flicking the whip of kingship. Deep in his addled mind, he lusted for the crown.

Rani's head reeled as she moved through the City streets. Unconsciously, her fingers crept to the metal band about her arm. She could feel the snakes' ruby eyes through the cloth. Now she was grateful that she had not had the opportunity to seek out Bardo after Bashi's silly show with the guards the night before. The younger prince certainly had not unveiled the sort of strength that his brother had just revealed.

Now, Rani longed to find Bardo, yearned to tell him that she knew the answer to the puzzle he had set for her. She knew who had conspired against the king, who had wanted to eliminate Prince Tuvashanoran. She wanted to announce that Halaravilli—a prince who, with scarcely a blink, could command a subject's thumb severed from his hand—Halaravilli was the one the Brotherhood sought.

Rani was so intent on imagining her brother's joy at her message, that she scarcely realized the princes were moving through the City streets toward the cathedral. Rani only looked up as they passed over the threshold into the nave, as she realized the soldiers were stepping back, making way for her because she was the First Pilgrim, and she was entitled to lead the way into this house of worship.

When Rani hesitated for a second, Bashanorandi started to grouse. "What is your point, Hal? Why did you drag us here? Cook will be angry if we don't get back home."

"Peace of Jair, guidance of Jair. Looking for the light of all the Thousand Gods." Hal made his way down the cathedral's aisle, ignoring the purported authority of the First Pilgrim. "Peace of Jair, guidance of Jair. The prince acts for justice, the prince acts for peace."

Lulled by Hal's babbling and by the familiarity of the path they walked, Rani almost did not realize that the crown prince was leading her directly down the side aisle, picking his way unerringly to the small stone altar that Rani had come to know so well. "Justice of Roat," Hal muttered. "Guidance of Roat." She watched in astonishment as Hal knelt before the familiar altar, and when she dared to look around the cathedral, she half-fancied she would see Bardo sitting in the shadows.

Of course, Bardo was nowhere to be seen. Instead, Rani's attention was captured by Bashi. As always, the younger prince had declined to follow his brother. Even as Hal knelt before the small altar, muttering a prayer, Bashi strode down the cathedral's main aisle, dragging with him the royal guardsmen, as if he were a lodestone attracting the heavy metal of their breast-plates.

Rani's attention darted back and forth between the princes. Hal lowered his head to the cold marble edge of Roat's altar, swallowing his whispered chanting as he clasped his hands before his brow. At the same time, Bashi clambered up the steps of the main dais, taking them two at a time, looking back at his guards as if they were all playing at some military campaign.

Rani could not keep her eyes from darting up to the fateful Defender's Window, to the glasswork that had brought death to Prince Tuvashanoran and ignominy on Rani's guild. The sun was almost at the same angle as it had been on that doomed day; Rani could see the streak of cobalt light that Instructor Morada had planned. She could see another prince ensnared in the glasswright's web.

She took a step forward, a cry rising in her throat, but before she could speak, Hal raised a hand to her arm. As if he knew she wore Bardo's bracelet, his fingers settled unerringly on the band of snakes, pinching the metal as tight against her flesh as Larindolian had done the previous night. The movement was effective; Rani swallowed her words before she had a chance to warn Bashi of the danger.

Of course, Bashi needed no warning. He stood for a moment in the cobalt light, tossing back his own cloak, letting the azure sunlight stain his hair, his face, his entire body. Then, he stepped out of the beam, all the time keeping his back to the main altar. Rani watched as Prince Bashanorandi joked with his guards, jested with his people. She was captivated as he stepped up to the main altar, and she stared in disbelief as he raised the golden chalice that was centered on a snowy white cloth.

The golden chalice—the cup that symbolized the Defender's gifts to his people. Prince Tuvashanoran had drunk from that cup. King Shanoranvilli was the only person living today who was worthy to drink from the Defender's cup.

And Bashi raised it to his lips.

The soldiers did not seem to notice. They were lolling about the cathedral, glad to be inside its cool confines, grateful to be free of the pressing crowds that made their jobs so difficult. When one of them did take notice of his young lord playing with the holy goblet, he merely uttered an exclamation, and then the other soldiers fell to teasing the Prince, joking with him, turning the sacrilege into a game.

Rani read volumes into that easy acceptance. The soldiers did not care how their leader acted; they were not going to question their chosen lord. Whatever Bashi did, he did in accordance with his royal entitlement, his birthright. Indeed, the men's easy camaraderie bespoke their feudal bonds— they were not bound to the abstract concept of the house of Jair, after all. They were *Bashanorandi's* men. They served him, and him alone.

As Bashi set the chalice back on the altar, Rani swallowed a bitter sigh. She had been a fool to think Hal the suspect prince; she had been led astray by the flurry in the marketplace, by the sight of a mangled hand, a bloody stump. Rani knew in her heart of hearts that Bashi was the youth who aspired to power. She saw it with eyes that had served the priests, binding Tuvashanoran's cold, dead body. She felt it with a heart that had lived in the Soldiers' Quarter, had swelled with pride at watching the military loyalty of good soldiers. Only her merchant's instincts had blinded her, temporarily, in the marketplace. Her longing to return to the quarter of her birth and the love of her family had deluded her, for one brief moment, into thinking that Hal was the scheming prince.

Now, Rani turned to find Hal watching her strangely, as if the prince could read her careful calculation, could tell that she had suspected him, however briefly.

"The light strikes the cup," Hal observed. "The light strikes the cup, the cup strikes the chord. The chord calls the men, the men guard the prince." Rani nodded, understanding the strange logic of Hal's sing-song mysteries. "The men guard the prince, the prince calls the men."

Hal rose to his feet, and the guard snapped to attention. Even Bashi stopped his capering about the altar, following his brother down the aisle and back to the Palace. Rani fought the impulse to look over her shoulder as she left the cathedral yet again. She hoped against hope that Bardo had been secreted in the shadows, that he had seen Bashi's brashness. If Bardo had been a witness, then she would not even need to name her suspicions. Bardo would know the traitor.

The royal procession managed to return to the Palace without event, and the three charges settled in the nursery for an afternoon of reading, studying, and quiet time. Rani ignored her supposed guild of the bards, forsaking the opportunity to spin out tales for the princesses or read great stories in leather-bound tomes from the royal library. Instead, she scrounged up a slate and a piece of chalk, whiling away the darkling hours sketching the nursery's residents.

She drew each of the princes with a spray of strong lines, forcing the youths' restless bodies into planes that would be easy to cut from sheets of glass, easy to read from a distance.

At first, Rani thought that she was drawing portraits, but she realized she did not yet have the skill to capture the boys in simple glasswrights' lines. The more she tried, the more frustrated she became, until she finally rubbed out all of her mistakes. Taking a deep breath and muttering an appeal to Lan for patience, Rani began again.

This time, the lines drew themselves on the slate, flowing from the chalk as if some divine force controlled her hand. As she completed her "portrait" of Hal, she almost laughed aloud. A young lion stared out at her from the slate, its eyes wise beyond its years. She sketched in a mane with a few lines, finishing off the feline grace. Halaravilli might be young, but his heritage was clear; he was a prince of the House of Jair, and the royal lion was his symbol.

Excited by her success at merging youth and animal, Rani turned her attentions to Bashi. The younger prince sat across the nursery, joking with the princesses and ignoring his studies. As Rani started to sketch the lines for his face, she again felt the supreme confidence, the easy flow of the chalk against the slate. This time, though, there was no royal lion that peered out from the drawing surface. As she sketched in the prince's hair, captured his eyes, etched in his cheeks, the crafty gaze of a fox stared out from the slate.

There was more behind the portrait, though. As Rani studied her strong lines, she realized that she had seen another cunning gaze; she had seen that vulpine hunger before. As if testing herself, she thought back to the previous night, when she had caused the commotion in the corridor. Then, she remembered her encounter in the shadowy hallways built into the city walls. Yes, she had been blind not to see it before.

The entire court must be blind. Prince Bashanorandi's features were a younger, softer version of Lord Larindolian's.

All of a sudden, a veil fell away from Rani's eyes. It all made sense—she was a fool not to have seen the pattern earlier. She, who prided herself on seeing patterns.... Larindolian had emerged from the queen's chambers. Prince Bashanorandi had the narrow, chiseled features of the cunning chamberlain. Larindolian had his fingers in every pie in the City—he had manipulated Instructor Morada, gaining access to the deadly scaffolding outside the cathedral. He had taken charge of Rani's life behind the palace walls. He had sworn Rani to secrecy within the Brotherhood.

Larindolian plotted to overthrow the king. How long before he took the final steps—murdering King Shanoranvilli, and the last true heir, Prince Halaravilli? How long before Bashanorandi became king of Morenia?

Rani's heart pounded. She needed to reach Bardo immediately. She needed to tell Bardo of the mistake they both had made, of their foolishness in trusting the chamberlain. She had been right all along—she had been wise to fear the man who had beaten Instructor Morada and turned the glasswright over to the Palace guard. She had been right to fear the man who had sliced open her veins, who had fed her blood to the snakes in the Brotherhood's hidden chamber. Rani knew that she had no choice; she must get to the cathedral now, without her dangerous guard-dog Marcanado.

While the princes still knelt at their prayers, Rani crossed the nursery floor. The family had become accustomed to her odd comings and goings, and she hoped that no one would notice that she was sneaking out early. Her heart thrummed when none of the nurses responded, and she slunk down the torchlit corridor, keeping to the shadows as if that would delay Marcanado from reporting for his nightly mission.

She dared to breathe a sigh of relief as she entered the main courtyard; perhaps Lan himself was watching her, keeping her hidden from her watchdog's stolid eyes. Darting across the cobblestones, Rani gained the gate, startling the kindly guard who kept watch for mischief in the night.

"What ho!" he exclaimed, stepping from the shadows of a small hut beside the gate. He slapped back the sword that he had started to unsheathe. "You're early tonight, young pilgrim!"

"Aye," Rani answered desperately, her words a little too sharp in the night air. "I need to reach the cathedral. The

Thousand Gods are restless tonight, and I need to pray for peace."

"Where's your soldier, little one? It's still not safe in the City streets." The man chided her.

"He's with the princes. The entire household is still up in arms over the marketplace today; even the princesses are out of sorts."

"I have strict orders..."

"It's more important that Marcanado stay with the princes tonight," Rani wheedled, turning her most winning smile on the man. "Besides, I know the way now. I could walk it in my sleep."

"It would be my job, if I let you go."

"Nonsense," Rani coaxed. "You can watch me from the gates—you can see halfway to the cathedral without taking a step."

"Well...." The man had already decided to give in.

"I'll be back before they even know I'm gone."

"Be quick, then, little pilgrim." The man grunted as he turned the heavy iron fitting on the gate. "I'll watch you move down this street, and I'll keep an eye out for your return."

Rani smiled her gratitude and stepped up to the gate. Just as she was about to escape into the City streets, a voice cascaded across the courtyard. "Close the gate, close the gate!" The metal clanged back on its hinges before Rani could register that Prince Halaravilli was the speaker. He darted into the shadows by the guardhouse. "Where are you going in the night? What gods do you pray to for right? For right, in the night, what is right?"

Rani was shocked by Hal's presence, by his sing-song accusations, and she sputtered out an explanation. "You know that I'm the First Pilgrim, Your Highness. You know that I must pray in the cathedral."

"Pray in the night, pray what is right. There is danger in the night, Pilgrim, danger in the City streets."

Rani shook her head, furious that she had been caught so

close to escape. "I'm the First Pilgrim, Your Highness. No one will harm me while I act to honor the Thousand Gods."

Hal's eyes flashed angrily in the dark. "There is danger everywhere, First Pilgrim. Danger in the night, danger in the day. Danger in the streets, danger in our rooms."

"The guard will watch me from the gate," Rani gestured to the disconcerted gatekeeper, who was clearly hoping that his decision would not be faulted by the prince.

"There is danger among soldiers. Danger among princes. Danger among merchants. Danger among priests." Rani tried to laugh off the bitter threats, desperate to make good her escape. Hal's chanting continued, though, gaining strength as he sailed on. "Danger from the lion. Danger from the fox."

Before Rani could react, Hal's hand shot out, closing around the bracelet that nestled against her arm. "Danger from the snake."

CHAPTER 14

Rani felt the blood rush from her face as Halaravilli closed his fingers tight about the metal band. The snakes burned into her flesh, and she set her teeth to keep from crying out. The prince took the measure of her pale face, and then he turned his suddenly steely eyes on the guard. Jutting his chin toward the gate, he commanded, "Keep watch out here. I must speak with the First Pilgrim."

The captain swallowed visibly and stepped away from his convenient little hut. Halaravilli dragged Rani inside the shelter and shut the door behind them, loosing her arm to thrust a poker into the heart of the small fire that the guard kept burning.

"Wh—" Rani annoyed herself by stammering. "Wh-what are you going to do?"

Hal traced her wavering gaze and then set the poker to rest on the hearth with an exasperated sigh. He seemed to make a true effort to gentle his words as he said, "Nothing, First Pilgrim. Nothing to you."

"Then why did you stop me?"

"You're in danger. It would be a sin to let you walk into that cathedral, knowing as I do what awaits you, First Pilgrim."

The ominous explanation heated Rani's words. "The only thing waiting for me in the cathedral is the peace of the Thousand Gods."

"The Thousand Gods?" Hal guffawed, as if he had never heard of such piety. "You poor thing—the First Pilgrim, an orphan and alone in all the City—yet still you can devote your nights to praying to the Thousand Gods?"

"Just because my parents are dead doesn't mean I can't pray!"

"Too true, First Pilgrim. Too true." Hal plunged the poker deeper into the fire, rearranging the logs that glowed red with embers.

"Stop calling me that!"

"What? First Pilgrim? It *is* your title, isn't it?"

"Of course, but you've never used it before. You make it sound like an accusation."

"And what would you rather I call you? Marita Pilgrim? Rani Trader? Ranita Glasswright? Ranimara? Rai?"

Rani's breath froze in her lungs. The tiny room tilted at a crazy angle, and she stumbled toward the prince in a mad effort to keep her balance. The patch of hearth, glowing with fire, soared up to catch her.

Before she could smack her head against the floor, Hal's wiry hands closed on her arms, catching her, pinning her, protecting her from her own headlong fall. "I—" Rani started, staring up into his questing eyes. "What are you saying? What do you know?"

"I'm saying more than we have time to talk about here in a guardsman's hut at the palace gates. I'm saying that I know who you are, and I know what you've done."

"I didn't kill Prince Tuvashanoran!" Even as the profession of innocence spewed from her lips, Rani fought to free herself from Halaravilli's grasp. His fingers tightened about her arm, about the bracelet Bardo had given her. She tried to pull away, but he merely pulled her closer, raising stiff fingers to her tunic lacings.

She twisted with the desperation of a cornered animal, nearly ripping her clothing as she yanked open the ties at her own neck. She scrambled to grasp the metal twisted about her right bicep, bruising her own flesh as she ripped off the twining snakes. There was little doubt that the prince could overpower her, but she'd be cursed by all the Thousand Gods before she'd let him shred her clothing in his single-minded search for the Brotherhood's symbol. "I did not kill your brother!"

"I didn't say you did." He plucked the copper band from her, holding it with his fingertips as if the metal had the power to burn. The snakes' eyes captured the hearth's flickering fire and cast it back at them. "I never said you killed my brother."

The sorrow in his words knocked Rani senseless. She stepped back from the prince with awe in her eyes, a hundred facts falling into place, only to be shifted aside by a thousand questions. "What *are* you saying then? Why are you talking to me normally? What happened to your chanting?"

He pinned her with his dark, shrewd eyes. "I don't need to play those games with you."

"What games?"

"And you don't need to play games with me," he chided. "I know that you're the First Pilgrim, and you've clearly been selected by the Brotherhood of Justice."

"You know what the snakes mean!" Rani hissed despite herself, and Halaravilli nodded.

"Aye, or at least I know enough to fear them, among all the rival powers in my father's kingdom." When Rani merely stared without comprehension, Hal smiled. "I know to fear the power, and I know to fear my brother. I know to fear the snakes, and I know to fear the fox."

"Stop it!"

Hal favored her with a twisted grin, but he fell silent. "I know that a chanting idiot is no threat to traitors who would murder all who stand in their way."

"Do you realize what you're saying?"

"Better than you, First Pilgrim. I know the penalty for treason even better than I know the penalty for a merchant who gives short weight." Rani vividly recalled the scales-master in the marketplace—was it only that afternoon? Then, Hal had commanded that a thief lose his thumb. The penalty for treason was harsher—a neck stretched in the balance. Hal sighed. "I know the weight of a brother who sees wrong and acts worse."

"My brother hasn't done anything wrong!" Rani protested hotly.

"Then you do *have* a brother, First Pilgrim?" Hal's eyes pinned her, as she fought for an answer.

She spluttered her protest in anger. "I do, and you can't keep me from seeing him!"

"Don't tell me what I can and cannot do!" Halaravilli waved the snake bracelet before her eyes. "I'm a prince of the House of Jair, and I could have you thrown into the dungeons without any explanation. I could put you in the same cell where your parents prayed for deliverance, before they met the hangman's noose. I could lock you up where the straw still stinks of the blood from your fellow glasswrights, where you still might find a thumb mixed in with the offal."

Rani's scream rose from the bottom of her soul, and she flung herself at Hal as if he were an ordinary youth, an ordinary human being and not a royal prince. She fought to gouge out his eyes, to pluck his hair, to rake her rigid fingers along his cheeks. The keening that rose from her belly was an animal sound, fed by her weeks of wandering in the City streets.

Hal's arms were iron bands about her chest; he had her subdued before the guard could fling open the door to the hut. When the prince addressed the soldier, he managed to add a quirky grin to his words, "Everything is fine, soldier, everything is fine. The First Pilgrim is just a little excited, a little concerned, a little perturbed. The First Pilgrim cries, the First Pilgrim sighs."

Rani was still squirming for freedom as the guard gave a nodding smile that stopped just short of a leer and withdrew from the small room. Twisting about like a fish on a line, Rani applied the careful knowledge of a youngest child and leaned her weight into Hal's chest, simultaneously raising her booted foot to crash her heel down hard on his instep.

The maneuver worked as effectively as it had when she had wrestled with her brothers, and she suddenly found herself across the room from the prince, panting and wild-eyed. "You lie," she gasped.

"Every word I told you is the truth."

"You murdered my parents! You tortured my friends!"

"I did nothing, Ranita."

"Don't call me that!"

"Rani, then, is that what you'd prefer? Or Rai?"

"How do you know these things?"

"I'm a prince. I'm next in line to a throne that is being fought over by jackals. If I didn't learn things, I'd be dead by now."

"Who told you?"

"Many people, in many ways. My private guard was known to you."

"To me?"

"Aye. His name was Dalarati."

Rani froze, unable to respond to the accusation implicit in Hal's words. She could see Dalarati, lying on the floor of his small, neat room, horrifyingly still as his blood spread into a wider and wider pool. But that was ridiculous. She was no longer in the Soldiers' Quarter. She was no longer risking her life as a Touched girl. She was Marita Pilgrim. Here. Now. In the palace. "Dalarati?"

"Aye," the prince confirmed, and his grey eyes cut deep. "He was a good man, and true. He worked to help me, to help the Crown, and never to place the kingdom at risk. Why do you weep, Marita? Ranita? Rani? Ranimara? Rai?"

Rani dashed at her tears with the back of her hand. "I'm not weeping! Why shed tears for a traitor?" She fought against her pounding heart and forced herself to look Hal in the eyes. "I'm late, Your Highness. I am a pilgrim; I am supposed to pray."

"You go into danger."

"I go to the cathedral. What danger could await me there?"

"If only I could ask my brother, Tuvashanoran."

"I mourn for your brother, Your Highness, but that changes nothing. I have to go to the cathedral. I'm the First Pilgrim."

"They're using you."

"We're all used. Your father uses you to secure the House of Jair. My guild used me before ... before my pilgrimage."

"And this?" He raised the snake-bracelet, dangling it before Rani's eyes, as if he would hypnotize her with the flash of fire on glass, fire on copper.

"That was lent to me by another. It is not mine to lose or give away."

"It is an evil thing, Marita."

"Things aren't evil, Your Highness." The response came to her as if Tole, the god of wisdom, were speaking in her ear. "People are evil."

"And your Brotherhood? Do you call them good, Marita?"

"They're not *my* Brotherhood, Your Highness." She held his gaze across the ugly twist of metal. "Don't you understand? I'm not one of them. I'm not one of anything. I have no caste, I have no family. The only person left to me in all the world is my brother, Bardo. Don't keep me from him." She took a step closer, holding out her hand for the bracelet. "Please. You know what it's like to lose a brother. Don't force me to lose the last one I have in all the world."

Slowly, as if he were enchanted by a power beyond his control, he handed back the entwined snakes. "Death is the sentence for all traitors."

She met his eyes above the twisted copper. "I'm not a traitor."

The snakes stung her flesh as she took the band. Despite her firmest intention, she could not bring herself to force it back on her arm. After a moment's hesitation, she tossed the bangle into the embers on the hearth. It fell, twisted and malignant, smothering the coals for just an instant before the flames leaped to new life, as if she had tossed fuel on the fire.

The metal had begun to glow when she turned to leave. Halaravilli avoided her eyes as she opened the door to the hut, and she did not look back as she made her way through the City streets, alone and unprotected.

* * *

The cathedral was cold, filled with clammy air and stale incense that made her think of the laying-out room in the cathedral close. She imagined she heard chanting mourners as she crept down the side aisle, and more than once, she paused in a niche, wishing she had her Zarithian dagger safe at her waist. A handful of candles flickered eerily on altars about the hulking stone building, and her hand trembled as she added her offering to Roat, the god of justice.

She had just sunk to her knees, when she heard footsteps approach behind her, and then soft words. "I thought you were not coming."

"Bardo!" She launched herself at his unsuspecting frame, almost toppling him before his arms could close around her.

"What is it? What's the problem, Ranikaleka?"

She shuddered. "Don't call me that! I'm Rani! I'm Rani Trader!"

Bardo shushed her as he led her to the nearest low bench. "Of course you are. Who would say otherwise?" His voice was soft and soothing, a reminder of her mother's gentle touch when she was a baby and awakened with nightmares. "What's gotten into you tonight? Why are you so late?"

"I can't do this, Bardo. They're princes—they're the royal family. I'm just Rani Trader, I'm a *merchant*!"

"What happened, Rani?" His voice hardened, and she heard the tone of a commander behind his words. "What did they do to you?"

"Nothing!" She wailed, and the two syllables echoed off the high stone ceiling. Bardo reached out to shush her, to remind her of their precarious position here in the cathedral. When his fingers closed over her arm and he felt nothing but flesh and cloth, he grabbed at her tunic lacings, stripping the cords from her neck like a hunter butchering a deer.

"Where is the bracelet?" When she could only stare at him, terrified, he clamped his hands down on her biceps, shaking her until her teeth rattled. "What have you done with the bracelet?" The hard callouses on his thumbs bit into her skin, and she saw the Bardo who had nearly killed her once before, nearly murdered her because of the Brotherhood's snakes.

"I gave it to him!" Rani squeaked when she could manage to gather breath. "Stop it!"

Bardo let her go with a suddenness that sent her reeling toward the stone floor. Even as she crouched on hands and knees, gasping for breath, she saw her brother's boot move, draw back as if he would send his hardened-leather toe careening into her temple. "Gave it to whom?" he demanded, as she scrambled against the wooden bench, trying to huddle into the smallest possible target. "Who has the snakes?"

"Prince Halaravilli! Bardo, listen to me! He's the good one, the one we have to save. The Brotherhood has to protect him, we have to save him, Bardo, please believe me!"

Bardo's breath came roaring, like a pack of wolves in the night-time hills, and Rani crouched against the bench, sending up prayers to all the Thousand Gods, begging her brother to come to reason. Bardo reached down and captured her arm, hauling her out from beneath the pew and forcing her to sit on the hard wooden bench. "Tell me what you know."

She began with a whisper, fighting back tears, struggling to remember that she was speaking to her brother, to her own kin. Bardo would protect her. Bardo would make it right. Bardo would keep her safe from harm. She told her brother about all that had happened during that long, long day, as she suspected first Bashanorandi, then Halaravilli, then Bashi again.

Bardo listened, initially in anger, then in disbelief. His fingers closed about her arm as she spoke, pinching tighter and tighter as she told him all that she had learned, living among the royal family. She concluded, "And so, when I was drawing my portraits tonight, when I saw the bones behind their faces, that's when I knew that Bashi was not a true prince." She braved her brother's eyes. "And I think I know who his father is. I know why he wants the throne."

Bardo's voice was dead. "Why? What is it you think you know?"

"Lord Larindolian," Rani whispered. "He has too much

power in the palace. He was in the queen's chambers, and if you look at the lines of Bashi's face...."

For just an instant, she thought her words would rekindle Bardo's rage, but then he sighed deeply, shrugging as he sank to the ground. She cringed away from him, but he settled an easy hand on her shoulder, confident, controlling, silencing.

"I told Larindolian he played a dangerous game. I told him you were no fool." Rani held her tongue, and Bardo drew out the silence, like wire pulled through a mold. When he spoke again, his voice was weary. "You will not understand all of this, Ranikaleka. It's the stuff of kingdoms, the stuff of nightmares. I'll try to explain, as I understand it, and then you'll know why I've done all the things I've done."

Bardo sighed and ran his hands through his hair, scrubbing at his scalp in a familiar gesture of contemplation. "It started years ago, when Father first ran for office, for the Merchant's Council. You won't remember that, you were hardly more than a babe at the time...."

But Rani did remember. She remembered her mother baking a sweet pudding for good luck, and she remembered the entire family sitting down to a roast goose, even though it wasn't the Feast of Pilgrim Jair. She remembered the pride in her father's eyes as he hoped for the recognition of his fellows. She recalled the way he held himself as he walked through the streets. That had been a good time, and Rani had found the patterns easily when she laid out their wares in the family stall. There had been much silver to place among the pewter, even an occasional glint of gold, or the cool, smooth flow of ivory.

"The good times, though, only lasted for a few months," Bardo continued. "After that, the Council made its decision. Father was denied. He was shamed before his fellows in the marketplace; he could not even go on buying trips. Instead, we needed to trade with other merchants, with the sort who make their deals in the shadows of the City walls. Our costs went up, and we could not pass that on to our customers." Bardo shook his head in remembered frustration, his fingers curling into fists.

"We had no funds in reserve, when one of those shadow-merchants cheated us. Father had gone to close the deal at night, when even a soldier would have hesitated to walk in the dark passages beside the City walls, but he had no choice. There was no other way to get goods. If I had gone with him, things might have turned out differently...."

As Bardo's voice trailed off, Rani realized that she remembered the night he spoke of. Her father had come back to the house, pounding on the door, his voice hoarse and his face bleeding. Rani's sisters had almost refused to open the door to him, thinking he was some madman roaming the streets. When he stumbled into the kitchen where Rani was playing with her rag doll, he tossed a cloth sack onto the floor, hardly noticing when it fell too close to the fire. Rani started to reach for it, to save it from the flames, but her father roared at her, knocking her aside with an open hand that sent her reeling.

Nursing her own injuries and wounded pride, Rani had watched as her mother sponged blood from her father's brow. Even now, Rani could hear her mother's soft crooning, her warning that he must calm down, he must relax, he must sip the willow tea that would dull the ache behind his eyes. Jotham Trader would not be solaced—he had lost six month's profit when the thieves set upon him, and he still had no goods for the spring season. They would be ruined.

Her father's rage that night, though, was nothing compared to his anger when he went to the Council for aid. They told him they had no funds to spare, no goods to make up for those he'd lost. The winter had been rough for every merchant. The Council could not spare anything for a man who sold from his own shop, from outside the marketplace. Rani remembered night after night of thin cabbage soup, of her father speaking in angry whispers with Bardo, with Rani's mother, with anyone who would listen to his tales of woe.

He finally swallowed his pride and went beyond the Merchant's Council, beyond the caste he had honored and served all his life. He appealed to the soldiers, to seek out the thieves and—when he got no satisfactory response—he asked for justice in the King's Court.

Bardo's voice was bitter as he gave Rani the pieces of the story she had never had before. "There was no one in the City to help him, no one at all. His own caste turned against him, and the other castes looked down on him, like he was chaff in a mill. I knew, then, that I would never serve a system that was so broken, so corrupt. And I haven't."

Rani recognized the proud jut of Bardo's chin as his calloused fingers rose unconsciously to the tattoo about his left bicep. It was the look of the brother she had worshiped all her life. It was the look of a man who would not be beaten.

"I spoke out before the Merchants' Council. That was where the Brotherhood first learned about me. I was invited to their secret meetings, in the chambers inside the City walls, where you've been. The Brotherhood believes in true Justice, in a Justice separate and apart from the castes that have always plagued the City. Do you see?" Even as Bardo spoke, he spread his hands before her disbelieving eyes. "The Brotherhood believes in the equality of all men. They taught me to fight with the weapons of a soldier, a nobleman, whatever I needed to survive." Rani stared at his calloused flesh and thought of their father's smooth merchant hands, punished by nothing more violent than the rub of coins. Bardo nodded as she touched the horny skin. "The Brotherhood trained me, made me all I am today."

"But who are they?" Rani finally asked, drawn into the story despite her fear.

"We come from all the castes. There are nobles, like Larindolian, and soldiers like Garadolo. We have members in the guilds—your Salina, of course. Merchants and Touched—we all work together to build a City that is strong, like Jair meant us to be, like Jair was himself, because he moved from caste to caste. That's why we use the symbol of a snake—because the serpent grows and grows, shedding its skin, like we will all shed our caste, becoming a new beast, ever more powerful."

Rani's voice was shuttered by the fanatical light she

saw in her brother's eyes; even if she had wanted to ask more, she would not have been able to force words past her awe, her fear. Bardo continued his lesson, explaining the Brotherhood as if he were chanting a prayer, here in the cathedral. "The serpent has fed well, grown long through the years. We are almost at our full strength, almost ready to make our last move, to shed our skin for the final time and unveil our true shape."

"When?" Rani forced out the word, dreading the answer.

"Before the new year." Bardo replied with a devotion normally saved for a prayer to all the Thousand Gods. "We have all our players in place. Our strongest ally is ready to shed her skin, ready to take up her place in the Brotherhood and lead us to a new age."

"Who is that?"

"Haven't you guessed?" Bardo looked at Rani with a patient smile, and she caught a glimmer of the loving brother who had been her idol. She shook her head, a little ashamed at her slow grasp. "Larindolian's lady. Queen Felicianda."

"The queen!" Rani gasped, but even as the words escaped her, she remembered the message that Mair had brought her, a lifetime ago, in the marketplace—"The doe runs faster than the buck, and she doesn't tangle her antlers in the brush."

Was it only a month ago that Rani had thought those words applied to Guildmistress Salina? Even now, she had trouble remembering the certainty she had felt in the crowded square in front of the cathedral, the absolute faith that the guildmistress was the one prophesied by the Core. Of course, she realized now. The *queen* was the doe; she was the fleetest, the fastest, the best. Queen Felicianda had set the wheels in motion to place her own son upon the throne, and she had manipulated the world around her so that there was no risk that her own name or reputation would be sullied by the struggle.

Even as Rani recognized the truth, she realized that Bardo was still talking, still confessing the history of the dark circle he had joined. "Queen Felicianda was our founder. *She* was the one who brought us the Brotherhood, who showed us the error in our ways, here in Morenia. In *her* land, in distant Amanthia, there are no castes to bind people. They do not even have a hereditary king; the strongest men in all the land fight for the title when it is time."

"And that is better?" Rani imagined the battles and the bloodshed—she had heard the bards' tales of warfare.

Bardo laughed and ruffled her hair. "Of course it's better. The best man wins! We will never again be forced to beg food from the Merchants' Council. We will never again need to pray for a shred of justice from castes who could care less, who hate us."

"But what if we're not the best?"

Bardo's laughter filled the cathedral. "Not the best! Such doubts, and in one so young!"

"What if the king is better? What if Tuvashanoran was the best?"

"You don't know what you're saying. The king is an old man, Rani. I know he's been kind to you, and I know that you feel you owe him, but he is an evil man. He is the reason the rest of the castes survive. He is the reason our father was so unhappy. Must I remind you that he killed our family?"

"But that was because he thought that we killed Tuvashanoran! The prince was all his hope! He would have been a very good king."

"Tuvashanoran would have continued the old caste system all his life," Bardo snapped. "He would have ruled supreme until he ran the castes, and himself, and all of us into the ground! Tuvashanoran was a liar and a cheat. He promised himself to the Brotherhood; he even bore our mark. But he strayed from our mission and forgot our goals. He did not want to compete to lead us; he thought the title of 'king' should come to him because of his birth status. When his father decided to name him Defender of the Faith, Tuvashanoran forgot all he ever knew of Brotherhood and equality."

Rani began to see the Brotherhood's twisted logic. She could find the pattern behind Bardo's words; she reconciled his thoughts and his actions. "So," she began slowly, "with Tuvashanoran gone, you can change the old system. If you can put your own king on the throne, you'll succeed in bringing the Brotherhood to power."

"Precisely!" Bardo congratulated her. "And that's where you come in. It is very important that the initial change look like happenstance. We know that the people aren't ready for the Brotherhood yet. The castes are still too strong. We need to put the right man on the throne, and then we'll have a lifetime, his entire rule, to consolidate our power. We know the Brotherhood won't lead the way in one year, or in two, or maybe even in ten, but with time on our side...."

"And the right man is—"

"Bashanorandi," Bardo completed her sentence. "He is liked by the people, and his mother has taught him all the ways of her folk. And when, in years to come, certain records come to light, showing that King Bashanorandi is not truly descended from the line of Jair, the people will come to realize that their old hierarchies, their old castes, are completely without meaning. The Brotherhood will win, without costing a life."

"Except," Rani corrected, "Tuvashanoran, who would have been the king. And Halaravilli—he's the Crown Prince, not Bashi."

"And, for that matter, King Shanoranvilli himself," Bardo agreed. "But now is the time. The Brotherhood is at its greatest strength, and we have you—*you*—in the Palace every day. You can weave the last threads into our pattern and make the end of the castes more than just a bard's tale. You can guarantee that Bashanorandi is our next king."

Rani stared at Bardo in disbelief. She must have misunderstood him. She must have misheard his words. Bardo could not be telling her to murder Hal. "I don't know what you're talking about, Bardo."

"I think you do, Rani. I think you understand the Brotherhood's mission. We are so close... You can join us, dearest sister. You can be a full member of the Brotherhood, if only you do this one thing. Kill the pretender. Dispatch Prince Halaravilli and join the Brotherhood."

"No!" Rani cried, protesting the suggestion, protesting

the Brotherhood, protesting the fanatical light in Bardo's eyes. "You don't know what you're saying! Hal is the *hope* of Morenia. He can grow to fill Tuvashanoran's shoes."

" Prince Halaravilli is a babbling idiot! He can barely string together ten words in a coherent sentence!"

"That's all an act," Rani pleaded. "He chants and rhymes to protect himself, to save himself from ..." she swallowed hard, but forced herself to complete the sentence, "from those who wish him dead."

Bardo's hands closed over her arms, hunching her shoulders close about her ears. "Listen to yourself, Rani. He is a liar, a cheat. Does such a man deserve to be king? With one quick thrust of a blade, with one draught of poison, you can change all that. You can save the kingdom!"

"She's already said no."

The voice rang out in the cathedral, deadly cold against the passion of Bardo's plea. Rani whirled toward the sound, grateful for an ally in this mad battle, but her heart froze as she saw the speaker.

"Let her go, Bardo. She's made her choice." Guildmistress Salina stepped into the pool of flickering light beside Roat's altar.

"Salina!" Bardo started guiltily, as if he and his sister had been caught in some immoral tryst. "What are you doing here?"

"Larindolian sent me. He did not think you had the power to bring this one into our ranks." Salina sniffed and leveled her agate eyes on her former apprentice. "We've waited long enough for her to come around. We'll end that all tonight."

"What do you mean?" Even as Rani choked on the chill pronouncement, Bardo maneuvered himself so that he stood between his sister and her guildmistress.

"She's had her chance, Bardo. You've told her all about us—more than any outsider has heard in all the existence of the Brotherhood—and still she hesitates. We can't take the risk. We can't endanger the lives of a hundred faithful followers for one mewling apprentice who refuses to listen to reason."

"She'll listen, Salina!" Rani had never heard Bardo plead before. "I had not finished explaining."

"You've told her more than any *true* follower of Justice should need to hear. Step aside, Bardo." Salina raised one arm, and a troop of armor-clad men stepped from the cathedral shadows, coalescing like a deadly midnight fog.

"Guildmistress Salina," Rani began.

"Silence!" snapped the old woman, and Rani was obedient enough to her former caste that she held her tongue. Bardo, though, was not so constrained.

"We *need* Rani, Salina. You argued for her recruitment yourself. You said that we needed to get a pilgrim into the Palace, that we needed to plant an agent who was above suspicion."

"Ahhhh," sighed Salina. "I feared as much." Her words were heavy, like iron, like death. "You are willing to set aside the bonds of Brotherhood for her."

"I'm not doing any such thing!" Bardo protested, pulling Rani close to his chest. She felt hardened leather beneath his tunic, as if he had feared this ambush in the cathedral.

"Enough of this foolishness!" Salina clapped her hands, and the ring of soldiers tightened around Bardo and Rani. Long steel knives glinted in the flickering candle-light, poisonous tongues darting back and forth like serpents. "Make your choice, Bardo. The Brotherhood, or that treacherous rat!"

Rani squirmed, fighting against Bardo's sinewy arm to look into his face. His breath came harsh, as if he had raced the wolves outside the City, as if he had rung the Pilgrims' Bell with all his might. He did not look at her; instead, his eyes stared into the cathedral's dark heart, as if he were seeking advice from First God Ait and all the Thousand Gods.

Rani felt the pulse in his arm, felt the desperation in his breath. She longed to speak, but she was afraid to topple the balance, afraid to unravel the pattern she could only hope was forming. As she glared daggers at Salina, the guildmistress measured Bardo's response with her own narrowed eyes. "Choose, Bardo, or I'll take the choice from you."

The soldiers shifted restlessly, and Rani saw the fire lick their knives. There was no choice. There was no decision. Bardo could hand her over to the Brotherhood, or he could accept her fate for both of them. The Brotherhood's soldiers would not be content until they had sheathed their blades in blood.

Bardo read the same message in the eyes of his erstwhile allies. His fingers were icy tongs as he turned Rani to face him. "Go with them, Ranikaleka. They'll keep you until we have finished our work. When the Brotherhood is done, you'll be free to join me."

Salina rolled her eyes in exasperation, and the soldiers shifted nearer, using their long knives to herd Rani from her brother's side. "Go, Rani!" The command was spoken with the power that Bardo had had over her entire life—the power of a favorite brother. "Go with them, Rani, and all will be fine!"

"Bardo!"

Her anguished cry was cut off by a new clatter of mail-clad soldiers, by countless boots on stone. "Halt!" The command rang out in the cathedral, and the space was suddenly filled with torches. A company of guards, all dressed in the king's livery, streamed down the aisle. "Halt in the name of King Shanoranvilli!"

Rani was so relieved that she nearly collapsed by Roat's altar. Before she could speak her gratitude, the captain of the guard signaled for his men to surround the Brotherhood's soldiers, to close ranks around Guildmistress Salina and Bardo. Only when the Brotherhood's threat had been quelled did the captain pay attention to the quaking apprentice in the middle of the cathedral aisle.

"Ranita Glasswright!" he announced, leveling his own heavy sword at her throat. "Stand forth and submit to the justice of the rightful king of all Morenia. Answer to King Shanoranvilli for the death of Prince Tuvashanoran!"

CHAPTER 15

"Eat, girl. Build your strength for the questions you'll be asked today." The soldier laughed harshly as he flung a bowl of thin gruel through the iron bars of Rani's cell. A tin cup of water followed, sloshing as the guard made his hurried way along the dungeon's dank corridor.

Rani barely looked up at the voice. In the—how long had it been? three days?—that she had been imprisoned in King Shanoranvilli's dungeons, she had not been able to swallow more than a bite of the poor fare that passed as breakfast, lunch, and dinner. In her fitful sleep, she remembered fine meals she had enjoyed, even the riches that Narda had shared with her so long ago in the marketplace, but she could not force her belly to accept the watery porridge.

"Aye," came a sarcastic voice from the cell across the cramped corridor. "There's a good girl. Your family would be proud of you."

Her family. The guards had made no secret of Rani's identity as they dragged her into the dungeons. The other prisoners had reacted with the patriotism of the bored; Rani had been spat at and called foul names. More than one wit made a two handed fist, waggling a single thumb in her direction as an obscene reminder of the glasswrights who had been methodically tortured while Rani roamed the city streets.

The prisoners knew that she had murdered Prince

Tuvashanoran; they needed no silly formality like a trial. Rani had not tried to defend herself as she walked along the stinking, damp corridor. She hoped there would be time for that later, time to tell the truth before King Shanoranvilli passed sentence on her.

Of course, the other glasswrights had had no trial. The prisoners made sure she learned the details. The apprentice glasswrights had been dragged from their cells, screaming, and returned to the cold stone rooms with bloody stumps where their thumbs had been. It had taken weeks, but finally all the glasswrights were maimed—the apprentices butchered, the Instructors questioned and bled until they were little more than ghosts. Some had died and been buried in the criminals' graveyard outside the City walls, forever denied the purification of a funeral pyre. Others had at last been set free, to forage whatever life they could in the hostile City streets. Not a glasswright remained in the dungeons.

Rani's family had had no trial either. They had huddled in their cell, crouching against the back wall so that the other prisoners could not witness their shame. The jailed scum had seen enough, though, to tell Rani details she had hoped never to learn. She knew the order in which her brothers and sisters had been taken from the prison. Now, she could recite the tortures they had suffered as they refused to divulge the absolutely unknown whereabouts of their missing daughter-sister, and Rani's far-too-active imagination taught her the feel of the rough rope about their necks before they were hanged like common thieves. Over and over again, she pulled her imagination away from their graves in the cold, winter earth. Unsuccessfully, she forbade herself to think of worms and dirt and putrefying flesh.

First her brothers, then her sisters. Her mother. Her father.

And now she had only one brother left alive—Bardo, who had been willing to hand her over to the harsh mercy of the Brotherhood of Justice. Rani found small comfort in the knowledge that the soldiers who had dragged her back to the dungeons had rounded up the Brotherhood as well.

Bardo and Salina's armed guards were penned elsewhere in the warrens beneath the castle.

Guildmistress Salina had been here also, in this desolate dungeon full of women and the rare unfortunate family. After the woman had shouted herself hoarse, she had taken to banging her tin cup against her cell's irons bars. The guards wrestled away the cup, only to be serenaded with a hard-soled leather shoe. At last, the guildmistress had been carted off amid much swearing—her teeth had found at least one soldier.

Even though Rani had come to despise the old woman, she longed to cheer the spirit of such rebellion. Then she remembered the evil that Salina had directed toward her, the concerted decision the guildmistress had made when she permitted Rani's fellow apprentice, Larinda, to be maimed. Salina had had the power to stop the madness even then, but she had not acted. Now, Rani was certain that the guildmistress had drawn on the Brotherhood's dark loyalties to arrange her own escape, weeks ago, when all the glasswrights were first imprisoned. She had been freed to work her continuing evil in the City streets, and all of the guildsmen she had sworn to lead were maimed as Salina prowled the Brotherhood's warren inside the City walls.

Rani took another look at the thin gruel in her bowl and felt her empty belly contract in rebellion. She drank the cup of tepid water, but she sent the bowl sliding across the flagged stone floor, watching with sad satisfaction as it came to rest against the bars of the cage on the opposite wall. The prisoner in that cell crowed with victory and snatched up the bowl before a guard could stumble in to spoil the fun. Rani tried to close her ears to the prisoner's gurgling satisfaction.

She was cold in her cell, but she was loath to curl up on the filthy straw that turned to slime on the stone floor. Every time she touched the sodden stalks, she remembered Prince Halaravilli's words. "I could lock you up where the straw still stinks of the blood from your fellow glasswrights, where you might find a thumb mixed in with the offal."

Well, he had certainly done that. She had no doubt that Hal had sent the guards after her in the cathedral. He had proven that he was superior to a mere masquerading apprentice. With the power of all the palace guards, he had succeeded in showing Rani who was in control. She was certain that Hal had had her arrested, seeking vengeance for the deaths of both Tuvashanoran and Dalarati.

Rani sighed deeply and closed her eyes as she leaned her head against the stone wall. Even if she denied killing the eldest prince, she could not duck responsibility for Dalarati's death. She had blood on her hands, and no amount of protest would wash it away.

Her mind began to wander, freed by the hunger in her belly to roam strange hallways. Blood on her hands.... She had seen other people with literal blood on their hands. Instructor Morada for one. The glasswright had cut herself often enough as she plied her craft. Even now, Rani remembered the Instructor's fury on the platform outside the cathedral. Who had been lurking beneath the scaffold that day?

As if in answer to her idle query, she pictured Bardo in the cathedral, remembered the rough patches on his hands as his fingers closed around her throat. In her struggle to escape his rage, she had scarcely noted the callouses on his fingers. Now, though, with nothing to do but think on what Bardo had said and done, she connected up his roughened hands with his words. The Brotherhood, he believed, had given him a chance, an opportunity to grow beyond his caste. He had learned to use nobles' weapons—like the bow? Rani knew, deep in her heart, that the callouses she had felt against her windpipe were the result of a rubbing bowstring.

Try as she might, Rani could find no reason to believe that Bardo had *not* killed Tuvashanoran. The thought made her laugh, but it was a laugh of madness. Her family had been tortured and killed so that they would divulge a murderer's whereabouts. They had thought the guards sought Rani, thought they had been betrayed by the youngest child in the family. In reality, the Traders' disaster had been brought about by Bardo, the eldest son and brother who had been lured away by power. By murderous, thieving power.

Perhaps Halaravilli was right—in a manner of speaking, Rani *had* killed Prince Tuvashanoran. If she had stayed on the scaffold that day, if she had ignored Instructor Morada's command to leave, she might have been able to persuade Bardo that he was wrong…. Even if she had returned to the guildhall like a good apprentice, if she had held her tongue when she saw the bow silhouetted against the window, she might not have aided Bardo in his deadly mission….

Rani strung together the beads of disaster as if she were creating another pattern in the wares at her father's stall.

The clank of metal interrupted her mawkish thoughts, forcing her to full wakefulness with a sudden heart-pounding terror. The guards could be coming for any of the prisoners. They could be bringing some new unfortunate. But Rani knew the soldiers came for her.

They were rough as they pulled her from her cell, and their exclamations were even harsher as the leader exclaimed, "Put her in chains! She'll not be a threat when we take her before the king."

The iron shackles looked evil in the soldiers' hands, and the men had no compunctions against using brute force to place them on Rani. The nearest soldier pulled her upright with a force that nearly yanked her arm from its socket, and then he hurtled her across the damp stone corridor until she fetched up hard against the iron bars of the opposite cage. She was still trying to draw a breath into her bruised lungs when he jerked her arms behind her, twisting lengths of chain about her neck and waist before he secured the links with a giant padlock.

Rani shook her head dazedly, trying to clear the cobwebs from her mind. Lan protect her, surely the soldier did not need to be so rough. He must be putting on a show for the benefit of his men. Show or not, Rani's arms settled into a dull ache as the unaccustomed weight pulled at her joints.

The soldier, though, was not finished. As if Rani were the most dangerous of criminals, the guard produced another length of chain. This time, two of the armored men pressed her against the prison bars, crushing her narrow chest against the cruel iron as their leader wove the links about her ankles, clasping the shackles to the chains at her waist.

One of the soldiers dug a mailed fist into the nape of her neck, forcing her to turn her head to the side, to gasp for air. Out of the corner of her eye, she could make out the occupant of the cell she pressed against, an ancient bundle of rags, more filth than human. As the soldiers tugged at their handiwork, testing the locks, the other prisoner looked up, snaring Rani's eyes with a surprisingly clear gaze. "Mind yer caste, little one. Mind yer caste i' th' court o' th' king."

Rani knew the voice; she knew the all-seeing eyes that peered from the heap of filthy rags. She remembered the ancient Touched creature who had spoken to her on the doorstep in the abandoned quarter where Larindolian had betrayed Instructor Morada. "You!" She managed to breathe, before a soldier's open-handed slap sent her head careening into the cell's bars.

"Silence!" bellowed the soldier, and the ancient Touched creature began to cackle. Rani was led away before the guards could retaliate against the other prisoner.

It took all of her concentration to keep her feet amid the tricky chains. More than once, a soldier reached out to steady her, jerking her upright as she over-compensated for the weight slung about her chest and ankles. She was so disconcerted by her bonds that she did not pay attention to the corridors they strode through. The tall doors of the royal audience hall were a complete surprise.

The soldiers, though, did not waste time for their young charge to gape in amazement. Instead, they knocked the doors back on their hinges, sending a shudder through the hall's stone walls. Silence collapsed over the room, and Rani immediately became the focus of dozens of eyes.

The audience chamber was lined with fluted columns, and a well-armed guard stood between every two posts, sword drawn, mailed hands caressing imminent death. More threatening by far, though, were the black-robed figures standing at the base of each column—Jair's Watchers.

Rani's heart sank. She knew now that she would be subjected to the Defender's Judgment. No council would sit to judge her; no disinterested panel would determine her fate. King Shanoranvilli, as Defender of the Faith, would decide the punishment for the girl he believed had murdered his son. He had such jurisdiction because the murder had taken place in the cathedral, because the victim had been prostrate before the altar. The Defender could act without explanation, without justification, so long as he acted in the sight of Jair's Watchers.

If Rani despaired at the black robes' message, she nearly cried out when she looked at Shanoranvilli on his dais. Gone was the grandfatherly lord who had welcomed her into his family, into the bosom of his household. Now, the king wore his heavy crown of state and a robe of bloody crimson. His eyes were red-rimmed, sunk deep above his collapsing cheeks, and Rani imagined that she could hear the rattle of his breath across the hall. His chain of office lay across his chest, the heavy golden J's smothering him.

Weak as he was, the king did not stand alone. On his right side, ready to do the royal bidding, stood Lord Larindolian. Rani's eyes narrowed as she met the noble's vulpine eyes, and she barely resisted the urge to spit at the chamberlain's feet. Larindolian, for his part, merely nodded once, as if Rani were a faintly disgusting specimen he had seen delivered to the royal menagerie.

On Shanoranvilli's left side, perched on the edge of a straight-backed throne, sat Queen Felicianda, flanked by her son, Prince Bashanorandi. The noble woman's chin jutted forward as she surveyed Rani, and her fingers tightened on her husband's arm. Even now, as Rani knew she should hate and fear this conspiring traitor, she found herself snared by the queen's fragile beauty, by the grace of a doe caught unawares at the edge of a forest.

Before Rani could embarrass herself by appealing to the queen's mercy, the captain of the guard saluted his liege.

"The prisoner, Your Majesty." Rani had only an instant's warning before the soldier's mail-clad hand spread across her back, propelling her forward with a vicious thrust until she tripped and landed hard on her knees.

"Your Majesty," she whispered, licking her lips to help force out the words. "My lady," she inclined her head toward the treacherous queen.

"Silence!" ordered the guard. "You'll not speak until the Defender of the Faith gives you leave!"

Larindolian nodded his head in support of the brutal suppression, but King Shanoranvilli scarcely seemed to hear the command. Instead, he looked down at Rani with a fog of sorrow across his gaze. "First Pilgrim.... I had thought to make you one of my family, to bring you into the house of Jair. I believed you were true to the Thousand Gods."

"Your Majesty," Rani responded, ignoring the frustrated shift of soldiers' boots on stone. "I *am* true to the Gods, and loyal to your House as well."

"You show your loyalty in strange ways, First Pilgrim. You murder my son and then you conspire against me inside the very walls of my palace."

"I—" Rani started to interrupt in protest, but she was cut off by another voice.

"Begging your pardon, Sire." All eyes turned toward the speaker, captivated by his smooth and respectful tone. "Begging your pardon, but by the laws of Jair, you may not condemn the First Pilgrim for murdering our brother until she has been formally judged guilty of that heinous crime. First, we must question the prisoner and determine the truth. With your approval, Sire, I will serve as Chief Inquisitor."

Rani knew the voice, but she was amazed at the steady force of the words. Squaring her shoulders and bracing herself against her strangling bonds, she turned to face Prince Halaravilli. A shudder wriggled through her as she realized that Hal had wholly set aside his sing-song chants. She met his eyes boldly, and after a moment, she managed to say, "Your Highness."

"Your Majesty," Lord Larindolian interrupted as Hal

acknowledged Rani's greeting with the slightest of nods. "I renew my protest. Need I remind you that we are dealing with a traitor here? A murderess who has royal blood upon her hands? It is one thing for you, Sire, to sit in judgment, on the seat of Jair.... But to hand over the reins to one so ... so inexperienced as Prince Halaravilli...."

The king sighed deeply. "Prince Halaravilli is my heir, Lord Larindolian. The one I would have bear this weight for me is the very one who cannot be here today. Prince Tuvashanoran has been gathered to Jair's breast, and I must see that my other sons are prepared to follow in my footsteps."

"But, Your Majesty, it would defame Tuvashanoran's memory if his murderer's trial were conducted by the prince," Larindolian pushed. Rani thought she heard a note of desperation behind the chamberlain's tone; she was not the only person who had heard the steel in Hal's formal invocation.

"Lord Chamberlain," sighed the king, "you know the rules as well as I. I may appoint a Chief Inquisitor, so long as Jair's Watchers preserve the trial's fairness." Larindolian started to protest further, but Shanoranvilli raised a quaking hand, lowering his voice and pulling his chamberlain closer. Although Rani could just make out the king's whisper, she was certain his words were lost to the more distant witnesses in the vast chamber. "My lord, I am old. I am tired. I still mourn the loss of my eldest son, and this new loss of the pilgrim I took into my house. I dare not harness the power of the Inquisitor's Orb."

The king should never have made such a confession in open court, before soldiers and scribes and the anonymous subjects of Jair's Watchers. Rani saw a light spark in Larindolian's eyes, a glint of joyful confirmation that he was correct, that the Morenian throne was ripe for the plucking. For now, though, the conspirator was left with no choice but to bow in submission. "Of course not, Your Majesty. I was only concerned for the prince; you know he is of tender years. I had thought to spare him the weight of these decisions. Perhaps he should share the burden with his brother."

Bashi, standing beside his mother's throne, creased his handsome face to a frown as he eavesdropped on his elders' conversation. He spared a worried glance at Larindolian, just a flash across the king's seated figure, but Rani read volumes in that look. Bashi expected Larindolian to win the day.

As if to echo her son's desires, Queen Felicianda settled a hand on the king's arm, and for just a moment, Rani thought the chamberlain might succeed with his suit. If the king felt he must prove his trust in his lady, his faith in her line, then he might indeed let the reins be shared by the princes.

Before Rani could calculate the cost of letting Bashi sit in judgment over her, Hal cleared his throat. "Begging your pardon, Sire, my lord." He inclined a respectful bow toward the chamberlain as he interrupted, and Rani wondered if she were the only person in the hall who could see the prince's hand clenched into a fist at his side. "With all due respect to Lord Larindolian, the crown is a heavy weight, and it will not sit on two heads when you walk with Jair in the Heavenly Fields, may that be long in the future." Hal paused to make a religious sign, and there was a noticeable delay before the spellbound watchers also invoked Jair to spare the king for many years. Rani struggled to follow suit, fighting her massive iron chains. "I can do this, Sire. Trust me to avenge my eldest brother."

The fire behind Hal's words burned to the edge of the audience chamber, and even Bashi stepped back in surprise. The court had become so accustomed to Hal's sing-song games that they were overwhelmed by his calm, insightful logic. Shanoranvilli eyed his oldest living son for a long minute and then nodded his head in slow approval. "Go ahead, my son. Seek justice with Jair's guidance."

Again, Hal made his religious sign, invoking the Pilgrim's support and the light of all the Thousand Gods. Then, he raised his eyes and proclaimed directly to his father, "First, we are missing two prisoners. Guard!"

There was a moment of confusion, and then the doors to the chamber crashed opened once again. Two clusters of soldiers swarmed into the room. Rani craned her neck, ignoring the heavy pressure of iron against her jugular as she took in her fellow accused—Bardo and Guildmistress Salina.

Then, before Rani could fully think about what their presence meant for her, for the City and the Brotherhood, Hal raised an imperious hand, gesturing for the nearest of Jair's Watchers to approach. Two black-robed figures flowed from the embrasures between the nearest columns. The first Watcher bore a wrought iron stand, an intricate piece of darkest metal, which settled on the stone floor on four steady legs—one leg for each of the four castes of noble-priest, soldier, guildsman, and merchant.

As soon as the stand was level, the other Watcher stepped near, balancing a head-sized globe on the top of the metal holder. Rani had heard of the Inquisitor's Orb before—all the people in the City knew its power. Like the glasswrights' globe that had been shattered so many months before, this sphere had been crafted by Jair himself, at the beginning of the Pilgrim's reign. It incorporated all the power of that great age, when the Thousand Gods had watched over Morenia with a vengeance.

The globe was made of a glass-like substance, although Rani could see that it was like no other glass she had ever handled. The smooth surface was finer than anything the glasswrights could ever have fashioned, solid like crystal, but translucent, swirled with colors, and utterly flawless. Rani thought of the last time she had settled her hands on a similar orb, the day she had spoken her apprentice oaths before Guildmistress Salina.

Now, at Halaravilli's bidding, Rani placed her hands on the smooth surface of the Inquisitor's Orb, fighting her iron chains to bend her wrists. At the touch of her fingers, its swirling colors coalesced, merged into each other like ink feathering into water. Blue, green, yellow—all were swallowed up until the orb glowed with an inner light, a deep crimson like the shade of Rani's blood. Like the garnet eyes on the Brotherhood's snakes. Rani tried to swallow with her suddenly dry throat, and she barely managed a silent plea to Lan.

The Inquisitor's Orb would sense the truth of the answers she gave today. If she lied, the crimson light would change, and all the world would know that Rani was a traitor. A conspirator against the king. A murderer.

Halaravilli waited until Rani's palms were flat against the sphere, and then he gazed at her evenly. "The Inquisition shall now begin. What is your true name?"

She stared at him in confusion. Her *true* name? Was that the name she had been born with? The name she had earned through her slavish labor in the guild? Was it the one she had claimed for herself when she ran in the streets with Mair's troop? The name she had been granted by the Thousand Gods, when they permitted her to serve as the First Pilgrim?

"I—" Her voice squeaked out, high and shrill, and she forced herself to swallow, to gulp down a calming breath. "Your Highness, I am called many things. Marita, Rani, Ranita, Ranimara, Rai—" *Ranikaleka*, she thought, not looking at Bardo. "Many things," she continued. "But those names are all unimportant, for whatever one calls me, I am always the same. I remain the same poor pilgrim in search of the guidance of all the Thousand Gods."

Hal's eyes remained deadly serious, and he intoned in a voice like death, "Then we shall call you Ranita Glasswright, for that is how you stand accused before us." He continued after a long minute, "So, tell me Ranita. How did you come to be in the Palace?"

Rani's first thought was that the question was silly—everyone in this room knew how she had been selected as the First Pilgrim. Nevertheless, she should hardly duck out of easy questions, not when the orb pulsed beneath her hands, not when she knew the hard questions Hal might ask of her. If *this* was Hal's idea of an Inquisition, perhaps she could answer and emerge unscathed, with her reputation untarnished. Rani offered up a fleeting prayer to all the

Thousand Gods that she might be able to clear her name and avoid incriminating her sole surviving kin.

Taking a deep breath, she launched into a spirited recitation of her coming to the cathedral, of the hundreds of bodies pressing in close upon one another. She explained how she had been distracted, held back in the crowd, as each of the pilgrims was greeted in the name of one of the Gods. She recounted how luck—luck, and the all the Thousand Gods—had brought her to the cathedral portal at the right time, in the right place, just as the priest was ready to name the First Pilgrim.

Hal listened to every word, nodding as if in confirmation when she spoke of her wonder at being chosen. He looked neither to right nor left as he listened, and Rani found herself wanting to tell him more, wanting to share with him that it was *Salina* who had detained her in the square, it was the guildmistress who had held her back until the right instant. Still, Rani held her tongue. If she were forced to name Salina, then she'd be forced to name the Brotherhood, and then many others would suffer—not least, Bardo.

The globe under her hands tingled, as if a low fire burned in its core. The warmth was beckoning, comforting after the dungeons' chill.

She should have been prepared for the prince's next question, even though it was delivered in an easy, off-hand manner. "So, Ranita, were you in the cathedral square often?"

"Oh, no!" Rani remembered that she was supposed to have come to the City from far-away Zarithia, even as she recalled that she was bound to speak the truth. She swallowed the easy lie—"Never"—and managed instead the truthful, "Not often at all."

Hal rounded on her, like a wolf cutting a lamb from the herd. "And when was the last time you had been in the cathedral, before your selection as First Pilgrim?"

His grey eyes were so penetrating that Rani could not help but wonder if he had noticed her on that day, when Tuvashanoran had been presented as Defender of the Faith.

Rani's mouth went dry, and her heart began to constrict in her chest. She had no ready lie, no half-truth for this prince who had befriended her. Befriended her, or so she had thought. Perhaps he had merely been playing her for a fool, feeding her a tale, as he had fed the entire court, making them believe that he was a babbling idiot.

"Ranita Glasswright, I asked you a question. When were you last in the cathedral, before the day you were selected as First Pilgrim?"

Rani swallowed hard, but she could produce no more than a whisper. "On the day your brother was to become Defender of the Faith, Your Highness."

There was a rustle among Jair's Watchers, the murmur of a crowd that was pleased by the play it had come to witness. Hal raised a commanding hand to the captain of the black-clad contingent, and persisted as if he were unaware of Rani's inner struggle. "And what were you doing in the cathedral on that day, Ranita?"

Ranita. Her name as an apprentice, a glasswright. A name her family had sacrificed for. A name her family had died for. She swallowed hard, raising guileless eyes to meet the prince's. "I did no evil that day, Your Highness."

Taking a deep breath, she plunged into the story, careful to tell only the truth, even as she excised any part of her tale that would implicate Tuvashanoran's true murderer, Bardo. Her story was the last offering she could make in honor of her family.

She told how she had come to the cathedral, and how the sunlight had shone brilliantly through the stained glass. She told of the beauty and the glory, watching Prince Tuvashanoran kneel before the altar. She captured the pageantry, the gallantry, the knowledge that she was in the company of one of the greatest men in the history of all Morenia. And then, scarcely pausing for breath, she told how she had seen the bow outlined against the Defender's Window, and how she had cried out to save the prince. To *save* Tuvashanoran. Not to kill him.

As Rani spoke, the globe beneath her fingers grew warm.

At first, she thought that was the normal property of glass growing used to human touch. But as she chose her words, as she remembered the fervency of her faith on that autumn day, the globe pulsed beneath her hands, radiating heat like an oaken fire.

"And, Ranita, did you know anyone in the cathedral that morning?"

Her carefully constructed tale shimmered in the air between them. With her fingers poised over the globe, there was no possibility of lying, no chance of dodging the question that called for a simple yes or no. She thought of taking her punishment and ending this entire sad charade. She thought that she should answer in the negative, do her best to preserve the last member of her family, to save Bardo. She should speak words that would permit her brother to live, would permit Guildmistress Salina to survive, as her true flesh-and-blood mother no longer could. This was the moment she had waited for, the moment that all the Thousand Gods had guided her to—this was her chance to salvage life from the horrors of death that she had witnessed.

Hal looked directly into her eyes and repeated his question. "Ranita Glasswright, did you know anyone in the cathedral?"

"Yes." She braved his gaze, pleading with him to release her from the next, inevitable question, but knowing that she had already made her decision. She had already chosen truth, and justice, and the light of the Thousand Gods.

"Who?"

Rani's heart pounded in her ears, and she longed to raise her fingers from the tell-tale globe. Her palms were burning now, scalding against the blood-red orb, and she imagined that her flesh would soon begin to curl. One little lie. One little denial of fact, twisting of the truth. Surely, the Thousand Gods would understand, would commend loyalty to family and caste.

But, looking into the strong lines of Hal's face, seeing the ghost of Prince Tuvashanoran, she realized that she would not lie. She would not try to save Salina. Salina, or Bardo, or the Brotherhood. Larindolian, or Felicianda, or Bashi. She would tell her story. She would tell the truth, set out the pattern, trade her words for whatever the prince would give her in exchange. She must mind her true caste—her merchant caste—as the Touched creature had ordered her to do so long before.

"Salina. That woman there."

"You stupid cow!" Salina's poison spewed across the audience chamber.

"Silence her!" Hal snapped immediately, and one of the soldiers produced a gag, using it efficiently on the writhing, foul-mouthed guildmistress. The black-robed Watchers at the edges of the chamber took a step closer, but Hal waved them back to their places.

"Salina, you say," he turned to Rani when a semblance of peace had returned to the room. "And how do you know Salina?"

Even now, before she spoke the words, Rani could feel the globe cooling beneath her fingers. She could feel the Thousand Gods hovering about her, waiting for her to speak the truth. Now, Jair was standing beside her, resting his calm hands on her shoulders.

Jair, the First Pilgrim, the man who had lived his life in each of the City's castes. She felt his presence, like she had felt the power of her father, the force of her brother. Jair comforted her, even as he laid out the rough road she must follow. She was a trader by birth. She saw patterns and harnessed them, trading to preserve herself. Minding her caste, minding her birth right, Rani Trader began to tell the court all she knew about Tuvashanoran's death, about the Brotherhood, about its plots for power and control in the City.

When she started to speak, she was conscious of the people around her. She could see Hal's lean face studying her intently; she could catch a glimmer of the old king, watching her confession with rheumy eyes. Larindolian, Felicianda, Bashi, even Bardo and Salina behind her—they all paid attention to every word she chose.

As she spoke, though, she ceased to be aware of her companions in the hall. She told of her sick realization in the cathedral, of the instant she knew that everything had gone most horribly wrong, and then Tuvashanoran was slain, cut down by the cruelest arrow because he had turned at her innocent words of warning. She told of her terror when she had found her family home burned, her shame and anger when her childhood friend, Varna, denounced her. As she related all that had happened in the City streets, she remembered more and more details—a glimpse of truth buried deep in Mair's words, a glimmer of reality shielded behind Dalarati's dedication to the Crown and to chivalry.

She spared nothing and no one in her telling, confessing even to murdering the proud young soldier in his barracks room. As she related that greatest crime, she stared at her own hands, amazed that they did not still bear the mark of sacrificial blood.

The first time she mentioned Salina's name, the guildmistress stiffened. When Rani identified Larindolian as the man in the deserted quarter, berating Instructor Morada, the chamberlain gasped and started to choke out a denial. As she labeled Bardo as the Brotherhood contact whom she had met in the cathedral, the very member of the Brotherhood who had encouraged her to execute Prince Halaravilli, Bardo had cried out her name, but his voice was faint in her ringing ears. He was silent when she reported the callouses on his hands, his boasting that he had learned noble weaponry under the Brotherhood's tutelage. When she named the queen as the leader of all the Brotherhood, Felicianda spoke no word at all; she merely tightened her fingers on the arms of her throne.

By the time Rani was finished, there was nothing but silence in the audience chamber.

"And so," she said at last, inclining her head toward Prince Halaravilli, "I stand before you today. I have failed in everything I tried—I left my father's home never to return, I destroyed the glasswrights' guild, I murdered a soldier, and I defiled the good office of the First Pilgrim. I have no choice but to throw myself upon the mercy of this court and the good graces of the king."

In the silence that followed, Rani spread her fingers across the surface of the crimson orb. Where it had beat hot as blood before, now it was cool to the touch, soothing, like the whisper of a mother's hand across her fevered brow. Rani drank in that comforting chill, remembering to breathe, trying not to think.

And Halaravilli himself seemed captured by the same awe that commanded her. The prince looked out at the assembled witnesses, but he appeared unable to speak, unable to command the convened court.

Unable that was, until Larindolian recovered his voice. "Lies!" the chamberlain hissed. "All lies!"

"And what reason would I have to lie!" Rani cried, stung back to life by the desperate denial.

"Who knows what reason a gutter rat has to do anything! You are an ungrateful beast! This royal family has taken you under its wings, nursed you at its breast, while all the time you were the stinging serpent. You place the blame on Instructor Morada, a woman who is dead and cannot speak for herself. Why should we believe you?"

"I have shouldered blame for myself, my lord," Rani answered, the chill from the orb seeping into her words. "I confessed to murdering Dalarati, although even then I acted on your command."

Larindolian spluttered, but Hal interrupted before the chamberlain could fling more accusations about the room. "Ranita's story is easily tested. Let us see who bears the mark of the snake."

"What!" bullied Larindolian. "Would you have us strip here in the audience hall?" The chamberlain tried a haughty laugh.

As Hal raised a commanding hand, the soldiers stepped forward from the columns, bristling with drawn swords. A quick shake of the prince's head froze the traditional fighting men in their stance of readiness, and then a hand signal freed Jair's Watchers to step forward from their marble columns.

Rani could not make out their faces inside their black cowls; rather, she could only watch as two black-robed figures approached each of the accused. A pair flanked the queen, ready to lay hands on royal flesh, but King Shanoranvilli finally broke his silence. "No, son. You go too far."

Hal stared at his father solemnly, pity deep in his eyes, and he gave a tight nod to Felicianda's Watchers. "Don't let her move," he instructed, and the two figures drew closer, even as the queen raised her imperious chin. Before she could speak, Hal glanced at his pale younger brother. "Him, too." Bashi started to protest his innocence, but Hal ignored the prince, gesturing tightly with his hand.

No one dared to breathe in the chamber, in the instant after the command. Then, the audience hall was filled with the sound of ripping fabric. Rani whirled about, staggering in her iron chains, as first Bardo's arm was bared, then Salina's snake-encircled calf. Even as the assembly gaped at the writhing snakes on the naked traitors' flesh, Larindolian fought for freedom, twisting beneath his captors' hands as if he were a fish on a line. The black-robed figures moved in an intricate ballet, though, and in a few heartbeats the chamberlain had been bared to his smallclothes. The snakes that twined about his chest were all the more fierce for his flushed skin, for the rage that made him pant, made the serpents writhe like living beings.

Even Halaravilli was unnerved by the spectacle, by the nest of serpents that seemed to engulf the lord chamberlain. When the prince could find his voice, he turned to his father. "My lord," Hal's voice was respectful, even as it was filled with awe, "As Chief Inquisitor, I present to you five traitors, members of the so-called Brotherhood of Justice."

King Shanoranvilli seemed almost not to hear his son. The old man stared in amazement at his chamberlain, steadfastly avoiding any other sight in the room—Bardo or Salina or Bashanorandi, or, especially, Queen Felicianda. When he finally spoke, his voice was old and tired. "And Lord Chief Inquisitor, what sentence would you have me pass?"

Hal did not hesitate; he knew the rules. "Death is the

sentence for all traitors. Let these mongrel dogs hang by their necks on a slow rope, until they are dead, and then let their bodies be cast into an earthen grave, denied forever the purification of the pyre."

Felicianda gasped, drawing all eyes in the chamber as she fell to her knees, ignoring the black-robed figures around her. "My lord, I beg of you! Prince Bashanorandi is not one of us! He does not bear our mark of the snakes! He is innocent in all that has happened."

The queen's plea crumpled Shanoranvilli's face, and Rani realized that until then, the king had held out hopes that he could save Felicianda, that he could spare the woman he loved. Her cry, though, amounted to a confession, and the king merely shook his head in wordless sorrow. With difficulty, he whispered to his loyal son, "Your words are harsh, Lord Chief Inquisitor."

"My words are fair, Your Majesty. Death has always been the sentence for traitors. These folk knew that when they first nestled the snake to their breasts. They knew it when they plotted against the crown. They knew it when they murdered my brother, your son, when they planned to murder me and set my brother Bashanorandi on your throne, perhaps even before you were ready to leave it."

"My lord," Felicianda began, ignoring the cold-eyed prince. She spoke only to her husband, to the king she had wed fifteen years before. "You cannot listen to this child—"

"Silence!" Shanoranvilli's voice echoed in the hall. Rani's ears rang, and she wondered how the king's ancient lungs had produced such volume. It seemed as if another man spoke when the king said to his son, "But what about the Brotherhood? What about the members we do not know?"

"Your Majesty," Hal responded, and Rani could hear that he had already planned his words. "If you cut off a snake's head, it dies. The Brotherhood will be powerless without its brain, without its eyes, without its fangs."

For a long minute, Shanoranvilli looked at the traitors. At his wife, who had brought him love and children late in his life, and no small amount of riches with her dowry from the North. At his chamberlain, who had stood beside him through the years of ruling a kingdom. At the strangers who had brought such sorrow to his court—the guildmistress and the merchant, now trembling before his royal might. Rani watched the king, and she knew his decision before he did. She saw the pattern, knew there was only one way for order to be restored.

"So be it," the king said at last, and his words were almost lost in his beard. Sighing, he repeated, "So be it. In the name of all the Thousand Gods, and in the name of Jair himself, I declare that the lives of these four traitors shall be forfeit."

"My lord—" Felicianda exclaimed, and she would have fallen to the stone floor if Jair's Watchers had not held her upright.

"The Lord Chief Inquisitor is right, for time out of mind, there has been no other sentence."

"Have mercy, my lord!" Felicianda's voice clogged with tears. "In honor of our son, Prince Bashanorandi, have mercy!"

"Mercy you shall have," replied the king, after a long, painful silence. "On two counts, mercy. First, you will all meet the headman's axe, and not the gallows-rope. Second, your son ... our son ... will be spared, for he knew not what you did for him. That is one soul's blood you need not explain to all the Thousand Gods."

"Your Majesty," began Larindolian, who had paled to a sickly shade of white at the king's pronouncement. Now, the serpents on his chest stood out like great bruises on his flesh, cast into death spasms by the nobleman's panting.

"No word from you, Traitor," snapped the king. "You have cost me two who were most dear to my heart—my firstborn son, and my queen."

"But my lord—"

"Silence!" At a quick hand gesture, the nearest black-robed Watcher leveled steel against Larindolian's throat, and the chamberlain gave up his plea. Shanoranvilli waited one interminable moment and then nodded to the captain of the palace guard. "Let it be done now, before they can work more evil. Let the sentence be carried out in the central courtyard, before the sun reaches noon."

Rani watched in shock as the prisoners were escorted into the courtyard. She was horrified at the machine Hal had created, at the engine she had set in motion with her testimony. Hal spoke quiet words to the captain of the guard, and the soldier freed Rani from her iron bonds, leaving chains and locks in an ugly pile on the flagstones. Rubbing her wrists, Rani followed the royal party to the courtyard, surrounded by black-robed Watchers.

She should not have spoken. She should not have given Hal the fuel to feed his fire. She should have found another way to save the king, to tell the truth, to protect the crown from the Brotherhood.

When they reached the courtyard, Shanoranvilli's soldiers moved with great efficiency. Loops of rough hemp were cast around each of the prisoners, binding their arms to their sides. Rani imagined the rope against her own flesh, felt the fibers burrowing into her skin. She was snared by the expressions on the traitors' faces.

Felicianda, gazing at the king in utter disbelief.

Larindolian, false confidence returning, looking out at the growing crowd with vulpine superiority, as if he still scented escape.

Salina, glaring at Rani as if she had broken yet another piece of cobalt glass, as if she had upset a crucible of solder and was confirming yet again that she was a failure, a mistake, a miscreant who never should have been admitted to the glasswrights' guild.

And Bardo. "Rani," he whispered, and she imagined she could hear her name across the cobblestones. She heard the confession behind the two syllables: "I never meant for you to be caught up in all of this. I never meant to harm you, to harm the king, to harm Tuvashanoran. I never meant to destroy our family. I never meant for Salina's men to take you in the cathedral." All that he told her, and more, in the silence of his gaze across the courtyard. "Ranikaleka ..."

The end was fast. The executioner appeared from

nowhere, his chest bare in the freezing winter air. He carried the largest axe that Rani had ever seen. Shanoranvilli gave the commands, his voice bleak and hopeless. First, Felicianda, in recognition of her status. "Hail, Jair, and all the Thousand Gods, take this traitor from our midst." The actual command was a wordless cry, answered by the wet crash of axe on wooden block.

Then Salina, in deference to her gender. Then Larindolian, in honor of his caste. Then, last of all, Bardo.

Rani watched as her brother looked out on the assemblage, his eyes empty, his chest heaving in terror. He caught her gaze as he knelt, managed to hold her in his sight as the axe was raised. Shanoranvilli proclaimed the formula, and Rani cried out, almost as if she were giving the executioner his command.

She lurched forward, and Jair's Watchers swarmed around her, catching her as she plummeted to the cobblestones. As Rani collapsed under the stagnant waters of consciousness she thought that she saw the old Touched crone wreathed in a Watcher's black cowl. And Mair.... And Borin, the aged tradesman who controlled the Merchant's Council, who had sat in judgment of her so long before.... All so long ago, all in another life.... The Fellowship of Jair that Bardo had warned her about, had tried to save her from. The Fellowship of Jair in new robes, a dozen blackest garments. Absurdly, Rani remembered crouching in the marketplace, giving Mair a golden slip of paper, giving the Fellowship of Jair the power they now held over her, over Bardo.

Then, Rani was reeling, spinning, sinking under the tide as the headman's axe bit one last time into the block.

CHAPTER 16

Rani stood in the windowed embrasure of the royal nursery, looking out at the snow-blown landscape through her scavenged piece of cobalt glass. Yet another winter blizzard had whistled through the City the night before, and the central courtyard was knee-deep in snow. Icy paths had been tromped across the cobble-stones.

"You won't change anything by catching cold there."

"Your Majesty," Rani managed dully, not bothering to drop a curtsey as she turned from the unglazed window. Hal was clad from head to toe in black, the mourning attire he had worn for the past month, since Shanoranvilli slipped into the Heavenly Fields, giving in to the depthless sorrow of betrayal.

"Must I command you to call me by my name?" Hal kept his voice light, but his hands were firm on Rani's shoulders as he guided her away from the window. He closed the wooden shutters, pointedly not noticing the pool of blue glass in her palm.

"I'm sorry, Hal," she mumbled. "I'm tired this morning—the Pilgrims' Bell rang all night, through the storm, and it kept me awake."

He eyed her thoughtfully, obviously making a conscious decision not to challenge her truthfulness. Instead, he leaned back on one of the two facing stone benches, stretching out his legs to rest against the opposing bench. Rani could not help but notice that he had grown inches in the few months since her trial. Small surprise—she had grown as well. The nurses were constantly clucking about the need to find her new clothes, *mature* clothes. She sighed. Hal's motion, more than showing off his new-found height, had effectively cut off any escape from the alcove.

"Sit, Rani." He nodded, as if he read the realization in her mind. In this past month, he had taken to calling her by her birth name. "The nurses tell me that you cry out in your sleep. You're disturbing the princesses."

"Well, I certainly wouldn't want to do that!" Her words were hot, despite her resolution to stay in the good graces of the king of all Morenia. "We can't have children disturbed by nightmares, not when they live in a world so free of treachery and murder and lies." Hal did not react to her bitter words, and she forced herself to take a deep breath. "I can be out of here this afternoon, Your Majesty. If you'll just let me by—"

"What is it that you see, Rani? Why do you scream in your sleep?"

She stared at him as if he were mad, and it took her a moment to find incredulous words. "Can you truly ask me that, after all that has happened? Not three months ago, we watched four people executed in the courtyard below!"

"The nurses say you never call out the names of the dead. You never name my brother or your own, or even Dalarati." Out of habit, the prince made a holy sign, and Rani impatiently followed suit. "They say you speak other names—Mair and Borin."

Rani's eyes filled at the quiet compassion in Hal's voice. "You'll never understand," she sighed.

"Try, Rani. You've made me understand much in the past. Tell me."

She shuddered and forced herself to meet his grey eyes. "I grew up in a family, Hal, a large family. I was surrounded by brothers and sisters, and we all made and broke our alliances, every day and every night. But throughout all that,

I always thought that Bardo was true. I always thought that Bardo was good."

Drawing strength from Hal's silence, Rani continued. "When I learned of the Brotherhood of Justice, I still believed Bardo. When I heard of the Fellowship of Jair, I still believed Bardo. No matter what evidence I was given, what truth I was shown, I still found a way for Bardo to be good and true."

Hal started to speak, but Rani hushed him with a curt shake of her head. "No. That last day, that last terrible day.... When I saw Jair's Watchers in the black robes that *I* had given them, the black robes that *I* took from the merchants' tithes.... Mair and Borin and the others—*that* was the moment that I fully realized that I had made a choice. Surrounded by the Fellowship of Jair, I betrayed Bardo. I gave up my perfect brother." Rani sighed and dashed the unwanted tears from her cheeks, steeling herself to say the last bit, the worst words. "I don't deserve a family. I don't deserve to belong to any group. And so, I don't speak the names of the dead. They have no power over me; they had no power, even in the audience chamber. It is the living who torment me, who remind me that I'm alone now and forever."

Rani's silence stretched out until Hal finally asked, "May I speak now?" She nodded, directing her gaze at the cobalt glass, willing her eyes to stop welling up.

"You've lost one family, Rani, and nothing I can say or do will change that. But just as you found other names, other castes for yourself, so you can find other families. You can join us, join the Fellowship of Jair."

Foolish hope kindled in Rani's breast, but she doused it with the thought of all that she had done. Hal must have read her mind, because he continued: "We have an open space, you know. The one that belonged to Dalarati."

Familiar guilt twisted through Rani, and she repeated the soldier's name. "Dalarati."

Hal nodded. "Although, it's not fair of me to phrase our invitation like that. We were already waiting for you, before Dalarati died. We'd been watching you."

"Me! Why would you watch me?"

"Because you were where we needed eyes and ears. You came to our attention after you joined the guild. You were close to Salina; you maintained a link to Bardo. You were our ideal agent. That's when the Fellowship first spotted you, when we came to believe that you might be one of us." It was Hal's turn to cut off Rani's protest as he continued, "After Tuvashanoran was murdered, when we knew that the soldiers were looking high and low for you in the City, we feared that we would lose you. Mair made direct contact. You were brought before Borin, and he managed to keep you in the marketplace, to keep you safe from harm. Even so, after you served that egg-woman, the soldiers almost found you. Only Mair's early warning saved you."

Rani blinked and could see the Touched girl slipping from Borin's portico, just before the Councilor sent Rani off to the cathedral. "But she sent me *into* danger. The Brotherhood attacked the cathedral!"

"We had no way of knowing they would do that, that they were so desperate to retrieve Morada's body. Mair arranged with Borin that you would bear the tithes, and then she went on ahead, to the cathedral. She was working with others in the Fellowship to make good your escape from the City. My father's guards had just come too close."

"But why so much effort to save *me*?"

Hal was quiet for a long moment, and when he did speak, he chose his words carefully. "You were valuable to us, Rani. Once things quieted down in the City, we hoped to call you back from your refuge. We hoped that we could bring about the plan we'd hatched long ago. We wanted you to go to Bardo and be our agent within the Brotherhood."

"You wanted to use me."

"We wanted you to join us. We still do, Rani."

"Join you! But I killed one of your number!"

"All unknowing. You reacted to the lies you were told, to the evil you were fed. I am still authorized to invite you to join us."

"'Authorized'? Who gives orders to the king of all Morenia?"

"You know our leader—Glair. The wise old woman who watched over you at the beginning of your quest, who kept guard over you in the dungeons."

"The Touched crone!"

"Aye, or so she appears." Hal nodded respectfully. Rani turned away from the king, questions boiling in her mind. Mechanically, she opened the shutters, stared out at the winter scene below. In the snow-blown courtyard, she could not make out the chopping block, could not see where the executioner's axe had forever changed her life. After a long minute, Hal spoke, so softly that she almost missed his words. "Will you join the Fellowship? Will you join us, Rani? Ranita? Ranimara? Rai?"

Rani—the name belonging to her family, the relatives who were executed at the royal command. Ranita—the name belonging to her lost guild, to the glasswrights who were scattered or dead. Ranimara—a soldier's name, like the soldier she had murdered. Rai—the name belonging to the Touched, the City's anonymous chaff.

She had no caste; she had no name; she had nowhere to go in all the City.

"We need you with us," Hal whispered. "The Brotherhood may be vanquished, but Jair's way must still be tended."

"I know nothing of Jair's way. I've got blood on my hands."

"These are bloody times. The Fellowship will teach you about Jair."

"I'm a thirteen-year-old orphan, without a caste."

"You're one of us, if you desire."

He took the fragment of blue glass from her reluctant fingers and set it on the bench before enfolding her hands between his own, like a liege recognizing a vassal. "Rani, when I saw you in the guard's hut, when I knew that you were going alone, to face the worst the Brotherhood could offer, I knew I had to take some action. I had to save you, in any way I could. Even as I issued the orders, I knew that it would not be easy for you, being arrested, submitting to the Defender's Judgment. I could not let you go, though, could not set you loose in the City streets, to face what the Brotherhood had in store for you."

"But I'd been alone since the guild was destroyed." She sighed, tasting yet again the bitter realization that the glasswrights had been ruined for nothing, all for a grand mistake. "That was a crime, Hal. The guild did nothing wrong; they knew nothing of Salina's plots."

"It was wrong," he agreed.

"Sometimes, I dream of rebuilding the guild, of gathering together the glasswrights who are still out there...."

"I'll issue the orders today."

"That's it? Just issue the orders and gather them in?"

"That's only the beginning of the work. But they can start over again, and you can help them." Rani read the seriousness in his eyes, knew that he would send out the royal proclamation that afternoon.

"Just like that," she shook her head, a little dazed. "Command the forces of the kingdom with a snap of your fingers. Just like when you sent the soldiers after me in the cathedral."

He nodded seriously, not taking his eyes from her, not shirking from his role in bringing the Brotherhood to justice. "It was all that I could think to do."

"So that doesn't leave me much of a choice now, does it?" A growing smile softened her words. "If I leave the Palace, I won't get as far as the cathedral close before you'll send soldiers after me?"

"Maybe a little farther," he admitted. "The snow wreaks havoc with their armor."

"We couldn't have that—rusty armor for the king's crack troops."

Silence for a moment, and then Hal asked, "You'll stay?"

Rani nodded and spoke her words as solemnly as a vow. "I'll stay."

Hal smiled as he released her hands, and then he reached behind her, closing the wooden shutters on the snow-filled courtyard, the City beyond, and the kingdom of all Morenia.

A SNEAK PEAK AT THE GLASSWRIGHTS' PROGRESS

Volume Two of the Glasswrights Series

Rani Trader swung down from her tall bay stallion, taking a moment to pat the animal's muscled neck and catch her breath. The wind had torn at her lungs as she raced to the top of the rise, and she gasped for air, more than a little surprised that the past two years had given her the skill to ride so wildly. Behind her, several riders were strung out, flung across the tall grass like discarded chessmen. At the distant edge of the long, long plain, Rani could just make out the top of the City's tallest tower, already flecked with gold in the late afternoon light.

Rani's thoughts were not on Moren's towers, though. Instead, all of her attention was focused on Gry, the master falconer of Morenia. Rani's heart pounded as she stepped closer to the cadge that the falcon-master had set on the hilltop. Gry had left Moren early that morning, transporting by cart the sturdy birch enclosure and two prize falcons.

When Rani saw her kestrel's red and brown feathers, stark against the weathered supports of the cadge, she caught her breath. She was so pleased by Kalindramina that she scarcely spared a glance for the other raptor perched inside the enclosure. That bird was a peregrine, a falcon that merchant-born Rani would never be permitted to fly.

"Is she all right?" the girl asked the master falconer as she leaned over the kestrel. "Did the trip hurt Kalindramina?"

Gry snorted his gruff laugh and pulled at his right ear out

of long habit. "Nothing will hurt that little falcon, my lady. She's too mean to be hurt. It's no wonder the king doesn't fly kestrels! *I* expected you to get here earlier in the day, though." He weakened the implied criticism with another laugh.

"I wanted to." Rani frowned. This was the first day in ages that she had managed to break free from her obligations in King Halaravilli's court, free from the endless parade of ambassadors and nobles, guildsmen and soldiers, all intent on bringing the greatest glory to the kingdom of Morenia. Rani could barely remember the time, only a couple of years before, when she'd been afraid to leave the City walls, when she'd feared bandits and plague and all manner of disaster outside Moren. Now, scarcely a morning passed that she didn't dream of escaping the palace and all her courtly obligations. She took a deep breath, filling her lungs with the sweet aroma of autumn grass.

And she wasn't even supposed to be free this afternoon. Rani had promised to work on her embroidery. Nurse frequently assured her that she'd never find a husband if she did not master neat, even stitches in her handwork. Bristling against the injustice that made her old enough to waste her days entertaining visiting nobles but young enough to be subject to Nurse's jurisdiction, Rani had nodded in reluctant agreement and promised to try harder. Promised, that was, until Nurse had bustled out of sight.

Of course, Rani justified, Nurse *might* have relaxed her vigil if she'd known that Kalindramina was ready to fly. Even though the old woman knew nothing of falconing, Rani might have convinced her that the small raptor was a needy creature in the world of the Thousand Gods, a poor soul that required human contact. Besides, Rani could have explained, she herself must learn to watch over man *and* beast if she were eventually to count herself a good guildmistress.

For Rani held the future of the glasswrights in her hands, as surely as she had recently gripped her stallion's reins. It would likely take decades, but the former apprentice intended to rebuild the guild that had been destroyed two years before. The stained-glass makers had fallen victim to rumors and lies, to the king's mistaken belief that the artisans had been responsible for the Crown Prince's assassination. The new king, Halaravilli, had held true to his word, though, and he had sent a notice throughout his lands that the glasswrights had been forgiven, that they could return to Moren. Unfortunately, few of the guildsmen had trusted the royal proclamation. They remembered bloodshed and torture; they remembered betrayal and death.

Rani was determined, though. Even if she had to temporarily leave the comfort of Morenia, even if she had to travel to some distant land to learn her craft, she *would* see the glaziers return to Hal's court. And years from now, Rani would be responsible for her own master craftsmen, for the journeymen and apprentices. Of course, she'd also need to watch over their horses, over the cats that she would keep in the granary to chase the mice, over the caged birds that would inspire the masters with their song. A kestrel would fit well into the menagerie.

If Rani learned to manage the wild raptor.

Drawing her thoughts back from the beasts that would eventually sleep by the hearth in her own guildhall, Rani stretched her fingers toward Gry's hound. Soon, she would learn how to hunt with her own dogs. For Kalindramina's first flight, though, Rani would rely on the falcon-master's experienced hound to flush autumn-fat grouse from the brush. The dog sniffed at Rani's hand curiously, but he jumped back toward his master as another horse gained the crest of the low hill.

A young woman clung to the reins, sawing back on her mount's mouth as if she would decapitate the poor beast. The girl's shoulder-length hair was whipped by the wind of her passage, and her narrow features were pulled into a grimace. "Ye might've waited fer me!" she squawked, before Rani could step forward to help her. "Ye might remember that some o' us aren't used t' perchin' on a cursed animal's back!"

"And you might remember that you're supposed to be a

lady, Mair." Rani grinned. "You promised His Majesty that you would stop squawking like a Touched hen every time you speak."

"And *you* promised His Majesty that you would stay within sight of the city walls when you go out riding. There's a whole lot of lying going on in the royal palace, isn't there?" Mair's retort was quick, but Rani noted that her companion slipped back into the cultured tones of the court. Two years of living in the palace had smoothed Mair's rough brogue, but Rani was still a little surprised every time she heard the Touched girl speak in the round, soft tones of Morenia's nobility.

Of course, Mair was a quick student. That skill had kept her alive for more than sixteen years, years that had been astonishingly rough in the City streets. Mair refused to talk about her childhood, about the parents who had abandoned her to her life among the City's teeming population of lawless, casteless children. All that Rani knew was that Mair had gathered a group of loyal Touched around her, children who were willing to lay down their lives for their leader. In exchange for that devotion, Mair had kept her troop safe and warm and fed, even when the king's guard had tried repeatedly to drive out the group of casteless urchins.

"Cursed beast! Stand yer ground!" Mair swore at her mount as it shied away, and she sawed at the animal's tough mouth with arms that trembled on her reins. Rani's falcon, Kalindramina, shifted her talons on her bow-shaped perch, ruffling her feathers at the disturbance. The peregrine, though, remained aloof beneath its buckskin hood.

"Mair," Rani chastised. "Don't frighten Kali. You know you won't get anywhere if you manhandle your horse like that. Hold the reins firmly, and don't pull sideways."

"Mind your own horse," Mair snarled, and Rani swallowed a laugh as she turned her attention back to the falcon-master, who had watched the entire exchange with an indulgent smile. "Gry, can we fly Kali now?"

The old man's eyes darted to Rani's hand as she pulled on her heavy buckskin falconing glove. He tugged at his ear and gazed out across the plain toward Moren. "We'd best wait for the prince, my lady. He'll be offended if we start without him."

"He could have been here already, if he didn't ride like a noble reviewing his troops," Rani grumbled. "Besides, the prince already knows that his Maradalian will fly well. Please, Gry! I don't want to look like a fool in front of him."

The falcon-master glanced at the hooded peregrine, perched next to Kalindramina on the sturdy cadge. He tugged at his ear again, and a frown creased his forehead. "It's not a contest, my lady. You must respect the bird, as she's learned to respect you. You're not competing with Prince Bashanorandi today." Shaking his head in rebuke, the falconer stepped away from the two girls, becoming unusually interested in the raptors' jesses, the strips of leather that tethered them to their perches.

"She's *always* competing with Bashi," Mair noted dryly to the back of Gry's head as she finally slipped to the ground from her jittery mount. "You know, Rai, you were wrong to speak so harshly to the soldiers when we rode through the city gates."

"They were taking too long to pass us through. They *know* we're allowed to come and go. They were only dragging their feet because Bashi was there too."

"They were doing their job."

Rani glared at Mair. "So, it's come to this? You're going to tutor me in being kind to *soldiers*?"

Mair grimaced at Rani's sharp tone. "I'm telling you to be kind to *people*. I don't care what caste the men are, they don't deserve the cheek you offered them."

"Cheek! I haven't been cheeky a day in my life!"

"Call it what you will. Some of us adapt better to our life in the castle than others."

"You take that back, Mair! I didn't do anything wrong with the soldiers!"

"Of course not." Mair paused. "My lady," she added sweetly.

"Mair, if you want to criticize me, do it outright."

"You'll know when I criticize you, Rani Trader."

The words bit hard, spiced with deep-rooted anger, and Rani blinked back sudden tears. "You used to call me Rai."

"You used to act like one of the Touched."

Rani spluttered, digging for an answer, but no retort came easily. Instead, she glared at Gry's back, taking in the falcon-master's supposed interest in one of the joints of the portable cadge. Gry had been born one of the casteless Touched, like all of the nobles' servants. Through the years, he had worked hard to gain his employers' trust, to earn his success as master falconer. Rani looked away from the silent condemnation of his still back, turning her attention to the four soldiers who finally drew near the top of the gentle rise. "My lady," called the captain, bowing slightly from his saddle. "It's dangerous for you to ride alone."

"I'm not alone!" Rani exclaimed, and her voice was sharper than she intended. She swallowed hard and forced her words into a less shrill register. "I rode with my lady-in-waiting, Mair. And I rode to the king's own falcon-master. Besides, we were never out of your sight, Farantili."

"Much good it would do me, if I had to watch enemy troops ride out of those trees and carry you off." Farantili nodded his grizzled head toward the copse that bled across the bottom of the hill.

Rani covered a shiver of concern with scornful words. "What enemy would come so close to Moren? We're near enough to hear the Pilgrims' Bell from here. By all the Thousand Gods, you worry too much, Farantili."

"I'm paid to worry, my lady." The soldier's words did nothing to ease Rani's roiling temper, especially when he edged his horse between hers and the trees. "I'll send one of my men down to check out the woods, before you fly the kestrel."

"Farantili, that's ridiculous. It's already getting late in the day. If we have to wait for your scout, we won't get back to the city until after dark."

"Of course, my lady. We should turn back now. You can practice your falconry another day."

Mair did not bother to disguise her smirk of amusement as Rani yelped in frustration and whirled on Gry, ready to plead her case to the master. Before she could speak, though, the last handful of horsemen rode up. Farantili bent low in his saddle and Gry swept into a deep bow, but Rani scarcely inclined her head.

"Bashi," she murmured, and she watched anger flare across the prince's pale face. Prince Bashanorandi had no use for childish nicknames, particularly names that had been bestowed by the current king, when both boys had lived in the royal nursery.

"You had no right to leave me back there!" Prince Bashanorandi scowled as he fought to rein in his feisty brown stallion. "You *know* that Hal would not want us riding this far from Moren's walls. He'd have your hide if he saw you jump that creek! When will you stop to think, Ranita? You're not a merchant brat any longer."

But you're a brat, all the same.

No, Bashi was not fool enough to utter those words, not in front of the master falconer and the soldiers. Nevertheless, he thought them so clearly that Rani's hands curled into fists as expressive as Kali's talons. She bridled at the bitterness in Bashi's superior tone, even as she tried to remind herself that the past two years had not been easy for the bastard son of two proven traitors.

Bashi had been indirectly implicated in the plot to assassinate Morenia's Crown Prince. Many thought that the bastard should have been executed like his scheming mother and father. King Shanoranvilli, though, had mandated from his death bed that the boy he had always known as his youngest son should live. Even after the heartbroken old man died, Halaravilli had not withdrawn that sanctuary. In fact, Hal had left Bashanorandi the title of "prince," figuring that the appellation might help rein in the rebellious youth.

But Bashi had continued to be difficult, refusing to assume any responsibility in administering the kingdom. Hal had rapidly found himself snared in a paradox: he could have forced his so-called brother to act as a councillor, to be responsible for Moren's day-to-day administration, as was typical of a Crown Prince. But everyone knew that Bashi *wasn't* the Crown Prince. He wasn't of Morenian royal blood at all.

The situation was frustrating, and Hal took out his aggression with his sometime brother in a thousand ways, berating Bashi in the dining hall when the youth arrived late for supper, ridiculing Bashi's notions for a feast-day honoring all the Thousand Gods.

And Bashi took out his anger in ways that were safe, especially by tormenting the lower-caste Rani. The prince had arranged for her apartments to be on the darker, southern side of the palace compound, and he had snagged the best palace seamstress for himself. He had even managed to snare the treasured dinner place at Hal's right hand.

Rani was forced to grit her teeth and accept the ignominy. She was, after all, a merchant girl who only teetered on the edge of the noble caste. Now, painfully aware of all the limits on her rights, Rani harnessed her self-control. "I didn't leave my escort 'far behind,' my lord. You must not have noticed that we're at the top of a hill. The soldiers could see Mair and me, as we rode to this vantage point."

"A lot of good it would have done, if you'd been attacked."

"And who's going to attack us, this close to the City?"

"Ranita, you know there've been tales of marauders," Bashi sneered. As his face twisted around his superior words, he looked younger than his fifteen years. "Even if you *haven't* been allowed in Council meetings, you can't have missed the stories in the streets."

"You may be frightened by tales meant for children, o prince, but *I* am not. I know the difference between a monster that lurks beneath a child's bed and an invading army."

"No one said that it would take an army," Bashi answered hotly. "A single soldier with a sharp blade could kill you, before you even knew that you'd been taken."

Mair cut in before Rani could spit out a reply. "Aye, Prince Bashanorandi. A single blade is all it would take to cut down any of us. That's why we all must stay united. Against our *true* enemies." Mair accented her pious declaration by settling her right hand on the hilt of the dagger she wore at her waist, contrary to the delicate customs of the noble caste. There were, after all, advantages to being one of the casteless Touched.

"Now, now," interrupted Farantili. The grizzled soldier had let his wards argue among themselves, accustomed by now to their squabbles. When hand touched steel, though, he apparently deemed it time to intervene.

"Lady Rani, Lady Mair," Gry took advantage of the broken hostilities to regain the young people's attention. The master falconer added the noble title to the girls' names, as if he were accustomed to following the polite form of address with only a few syllables, instead of a noble's long name. "It *is* getting late in the day. If these falcons are going to fly, they should do it now, before dark. It can be hard enough finding them at noon, once they've taken their prey in the high grass."

Rani bit back a sharp reply, swallowing her inclination to claim that *she* had been ready to fly the falcons hours before. Instead, she turned her back on Bashi, stepping toward the falcon-master with a nervous energy. "Do you really think Kali's ready, Gry? Do you think she'll come back?"

The old falcon-master shrugged, and his brows beetled ominously. He tugged again at his ear. "If I didn't think she was ready, I wouldn't have brought her out here. There's no way of knowing for sure, though, until you try."

"But –"

"You've trained her, haven't you? You've been around my mews long enough to understand that this kestrel won't be acting like a dog. She won't come back out of love for you. She's still a wild beast."

"I know that!" Rani protested, fighting the hot blush that stole across her cheeks as she heard Bashi choke on a guffaw. "It's just that after all the time and energy we've put into training her...."

The master falconer squinted as he settled a hand on the cadge. "She flies to your lure, doesn't she?"

"Of course."

"And she's stopped bating when you hold her on your fist?"

"Yes." Rani fought back a grimace, remembering her frantic struggle the first time the falcon had tried to fly away from her gloved hand, even though the bird had been held close by the leather jesses around her talons. Rani's face had been batted by the tips of the falcon's wings, and she had waved her arm in reflexive fear, upsetting the poor kestrel even more. Rani had been grateful for the thick cuff of her buckskin glove as Kali dug in her talons above her would-be mistress' wrist.

The master falconer persisted. "And you know your kestrel's hunting weight?"

"Yes." Rani struggled to keep doubt from her voice. Hunting weight – that had proven to be the hardest part of the discipline of falconry. Rani had held Kalindramina within minutes after the bird was first caught in Gry's snare. The little falcon had fought with the power of all the Thousand Gods, desperate to be free. Rani, though, had followed the master falconer's instructions with trembling hands. She had slipped a long band of leather about the wild bird's body, pulling the noose tight to cinch in the kestrel's desperately flapping wings. With Gry's help, Rani had managed to settle a hood over the falcon's head, barely cinching the soft buckskin tight before the bird's cruel beak could slash through the leather.

Kalindramina had quieted then. She had stopped thrashing her wings, and her talons had ceased their frantic opening and closing. Nevertheless, the kestrel's heart had pounded, quivering faster than an infant's as Rani pressed her fingers against the bird's breast-bone. "Aye," Gry had crooned. "You feel that? D'you feel the meat on her? We'll let her lose a little of that flesh, so that she'll fly when we ask her. A hungry falcon is a trapped falcon. A hungry kestrel stays to eat. A hungry bird can be recaught."

Rani had checked the breast-bone again, and one more

time, before she was certain that she knew the feel of Kalindramina's full fed weight. Then she had nodded, and Gry had taken the kestrel away to the mews.

Now, a breeze picked up on the hilltop as Rani pressed a gentle finger against her bird's chest. The girl had grown accustomed to the miniature thunder that pounded behind the deceptively fragile cage of bones. Kali's heart yearned to fly free, to soar above the grasslands. The falcon longed to bank against the wind, spying the ground, watching for prey. Rani nodded to Gry, registering the weight of the hungry kestrel. "Aye. She's ready to fly."

"Let's fly her then." The bow-legged falconer waited for Rani to step up to the cadge. The girl took a deep breath before settling the falcon on her gloved fist. She fumbled with the hood for a moment, but then Kalindramina was blinking in the late afternoon light, cocking her head to the side as she looked at Rani. The girl drew in her breath sharply, snared as always by the beauty of the tiny feathers that fanned out from the falcon's eyes.

Bashi pushed past Rani to the cadge. As he reached for Maradalian, he grunted, "Aye, let's go."

Rani squealed her protest. "No!"

"Gry." Bashi's single word held an entire argument.

"Bashi, you can't!" Rani complained. "You know Maradalian will catch the prey. She's faster than Kali, and larger. It's not fair!"

"The Thousand Gods favor the fast." Bashi stripped off his peregrine's hood, settling the bird on his gloved fist with brutal efficiency.

"My prince," Gry began, clearly uncomfortable. "You know how important it is that Kali succeed on this first flight. The bird is too valuable to break on a whim."

"Oh, all right!" Bashi exclaimed. "You have my word. I'll keep Maradalian on my fist until after Kali has flown."

"But –" Rani began to protest.

"Surely Gry has taught you enough about falconing that you understand Maradalian won't have a chance? Your kestrel will have the advantage of height and speed as she drops toward the prey."

"I *know* that!" Rani snapped, irritated that Bashi was instructing her as if she were a child. "It's just that –"

"What? You think that Kalindramina is too weak to hunt, even with the advantage of height?"

"No! I only.... Please –" Rani began again, but this time she was cut off by the soldier, Farantili.

"Perhaps, Your Highness, we should simply wait for another day." The guard addressed his comment to Prince Bashanorandi as he looked morosely at the lengthening shadows.

"Ranita?" Bashi bowed toward the former apprentice, ceding her the choice with a twisted smile.

"No," she answered miserably. "Let's get this over with."

Gry waited a moment for her to confirm her decision with an unhappy nod, and then he whistled at his hound. The little dog had watched the exchange with growing excitement, whining softly as both falconers settled their birds on their wrists. Now, he understood his mission, and he coursed out over the grassy hillside, nose low to the ground as he ranged back and forth. Rani followed, taking long strides in her riding leathers, remembering to croon softly to Kalindramina. The little kestrel *was* fast enough to get the prey, even if Maradalian were competing. Rani knew that. She just had to repeat it to the falcon a few times.

Bashi crashed behind them, the grass rustling loudly against his legs. Gry came next, then Mair and the soldiers.

An excited hush fell over the humans as they watched the dog. The sun was visibly lower in the sky, and the hound had covered half the distance to the shadowy copse of trees before he found his prey. Just as Rani was preparing to offer up a special prayer to Fairn, the god of birds, the little dog finally snapped to attention, all of his canine energy focused on a large tuft of grass. Gry nodded tersely and waved his hand, indicating that Rani should move around to the far side of the tussock.

Rani complied, aware that her heart was beating almost

as fast as her falcon's. She watched the hound, hoping, praying that the beast would remember its training, would wait until Kali was ready. The dog quivered with excitement, but he stayed low in the grass, head pointing at the hidden grouse like an arrow.

Rani's fingers were slick with sweat as she loosened Kali's jesses. She clenched the muscles in her arms and tossed the falcon gently skyward. The kestrel did not hesitate; instead, she caught a puff of breeze and began to climb above Rani, circling to use the wind to her best advantage. Rani caught her breath. This was the moment when Kali could choose to fly away, could choose to find her own meal, her own prey to satisfy the hunger that burned in her belly.

The kestrel did not flee, though. Instead, she reached a comfortable height above her mistress, banking into the wind and settling her wings against the draft, managing to stay even with scarcely any effort. Rani watched for only a moment, until she was certain that the kestrel was waiting on, and then she shouted a harsh command to the dog.

The hound leaped forward as if propelled by a spring, barking as grouse exploded from the tussock of grass. The birds flapped their wings desperately, struggling to clear the ground, to escape the slashing canine teeth. Rani's heart leaped into her throat, almost strangling her with its sudden pounding. Her glance flashed from the dog to the grouse to Kalindramina.

As if Rani were staring through a tunnel, she saw the falcon's wings pull in toward its body. The sleek red and brown feathers moved with precision, calm and quiet despite the turmoil on the ground below. Rani imagined she could see the kestrel's sharp eye; she felt it measure the distance to the grouse, calculate how far the slow prey could travel while the falcon plummeted. Then, Kali's talons were extended, and the kestrel plunged from the crystal sky.

Kalindramina never caught her prey.

Even as Rani watched, an ebony lightning bolt flew from the earth into the sky. The grey and white arrow caught Kali in the middle of the kestrel's plunge, knocking the bird aside. Feathers exploded in mid-air, and Rani's heart was sheared by her falcon's furious cry. Even as the grouse fluttered to safety, Rani tried to decipher the scene before her. The hound took up an excited barking as Rani ran forward. The girl ignored the dog, ignored the rough grass, ignored everything except the whirlwind that tore across the ground.

Maradalian, Bashi's peregrine, screamed from the tall grass, struggling to lift its prey to safety. That kestrel prey, though, thrashed about, shrieking its own desperate cry. "Kali!" Rani added her panic to the melee. "Gry! Stop them!"

The old falconer, though, understood the danger of getting between two fighting raptors. He knew too well their razor talons, their tearing beaks. Gry held his ground. Maradalian was the larger bird by far, and more experienced in flying with jesses attached. Kali was struggling to fight her way free, screeching her rage, flapping her red and brown wings.

Rani reached into the avian whirlwind, leading with her buckskin glove. Maradalian slashed at her with a sharp beak and Rani swore, grasping at the bird with both hands. Before the peregrine could react, Rani sucked in her breath; Kali had caught her unprotected left palm with a dagger-sharp talon. "Gry!" Rani panted again, desperate for assistance.

The falcon-master could not move, though, before the kestrel fought its way free from the ground. Even as Rani grasped at Maradalian's jesses, Kalindramina took to the sky. The red and brown bird pumped her wings hard to gain height, and Rani thought that she must be injured to labor so hard. "Kali!" she gasped, but the kestrel only circled once before she flew off to the east, pushing toward the copse of trees.

Rani raised her bleeding hand to her mouth, sucking at the jagged wound even as she watched her treasure disappear into the sky. Blood flowed freely from the slash, and the salty taste on her tongue made her stomach tighten.

Even as she fought the urge to gag, Gry stepped forward, managing to slip a hood over Maradalian's frantic eyes. The falcon-master stood still for a moment, blinking in disbelief, and then Prince Bashanorandi stepped forward to claim his falcon. His face was pale as he settled the bird on his gloved fist, and he sucked breath between his teeth when he saw the jagged slash across Rani's hand. For just an instant, he looked precisely like a fifteen-year-old boy, caught breaking the rules.

"Bashi!" Rani spat. "You did that on purpose!"

"Don't be ridiculous!"

"You wanted to kill Kali!"

The prince's tongue darted over his chapped lips. "I never wanted any such thing! I held back until Kalindramina had the height." His gaze followed the course that the kestrel had flown, and he shook his head. He swallowed hard before adding plaintively, "I assumed she'd have the skill to catch her prey." Bashi settled a protective hand against the dark grey feathers of his now-calm peregrine, then he reached into a pouch at his waist and pulled out a kerchief. "You're bleeding all over. Wrap your hand with this."

Rani wanted to throw the cloth at his feet, but she dared not. Mair stepped forward to bind up her wound, not bothering to disguise a hateful glance toward the prince. Bashi became absorbed with his peregrine's feathers, and he muttered, without looking up, "You have to admit, Rani, Maradalian didn't have much of a chance, flying from my fist."

"I don't have to admit anything, you bastard!" Rani sucked in her breath as Mair knotted the kerchief across her palm.

Prince Bashanorandi paled still further, and his lips turned to grim stone. Maradalian sensed his tension and the peregrine bated, trying to fly from his gloved fist, only to be pulled up short by her jesses. Bashi soothed the bird mechanically before he turned back to Rani. When he spoke, the words were pulled out of him like wool thread stretched on a spindle. "So you would remind me, merchant girl. Every single day, you would remind me."

Rani saw the raw anger in Bashi's eyes, recognized that the better part of his rage was because Mair and the soldiers had witnessed their altercation. For just an instant a chill crept up Rani's spine. Before she could reply, Bashi spun on his heel and marched up the hill toward the cadge. Gry followed close behind, but the soldiers waited until the girls were ready to make the climb. Rani lingered for a long moment, staring east into the gathering night-time gloom, toward the copse where Kali had disappeared.

Mair whispered, "Don't even think about it, Rai."

"She might be there."

"Why would she? She's frightened and hungry. And free."

"That kestrel is my responsibility, Mair. She might get tangled by her jesses. I trained her for four months –"

"Lady Rani," Gry called from the cadge. Even in the dim twilight, Rani could make out the falconer's impatience as he helped Bashanorandi settle Maradalian on a perch. The stocky man's voice was harsh as he spat out his frustration with Rani, with the royal prince, with the loss of one of his birds. "It's not likely that Kalindramina stopped at the trees. She'll be far away by now."

"I have to find out for sure."

"It's getting late, Lady Rani!" The falconer tugged at his ear as if he would rip it away from his skull. "King Halaravilli will be angry!"

"Aye, Gry. Bashi should have thought of that before he flew Maradalian."

The falcon-master shrugged. "Bashi wasn't thinking."

The prince moved before Rani could realize what was happening. Pulling a curved dagger from the top of his boot, Bashi slashed his blade across the side of Gry's throat. "My name is Bashanorandi, you Touched dog!"

Gry cried out and sank to his knees, even as Rani shouted the falcon-master's name. In a glowing ray from the setting sun, Rani could see Bashi's face, could make out the momentary horror etched across his eyes. The prince was clearly astonished by his own action, and his right hand trembled on his curved knife. Bashanorandi looked up at Rani, reaching toward her with his empty hand, grasping like a child.

"In the name of Fen, what have you done?" Rani croaked the question before she could think.

She saw Bashi register her words, saw him absorb the name of the god of mercy like a slap across his face. His cheeks flushed crimson beneath his ginger hair, and before Rani could speak again, he had whirled on the stricken falcon-master, drawing back his fine leather boot to sink his toes hard into the falconer's side. The stocky man curled up reflexively, the action making blood spurt from his throat. He pleaded with the prince, making a horrible gurgling sound.

"Your Highness!" barked Farantili, sprinting to the hilltop. "Leave him be!"

Bashi drew back, trembling with rage. Rani stared at the prince in amazement, unable to comprehend what he had done. Mair's eyes blazed in the twilight, and she rushed to the master falconer, tugging at her cloak in a futile attempt to rip it into bandages.

"Stand back!" Bashi ordered. He snatched at Mair's arms, dragging her away from Gry. "Don't get near that Touched dog!" Even as Mair fought against the prince's grip, Farantili stepped forward. "Soldier! Don't even think about helping him!"

"He's a finer man than you'll ever be," Farantili grunted, falling to one knee beside the stricken falconer. Gry's hands and feet twitched, and his body began to spasm.

"Leave him!" Bashi's throat tore on the shout, and he fumbled for his curved blade. "That's an order, man!"

For just an instant, Farantili stared up at his liege, his eyes dark with unspoken emotion. Then, the soldier turned back to the falconer, and he began to mutter soothing words, trying gently to view the wounded man's gaping throat. Bashi gasped in disbelief, and then he raised his curved blade. "To me!" he cried, flashing a glance over his shoulder at the other guards.

There was a moment's hesitation, while loyalties fought among themselves, and then a tempest broke over the hillside. Metal clanged against metal. Horses whinnied in panic, the sound high and chilling on the twilight breeze. Maradalian bated from her perch, fighting her hood and jesses. One of the soldiers crashed into the cadge, splintering the birch supports.

As Rani watched, Farantili was shoved to the ground amid the shambles of the cadge. Another soldier stepped up, menacing the fallen fighter with a short sword. Rani cried out, desperate to stop the bloodshed, but before she could make herself heard, another guard was cut down, bellowing as his hamstring was sliced by one of Bashi's loyal men.

Across the now-trampled grass, Rani could make out the sound of bones crunching. Two soldiers pinned Farantili to the ground, pressing his spine against the shattered birch uprights from the cadge. One of the pair straddled Farantili's chest and began to pummel the man's head, starting with closed-fist blows and ending with a simple rhythmic pounding. Farantili's limp neck hit the earth again and again and again.

Even in her shock, Rani realized that she was in danger. She knew that she needed to escape from these rebellious soldiers, from men who would attack their own sworn brothers, who would sanction the murder of a defenseless master falconer. She was not safe among men who would beat one of King Halaravilli's soldiers to a pulp and butcher another like so much meat.

Rani whirled toward her stallion, desperate to remount and escape.

"Stop!" Bashanorandi's order flamed across the twilight chill. In a flash, Rani saw that he held Mair close to his chest; she could make out a steel dagger leveled against the Touched girl's throat. As if to emphasize the command, Mair dropped her own blade. The prince kicked it into the high grass.

"Let her go, Bashi!"

"She's not going anywhere, and neither are you."

Even in these dire circumstances, the words rang falsely. "Are you going to keep us on the plain all night then? Like children lost in the countryside?"

"You may pretend this is a joke, Rani, but I assure you it is not." Bashi twisted Mair's arm behind her back, and the

girl's lips tightened over her teeth. She refused to cry out, but
her look spoke volumes to Rani. "You will not go running
to Hal with stories of what happened here. I don't want my
men to hurt you, Ranita, but I'll let them if they must."

"*Your* men? Those are King Halaravilli's soldiers." Rani
tried to force certainty past the image of Farantili's bloody
head, past the moans of the hamstrung guard.

"These soldiers are loyal to *me*, Ranita." Even as Bashi
made his pronouncement, one of his guards grabbed for
Rani's arm. Without thinking, she spat in the man's face.
He bellowed in rage, snatching for his sword, but his
fellow grabbed Rani and pulled her, hard, against his chest.
Through the Morenian livery, she could feel a hardened
leather breastplate, a foreign design that poked against her
spine. The full armor was stranger still because there was no
reason for the soldier to be wearing it, not for an afternoon
ride within sight of the City. The man she had spat at swore
and wiped at the mess on his face.

For just an instant, Rani thought that her eyes deceived
her in the twilight gloom. When the man pawed at his face,
he left behind a tracery around his eyes. Only when Rani
blinked did she realize that the man had not *covered* his
face with the strange design. Rather, his wiping motion
had removed a layer of color, a coating of flesh-colored
paint like the cosmetics that Nurse was always thrusting at
Rani. Beneath that false color, Rani could now make out
a distinct tattoo, the careful outline of a lion beneath the
man's left eye.

She caught her breath. She'd heard enough in Hal's court
for the past two years to know that the northern soldiers
tattooed themselves at birth, dedicating their lives to their
warrior existence. A northern soldier, then, from Amanthia.
From the executed Queen Felicianda's homeland.

"What have you done, Bashi?"

"That's Prince Bashanorandi to you!" Bashi nearly
screamed his rebuff, pulling hard on Mair's arm. The
Touched girl tried to bite back her cry of pain, but a little of
the sound leaked into the clearing.

"My lord Bashanorandi," Rani forced herself to say.

Bashi nodded, apparently placated. With a curt gesture, he passed Mair to one of his soldiers. "Kill her, if that one takes a single step amiss."

"Yes, my prince." The soldier locked his arm across Mair's windpipe, settling a long, curved dagger against her side. A curved dagger, Rani finally registered. Curved like the knives of the northern troops.

"What are you doing, Bash –, Prince Bashanorandi?"

"Once, I thought I'd wait to show my strength, but you've made that impossible. Get on your horse."

"What?"

"I know you're not stupid, Ranita. Get on your horse."

"I'm not riding anywhere with you."

"I'll kill you here and now, if I have to." Watching the pulse beat fast in his throat, Rani understood that Bashi was not making an idle threat. "I'm not going back to Moren, back to Hal. But if I sent you back to Moren directly, I'd never have time to get to Amanthia, before you'd have Hal's soldiers after us. I just might convince my brother to ransom you two sorry excuses for courtiers, though. Parkman, get the creances."

The lion-tattooed soldier strode over to the toppled cadge, swearing as the frantic Maradalian flapped her grey and white wings. The man extracted two long leather leashes from the collapsed structure. He snapped the creances between his fists, testing their strength as he turned back to his liege.

Bashi's eyes glinted in the last of the sunlight. "I don't want to do it, Ranita. I don't want to order you killed, but I will if I have to." The girl had no doubt that he *would* follow through on his threat. "Mount up now. We have a long ride ahead of us."

With a warning glance toward Mair, Rani turned back to her stallion. She grunted as she pulled herself onto her high saddle, trying to ignore the slash of crimson that painted the leather as her wounded hand opened again. Somewhere in the struggle of the last few minutes, she had lost her rough bandage.

Bashi jutted his chin toward Rani, and the soldier snapped the creances once again. "Lash her to the stirrups."

Rani immediately set her heels, ready to kick the horse and flee back to Moren. Before she could act, though, Bashi barked a command to the soldier who held Mair. The man tightened his grip on Mair's arm, twisting hard and pulling the limb high behind the Touched girl's back. The crack of splintering bone was audible above the rustle of the high grass, and Mair cried out through her clenched teeth. "Don't even think about riding off, Ranita. I'll kill her before you're out of earshot."

Certainly Bashi would use more violence to gain his way. The prince's face was coated with a sheen of sweat, and his hands clenched and unclenched repeatedly in the twilight. Mair began to moan softly, although she tried to swallow her pain. Rani sat still as Parkman tightened the falcon's leash about her, lashing first one foot to her stirrup then passing the leather beneath her stallion's belly and binding the other. "Get her hands, too," Bashi barked, and the soldier complied, using another length of leather.

Staring at Bashi with bitterness, Rani only just remembered to hold her tongue as the prince nodded and ordered Mair released. It was a simple matter for Bashi to have the Touched girl bound, to have her tied to her own mount. Then Bashi's soldiers seated themselves on their own horses. The prince glanced around the plain nervously, his eyes lingering on the dead falcon-master, the murdered soldier, the maimed one. The falcons' cadge was crumpled on the ground like a skeleton. Maradalian stood amid the ruins, blinded by her hood, uncertain of the disaster around her.

Bashi nodded to Parkman and pointed his chin toward the hamstrung soldier. "Get rid of that one, and let's get out of here. We can get to the coast by sunset tomorrow and find a ship to sail north, to Amanthia. With any luck Hal won't find this till then. We can demand ransom for the girls when we arrive in my mother's homeland."

Before Rani could protest, the soldier dispatched his one-time brother, slashing the man's throat with one even motion. Then the guards fell into formation, one riding at Rani's left side, one riding at Mair's right. Two of the armed men followed behind, flanking their prince. When Rani hesitated to spur her stallion, the soldier beside her drew his sword. Before she could decide whether she would take a stand, Mair swayed in her own saddle, moaning as the movement jarred her injured arm.

"You've got to help her!" Rani cried to Bashi. "At least let me put her arm in a sling."

"After we've ridden. You can help her after we cross the Yman."

"The river is two hours from here!"

"Then it will be two hours before her arm is set."

Rani heard the determination in his voice. In a flash, she remembered the Bashi she had first met when she arrived in the palace. That prince had been a spoiled boy, a noble who accepted his royalty with an unseemly arrogance. He had manipulated nurses and guards, played upon his supposed father's heartstrings. Now, he had these four soldiers bound to him, and nothing would convince him to take pity on two low-caste girls.

Sighing, Rani touched her spurs to her stallion's flanks. Mair moaned through lips that were grey in the twilight, but she jigged her own horse forward. As the riders moved east into the unfolding night, a breeze picked up, blowing from the distant city walls. Rani could just make out the rhythmic clang of the Pilgrims' Bell, summoning the faithful to Moren's safety, to the haven of King Halaravilli, to the lost comfort of home and hearth.

About the Author

Mindy L. Klasky learned to read when her parents shoved a book in her hands and told her that she could travel anywhere in the world through stories. She never forgot that advice.

Klasky's travels took her through multiple careers. After graduating from Princeton University, Klasky considered becoming a professional stage manager or a rabbi. Ultimately, though, she settled on being a lawyer, working as a litigator at a large Washington firm. When she realized that lawyering kept her from writing (and dating and sleeping and otherwise living a normal life), Klasky became a librarian, managing large law firm libraries. She now writes full time.

For years, Klasky's dating life was a travel extravaganza as well. She balanced twenty-eight first dates in one year, selecting eligible gentlemen from sources as varied as *Washingtonian Magazine* ads, Single Volunteers of D.C., and supposedly certain recommendations from best friends. Ultimately, she swore off the dating scene entirely. After two years of carefully enforced datelessness, she made one last foray onto Match.com, where she met her husband—on her first match.

Klasky's travels have taken her through various literary genres. In addition to her Red Dress Ink books, Klasky has written numerous short stories and six fantasy novels, including the award-winning, bestselling *The Glasswrights' Apprentice*. In her spare time, Klasky quilts, cooks, and tries to tame the endless to be read shelf in her home library. Her husband and cats do their best to fill the leftover minutes.

OPEN **(|)** ROAD

INTEGRATED MEDIA

Open Road Integrated Media is a digital publisher and multimedia content company. Open Road creates connections between authors and their audiences by marketing its ebooks through a new proprietary online platform, which uses premium video content and social media.

CPSIA information can be obtained
at www.ICGtesting.com
Printed in the USA
FSHW012102150119
55061FS